MW01608632

To: President of the United States of America   Date: April 15, 2025
Bernard S. Chambers

From: General George C. Paxton
Chairman of the Joint Chiefs of Staff

Re: Classified asset █████████

Dear Mr. President.

This memo is to inform you of a grave threat to the continental United States of America. The subject of this report had been previously classified at the █████████ level but with the transpiring of recent events has subsequently been reduced to █████ level for your notification.

The current events in █████, the destruction of ███████████████ by a previously ████████████████ is a fabrication to mask actual events that have transpired. The actual event is the catastrophic destruction of ████████████████████ ██████████████████ This destruction is presumably at the hands of ██████████ ██████████████

In the ensuing chaos, the operative was successful in the forceful acquisition of ██████████, an asset known as the ████████████████████████████████. The asset is able to ██████████████████████████████████████ It was believed that the development of this █████████ would have firmly tipped the scales of world domination back to the favor of the United States.

The recovery of this ████████ is top priority and is being driven by █████████ █████████████████████. ████████████ has stated his confidence that the weapon has not left U.S. soil and that he will quickly reacquire it and terminate the ██████████ █████████ whom he reports to be ██████████████████████. Russian authorities are vehemently denying their involvement in this event and offer their condolences for the ██████████████ that transpired █████████.

A follow up report will be conducted during the upcoming classified █████████████ scheduled in ██████████. It is my hope that I will have additional information to report at that time.

                    General George C. Paxton
                    Chairman of the Joint Chiefs of Staff

                    Classification: POTUS eyes only

GHOST MOUNTAIN
CREANDO NOVUM VICTORIAM
★ ★ ★
RESEARCH CENTER

TIME SHOT

R. K. JOHNSON

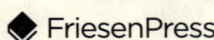 FriesenPress

Suite 300 - 990 Fort St
Victoria, BC, V8V 3K2
Canada

www.friesenpress.com

ISBN
978-1-5255-3143-9 (Hardcover)
978-1-5255-3144-6 (Paperback)
978-1-5255-3145-3 (eBook)

1. FICTION, ESPIONAGE

Distributed to the trade by The Ingram Book Company

FOREWORD

TO BEGIN, I MUST SAY THAT I WAS THRILLED WHEN ASKED BY THE Directorate to write a foreword for *Time Shot*. I asked them, "Who am I for such an honor?" They replied, "You're the agent who saved future reality."

Time Shot is an accurate historical depiction of future events – events that would rewrite the future history of mankind. *Time Shot*, a book written by R.K. Johnson, although under the premise of fiction, casts only a thin veil over the truth of the real soon-to-happen events that inspired it. What happens in this story are the true possibilities of what could really happen, what could actually be. The veiled truths of this book, and others to follow, threaten the very power structure of those who are genuinely in control. I don't speak of governments, clubs, or secret societies, who think they're in control, but rather of a deeper, more powerful force that governs everything – yesterday, today, and forever; an entity currently controlling all realities as we know them to be or soon to be. This story tells you about a single thread, woven into the tapestry of space, time, and infinite possibilities, that when pulled, nearly unraveled the future of everything.

From this book's very beginning, you, the reader, will be taken on a gripping thrill ride of scientific wonder and dangerous intrigue. You'll be given a glimpse into the best-kept secret of today: The Ghost Mountain Advanced Research Center. The story of this wondrous place on its own should be sufficient to capture your imagination, but then an unimaginable event occurs. A dark and sinister agent deceives his way into this sanctuary of discovery, and the resulting destruction of this agent's actions threatens the very future itself.

Orchestrating a theft that sets in motion perilous events, this dark agent forces our hero to engage in a battle not only for his life and sanity, but for your very future as well. This book culminates in a climax that will leave you exhausted from the thrill ride you just experienced.

Oh, but I must stop here because I don't want to give away too much. I just want to say that you, the reader, will enjoy this account. I know I did. The very reason you're able to read this at all testifies to the success of our hero in his mission and of others to come in theirs. Who am I to say this, you ask? Let's just say, for now, you can know me as the mysterious blonde woman.

Dedicated to those who are believers.

CHAPTER 1

Monday, April 14, 2025

"We've lost power to reactor containment!" Dr. Carrie Boulos braced for the next shockwave. "Instruments indicate a runaway chain reaction in the core. We're straining the onion, and systems are blowing everywhere!" She looked up, "Surges are reaching locker containment!"

With that statement, she reported that energy pulses were bombarding the containment field of the anti-matter magnetic storage locker 2000 meters beneath their feet. Inside the locker sat fifty kilograms of pure energy in the form of anti-matter, waiting for the chance to be released suddenly in one immense torrent.

Dr. Wellington remained calm, "Can we bleed the energy?"

An answer came from the speaker on his console phone, "Negative. We've deployed all safeties, and they're ineffective. We've injected poison into the core, but we need more time."

Carrie listened to the answer, as the soft tone of the only alarm serving notice to the immense peril they were facing sounded. She felt the surrounding mountain shudder in a low and steady rumble, as if the rock was quaking in fear of what was to come.

Dr. Wellington looked at Carrie, "What's the locker field at?"

Carrie began to answer but was interrupted as the room violently reeled from an energy pulse that ripped through the mountain's power systems. After the final pulse, the mountain stilled its tantrum, giving up all hope. When the shaking stopped, Carrie sensed an eerie calm settle over the room; a calm that failed to give reassurance to her that the crisis was over.

She watched as her coworkers exhaled in nervous laughter, as they slowly convinced themselves the emergency was over; the danger had passed. Carrie stood in silence for a moment, speechless in fear. The room was silent except for the persistent warning of the overhead speaker. Carrie came to her senses and looked at Dr. Wellington. With an expression of dread and a quiver in her voice, she whimpered in the quiet, "Zero."

Carrie's reply erased the smiles and drained the color from their faces. A sudden terror flooded over the assemblage of scientists, as they fleetingly beheld each other. Suddenly, she and the others noticed the floor rise up in a slow and steady motion, as if a dreadful monster was forcing itself from its underground prison to freedom where it could execute a destructive rampage. She watched the result of the pressure wave from the immense explosion that occurred two kilometers beneath their feet. The force had rapidly worked its way through the solid rock of the research base and quickly overtook the scientists, who had foolishly believed that they could tame the untamable.

She stood helpless, looking at the others for redemption from their collective fate, only to realize that they were all powerless to do anything except submit to the inevitable. Without time to speak the words, their final expressions conveyed a silent goodbye to Carrie and each other for the very last time.

CHAPTER 2

"WHAT A BEAUTIFUL MORNING," THE SMILING STEPHAN KRUEGER SAID. He stood and surveyed his five-foot-eleven-inch frame in the hall mirror. He looked at the clock on the shelf beside him. "Monday, April 7, 2025. Remember this date. It's the day our lives changed and got better." He turned back to the mirror. "Everything needs to be exactly in the right place."

"Hair." He gently patted his thick black hair. "Check."

"Beard trimmed nicely." He rubbed his close-cropped full beard, testing that it was just right. "Check."

"Shirt cleaned and pressed." He twisted and turned to see every angle. "Check."

"Pants neat and…Uh-oh". He paused and ever so meticulously picked off a tiny piece of lint that of course would have ruined his whole ensemble. With an over-exaggerated motion, he hurled it into oblivion. "That's better. Check."

"Don't be so silly, Stephan."

He looked up and smiled after hearing the familiar voice of his wife, Anna. He watched as she approached him from the kitchen. When she reached him, she leaned in and planted a sweet kiss on his cheek. "You always look amazing, my love." She poked his hard stomach, "Oh, and fit too."

"That's only because I have you, Anna," he said, as he kissed her in return. He took a deep breath. "I'm nervous. I don't want to mess this up."

"What's to mess up? They've hired the best systems engineer in the world. I'm just surprised it took so long for someone to recognize your talent."

"I appreciate that, Anna. I've been feeling down these past few years. I've tried to find work for so long that I forget what it's like to have a job, a real job that is. After all, I'm not so young anymore."

"What do you mean not so young anymore? You're only forty-one." She brushed his shoulder, "Besides, you have a job now." She cocked her head, "Who is it that you work for now?"

"They tell me it's an army base."

"Well, I'm not too happy about that, Stephan. After all, look how the navy dumped you six years ago after you faithfully served them for ten years."

"Don't be angry with them, Anna. They paid well for the time I put in. Thanks to them, we at least had shelter over our heads and food on the table for the children and us. Speaking of the children, where are they? Are they awake yet?"

Stephan heard a soft giggle from behind the couch, followed by a, "Not yet." He turned to the sound and said, "Who am I talking to then? You must be monsters hiding behind the couch, coming to get me." He playfully lunged toward the couch, growling at the dangerous monsters behind. The girls jumped up and screamed as Stephan grabbed them and hugged his beautiful twins.

"Oh, Daddy, please stop. We don't want you to mess up your shirt." The girls spoke in stereo.

"You're worried about daddy's shirt? You girls are sweet." He hugged them again tightly and kneeled down to their height to assure them. "Things are going to get better around here now, girls. I know that you've had to give up a lot lately, but it'll be better now."

"It is already, Daddy," Antoinette said. "Ally and I love not having to share a bedroom in this big house we've moved into."

Allyssa added, "Yeah and I like our new town too. Letti... Lexi... Lavi... Oh never mind, did you know we can go to two ice-cream shops here?"

Stephan laughed, "The town is Leviville, pumpkin. Two ice-cream shops, hmm? I didn't know that. I guess Mommy and I will have to take you two down there soon, but first, you must go to school."

"Aww," the girls frowned in stereo protest.

Anna rescued Stephan before he had to mount his defense. "Okay girls, let's go and leave Daddy alone to get ready. He has a big day today."

4

"Okay, bye, Daddy," they sang in unison. They scurried up the stairs to ready themselves for school.

Stephan smiled, "They're so sweet, Anna. How is it that we've been so blessed these past eight years, and wasn't it crazy for them to be born on the day of that big solar eclipse in '17."

Anna smiled in agreement. "Yes. I missed a great show, but I wouldn't have had that day any other way." She smiled as she looked up, and then turned back to him, "So, what does your new employer want you to do today?"

He walked to the kitchen and lifted a package from the table. "I'm supposed to report to them at eleven o'clock today. I've all these papers to bring and fill out too."

"Where do you have to go?"

"All they gave me were GPS numbers. It's a secret base, so I guess they don't have an address." He laughed. "Make sure you don't tell anyone I work there too."

"Did you find them when you went for your drive yesterday?"

Stephan pondered for a moment, "I think I did, but I'm not sure. There was a shack and a gate, but that man I told you about – you know – the one who drove up behind me so quickly? He scared me so much that I left before I could find out for sure."

"Yes, the man you told me about. Do you still think he looked like you?"

"Honestly, Anna, I don't know. It all happened so fast; I'm not sure. It just looked like it when he sped past me. Strange isn't it?"

"Strange, indeed," she echoed.

"What's also strange is how I got this job at all."

"What do you mean, dear?"

"What I mean is: How did that employment agency know about me? Where did they learn about me? What did…"

"Stop questioning and be grateful that they did, Stephan. You deserve this. You aced every interview and test." She caressed his face, "You're smart, and if I must say so, handsome too."

Stephan laughed, "Yes, dear, I'll stop questioning it."

"Well, I better check on the kids. You ready yourself for your new job." Stephan smiled and returned to his preening.

CHAPTER 3

"WHY DID YOU NOT FINISH THIS YESTERDAY, SASHA?" A SULTRY VOICE on the phone asked in a thick Russian accent.

"He led me to the base."

"How do you know it was base?"

"I saw the gate and sentry shack. He stopped right in front of them. I barely made it out without being detected."

"Are you going to be able to complete your mission, Sasha?"

"Yes Galina, I'm going there now." He raised his hand to block the early morning sun. "This blasted sun is blinding me." A short distance ahead, he spotted the hidden sheriff's car. "It's a trap." He noticed the hidden stop sign and stomped the brakes of his SUV, skidding to a halt. Suddenly, an enormous truck thundered across his path.

"What was that, Sasha?"

"I was almost hit by a truck."

"That would have ended everything right there, Sasha. You must focus!"

"Galina, don't lecture me, I am focused. I am operative now for twenty-five years, almost as long as you are alive. Bring Pavel and meet me at the house. I, Sasha Valintinovich Mishkov shall be the first to infiltrate Ghost Mountain."

"Yes, Sasha, and I, Galina Maksimovna Saranova and Pavel Ivanovich Antonovia shall be there soon," she playfully mocked.

"Funny," he huffed. "See you in one hour." He ended the call. He continued and drove past the parked police car, nodding as he passed the oblivious sheriff's deputy. *I must get there quickly.*

Stephan gathered his belongings and piled them onto the kitchen table. "I think that's everything." The wall-mounted telephone rang. He rushed to it in anticipation and picked it up. "Hello?"

Stephan listened intently. He quickly grabbed a piece of paper and a pen and jotted down instructions. The phone clicked off. Stephan held it up and looked at it, "Weird."

"Who was that, Stephan?" Anna said from upstairs.

"Nobody, dear." He replaced the receiver into the cradle and picked up the note he had just written. Suddenly he heard a knock at the front door. "Wow, busy morning." He placed the note back on the counter and walked to the front door to open it. His eyes widened as he saw his doppelganger standing before him.

"Good morning, Stephan."

"Good morning?" Stephan looked confused. "How may I help you?"

"My name is Sasha, and I'm here to talk to you about your new job. You look surprised." Stephan nodded. Sasha smiled, "Please, may I come in?" Stephan stood still, not knowing what to say. "Let me repeat; may I come in?" Sasha lifted his jacket to reveal a holster containing a silver pistol. Stephan stared at the gun and eased back, allowing Sasha to step inside.

"What do you want?" Stephan's voice quivered.

"Stephan, take it easy my friend. I simply wish to talk." He backed Stephan into the kitchen away from the stairs and slid a chair toward him. "Please, sit."

"Talk about what?" Stephan settled into the chair at the urging of the intruder.

"Well to begin, I want to congratulate you on your new job at the base."

"Congratulate me? … on my? …Who are you? What do you have to do with my new job?"

"More than you know, Stephan. We helped you to get it. We found you for them."

"You're from the employment agency?"

"Yes, I'm from an agency, but it's not for finding employment. Stephan, we've had our eye on you for a long time. When you left the navy, we knew we had to have you. We had a plan for you. Why do you think you couldn't find work until now? It wasn't easy fending off so many people who were interested in you. We wanted you for our purposes, so we've been saving you just for this occasion."

"You've been saving me?" A hint of understanding appeared on his face. "This is why I couldn't find work? You wanted a commission?"

Sasha laughed, "For such an intelligent man, you're pretty stupid. Haven't you noticed how much we resemble each other?"

Stephan nodded, "Yes, I have. In fact, we look exactly the same."

"My agency does far more than find people jobs. We find the right people for us. We're an infiltration unit. We find people like you, who look like people like us, and find the best place for them…for us. We get someone hired and take their place at their newly acquired work. We've been doing this for years and are in many places, even the Pentagon and the White House. We were not, however, able to get into Ghost Mountain, until now. We've even made pretty good money doing this."

"I don't understand. How do you walk in and take over a person's life…" His voice trailed off when he heard a loud thump from upstairs, followed by laughter. "I think I'm beginning to understand. I'll answer any of your questions; please, don't hurt my family."

Sasha glanced upward, "Let's not worry about that right now. I do have some questions for you though." He walked around the kitchen and spotted the envelope on the table. He picked it up. "Is this the package from Ghost Mountain?"

Stephan nodded, "Yes, yes, it is."

Sasha dumped the contents onto the table and sifted through them. "Let me see: temporary ID card, information forms, medical forms, offer letter. Oh, I see here that they want you there today at 11:00 a.m. That doesn't give us a lot of time to get acquainted." He picked up a small black box. "What is this?"

"They told me it was a transponder for my truck and said if I didn't have it, I could get shot."

"Good to know. What else is here?" He rummaged through the contents and picked up a small fob. "What is this?"

"I don't know; they didn't tell me." He heard another thump and more laughter from above.

"I don't like getting answers like that. Again, what is this fob? Are you trying to get me captured?"

"I don't know; they didn't say what it's for, just that I need to have it."

Sasha pulled a silencer from his coat and threaded it onto his gun. He stepped toward Stephan and pressed it against his kneecap. "I don't believe you. What is the fob for?"

"I don't know..." Sasha pulled the trigger and blasted Stephan's kneecap from his right leg. Stephan screamed in pain and dropped to the floor holding his bleeding knee. Sasha casually picked up a kitchen towel and wiped the blood splatter from his gun, all the while listening to the hastened footsteps of Stephan's family rushing down to see what happened.

"NO...Please!" Stephan screamed as he saw Sasha watching for his family. Seconds later Anna ran into the kitchen, closely followed by the twins. "Anna! No! Turn around! Take the kids and run!" Anna stopped when she spotted Sasha.

"Too late," Sasha said.

The girls ran in and screamed at the sight of their father on the floor, "Daddy, Daddy, what's happening?"

"Hello, family. Please, come in and join us." Sasha waved his gun. "Please settle the girls down."

Anna grabbed her children to cover them with her protective arms. "Who are you? What do you want?"

"I'm Sasha. I'm trying to get the truth from your husband, but he's not cooperating."

"Stephan, tell him what he wants to know."

"I have, but he doesn't believe me." He forced the words past his pain.

Sasha held up the fob, "I *want* to believe you. I *need* to believe you. So, tell me. What is this for?"

"I..."

"Careful now," Sasha lifted the gun and alternated his aim between the two children, "Your answer decides what happens next."

Stephan looked Sasha squarely in the eyes. He shifted his gaze back to his children and fought back his tears. "I don't know..."

Sasha firmed his grip and pressed his gun against the forehead of one of the girls. He watched Stephan closely. Crying, Stephan didn't change his answer. Sasha lowered his gun and placed it on the counter, then reached into his pocket and pulled out his pack of cigarettes. Drawing one out, he lit it with the final match from the now empty book, which he tossed onto the table. He took a long, deep inhale from his cigarette and held it in his lungs for a moment. Exhaling, he said, "I guess I must believe you." He quickly picked up his gun and fired three rapid shots, each into the foreheads of Stephan's family; their lifeless bodies fell to the floor in a series of sickening thuds.

Stephan screamed, "You bastard! You killed..." Sasha fired a fourth and final bullet, silencing Stephan.

CHAPTER 4

MAJOR GENERAL ISAAC TREMAINE SAT AT HIS DESK AND GENTLY PUSHED the enter key on his keyboard. "Let's see… who gets this again?" He looked at his list and typed in the names of Secretary of Defense Robert Maxwell and Joint Chief of Staff General George Paxton, among others. He clicked on the send button and watched as the program encrypted his report. When finished, it vanished from his screen into cyberspace. "There, that should make them happy."

He took a piece of candy from the bowl on his desk and popped it into his mouth. The general sat quietly pondering when his conference bridge rang. He clicked the answer button and watched as an image appeared on the wall-mounted screen. He recognized his friend, General Simon Glendall. "Simon, my old friend, how are you?"

"I'm great, Isaac. How 'bout you?"

"I couldn't be better. I wish I could tell you why."

"I know, majestic clearance, we can't talk about that stuff on here. Too bad you're not at your old desk next to mine like in the old days. I can't believe it's been nearly ten years already. Was it worth it? You know, leaving the field as you did?"

"Simon, at first I thought it was a punishment promotion because I pissed on the wrong shoes or something. I felt like I had flushed thirty years down the drain. When I got here though and learned what I was commanding, I thought I'd died and gone to heaven."

"Glad you feel that way, buddy. You've been through the crap and deserved a break."

"So, to what do I owe the honor of a call from the Head of Army Intelligence, not just a social call I imagine?"

"No, I wish. I wanted to let you know that we're picking up some chatter on the Russian stream about Ghost Mountain. We don't know what for – just that the name keeps popping up. We're looking into it but so far nothing. If we do find out anything, you'll be the first to know. All I can say for now is, keep your eyes peeled."

"Chatter, huh? Well, thanks for letting me know, and if you hear anything, call me anytime."

"Will do. Hey, by the way, how's that loaner doing?"

Tremaine chuckled, "Loaner? Perez? He's doing great. I'm thankful that you released him to me. He's a keeper though, if I can have him."

"No can do, Isaac. I'll need him back. Sorry if it pisses off your daughter, but son-in-law or not, I could use him in the field again, soon."

"Well, I need him here for a bit yet. He's on a special project right now that couldn't do without him."

"Well, don't keep him too long. I don't want him getting rusty or soft in that cushy job you have him in." Simon laughed.

"No worries, I'll keep him on his toes. Thanks, buddy. We'll talk again soon." Tremaine signed off as Glendall waved goodbye. "Chatter, huh?" He picked up his phone.

"My name is Colonel Joseph Perez, and I'm looking for a few good men…or women." Colonel Perez stood his six-foot-one-inch athletic frame at attention in front of the crowded room filled with a combination of scientists and soldiers, each who had their gazes fixed upon him. "…A few good men or women to bet on whether I can make this awesome shot. Daddy can use a new seat for his Honda."

The crowd laughed and heckled back: "Not a chance, Perez, I'll take that bet." "You must be crazy thinking you can pull that off." "Like taking candy from a baby."

The solo voice of Lieutenant Stanley Thompson spoke up, "I'll bet he can do it."

"You're on, Chugger," was the reply.

Captain Melanie Short walked into the lunch room, "On for what?"

Chugger said, "Perez is betting that he can hit the old road sign across the pass from here. I think he can do it." He winked.

"Are you kidding? It has to be three and a half kilometers. I know he's good, but that good? I'll take that bet."

"Okay, everyone, pony up. Money talks and…the Captain can hold the money." Chugger turned to Perez, "Okay, buddy, you got this, right?" He leaned into his ear, "I can't lose this much money, Perez. I'm counting on you."

"Oh, ye of little faith. Follow me and behold." Perez walked through the airlock to the balcony of the third-level lunchroom.

"Can someone clear the deck here?" Perez said. He watched as eager helpers cleared all of the tables, save one, from the balcony for him to rest his fifty-caliber rifle.

"Get on the phone and ask Dunbar to zoom in on the sign and patch it down here," Chugger asked a private in the room. Chugger lifted a spoon to his mouth and pretended to be a sports commentator.

"Colonel Perez hoisted his trusted rifle and gently placed it on the table. Oh, the thoughts that must be racing through the delicate mind of this awe-inspiring warrior: 'Can I do this? Will the crowd laugh at me? Will I lose…'"

"Will you shut up, Chugger? You're not helping me."

"Sorry, buddy, I'm just trying to set the mood. I guess I'm getting caught up in the moment."

Perez looked through his scope and adjusted his aim. Behind him, a TV monitor switched to a telescopic view of the sign on the other side of the pass.

Captain Short said, "The screen's up. Look, Dunbar put the distance on it too, thirty-six hundred and fifty-three meters. That's a world record. Perez, are you for real?"

"Well hopefully, third time is a charm," Chugger said. He held his hands far apart and whispered, "Missed by a mile the last two times."

"I heard that, Chug. I thought you were on my side."

"Yeah, for sure, I'm on your side."

"I'm beginning to think you bet the other way."

"You'll never know, Perez."

"Okay, quiet everyone. He's about to shoot." Chugger lifted the spoon again. "The tension is mounting here on this auspicious occasion where two worlds are about to collide. The first being…"

Perez looked up at Chugger, who sheepishly quieted down, "Sorry, buddy. Hey while I have you, will your old eyes even be able to see the target?"

"Hey, my eyes are just fine."

"Bad sight is nothing to be embarrassed about. It comes at your age."

"My sight is fine, Chug. I'm only forty-three. Listen, will you stop." Perez smiled and threw a saltshaker at him, which Chug caught and set down. He laughed. Perez looked through his rifle scope. "Oh, nuts." The target was so far away that he could barely see it, even with the scope.

"What's wrong, buddy?"

"Nothing, Chugs, nothing at all." Perez drew a bead on the target and inhaled. He held his breath and slowly allowed air to trickle out until he felt the sweet spot and stopped. He gently pulled back on the trigger.

The shot rang through the corridors of the base. General Tremaine heard the sound from his office. "What the? ...Perez."

The solitary shot traveled the distance in four and a half seconds. All eyes watched the image on the TV screen. The wooden post holding the sign exploded into a cloud of splinters, and the room erupted into a loud cheer.

"Are you kidding? Damn, I bet against you! How did you hit it? How? ...Hey, what's that in your hand?"

"Nothing, Lieutenant. Carry on."

"Wait a minute. Is that a remote detonator? You son of a... You rigged the sign. Did you even aim? All bets are off, Perez cheated!"

Captain Short was on the phone with Dunbar. "Can you rewind to the spot? Okay, we'll watch. Hey everyone, look again. Dunbar's going to play it back in slow motion." Everyone sat, eyes staring at the screen, when suddenly a dot appeared in the metal part of the sign. Seconds later the post exploded.

"I'll be pickled," Chugger said. "He hit the damn thing. Perez, you just set the world record, kickin' that Canadian's butt. Way to go Special Forces."

Perez sighed, "Too bad nobody will know about it. The Canadian is still the official holder, although I do recall another shooter in Russia who unofficially beat it too."

"Here, you deserve this." Captain Short thrust a handful of cash in the face of Perez.

He smiled, as the winnings were a consolation for fame never to come. "Oh well, at least my butt's going to be enjoying a new seat soon."

The phone rang, and Captain Short answered it. After a moment, she said, "Yes, sir."

"Well, my butt's gonna to be hurtin' from all the kickin' I'm gonna get from my wife for losin' this much money," Chugger said.

"Shudda' bet on the winner, Chug." Chugger groaned at Perez's statement.

After a few seconds, Captain Short hung up. "Excuse me, but both of your butts are going to be in a sling. The general wants to see you both, sir, and he emphasized the word – *Now*."

"How did he know?" Perez said.

"I guess he knows you, Colonel. And Chugger too," she smiled.

CHAPTER 5

"SO, TELL ME WHO YOU ARE, STEPHAN." SASHA RUMMAGED THROUGH his things. "Whatever you can share would be greatly appreciated." He fingered through photo albums, DVDs, even magazines trying to get a picture of Stephan's mind. A knock came from the front door. Sasha picked up his gun and walked to it.

"Who is it?"

"Sasha, it is Pavel and me."

He opened the door. "Finally, what kept you?"

"Big boy here needed his coffee."

"Hey, American coffee is taste good," Pavel said.

"Should you be drinking so much at your age?" Galina said.

"I am only fifty-five, kitten. Coffee keeps me alert."

"Enough talking about coffee you two, did you bring everything?"

"Yes, we did." Pavel threw the supplies on the floor. "I am top Russian agent. Why must I do such tedious work and clean your mess always? I am not janitor. I have not killed in a while, and I am getting withdrawal."

"Do not fret Pavel. With your muscles, we will have this done in but a few moments. As reward, I will buy you an espresso, big boy."

"Dah, I would like that, kitten. How did such beautiful girl like you do this work?"

"Like Sasha, I was created for this work by the state. I have known no other life in my twenty-eight years."

"Pity, I wished to be baker before this, but became butcher instead." He lifted Stephan's bleeding body from the floor.

"What was that?" Sasha said after he heard a loud hiss coming from the front of the house. He walked to the front window and peered outside. "It's a delivery truck. Someone is coming." He watched as a tall, heavy man jumped down from the truck and strolled to the house. "Quickly, clean up bodies and put them in there." Sasha pointed to the laundry room next to the kitchen. Pavel moved Stephan's body and tossed it into the room while Galina dragged Anna's. A knock came at the door.

"Keep going, I will answer it."

Pavel grumbled and picked up a child in each hand. He tossed both like rag dolls into the laundry room and closed the door. Sasha watched as his backup agents drew their guns and waited in the kitchen.

He opened the door, "Hello."

"Good morning, sir. I'm sorry to disturb you, but we've got a delivery for Anna Krueger."

"I'm Stephan, her husband. Can I help you?"

"We're here to deliver a complete set of new appliances that your wife won. I simply need to verify her identity before I can leave the items."

Galina quickly pulled the elastic from her ponytail and allowed her long, balayage-style blonde hair to flow over her shoulders. She gleefully burst from the kitchen, tossing her hair. "Hello there, I'm Anna Krueger. I still can't believe I won."

"Hello, Mrs. Krueger. My name is Paul, and I've got these appliances you won when you entered the Flour-Corp baking contest. But before I can unload them, I need to verify your identity."

"Certainly, please follow me while I get my purse from the kitchen." Sasha trailed the two as Galina led the mover into the kitchen.

"What the hell happened in here? Is that blood?" Paul said.

Suddenly and with immense force, Pavel seized Paul from behind and wrapped his massive arms around his neck. In a swift and effortless motion, he snapped his neck, killing him instantly. Pavel released Paul's large frame allowing it to drop to the floor. "We need to get rid of the other man too." Galina nodded and skipped to the truck and easily propelled her muscular body up onto the step of the truck. When she saw the driver, she flashed her intoxicating smile. She could see him relax his countenance as her beauty charmed him.

"Your friend asked that I bring you inside to help move the old appliances out."

"Normally we don't move the old ones out, ma'am," he smiled, "but in your case, I'll make an exception."

"Another victim of Galina's siren charm," Sasha said, as he listened from inside. Pavel chuckled.

"Right this way." She used her voice to lead him to his doom. Galina sauntered back into the house, giving the best show her voluptuous figure would do for the following, hapless driver.

"He's in the kitchen." Galina watched as the driver plodded past her to the kitchen. As he pushed the door open, he met a hulking Pavel looming over his dead partner.

"What happened?" The driver stopped. Galina brought her gun up behind the driver as Pavel grinned and drew his finger across his throat. The driver panicked at the sight and quickly spun around to run, but was greeted by the silenced barrel of Galina's gun pressed against his forehead.

"Goodbye, Mr. Truck Driver." She pulled the trigger, ending his life instantly, scattering his last thought across the kitchen.

"I love doing that," she smiled.

"I think it is getting crowded in here," Pavel said, shaking his head as he looked around. He took the bodies and piled them in the laundry room with their other victims.

Sasha looked outside and saw a neighbor working in his garden. "We cannot move any bodies right now. We need to get rid of the truck too."

"I, Pavel the janitor, will clean this mess for you too. I will take truck and leave unlocked at next stop. American thieves will take and throw off police. Better get freshener for air, too."

Pavel stripped off the larger delivery man's overalls and squeezed into them.

"You look like stuffed sausage in those, big boy."

"Comical, Galina, very comical. Follow me." He lumbered out to the truck and climbed in, careful to not tear the strained coveralls. He clumsily drove away.

"How are you getting to the mountain, Sasha? Are you using his truck?"

"No, I'll bring SUV. I had registration changed to his name by our agent in DMV."

"Okay. I'll be back soon. Will I see you?"

"No, I will be gone."

"Good luck, Sasha."

"Thank you, Galina. Whatever happens, happens. I will see you tonight, I hope." Galina left and followed the truck.

"Okay, back to business now. Where was I? Oh, yes." His watch beeped. He looked at it and sighed, "Time to go." He gathered everything he needed to bring to Ghost Mountain, including the mysterious fob. As he collected everything, he spotted a paper on the counter. "What is this?" Lifting it, he briefly examined it and then casually discarded it. He then turned and left for Ghost Mountain.

CHAPTER 6

SERGEANT TREY DUNBAR SAT AT HIS STATION, SURVEYING THE VAST array of video screens and security systems before him. Corporal Tiffany Swan entered the room and sat at her station.

"That was some shot today, wasn't it, Trey?"

"That's for sure. I never seen anything like that before."

"Good thing you were bird doggin' it for 'em too. Otherwise, we wouldn't have seen Perez hit the sign."

"I don't know why he blew it up, although it does explain why he asked for that entry charge a few days ago," he laughed.

"You know Perez, drama king."

"Yeah, that's for sure. On to business now, you got today's log?" Swan handed him a list on a clipboard, which he took and scanned. "Looks like we've got a newbie coming in today," Dunbar said.

"Better he's here today than yesterday. That was the shift from hell. All systems were down for an hour; anyone could've gotten in. I thought we're supposed to have top security here; you know, better than all the rest combined, even Groom Lake. We even got a dedicated satellite for crying out loud."

"Well, what do you expect for a few measly trillion dollars?" Dunbar said.

"At least, it's better today," she said.

"That's because I'm here. Besides, we don't have all those pesky UFO wing nuts trying to break in all the time." Swan laughed at Dunbar's comment. A beep came from Dunbar's console. Cameras automatically zoomed in on the approaching threat.

"What do we got?" Swan said.

"Looks like a black SUV coming up the road," Trey said.

"Do they have a transponder signal?"

"Affirmative, the computer's checking it now."

"I wonder if it's the same one from yesterday – you know – the one I logged? It was here the same time as that beat-up pickup truck."

"Don't know," Dunbar said. The computer beeped. "Transponder's coming back as Stephan Krueger. It's that newbie on the sheet, but it's the wrong vehicle. He's supposed to have a pickup, not an SUV."

"So, it could have been him yesterday when systems were down."

"Two cars, one person – don't work that way usually. I think I'm gonna get Chugger's team up." Trey keyed the radio, "Welcome Mat to Welcome Wagon, come in."

"Welcome Wagon here."

"We need a reception at Echo Gate for one bogie."

"Roger that. Team Echo is responding. What's the Threat-Con?"

"The general has us at Bravo, but I'm declaring a local Charlie."

"Roger. Threat-Con Charlie."

"Okay Swan, keep sharp. They're pulling up. Scan peripherals."

"Hey Trey, the plate's coming back as Krueger's."

"Great, thanks. It looks like Krueger has a passcode for today too."

"Let's see if today is this guy's lucky day," Swan said.

Sasha pulled up slowly to the gate. He let out a deep breath. "Whatever happens, happens." He reached out with his hand and pressed the call button on the gate intercom.

The speaker crackled, "What's today's passcode?"

Sasha fought back a brief moment of panic. *Passcode? No… I eliminated him too quickly. What could it be? Did I miss something in the package?*

Seconds ticked by that felt like hours. The speaker repeated its question. "What is today's passcode?" Sergeant Dunbar signaled Swan to activate the gate team.

"Echo Team, surround and prepare to engage on command," Swan ordered.

"Roger. Uncloaking now." Sasha froze as several heavily armed soldiers surrounded his SUV, seemingly from thin air.

"I'm new, and I was told to report here today. I don't remember any passcode." Sasha started to sweat.

"Until we hear your passcode, sir, you're considered a trespasser, and we are authorized to use deadly force. We suggest you remember. You have thirty seconds to comply."

What is it? Think, Sasha, think! He remembered a word he read in the documents, "Is it – rendezvous?"

"Negative. Sir, you're not playing a video game here; you don't get three lives, but because you're new, I'll give you one more chance. You have twenty seconds left."

Sasha racked his brain as the clock ticked down, second by second. The surrounding response team stood poised to attack. He remembered the note by the phone. *What did it say again?* He thought hard and finally recalled what it read. *It could be a grocery list for all I know.* He looked at the soldiers pointing their weapons at him. *What I do know is that I've only seconds left.* Sasha opened his mouth to speak as the last few seconds ticked down, "Laundry Detergent!" Inside the security office, Trey looked at Swan.

Sasha waited, preparing his response to the attack. He watched as the leader of the team touched his earpiece and listened to the judgment of Sasha's intrusion.

The leader keyed his mic, "Ten-Four." He raised his hand and with his finger pointing up, swirled it around and said, "Stand down, Echo team." Each slowly lowered their weapons and backed away, seemingly fading into thin air again.

Sasha was shocked. Not realizing he spoke aloud, he said. "Where did they go? Were they real?"

The voice on the intercom spoke, "Oh they're very real, sir, don't worry about them. Your passcode is acceptable. Why don't we have this vehicle on file for you?"

"I bought this in honor of my new job. I also heard that winters could be harsh too." Sasha held his breath.

"Ain't that the truth," the voice said. "Were you here yesterday with both of your vehicles?"

Sasha scrambled for a quick answer, "Yes, I was here with my wife. We drove both here to see if they could make the trip."

"You realize this is a classified location, don't you? Your wife isn't supposed to know about us here."

Going all in, Sasha said, "Yes, sir. I'm sorry. I'll make sure to kill her tonight when I get home."

Dunbar laughed, "Okay, I'll let it go this time. Please make sure she tells no one or your joke will become real." Sasha exhaled when the gate began to open. "When the gate's fully open, move forward down the road to the main hangar. Once there, follow instructions."

When the gate was fully opened, Sasha entered and drove down the road. He rounded a bend and saw an old airplane hangar. It looked as if it had been built in the late 1940s – all rusted and most of the paint chipped away. He approached the building, and as he did, the hangar doors opened wide enough for his SUV to pass through. From a speaker above, he heard the verbal instructions: *Drive in and proceed to the right.* Sasha complied and drove in. When he entered the hangar, fixtures activated, bathing him in bright light. Before him, he saw an LED display that read: *Enter tunnel # 1 and report to office C.*

He glanced at his compass and odometer. He mentally noted his position and direction to estimate where he was going as he traversed the tunnel. Sasha gauged that he was driving toward and under the mountain. Watching his odometer, he noted that he had traveled about a mile and a half inside when he came upon a cavernous area with several large buildings. Sasha scanned the structures and found building C. He pulled up to it and parked. Sasha sat for a moment and practiced. "Hello, I'm Stephan Krueger. Hello. I am Stephan Krueger. Hi. I'm Stephan." He got out of his vehicle, and at that moment, while walking toward the door – Stephan Krueger became resurrected. "Whatever happens, happens," he whispered. Sasha entered the building.

"Right on time, Mr. Krueger." A stout, middle-aged woman extended her hand toward him. "I'm Captain Fiona Mitchell, Ghost Mountain's human talent director." Sasha played dumb and saluted her after shaking her hand. Captain Mitchell laughed. "No need to salute me, Mr. Krueger. You're a civilian. One of three thousand I look after."

Sasha stammered, "Three thousand?"

"Yes. I also represent six thousand military personnel."

"Six thousand?" Sasha said.

"Yes, we're a big base. That's why I hired you through an agency. I apologize for not personally being involved in hiring you."

"That's fine, Captain. I'm sure you're a busy person," Sasha said, but thought, W*e counted on it.*

"We won't take long today. Have you filled out all your forms?" Sasha nodded and handed her the envelope. She peeked inside. "Excellent. Oh, wait, I need this." She took the fob. "Come with me, please." They walked. "How was your reception at the gate?"

"Good, I guess, although, I did almost get shot."

"Well, I'm glad you didn't. I'd have to go to all the trouble of finding another replacement for you." Sasha smiled. *I like her spirit.* He followed her to an office with a big machine sitting on a table. "Ordinarily, this should be done by now, but we had a problem processing your DNA sample. We need to do your fob sync again."

Sasha's body tensed slightly. *Do they have his DNA?* "Problems?" he said.

"Well, by a problem, I mean we lost it somehow. It may show up some time, but we'll do this here and now." She inserted his fob into a slot in the machine. "May I have your left pointer finger, please?" Sasha lifted his finger to her. She grabbed his hand and guided the finger into an opening in the machine. "Sorry, this might sting a bit." Before he could respond, he felt a stab in his finger, followed by a slight suction pressure as it drew his blood. "You can remove your finger now." She handed him a bandage and the fob.

"What just happened?"

"We just took your fingerprint and blood for DNA synchronization."

"Aren't you supposed to ask me first for that sort of thing?"

"Why? You've already permitted us. In fact, you already gave us a sample."

"Sorry, you just startled me."

"Not too tough are you, big fella? Here, have a lollipop." She offered him one from a jar.

"No, thank you," he grunted.

"Just having fun, Mr. Krueger. Your profile said you were amicable. I'll change it if you like."

"No need. Captain, I'm sorry. I'm just a bit nervous right now." He smiled.

"That's fine, Mr. Krueger. The fob is going to take at least twelve hours to merge with your DNA. Make sure you have it with you at all times when you're at the base. We synchronize them to your DNA, so it's good for you and only you. If you ever forget it, turn around and get it. If you ever lose it, report here immediately for a replacement. Come with me, please." They walked to the next room. "Stand on those feet stickers and look here."

"Where..?" *Flash.* Sasha's question was interrupted by Captain Mitchell taking his ID picture. She waited thirty seconds for the machine to process the ID while Sasha rubbed the blind spots from his eyes. She handed the ID to him. "Here you are. Don't lose this either."

"Yes, I know, or you'll blind me again."

"Sorry about that. I'm in a bit of a hurry."

"I can tell."

"Okay, I think that does it. Consider the rest of the day as a free day off. You can go home now and return tomorrow at 7:00 a.m. The reception at the gate should be a little more pleasant for you now. Present your card to the reader and then your left pointer finger. It'll beep, and the gate will open. Follow the displays, and they'll guide you to your station. You'll be reporting to Ryan Jones in the maintenance bay. Do you have any questions for me?"

"Yes. What is this fob for?"

"Beats me. Any other questions?"

"No, I'm good, thank you."

She escorted him back to the building entrance. As he walked to his SUV, he turned and saw the Captain pick up a phone. He could see her mouth the words, "Follow him."

On his way home, it was easy for him to spot the surveillance following him. He texted Galina, "Success, I'm in. Meet me at house. We're married now." A minute later his phone beeped with a text reply. *We did not even have honeymoon. Is Pavel our crazy uncle too?*

"He is the crazy part, for sure," he snorted.

CHAPTER 7

"GOOD MORNING, MR. SECRETARY." GENERAL TREMAINE EXTENDED HIS hand. "Welcome to Ghost Mountain."

"Good morning, General." U.S. Secretary of Defense Robert Maxwell firmly shook the general's hand.

"I trust your journey was pleasant, sir?"

"I love flying no-frills military aircraft. No peanuts for me, please, just get me there fast."

"Speaking of fast, Mr. Secretary, we have a busy morning scheduled. Should we skip the chitchat and get to it?"

"That's the way I like it, General."

"Please follow me, sir." General Tremaine led Maxwell to an elevator door flanked by two armed guards.

"Do you have the fob we sent you, sir?"

"You mean that thing you poked my finger for?"

"Yes, sir."

He pulled it from his pocket. "I didn't like that poke."

"Most don't, sir." Tremaine placed his hand on a flat panel. A light scanned it, and when completed, the scanner turned green and emitted a gentle beep.

"Sir, could you place your hand on the scanner, please?"

"I'm curious. What if I didn't want to, General?" Maxwell smiled mischievously.

"You would be arrested and detained, sir."

"What happens if I resist?" He looked directly at a guard for the answer.

The guard looked squarely at the secretary. "That's easy, sir. I'd shoot you."

Maxwell's smile faded, "Oh." He placed his hand on the scanner and held it until it beeped. Trying to hide his smile, Tremaine summoned the transport, and they stepped in.

"Time Shot lab. Voice authorization Tremaine-Alpha-Three-One." The transport chimed and responded with motion. "Have a seat, Mr. Secretary. The ride will take about ten minutes."

He sat. "That's a long elevator ride. How high are we?"

"This is a rather large base with a complicated tube transport system. We need to descend about one and a half kilometers and laterally traverse about two." Maxwell felt the transport stop its downward motion and move sideways.

"Just how large is the base?"

"About eighty-four million cubic meters, all blasted out of solid rock. The base has a vertical span of five kilometers, and horizontal spans of twelve kilometers in length and two kilometers in width."

"That doesn't leave a lot of this mountain left, General."

Tremaine chuckled. "Not solid, sir. Imagine a giant anthill, with its chambers and tunnels. Only this one cost three and a half trillion dollars."

"So, this is where you spend all the budget money."

"Well, a good chunk of it, sir. We also have the world's largest particle accelerator built in here."

"Is it as powerful as that one overseas?"

"It makes that one look like a child's toy, sir."

"Good." Maxwell puffed his chest a little. "So, what's come out of all this money we've spent here?"

"We have several classified projects currently under development that I unfortunately can't discuss, but I can mention a few others."

"Such as?"

"We've developed cloaking armor for infantry soldiers. We've also developed scaled energy beam weapons that soldiers can carry. We use both here at the mountain at our gates and with roving patrols. We power them with anti-matter energy cells—also developed here."

"Impressive. I look forward to more."

"That's why you're here, sir."

"Where are we going now?"

"We'll first meet with Dr. David Wellington, the project's creator. He'll explain everything to you while we tour the lab. After that, we'll go to the range to watch a scheduled test this afternoon."

"Excellent. I look forward to that too. Can anyone try the weapon?"

"I'm afraid not, sir. We've only tested it remotely so far. Today will be the first human test of the weapon. Colonel Joseph Perez will execute the shot."

"Can I at least watch from inside the range?"

"I'm sorry, sir. Only the colonel is permitted due to the range quarantine. We don't want a stray bullet hitting anyone, especially you. Today's shot will be the longest-range shot taken so far, and we're uncertain of the accuracy. We plan to shoot for five consecutive days – all to converge on day five."

"It sounds exciting; I can hardly wait." The transport changed direction again.

"What is this Colonel Perez like?"

"Top notch, Mr. Secretary. He's career army from an army family of eight brothers and sisters. He opted in at eighteen and has been Army since. He was Special Forces for several years and is currently INSCOM. I wish I could steal him permanently from Army Intelligence, but they need him back soon."

"Why do you need him so much?"

"To begin, he's smart, loyal, faith-filled, and tough as nails. His body can take a pounding, so he's ideal for our little projects here. He's also the best shot in the world. In fact, just yesterday, he unofficially broke the record, which I had to reprimand him for."

"Reprimand him, why?"

"It's a long story, sir. Regardless, there's no other man on earth I'd want testing this weapon."

"I see. Are we almost there?"

"We're almost there, sir." Tremaine activated a display showing the route and current position.

"Maybe you could have shown me that at the beginning of our trip?"

"Sorry, sir. I'll remember for next time."

"You should also consider serving peanuts on these things." Maxwell laughed. The transport slowed to a halt, and the doors parted, allowing the men to step out.

"Welcome to Time Shot, Mr. Secretary. Please follow me." Tremaine led him to a large conference room. As they entered, the general noticed Dr. Wellington sifting through papers at the podium. The men approached him.

"Dr. Wellington, I'd like to introduce…"

"Mr. Secretary." He grabbed Maxwell's hand, vigorously shaking it. "It's an honor to meet you. I'm Dr. David T. Wellington. You've done so much for our country."

"Wow, fishing for more money already?" Dr. Wellington's face contorted into a puzzled look.

"Sorry, Doctor, capital humor."

"Oh," he clumsily laughed. "I was referring to when you were education secretary."

"Shall we, gentlemen?" the general interrupted the awkward exchange.

Maxwell leaned toward Tremaine. "Thanks. Not much for humor, is he?"

"Most people with 280 IQs aren't, Mr. Secretary."

"Noted." He shifted his gaze to Wellington. "What can you tell me about this project, Dr. Wellington?"

"I'll try to explain in terms that you and the general will understand." Maxwell winced, "Ouch."

"In the simplest terms, Mr. Secretary, we've developed a system that can shoot a bullet through time."

"You what?"

Wellington let his statement sink in. "We can shoot a bullet through time using wormholes we temporarily create."

Maxwell was stunned and turned to the general. "That's what you meant by 'converge on day five'. How?"

"It started with a discovery I made several years ago using the base's accelerator. I discovered a particle that's responsible for time or at least how time works."

"There's a particle that does that?"

"Yes sir, if I may finish."

"Sorry. Please, if you will."

"The particle was theorized ninety years ago but wasn't proven until I found it five years ago."

Tremaine chuckled. "Yes, by almost blowing up the mountain in the process."

Wellington exhaled. "Maybe so, but I didn't. Instead, I found a particle that fit the characteristics of the long-sought-after chronon. You see, Mr. Secretary, time is not infinitely divisible. It has a minimum value.

If we scale below that value, reality ceases. This discovery aligns with Planck's constant of 10^{-44} seconds."

"Meaning?" Maxwell's face showed apparent bewilderment.

"Everything we know is a digital projection into a quantum probability field. We exist in that projection by perceiving it. It's digital because of these time divisions. A chronon is a particle that interacts with a seventh-dimension probability cloud. Our existence is a wave traveling through that cloud. When it encounters a chronon, the interaction creates the matter and energy for that time and space moment from the probability field. The length of the time segment is the duration of the particle interaction, which is 10^{-44} of a second."

"Let me get this straight; you're saying that reality recreates itself every 10^{-44} of a second?"

"Yes, that's what I'm saying. Wherever these two meet, matter and energy pop into existence. We're not creating energy but rather perceiving it. What we observe is recreated for that moment. The theory can also explain the double-slit experiment."

"Explains the what? Oh, never mind. Please continue."

"As I said, our existence is a wave. It travels through a seventh-dimension probability cloud, where a particle can interact with the wave. The two combine to create what we know as reality. When the particles decay after their time, a wake is created that we can detect and traverse. We can read the wake both forward and backward through time."

"Could we go back and see who shot Kennedy?"

"We're not quite that far yet, Mr. Secretary. It is limited. We're not sure how far we can go, as we haven't developed instruments sensitive enough yet."

"How does a bullet go through time?"

"I theorized and later proved that we could enrich these wakes with dark energy fields created by the decay of anti-matter, which we then tuned to illuminate."

"Like a black light and a white t-shirt?"

"That is a very close interpretation, sir. We're able to direct an energy pulse to an identified point in time and create a quantum entanglement between the two times. We create a time wormhole that bores through the time portion of the space-time continuum. Once established, we inject anti-matter to stabilize it long enough for the bullet to travel the time difference. When we shoot a bullet, it bridges the two times using the wormhole."

"Can you shoot this at any place and anytime?"

"Not any place. We can shoot through time, but we must be aiming at a predetermined space. For example, if we knew a target was going to be at a certain place in a week's time, we could go set up at the location, shoot, and walk away. The bullet would travel the week in time and strike the target a week later when it occupied the space selected. An observer would see the shooter aiming at nothing, but the shooter would see his target in the Chronoscope we developed."

"Wow, it would seem that nobody's safe anymore."

"This is the reason for our extreme secrecy in this project. Other than the General here, Perez, me, and my staff, only about fifteen people in the entire administration know about this, including you. The President doesn't even know about it."

"I'd like to see more. Please, show me around."

"We would be delighted to, sir." They set off to tour the lab.

CHAPTER 8

THAT SAME DAY, SASHA SWIPED HIS CARD AT THE READER. THE BASE'S security scanned and recognized his fingerprint, and in response, opened the security gate. When it opened, he drove to the hangar. As he entered the hangar, he read the digital display: *Enter tunnel #2, proceed to Building M-3*. He entered the tunnel and drove about three miles until reaching an enormous chamber, carved into the rock. He looked around and noticed buildings and maintenance equipment arrayed throughout the space. As he scanned, he saw a slender man in his mid-fifties standing in front of a building.

"Over here." The man pointed to a parking spot. "Park here." Sasha pulled into the space. As he got out, the man approached him.

"Stephan Krueger?"

Sasha nodded, "Yes."

"Hi, I'm Ryan Jones, the maintenance supervisor. It's nice to meet you."

Sasha extended his hand to shake, "It's nice to meet you, too."

Ryan reeled back, lifting his hands. "Sorry, I don't like to touch people, nothing personal. I'm funny like that."

"That's alright. I understand." Sasha suppressed his laugh.

"Follow me to my office." They entered the large maintenance building. Sasha memorized his surroundings as Ryan led him to his office. "Please sit down." Sasha sat in a chair across from Ryan. "So, how long have you been in Leviville?"

"Not long. I recently moved here with my family."

"I've been here since the base opened twenty years ago. We were a lot smaller then. I've lived in Leviville all that time too. I was married, but lost my wife, Penny, to a sickness that she picked up from a handshake. She was a nurse. That's why I don't touch anyone."

"I'm sorry about that."

"Thanks. At least I know where she is."

"I don't understand. Where she is?"

"Heaven, she's in heaven, waiting for me."

"Oh." *This man is crazy.*

"Anyway, welcome to maintenance shift A. There are six shifts here: A, B, C, D, F, and G." Sasha opened his mouth to speak. "Don't ask why, just go with it." Sasha closed his mouth. "We work twelve-hour shifts, seven days on, seven off. We work that cycle twice, then cycle on for a single set of night shifts. There're two teams on days and one on nights, and they overlap. I work straight days as the supervisor."

Sasha soaked in everything. "What will I be doing?"

"Slow down, speedy. We'll get there." He handed him a package. "Here's the shift schedule and your union papers. Read these regulations when you can. They tell us what we can and can't do, like bring explosives to work and all."

Sasha smiled. *I'll be breaking that one for sure.*

"The locker room is down the hall to your left, showers too. You can pick a locker later. The lunchroom is upstairs; I'll show you that later too. If you ever forget lunch, there's a base cafeteria on level three. We get a ten percent discount if we respond quickly to their maintenance calls too." He winked. "There are four guys per team, including the team leader. You'll be working with me for now, until you learn your way around, then you'll be allowed more independence." Ryan spun around in his chair and turned on a large monitor.

"Okay, here's the schematic of the base. We call it the Ant Hill for obvious reasons."

Sasha again opened his mouth to speak. Ryan interrupted again. "Yeah, I know, kind of looks like one, doesn't it?" Sasha was at least able to nod in time. *This guy talks fast.* "Okay," Ryan pointed to the bottom level. "We're right here. This is level one. We've access to the entire base from here. We have dedicated maintenance tunnels that only we and security can access. We also share level one with security."

"We're level one, check, security level one also, check," Sasha repeated back.

"This is the nuclear power plant area. We're on a separate private grid. We use as much power as New York City, so we need to generate it ourselves. Leviville would look a little suspicious using twelve thousand megawatts of power." Ryan laughed at what he thought was a funny joke. "Anyway, this is a new type of reactor – smaller, more powerful, and uses thorium and helium-3 as a booster. It's called a – let me think here – Colliding Beam Fusion Reactor. It also has a second system we nickname the onion because of its multiple layers. It's an X-ray collecting current generator that surrounds the reactor core. Overall, the station is five percent of the size of a regular nuclear station of the same capacity."

"What's this big area at the top?"

"Oh, that's the Air Receiving and Departure Deck; we call it the Air Deck. It's an indoor airport, and we maintain the systems in there too."

"And here?"

"Those are project areas. We do go there, but only when requested and escorted by security." Ryan pointed to the screen. "Here's the shooting range, and it's under quarantine right now. We aren't to go in there unless requested."

"It's under quarantine?"

"Don't ask." Ryan waved his hand over the entire screen. "This is the particle accelerator; we take care of that too. It's the biggest in the world. It can sustain energies up to 100 PeV and short burst peaks to 10 EeV, whatever that means. I only fix it."

"What's the grey area?"

"We don't go there. Never have, never will."

"Oh." This caught Sasha's attention.

"Okay, since you're my nuclear guy, why don't we start there? I'll take you to the control room and introduce you to the operators. You'll be talking a lot with them. After that, I'll show you around."

"This is an impressive facility," Sasha said, saturated with information.

"Wait until you see it. Let's go."

"This is an impressive facility, gentleman, but truthfully, I'm here to see the weapon."

"Right this way, Mr. Secretary." The trio walked across the lab and entered the weapons vault. Perez was already in the vault preparing the weapon for transport. "Good morning, Colonel Perez."

Perez snapped to attention and saluted, "Good morning, General."

Tremaine saluted back. "Stand easy."

He relaxed. "Good morning, Doc."

"Good morning, Colonel."

He thrust his hand toward Maxwell. "Colonel Joseph Perez, sir. I'm pleased to meet you."

Maxwell shook his hand. "Secretary of Defense Robert Maxwell. Likewise."

Perez looked at Tremaine. "Is this the V.I.P. you asked me to behave for, sir?"

Tremaine rolled his eyes. "Yes, Perez, this is he."

"I can't promise anything, sir, but I'll do my best."

Maxwell laughed. "Looks like we're off to a good start already."

"I was hoping, sir."

"What do we have here?" Maxwell scanned the weapons shelf.

"That's the…" both Wellington and Perez began to answer and stopped.

"Please, Doc. It's all yours."

"As I tried to say, this is the Time Adjustable Tactical Engagement System or TATES. It fires a bullet through time."

"Colonel Perez, please hand the weapon to the secretary."

"Yes, General." Perez picked up the TATES and held it out for Maxwell. "Don't break it, Mr. Secretary. It's worth $185 million." Maxwell froze. Perez motioned him to take it. He took hold of it but with the tenderness of picking up a newborn baby.

"It's light. How much does it weigh?" More confident, he bounced it in his hands. "Ten, maybe fifteen pounds?"

"You're close, sir. It weighs a bit over twelve pounds; four pounds more than an M4, but a lot lighter than a standard fifty caliber," Perez said.

"Is this strong enough? It feels flimsy."

"It is sufficiently strong, sir," Wellington said. "We've combined osmium, tungsten, and titanium and molecularly laminated the alloy to a carbyne-base structure. The blend also contains a few exotic materials such as nano-cellulose and an element that's not of this world."

"Oh, you mean that unknownium stuff we gathered from Hyperion? What a stupid name, by the way. I wonder who named it that."

"The moon or the element?" Perez said.

"The element of course."

"I did," Wellington said.

Maxwell winced at his claim. "Sorry."

Perez laughed as Wellington continued. "The materials combine to make a hyper-strength frame. It has to be strong to handle the torsional stresses of the propulsion system as well as the time displacement fields."

Perez leaned in. "Basically, Mr. Secretary, God would break a sweat bending this."

"Oh, I see." He looked at the bore, "How big is the bullet? It looks like a bowling ball could fit in there."

"Maybe not quite that big, sir, but it does use a non-standard projectile." Perez pointed to the barrel.

Wellington interrupted, "The barrel is an assembly of powerful magnets, which suspend and propel the round through their center. There is no need for rifling as the field causes the projectile spin. A projectile is suspended in the breach by magnets. When fired, the barrel creates field strengths up to 2500 tesla."

"What's that in English, Doctor?"

"Enough to twist a Buick into a licorice stick, sir."

"Thank you for the eloquent example, Colonel."

"Anytime, Doc." Perez smiled and touched his brow in mock salute.

"It is also enough to twist space-time into a near singularity, triggering the wormhole. When the weapon is activated, a visible distortion appears in the air. When the TATES establishes a wormhole, it injects anti-matter to expand and stabilize it long enough for the bullet to bridge the time gap."

"I thought anti-matter was extremely rare?"

"Historically, it has been, but since our discovery, we now have it in abundance."

"How?"

"It's complicated, however simply put: We reverse the time of ordinary matter to create it."

"I see. How do you control what you shoot at?" Maxwell handed Perez the rifle.

"That's where this comes in, Mr. Secretary." Perez placed the TATES back into its cradle and picked up the targeting mechanism. Maxwell reached for it, but Perez pulled it back. "I'm sorry, sir, but I won't even let Dr. Butterfingers here touch it. This scope is a $230 million one of a kind."

"Would you care to explain the complicated science of how it works, Colonel Perez?"

"I'd love to, Doc. I mount the scope here on top of the rifle. This end is a signal emitter, and this end is where I look. When I activate it, I see the present, but when I turn this dial, I see time scroll past. Do you remember the old reel-to-reel videotapes?"

Maxwell nodded. "Yes, I'm that old."

"Just like the tapes, I can scroll the time back and forth until I see what I want in the viewfinder. When I do, I lock it in, and it does this quantum entanglement thingy, linking the two places in time. It also primes the path for the wormhole. The viewer goes fuzzy because of quantum uncertainty but the projectile usually hits the target. How was that for scientific talking, Doc?"

"Very scientific, Colonel, except the entanglement-thingy part."

"What about the bullets? I'm guessing you don't buy them at your typical sporting big box."

"They're as customized as you can get, sir." Perez picked up an uncharged round. "We use a similar composition of material as the rifle, including unknownium. They begin as simple bullets, but when they're placed in the accelerator and bombarded with dark energy and chronons, they become time projectiles. The official name for them is a Chronon Augmented Projectile or CAP."

"Let me guess? You've always wanted to pop a cap into someone?"

"I wasn't going to say that, sir, but I do like it. Can I use that?"

Wellington groaned, "Please don't encourage him, sir."

"Because CAPs can't touch the air, they're contained in these." He handed an empty container to Maxwell. "These are containment cartridges. They only hold a single round, but that's all we need. The round is suspended magnetically in a vacuum. When engaged with the TATES, the round is lifted magnetically into the breach chamber where the gun takes over."

"What would happen if I touched one?"

"Not much, your body just would melt and be scattered through time."

"Don't be so crass, Colonel. I lost a technician that way, remember?"

"I'm sorry, Doctor. I forgot about Marcy."

"Mr. Secretary, as with what happened to my lab assistant, an unspent projectile will disrupt the nuclear bonds of any organic material touching it. The dissociated matter gets converted back into quantum condensate, which ends up being dispersed through time."

"That's horrible! Does that happen to a target as well?

"No. Once spent, the round exits the wormhole as a regular bullet to perform its regular killing."

"It sounds like you don't approve of this weapon?"

"Personally, I don't approve, sir, although I do believe this will save lives overall. Just like Trinity did."

"Let's hope so."

"It's almost 13:30, gentlemen. We must prepare for this afternoon's shot. Mr. Secretary, would you please accompany the doctor and me to the range, while Colonel Perez prepares the weapon?"

"Certainly, General."

Perez returned to packing the weapon. "I'll be there in twenty minutes max, sir."

General Tremaine led Maxwell and the doctor to the transport tube. "Another three-hour ride?"

"No, sir. Only five minutes." He pointed to the activated screen.

Maxwell broke the silence after four minutes of their ride. "You say you use unknownium. How much do you have?"

"They brought back about 150 kilograms during the first remote mission, and we have possession of all of it here."

"What about the sample on display at the Smithsonian?"

"Sorry, sir, it's a replica."

"Well doesn't that step on a frog? That takes all the excitement out of my visit next week."

"I'm sorry to ruin it for you, sir. We're expecting a delivery of another 500 kilos soon. We can spare some for the real display at that time."

"From where? How?"

"Long story for another time, sir, we're here." The transport stopped and opened up to a large room filled with scientists at their consoles.

"This is our test range," the general said.

"If you gentlemen will excuse me, I've matters to attend to before the colonel gets here."

"Yes, Doctor. I'll stay with the Secretary."

"Thank you for the tour, Dr. Wellington." Wellington smiled in response. "What can you tell me about the range?"

"It's a typical range, two-meter-thick concrete walls, one-meter-thick rubber absorbers around the perimeter. A unique feature of this one is the target delivery system. We employ a gantry crane to move targets anywhere in the room. They can range up to the size and weight of a tank."

"Perez is taking a shot in twenty minutes. Where are the targets now?"

"Starting today, we're taking one shot per day for five consecutive days. Each round is scheduled to arrive next Saturday at 14:00 hours. When we complete all the shots, we'll place the targets then."

"You don't need them now?"

"No, sir. Time bullets, remember? Perez will see the targets in the future."

"Speaking of seeing, that's quite a window to look through."

"Yes, sir. That's a twelve-inch-thick panel of transparent aluminum and diamond. It can resist a direct hit from a five-kiloton tactical nuclear artillery round. More importantly, it offers protection from our high-energy beams long enough to get out."

Maxwell pointed at several video monitors. "You can see everything from here."

"Yes, we have several cameras throughout the entire range. Infrared, ultraviolet, high-speed, you name the kind, it's likely there."

"Speaking of here, General, Colonel Perez is here," Wellington said. Maxwell turned and watched as Perez pushed a small cart from the transport into the firing area of the range. He watched as he closed a large door behind him and secured it.

"That cart is not too portable for the field, is it now?"

"We only need it for in here. Safety protocols for testing. Once in the field, it's very portable and can take a lot of abuse."

Maxwell watched as Perez set up the weapon on a table at the firing line. "It's already seven minutes to two. Will he be able to shoot in time?"

"Not a problem, sir. You can see that he has the scope mounted already and is about to attach a containment cartridge." He watched Perez lock a cartridge into the underside of the TATES. Perez pivoted a lever on the side of it, and a series of LEDs lit up in succession as the bullet lifted into the gun. A green light lit up on the gun just under the scope.

"He looks anxious."

"I would be too, Mr. Secretary. He's the first person ever to shoot the TATES. We've planned for every contingency imaginable, but who knows what could happen?"

Perez adjusted his aim and moved the dials on the scope. Maxwell could see movement in the viewer but not clearly. "How does he know he's at the right time?"

"There's a time display on the viewer, plus we have a display at the back of the range." He looked down range and saw the display. "Two minutes left."

"Target is locked in. I'm ready to fire on command," Perez said over his headset.

"Are you forgetting something, Colonel?" Dr. Wellington said.

"I don't think so; I've already said a prayer."

"Your fob, Colonel, you forgot your fob."

Perez quickly withdrew from the TATES. "Oh, yes. Thanks, Doc, that could have been bad." He pushed himself in his chair to the cart, grabbed his fob, and in one strong push coasted back to the table. He placed the fob next to him. "Hey, Doc, would you remind me to grab a carrier for this thing, so I don't forget it again?" Wellington nodded.

Maxwell held up his fob. "Why so much fuss about this?"

"Doctor, this one is all yours to explain," the general said.

"The fob functions in two ways. First, it's a field-damping device. Shooting the weapon without it would expose the shooter to a time displacement field that would kill them. It stabilizes the firing zone, counteracting the field. The second is that it's a warning device indicating a time-shot event has occurred."

"How?

"It reads the displacement signature and displays a number corresponding to the time difference of an event. It also displays the field strength in percentage. The value corresponds to the proximity of the event. The closer the fob is to the event, the higher the reading on the fob. This way if you are the shooter..."

"Or the target," Perez said into his headset.

Wellington sighed, "...or the target; then you'll see one hundred percent on the display. It beeps with a two-second warning."

"What can two seconds do?" Maxwell said.

"Sometimes, two seconds can be all you need, Mr. Secretary," Perez said.

"Okay, I'm ready again. On your command, sir."

"Dr. Wellington?" The general looked at Wellington, who nodded his approval.

"Fire at will, Colonel."

The gallery watched Perez intently. He gently squeezed the trigger, which activated the firing procedure. A small pulse of energy shot from the scope and the air in front of the TATES grew hazy. As the round spun up, the gun released a magnetic pulse that caused the air to spiral inward creating a singularity. The round was propelled from the gun at high velocity and entered the wormhole at the center. The disturbance then collapsed upon itself in concentric ripples radiating out from the center. The whole event was followed by a popping sound.

"It sounded like a paper bag popping."

"Yes, it does, Mr. Secretary. That is space expanding back."

Maxwell looked around the room at the celebrating scientists. "Okay, so now what? How do we know it worked?"

"We must wait until Saturday, sir."

Maxwell turned and looked at Perez. "Why aren't you whooping it up too, Colonel?"

"In my opinion, sir, it's a little too early to be celebrating."

"Why do you say that?"

"Just my gut, sir. Just my gut."

CHAPTER 9

"I CAN'T BELIEVE IT'S BEEN FIVE DAYS ALREADY." RYAN ACTIVATED THE transport controls. "Air Deck Voice authorization Jones-Sierra-One-One."

"It's passed quickly for me too," Sasha said.

Ryan read the control panel. "Twenty minutes? The tubes must be busy today. Better have a seat, Stephan."

"What do you think of the base, so far?" Ryan smiled.

"This place is amazing. How has it been kept so secret?"

"We have a top-notch security team here; they keep a tight wrap on any intrusions. We also scour the Internet for any hint of secrets leaking. Anything posted is usually found and destroyed quickly."

Sasha fought hard not to laugh. *No Intrusions, huh?* "How do you manage that? I can't even get my browser to work half the time."

"There's a central information-gathering network based in Washington. It's new. It was built to replace an old system that tried to kill the entire government. This one is a next-generation A.I., developed here, that's been implanted with a moral conscience."

"Really? How?"

"They gave it a moral compass based on the Decalogue."

"The what?"

"The biblical ten commandments."

"Oh. Interesting." Sasha was unfamiliar with them.

"Do you have any questions?"

Sasha shifted in his seat. "Yes, what do the numbers on this fob mean?"

"I'm not sure. All I know is that everyone must have a fob at all times."

"I see. Could it have anything to do with the one project we've not been to yet?

"Which one is that?"

"Time Shot. We've been inside every lab except that one."

"That one's beyond my security clearance. I couldn't tell you." Their transport halted, and the doors slid open with a chime. "Okay, we're here." Both men stepped out of the transport into a narrow hallway. Sasha noticed a large arrow painted on the wall pointing to the left. Stenciled inside were the words: *Air Deck / Locker Rooms.*

"Today you get to help me with some hazardous materials, but first I need to give you a safety orientation. You're about to enter the world's only airport carved inside a mountain. The official name is the Ghost Mountain Air Receiving and Departure Deck, but we call it the 'Air Deck'." Ryan and Sasha walked down the hall until they got to a small room where there were benches and equipment lockers. Ryan approached a locker and slid a nameplate with "Joseph Tines" etched on it from the holder. He placed it down and inserted a plate with Sasha's alter ego's name.

"This will be your locker. It used to belong to the man that you replaced." Ryan sighed. "He was a great guy. I miss him." He carefully placed the old nameplate in his shirt pocket. "Today, we'll be unloading an air transport that brought us some highly reactive materials, but first we need to suit up." He pointed to a safety harness, winter coat, and an air breather. Ryan showed Sasha how to get into the harness and how to put on the supplemental air breather. Once outfitted, they walked through the exit to a door at the end of the hallway. Ryan checked a panel beside the door. "Good, no arrivals for thirty minutes."

He opened the door. "Step inside." They both entered the small room, and Ryan closed the door. "Put on your breather now." Both Ryan and Sasha donned their breathers. He hit a button, and a hissing sound started, which caught Sasha's attention.

"What's that sound?" The breather muffled Sasha's voice, but Ryan still understood him.

"We're 12,000 feet up the mountain here. The air is frigid and thin – imagine mountain climbers. We need to go through an airlock to enter the Air Deck. The masks supplement our oxygen so we can breathe." The hissing stopped, and a light turned green over the door, followed by a click from the door lock. The two stepped out onto the Air Deck. Sasha stood motionless for a moment, "Oh, my..."

"Impressive, isn't it?" Ryan characteristically interrupted him. Sasha looked up and down the vast space of the Air Deck. It was massive. He estimated that it was at least 700 feet wide, 400 feet high, and at least 3000 feet long.

"How did they build this?"

"They had to rewrite a few engineering books to build this baby. There are another 2000 feet of mountain above us." Ryan pointed to the end. "That's where the planes come in." He pointed across the chamber. "See those windows?" Sasha nodded. "That's the flight control room and passenger receiving areas."

Ryan turned to a cabinet beside the doorway. He took a set of headphones and gave them to Sasha, then placed on his own. He pressed a red button twice, and a little door slid open. Two little robotic carts about the size of canister vacuums wheeled out and stopped. Ryan spoke, but Sasha couldn't hear him. He tapped his ear and shrugged. Ryan stopped talking, turned his head, and pointed to a button on the headphones.

Sasha reached up and pushed the button. When he did, he heard a beep followed by Ryan's voice. "Sorry about that, Stephan. I forgot to tell you about the communicator."

"Better. I can hear you now."

"What I was saying was that we need to stay tethered to these fall arrests anytime we're on the flight deck." He pulled a cable from the top of one robot and connected it to a line hanging from his harness.

"Why do we need these?"

"Walk with me." They walked to the opening of the Air Deck. The little canisters followed them like eager little puppies. "This is the garage door; it's the main entrance for aircraft." He pointed up. "If you ever see that red light over the door flashing, I'd advise against standing here for very long. The light means a plane is coming. The clock beside it shows how long before it does. Take a look over but be careful." Sasha leaned over to look down when Ryan gave him a little shove toward the drop. The push caught Sasha off guard, but before he could react, the cable tightened and reeled him back.

"Are you crazy? I could kill you for that!"

Ryan laughed. "Sorry, Stephan. I do that to all the newbies. I wanted you to know these things worked."

Sasha calmed down. "How does such a little thing weigh so much to hold me?"

"It's not the weight that holds you; it's strong electromagnets. If the unit senses anything unusual in your movement, it'll magnetically latch itself to the flight deck. It can hold five tons of pull. You never know when a blast of wind or a jet wash will send you flying. Look over the edge again." Sasha looked sternly at Ryan. "Don't worry; it's only funny once."

Sasha peered over the edge to see a sheer drop down the face of the mountain. "How high are we?"

"That's about an 11,000 foot drop there."

Sasha looked out. "Why is the view so funny?"

"That's because you're looking through a hologram cloaking the entrance."

"You mean the pilots can't see the entrance?"

"No, they can't. They rely completely on instruments as well as being a bit crazy."

"I guess so."

Leaning over and looking down again, Ryan chuckled. "I just remembered how your predecessor, Joey, used to BASE jump from here. He was every bit as crazy as he was fit." Ryan started walking back inside. "The man was a physical fitness machine, which is quite ironic because it was his exercise that got him killed. He was struck by a hit-and-run driver while running one day. Unfortunately, we never did find the bastard who did it."

You never will either. Sasha grinned under his mask. "Can just anyone land in here?"

"Only if they want to be turned into confetti. Above and below us are batteries of Phalanx Close-In Weapons Systems, particle beam cannon weapons, and batteries of Surface to Air Missiles (SAMs). Nothing is coming in uninvited."

"Do we maintain those?"

"Not directly. We maintain the power systems to them, but the armaments are military techs." Ryan turned and pointed to markings on the deck plating. "One of the systems we also maintain is the magnetics for aircraft launch and capture. Just like an aircraft carrier, we have catapults and capture systems, but ours are completely magnetic. We call it the Magnetic Aircraft Capture System or MACS. Each plane is equipped with an extra pod along the belly that serves as a magnetic grappling point." They walked toward the far end of the deck. "This is an auxiliary capture system, basically a big net to catch the planes if all goes wrong. It'll stop a plane but usually destroys it." They finished their walk, ending at the rear wall. Ryan pointed at a glass lens mounted on the wall. "This is one of the most important systems we maintain here. It's a laser guidance beam for the planes that come in."

"What does it do?"

"Regular ILS doesn't work here. A plane is coming in at 200 miles per hour straight at a rock face. They need our help to land, so we have this. Dual lasers hit a combiner and emit a beam that guides incoming planes. As far as the pilot is concerned visually, he's about to hit the mountain."

"It sounds complicated and dangerous."

"Not really. As long as the pilot keeps the dot in the center of his screen, he's golden. If not," he clapped his hands, "splat." Ryan paused for effect. "Okay, on to why I brought you up here today. We need to unload that plane over there." Ryan pointed to a mid-sized cargo plane in the hangar area. "There are four casks that we need to remove from crash containments and transport to the Time Shot lab."

"Yes, finally."

"What was that?"

"We're going to that lab?"

"No, we're not. We're just sending it via a hazardous material transport pod; the lab techs will unload it themselves."

"Oh, okay." Sasha hid his disappointment.

"We use a robot to unload hazardous materials. It's called a Robot-Assisted Material Handling System, or RAMHS. The acronym sucked, so we called it Rammy. I'll show you how to use it; it's pretty simple. The operator needs to wear a virtual reality visor and gloves to control it." Ryan touched the startup button on the visor, and Rammy sprung to life. Ryan lowered the visor over his eyes. "I can see what the robot sees, although it's a bit weird and takes getting used to." He drove it to the plane and stopped. "We manipulate the twin arms using these gloves to pick up objects just like you would if you were lifting it yourself. The gloves are designed with tactile feedback so you can feel the load in your hands." He picked up a container, pulled it from the plane, and placed it on the floor.

"How much can it lift?"

"About a ton." Ryan moved two containers as Sasha watched. He stopped and pulled the visor off. "Here you try, but first on the empty barrels over there. Put these on." Ryan handed the visor and gloves to Sasha.

Sasha put them on and swooned a little. "You're right; this is a weird view."

"Yes, they're stereo cameras, but they're mounted too far apart. It's a stupid design; kind of like being super cross-eyed, but you get used to it after a while."

Sasha practiced on the barrels, taking to the controls immediately.

"Wow, you're a quick learner. Okay, do the real thing now." Sasha looked at him, and Ryan pointed to the containers. "Go ahead, have fun." Ryan instructed him to move them to the Haz-Mat pod. Sasha moved the robot to the plane. Ryan tapped his shoulder from behind. "By the way, don't screw up or you'll kill us all." Sasha looked at him for a moment and then maneuvered the robot. He moved the remaining containers from the airplane to the transport pod.

"Okay, that's all of them."

"Great." Ryan hit a switch, and Sasha heard a hum emanate from the floor. He saw Sasha's look. "Maglocks."

"Oh."

He programmed the destination and set the transport pod for priority delivery to the lab. "There, that'll do it." The transport departed.

"So, what is that material?"

"The manifest calls it unknown. Personally, I think it's that fancy rock discovered near Pluto or something, you know, unknownium."

"It was Saturn's moons."

"Yeah, that's where. You watch the science channels a lot, don't you?"

"Sometimes."

"Okay, now…" Ryan's phone interrupted him. He touched his breather. "Maintenance, Ryan speaking." Sasha watched but could not hear the conversation on the other end. Ryan touched his breather again. "That was Dr. Wellington. He needs us in the test range immediately. Follow me; it's this way." They returned to the lockers and stripped off their gear. "Normally, we'd shower first, but they said it was an emergency."

They entered a passenger pod. "Test Range. Voice authorization: Jones- Bravo-One-One."

"I've noticed you use different codes when you set your destinations."

"Yes, it depends on where you're going. I had to use Bravo because of the quarantine. The highest access code is Alpha, which I don't have. The tubes are divided into several sectors and levels. The sectors are north, south, east, west, and central. Levels are one to ten. There are sub-levels, but we're not supposed to know about them. We don't have access anyway."

"The grey areas?"

Ryan nodded. "The grey areas."

CHAPTER 10

THE POD ARRIVED AT THE RANGE AND OPENED ITS DOORS. STANDING outside were two armed guards. "Jones and Krueger reporting as ordered." Both men showed their ID cards. The guards nodded them through.

"We need to find Dr. Wellington." Ryan scanned the room. "Wow, there's a lot of brass in here. I see General Tremaine, General Paxton, and Colonel Bryer. I'm not sure who the others are."

"I think those three are the Secretary of Defense, Robert Maxwell, Secretary of the Army, Patrick Milne, and Secretary of the Navy, Allison Beauregard."

"How'd you know that?"

"I used to be military."

"Oh…"

"There you are. I have been waiting for you."

"We just walked in, Dr. Wellington. I'd like to introduce…"

"Not now. I'd be happy to meet him later, but we have a crisis that needs to be dealt with now."

"Okay, Doctor, you're the boss. What's the problem?"

"The gantry crane isn't working, and we need to set targets soon."

"No problem, sir. We can wheel them down for you."

"No, you can't. The range is under quarantine."

"Oh. Do you need the targets or can you make do without?"

"No, I don't want a paradox."

"A what? Never mind. Okay, we'll get right on it. Are those the targets?" Ryan pointed.

"Yes. I thought about using the paper target scooters, but each target is 700 pounds, so they're too heavy for the scooters."

"How long do we have?"

"They need to be in place by fourteen hundred hours."

"Okay, we'll do our best." Ryan took Sasha to a wall panel. He touched a few buttons. "Here are the schematics for the range. Let's take a look at the power grid. By the way, sorry about his not wanting to meet you."

"That's fine; I'm sure Dr. Wellington is a busy man." Sasha was glad because the fewer he met, the fewer needed to believe his lies. "I didn't know we could access the computers anywhere. Will I be getting a login?"

"You will as you go out on your own."

"I could use it now to study the base."

"Okay, I'll get you a limited one. For now, can we focus on this?"

"Yes, sorry."

Dr. Wellington watched the two chatting, and his agitation grew. "Why are they just standing there talking?"

"Is there a problem, Dr. Wellington?" Maxwell said as he approached.

"Only a minor delay, sir. We hope to have it rectified shortly."

"Good. I'm very interested in seeing the back side of that shot from Tuesday."

"You will soon enough, sir."

"Doctor." Wellington became annoyed at the interruption.

"Yes?" He turned to see Ryan. "Oh, I'm sorry, Mr. Jones. Is it fixed yet?"

"Not yet. Everything checks out okay on the outside here, but we need to get inside to check a relay on the gantry itself. Is there any way…"

"No, not even the general can countermand the quarantine. What do we do now?"

"My new tech had an idea and said he'd be right back. He left with security."

Perez exited a transport pad and entered the range with the weapons cart. "Excuse me, Mr. Jones." Dr. Wellington approached Perez. "I'm not sure if we can shoot today, Colonel."

"Why? What's the problem?"

"The gantry crane is down, and we can't place the targets."

"Well, I was shooting at something this week, so I'm sure it'll work out."

"Unless we've entered a grandfather paradox," Dr. Carrie Boulos said in the background.

"What's that mean, Dr. Egghead?" Perez smiled at the young doctor. He nicknamed all the smart ones that, except Wellington.

She lifted her hands and mocked an explosion. "Poof."

"Don't be so dramatic, Dr. Boulos." He turned to Perez. "It means the bullets will either hit the back wall or not show up at all."

"Oh, that's all."

Perez walked away and entered the range locking it down. He began his setup. "Well, Doc, whether the targets are ready or not, I'll be ready." He set up the weapon and looked down range through the scope. "Hey, I think someone came up with an idea!" Just as Dr. Wellington was about to ask, Sasha emerged from the transport wearing the visor and gloves with Rammy trailing behind him.

"What are we supposed to do with that?"

Ryan assured the doctor. "We can move the targets with the robot. It's strong enough."

"We need to shoot in the next five minutes. How are we getting the targets down range that fast?"

Perez overheard. "Doc, give your head a shake. It's a Time Shot. I can do it now, and we can set up after. We have an hour."

"Yes, of course, you're right. Let's continue, quickly."

Sasha looked at Perez and froze. *Oh no, that's Colonel Perez. We've met before.* Sasha lowered the visor and made sure it was down when Perez was around. *What's he doing?* He aimed the cameras at Perez and zoomed in. *That's a rifle. Why is there all this fuss over a rifle?*

"Dr. Wellington. We need to get started. Are we good to go?"

"Yes, General. We have a plan."

"Good." The general turned to address the crowd. "May I have your attention, please? Could I have you all return to your seats? We wish to get started." The general waited a moment for all to take their seats. Sasha stood to the side with Ryan but was still in a position to hear what was said. He listened carefully but was cautious not to show too much interest.

"Good morning, ladies and gentlemen, officers, and secretaries. Welcome to the Ghost Mountain Advanced Research Center. Do we ever have a show for you today. I'm Major General Isaac Tremaine, and I'm the commanding officer of Ghost Mountain." Sasha took note of the information. "I'd like to begin today by introducing Dr. David Wellington, our project lead. Dr. Wellington has been with Ghost

Mountain from its humble beginnings when we were a mere $500 billion facility." Everyone except Ryan and Sasha laughed at the joke.

"With the doctor's discoveries, we've expanded into the world's largest and most advanced research facility. Discoveries here have taken America into the future and beyond, quite literally. I ask that you give honor where honor is due and welcome Dr. Wellington." The crowd gave the doctor a hearty round of applause.

Not accustomed to accolades, the scientist felt a bit uneasy about the attention, but shook it off quickly and began to speak. "Welcome esteemed and top-secret guests. This group represents almost the entire population of people who are privy to this project. We're about to witness one of the most important technological advancements ever seen by man." The doctor lowered a screen and projected a slide show. "Based on discoveries I made many years ago, we've developed a means of delivering a projectile, fired from a human-portable device, into both the past and future dimensions of time."

Sasha almost jolted the robot when he heard the statement. *They discovered WHAT? I must get this back to control.*

"Most of what I'm about to say is detailed in your briefing packages." He pointed to the screen, which displayed an animated view of the TATES. "The weapon itself is constructed from the strongest combination of materials ever created. It's powered by anti-matter which enables it to fire twenty-five rounds before needing a recharge."

He changed the slide.

"Targets are selected by using a sighting device that can visually read through time. It's called a Chronoscope. Anti-matter also powers the Chronoscope, enabling the operator to select a target in time. It sends a pulse connecting the present and targeted points in time."

Another slide.

"The weapon discharges Chronon Augmented Projectiles or CAPs, which travel to any target through a self-generated time wormhole. There are limits to the time we can traverse through. We can only go back in time to the point we manufactured the CAP."

Next slide.

"For example, if we manufactured the round that Colonel Perez is about to fire a week ago, then, it would only be able to travel one week into the past and accurately one week into the future. As it matures, the time range expands proportionally. Currently, our stock of CAPs enables us to travel seven days into the past and seven days in the future."

Sasha stood in awe and held in a gasp from what he had learned. *I can't believe the Americans have this! If they use this, Russia is in trouble. I have to see it work.*

"It's time, Doctor," Carrie said.

"Yes, of course." He looked at Perez. Perez nodded and gave the thumbs up.

"Colonel Perez is the marksman who has been testing the weapon all week. Today, we'll watch the final shot of five. In an hour's time, we'll witness all five shots converging at the same time, each from the five separate departure times. Colonel, when you're ready."

"Certainly, Doc. Okay, everyone, this is a containment cartridge; it can only hold one round." Sasha listened intently. *He's explaining everything, very thoughtful of you, Colonel. It'll be easier for me to use when I steal it.* "I take the cartridge and lock it into the undercarriage assembly like this." He inserted it with a click. "Next, I rotate this lever, and the round will magnetically lift into the breach." He touched the scope. "To activate the scope, I press this button here. I can now use these dials to adjust to one hour from now. I can see the current and target times on the display. When I'm happy with the target time, I lock it in with this button on the rifle."

He leaned into the scope. "With the target set, I can release the round with a pull of the trigger, just like a conventional weapon. After that, well, you'll see the rest." Perez gazed at the target and said over the headset, "On your command, General."

"Fire at will, Colonel."

Perez fired the weapon. Sasha watched as a haze formed in front of the gun. Suddenly the air twisted momentarily and rippled, ending in a popping sound. Every fob in the room beeped twice. The room erupted in applause. "Okay strange guy with the visor. It's your turn to be the hero. You have exactly one hour to get those targets down there." Perez unlocked the range. He stood and casually looked at Sasha but couldn't see his full features because of the visor.

Sasha looked back. *Does he recognize me?* When the range door opened, Sasha activated the robot. He reached out into the air, guiding it with the VR gloves. He felt for a place to hold the target and lifted it onto the cargo platform. Once secured, he drove down the range, "Where do they go?"

"It doesn't matter. Stick em' anywhere at the end. I've already shot at them." Sasha was puzzled by Perez's statement but continued. The robot ambled down the length of the range until it reached its first destination. Sasha carefully lifted the numbered target and placed it on the floor facing the gallery. He turned the robot around and returned for the next one.

When the robot had returned, Dr. Wellington said, "The first one took thirteen minutes to deploy. We're running out of time, can you go any faster?"

"He's going as fast as he can. You can't rush this," Ryan defended Sasha. Sasha gripped the second target and repeated the process.

"Twelve minutes, better, but please hurry."

He picked up the third target, this time with less caution. He turned and pushed the throttle to its limit. It clattered down the range to about the halfway point when it jerked as one of the tracks bound up. The jarring caused Sasha to lose his grip on the target. The spectators released a collective gasp as the apparatus crashed to the floor.

"That's why that one had a big chunk out of it," Perez said.

Sasha reached down and picked up the target from the floor. He placed it back on the platform and set out for the end once again. When set, he returned for the next.

"Seventeen minutes for that one. Only seventeen minutes for two targets."

"Thank you for the update, Doctor, but if you would, please let my man concentrate."

"Why isn't it you driving the robot? Could you be doing it better than he is?"

"Stephan is as capable as me, Dr. Wellington."

Sasha thought, *Thanks Ryan, I appreciate that. I may not kill you after all.* Sasha felt the pressure. He picked up the fourth target and continued down the range, pushing the robot hard, but mindful to not drop another target. He reached the end, placed the fourth target, and returned as quickly as he could.

"Twelve minutes. Only five left," Wellington said.

"Thanks for the play-by-play, Doc," Perez said. Wellington gave him a dirty look. Sasha picked up the fifth and final target. He turned and started down the range. Minutes counted down quickly as it clumsily tracked its way toward the end.

"Four minutes."

"Three minutes."

The observers all sat on the edge of their seats and watched as Sasha guided it closer and closer to the end of the range.

"Two minutes…"

"Thank you, Doctor, but that's quite enough."

"Sorry, General."

The robot was mere seconds away from the target location, when suddenly it stopped. A collective gasp was released as the robot failed. It refused to respond to any of Sasha's commands. Still ten feet short of deployment, it was as if something was blocking the control signal. Sasha lifted the visor, being careful not to allow Perez to see his face. Tensions mounted as the clock ticked away its final seconds.

The air turned hazy in the five distinct locations across the range. Suddenly, space twisted into the characteristic swirl, as the five wormholes established this end of their pathway through time. A bullet emerged from each swirl, which immediately collapsed into the ripple pattern as before. The collapse sounded off in five pops across the range. As each CAP appeared, they traveled the short distance to their targets, each striking dead center, including the fifth and final target, still held in the robotic arms.

The general looked at Perez, who smiled, "I didn't want to ruin the surprise."

The observation gallery broke out into laughter and cheers as the test fire was a total success. They'd just made history, although an account that would remain untold – still history nonetheless. Spectators extended their congratulatory handshakes to Sasha who tried to fade into the background of the celebration. Through all of the accolades, Sasha thought, *Laugh now people, for soon you will be crying.*

He watched as Secretary Maxwell approached the general. "General, I can't thank you enough for inviting me to see the test. I've been speaking with the Chairman of the Joint Chiefs General Paxton about the weapon, and he agrees that we need to get this in the field across all disciplines as quickly as possible. When could it be possible?"

"First, you're welcome, Mr. Secretary. As far as availability, we could scale it to fit many platforms including battleship rail guns. Deployment to field infantry could be in eight months with larger scale guns taking an estimated two years. Construction on that scale, however, is beyond our current capabilities. We'd need to expand our facilities again."

"Name the cost; we'll get it to you. I can already sense the excitement that'll come from the Hill. Wow, Ghost Mountain does it again. Do you realize how much this will shift the balance of power back toward the U.S. again?"

"Yes, I do, sir, and we're honored to be a part of it. I understand that after this test the project is being reclassified to below Majestic level. I feel it to be prudent to tighten our security around here if that's the case. With more people knowing the weapon is here, I sense an increased risk."

"About that, General, you're ordered to send it to Groom Lake for field testing. I want to see it in action in the field as soon as possible. Colonel Perez, of course, will still be the operator."

"When do you want that, sir?"

"As soon as possible, how's yesterday?" He paused. "That's a time joke, General."

"Yes, hilarious, sir. I'll begin the arrangements for a departure two days from now. We'll fly directly from here to Groom Lake. Would that be soon enough, sir?"

"That'll be fine, General. What if the weather is too bad for air transport?"

"We'll transport via ground convoy, sir, but if I recall correctly, the forecast looks good, so I don't foresee any issues."

"Thank you, General." Maxwell walked away lightly shaking his head, "Doesn't anyone here besides Perez have a sense of humor?"

Sasha stood silent for a moment to process everything he had just witnessed. *This weapon is the pearl I've been waiting to find.* He left the range with the now functional robot before Perez became too curious. He finished his shift and hurried home to report the day's findings. As he left the complex, he looked in his mirror. "Fly out in two days? We'll see about that."

CHAPTER 11

"YES, COMRADE GENERAL, YOU HEARD ME CORRECTLY. IT SHOOTS through time."

"Major Mishkov, we cannot begin to express our concern in this. We want you to retrieve the weapon and delay their efforts in any way possible. Make sure that you do not connect the theft to Russia. We will send whatever you need to help you do this. Can you stop the air transfer?"

"The airport is well defended Comrade-General, so a direct attack would be futile. I may have an idea though. I will somehow force a ground transport, so it will be easier to attack. As soon as I design a plan, I will send it to you for your approval, Comrade General."

"Very well, Major." The general abruptly hung up. Sasha looked at his phone and then to Galina.

"It must be an essential toy for Moscow to want so much," Galina said.

"You have no idea, Galina. You have no idea." He tapped his notepad. "Let's think now."

General Tremaine's intercom buzzed. "Colonel Perez is here, sir."

"Thank you, Jenny; please send him in."

The door opened, and Perez entered. He walked directly to the general and saluted, "Reporting as ordered, sir."

The general saluted back but skipped protocol, "Have a seat, Perez."

Perez relaxed and sat down. "That was quite the nail-biter yesterday, wasn't it, sir?"

Tremaine handed him a paper, ignoring his comment. "Perez. I'm sorry, but I need to cancel your leave for next week. We've been ordered to transport the TATES weapon off-site for further testing." Perez although visibly disappointed, did his best to remain composed. "I know this isn't what you wanted, but orders are orders. We'll be sending it by air transport to Groom Lake tomorrow. You'll accompany the weapon and operate it during the tests. It should only be for a few weeks. Do not, and I repeat, DO NOT let anyone take the weapon from your sight, understood?"

"Understood, sir." Perez scanned the transfer order. "May I speak freely, sir?"

"Of course, Perez, always."

Perez smirked, "Are you going to be the one who tells Sarah? You know, my wife, your daughter?"

The general laughed. "I was thinking of sending a Special Forces unit to do that, but I don't think they'd make it out alive."

They both laughed. "I'd be lying, sir if I said I wasn't disappointed. I could use the break."

"I know, Perez. I'm sorry. I'll make it up to you somehow." The general continued his briefing. "I've ordered the accelerator powered up to produce additional CAPs. We'll start tomorrow and then ship them when ready. In the meantime, take the remaining stock with you. How many do we have left?"

"Thirteen cooked, sir. Did you want to hold any in reserve, just in case?"

"No, let's use them all for now. I want the field test finished as soon as possible."

"Okay, sir." Perez nodded in agreement.

"At 0600 tomorrow, you're wheels up for Nevada. Say hello to the little green men for me, would you?"

Perez smiled. "Yes, sir. I will, and I'll even get you an Area 51 conspiracy t-shirt too."

"Again, I'm truly sorry about your vacation, Perez."

"No problem, sir. I'm sure the family will understand."

"You can go home early and prepare now if you like. Dismissed."

Perez rose and walked to the door. He grabbed the knob and turned it, opening the door a crack. "By the way, sir, who's the guy with the robot yesterday?"

"He's new here. His name is Stephan Krueger. He saved the day, didn't he?"

"Yes, sir, he did, but I can't help but think I've met him before. I just can't place where."

"He was former navy, maybe there?"

"Maybe, sir, but it's going to bug me until I figure it out."

"Please don't call me at three in the morning if you do."

"No, sir, I won't, maybe two in the morning?"

"Get out. I've real work to do now." The general laughed and put his head down to work again.

"Goodbye, sir."

Perez closed the door and went to his office to finish a few details before his trip. "Sarah is going to kill me." After he completed his duties, he left to prepare for his extended mission away and to break the news to his soon-to-be-unhappy family.

In another part of Ghost Mountain, Sasha poured over schematics of the Air Deck, looking for any vulnerability. "How can I shut the air transport down? There has to be a chink in the armor, but where?" He used his finger to trace line after line representing various cables and pipes all laid out in a complicated web of systems. "I could flood it?" He traced the pipes and drains. "No, it would simply drain off."

He turned a few more pages. "I could try a bomb in the weapons area, but I can't get too close." He touched the diagrams of the weapons room. "It can't be too big; it would send everything into chaos. I'd be the first they looked at too." He closed his eyes. "Think, Sasha, think." He paused for a moment, and then his face lit up. "That's it! I know what to do." He quickly cleared the screen of all of the prints. He went to an out-of-the way storage room and retrieved several devices that he had smuggled in over the first few days. "I better work fast. I think today's my last day here."

"Good afternoon, folks. Captain Bob Brooks here with Lieutenant Gary Connors in the co-pilot's seat. We'll be your flight crew for your transport to Ghost Mountain today. For those who might be interested, you're currently sitting in an Airbus C-295 air transport." Captain Brooks paused for a moment to check an indicator.

"We're on hold for a couple of minutes, waiting for takeoff. Please ensure your seatbelts are connected, and all loose items are secured." Brooks keyed off the intercom.

"Gary, could you open the flight plan when we're up, please?"

"Yes, sir."

A soft tone sounded in the pilot's ear. He keyed his mic. "Yes, Susan."

"Hello, Captain. All sixty-two passengers are prepared and secure for takeoff."

"Roger that, Susan, thanks. We'll be departing in about one minute." He keyed the mic off.

"Is the pre-flight checklist completed, Gary?"

"Yes, Captain, all pre-flights completed."

"Tower, Ghost Transport zero-one-seven holding position zero-six-left."

"Ghost one-seven, you are cleared for takeoff, runway zero-six-left, contact departure one-three-six decimal six in the air."

"Roger. Ghost one-seven clear to go; contact departure one-thirty-six-six in the air."

He positioned the aircraft for takeoff. "Here we go." Captain Brooks pushed the engine controls forward. The plane rapidly built up its speed to where both pilots could pull back on the yokes, causing the plane to lift from the ground.

"Departure, Ghost transport zero-one-seven out of one point three for five thousand."

"Ghost transport zero-one-seven, radar identified, maintain seven thousand."

"Roger, maintain seven thousand." He closed the mic. "Airspeed, 140 knots, waiting on gear."

"I'm raising the gear now, Captain."

"Roger, you're raising the gear. Adjusting flaps from ten degrees to zero." They felt the clunk of the landing gear as it locked into place.

"Flaps are coming to zero; gear confirmed up and locked, sir."

"Ghost transport zero-one-seven, Departure. After noise abatement, turn heading two-six-zero."

"Roger, right heading, two-six-zero after abatement."

"Flight plan activated, sir."

"Perfect, thanks, Gary."

"Ghost transport zero-one-seven. Climb to one-nine-zero and maintain."

"Roger, climb to one-nine-zero, Ghost one-seven."

"Ghost transport zero-one-seven, once at altitude turn heading two-seven-zero, set your cruise for two-one-zero knots, all follow-up headings are now according to your plan. Be advised, traffic at three o'clock high, three miles is a Dash 8 at heading one-seven-zero at two-one-zero feet and three-one-zero knots."

"Departure, Ghost-one-seven. Roger, turn heading two-seven-zero, cruise set to two-one-zero knots. We will execute our filed plan at one-nine-zero." He looked out the window. "We have a visual on inbound Dash 8. Thanks, departure. Ghost one-seven out." Captain Brooks keyed the cabin intercom.

"Hello, folks. Captain Brooks here again. We're approaching our cruising altitude of 19,000 feet and are traveling at 210 knots. The way looks clear for weather, and we're not expecting any concerns for the trip. We'll be arriving at Ghost Mountain in one hour and twenty minutes, right on time for your afternoon shift. Please enjoy the flight." He flipped the switch off. "Okay, Gary set the autopilot and let's break out the bubbly."

"Autopilot set. Bubbly? What do you mean by that?"

"Nothing, just kidding. This is a milestone flight for me."

"Really, what milestone is that, sir?"

"This'll be the ten-thousandth landing for me at Ghost Mountain."

"Wow, you've hit that much?"

"Three times a day for fifteen years now. How about you?"

"I've never counted, sir, but I'd say it could be a couple thousand."

"You know, Gary, no matter how many times I land these planes, I never get used to flying into a solid rock face."

"Yes, sir, it freaks me out a lot too."

"It's like trying to throw an egg through a small window that you can't see, and you know what happens if you miss."

"I know, scrambled eggs."

"I wonder whose crazy idea it was to put an airport inside a mountain anyway, especially with only a dog door to go through?"

"I'm not sure, sir, but at least they gave us a laser guidance system to help."

"Yes, I don't know what we'd do if we didn't have that."

"That's easy, sir. We'd crash."

Sasha climbed out of a maintenance tunnel just below the Air Deck landing field. "That should do the trick. Let's see them keep this open after a crash. A couple more stops and I'll have my work finished." Sasha carried on to his next destination, looking around for anyone who might have seen him.

CHAPTER 12

"IT'S ABOUT TIME YOU GOT BACK HERE, YOU LAZY BUM." CHARLIE Walsh leaned back in his chair, sporting a huge smile.

"You know I could have you court-martialed, drawn and quartered, set on fire, and thrown out of the mountain, right?" Flight director Jack Farmer said as he set his heavy frame back into his chair.

"I doubt it. You're too lazy even to pick up the phone, compadre."

"You're probably right, Charlie." Jack laughed. "How's the pattern look, ace?"

"Not too full; quiet day today. We've got Ghost one-seven about fifty miles out, heading two-seven-zero at two-one-zero knots and Ghost one-nine at 150 miles out at heading three-zero-zero, two-two-zero knots, both at one-nine zero feet. There's also Groom transport One-One coming here for the special tomorrow morning, entering radar at 250 miles, heading zero-nine-zero at two-two-zero feet and three-five-zero knots."

"We should be hearing from one-seven any minute now," Farmer said.

"Ghost TRACON, Ghost Transport zero-one-seven on final approach, request approach vectors."

"Speaking of them, there they are now."

"Ghost one-seven, TRACON here. Jack Farmer talking at ya, who's this?"

"Hey Jack, Bob Brooks here. I haven't heard from you in a while. Where've you been?"

"Trying to avoid you." Jack laughed. "I still owe you fifty bucks for that last game I lost."

"It was like taking candy from a baby, Jack."

"Yeah, I know, a sucker born every minute, but I was sure they were going to win."

"I would love to talk about getting money, Jack, but I may not get to spend it if I don't get my vectors soon. I'm flying a plane toward a wall of rock, you know."

"No worries, Bob. Descend to one-seven-zero. Set heading two-six-zero at first marker. I show you currently forty miles out."

"Roger, one-seven-zero feet, set heading two-six-zero at the thirty-mile marker."

"Landing guidance, what's your status?" Jack turned to Charlie.

"Laser active one hundred percent. MACS online and ready for capture. The Hail Mary net is activated and ready."

"You know, I don't like that nickname."

"Sorry, Jack. The Kinetic Capture Curtain is activated in the event of a MACS failure. Whoa! The laser guidance system just blinked."

"What do you mean L.G.S. just blinked?" Jack swiveled his chair to face Charlie.

"It just winked off for a second. It's back now though."

"Should we abort their approach?"

"The system looks okay now. Both emitters are active; it may be a monitor glitch."

"Okay, but watch it closely. If it blinks again, we abort immediately."

"TRACON, Ghost zero-one-seven at first marker, turning to heading two-six-zero. Request final approach vectors."

Jack turned back to the radar. "Ghost zero-one-seven. Roger that. After heading change, descend to one-five-zero feet, until past the curtain, then fast descent to one-two-zero feet. LGS ready for approach assist. MACS primed and ready to capture."

"Roger, Ghost zero-one-seven reducing to one-seven-zero knots, flaps at fifteen degrees, twenty miles out. We're at one-six-zero feet and dropping. Have you turned off the reception committee yet?"

Jack waved his hand to Charlie who advised security to deactivate air defense systems.

"Air defense systems disengaged. I show you fifteen miles out at one-five-zero feet."

"Roger that, confirmed at 15,000 feet ready to drop to 12,000 in five miles."

"Cue overhead landing lights and approach warning siren." Charlie initiated the warning light over the entrance. It began to flash followed by a ten-second blast from a siren, warning anyone on the deck that a plane was coming.

"TRACON, we're now descending to one-two-zero feet. Instruments have locked onto LGS, coming in for final approach. Slowing to one-forty knots, flaps at twenty-three degrees. We're deploying landing gear now."

"Roger, we're ready for you. You're sixty seconds out."

"Ghost one-seven we're at Rubicon, past the point of no return. Gear is locked, and we're on landing approach. Hold it, what's that, Gary?"

"Jack, LGS just quit!" Charlie jumped out of his chair to reach for the hologram shut off control. He slammed it with his palm.

"Ghost one-seven. Mayday! Mayday! LGS has failed, we've no approach assist, and we're flying blind. Thirty seconds out."

"Cloaking is off!" Charlie keyed the mic. "The garage door should be visible now."

"Okay, we see it. Crap! We're running fifty feet low, pull up ,Gary, pull up!"

The flight control crew collectively held their breath as they helplessly waited for the plane to close the gap in its final seconds. "Ready emergency services!" Jack hit the alarm horn.

Suddenly, they saw the nose of the plane scrape over the bottom edge of the entrance. Sparks and parts flew in all directions as the front and port landing gear of the aircraft were sheared off. The plane dropped to the deck hard, and metal ground against metal as the nose scraped along the deck. The propeller tips snapped like twigs on the port engine as each one rounded in its cycle. The plane skidded across the Air-Deck at an angle. The MACS engaged and attempted to slow the aircraft but couldn't do it without the brakes and reverse thrusters.

"Deploying the capture net!" Jack reached for the control and hit it with force. The net instantly stiffened, readying itself to absorb the full force from the impact of the sliding plane. Jack prayed under his breath as he watched it hit the net at an angle. The curtain heaved under the enormous strain and automatically slackened to release the force in a controlled manner. The plane decelerated, quickly coming to a halt.

Completely stopped now, the aircraft had entangled its broken front landing gear and damaged port engine on the net.

A low rumble emanated from under the deck. "Jack, the MACS has just re-engaged in launch mode." Charlie frantically reached for the emergency cutoff, but it didn't work.

"I know, look at the plane. It's inching backward." The starboard engine was still running on the plane.

"Captain, are you alright?" Gary reached for the shoulder of the unconscious Brooks and shook it. He didn't respond. He felt the captain's neck. "Okay, he has a pulse." Suddenly Gary felt the plane move backward. "What the?" He keyed the radio, "TRACON we're moving backward! What the hell are you doing?"

"I see you're talking, but I can't hear you. We can't shut off the MACS, and it's trying to launch you back out. The net is holding you, but I don't know for how long."

Gary pushed the starboard throttle arm forward, but the broken lever sprang back. "Bob, wake up!" Gary sat in his chair and pushed the throttle ahead, this time holding it in place. He keyed the cabin mic. "Attention, attention. Evacuate the plane immediately at exits on the left side only." Gary could hear the screams and confusion in the rear of the plane but had to stay and force the throttle forward to buy the passengers time to escape.

Minutes passed like hours as passengers jumped from the plane caught in the deadly tug-of-war. Emergency crews ran out and helped them to safety but could do nothing else. He strained to look out the window and see if the evacuation was complete.

"Is everyone out yet?" He called on the radio. He waited, but the radio stayed silent. "Answer me, damn it!" He forgot they couldn't hear him. He waited another minute, pushing the throttle.

The radio crackled. "Ground crews say the plane is clear. What are you still doing in there? If you can hear me, you two need to get out now." Gary heard the warning. He let off the throttle control, and the plane lunged backward. Quickly, he released his belt and jumped from his seat. He reached over and unbuckled Captain Brooks. He pulled hard and dragged the unconscious captain from his chair while the MACS strained the net tighter and tighter as it drew on the plane.

The plane jolted after it tore away a piece of the net causing Gary to fall backward with the captain in his arms. He quickly got out from under the unconscious Brooks and stood up, gazing at the waiting exit only steps away. He shook his head, grabbed each of Brooks' wrists and dragged him closer to the door. Suddenly, another piece of the net broke, which caused the plane to lunge backward, once again knocking Gary to the floor.

"Come on, Bob, wake up! I'm not leaving you here." He stood up again and was mere steps from the exit when the net finally lost its battle with the MACS. The restraint released its grip on the plane, allowing it to quickly accelerate toward the mouth of the cavern. Gary lost his footing again and held on, trying not to be pushed backward by the acceleration.

"I have to get you out of here." He strained to roll Brooks toward the exit, as the plane slid faster and faster toward the waiting 11,000-foot drop. He couldn't pick himself up, much less the captain, to drag him to safety. In a final valiant effort, he planted both feet firmly against the unconscious captain and pushed him from the plane onto the deck. "Have a good life, Captain."

The captain landed within feet of the edge. Gary watched as the plane shot through the exit, callously ejected from the base. As it plummeted, he lay back motionless and peacefully awaited his fate.

CHAPTER 13

"HONESTLY, GENERAL, I DON'T KNOW WHAT TO SAY. IT ALL HAPPENED so fast we couldn't respond. One thing I will say though is that if it weren't for Charlie shutting off the hologram, we'd have sixty-five dead right now."

General Tremaine stood in the now pressurized Air Deck with the flight control crew. "I know, you're right, Mr. Farmer, but I still don't like writing letters to grieving families no matter how few. I want this investigated right away. As far as the Air Deck is concerned, it's closed for business until we get to the bottom of this."

"Yes, sir. What about the special that's supposed to come today?"

"Reroute it. We'll have to change the plans and take it by ground."

A door opened behind the general, and Ryan Jones walked out. He approached the group holding something strange in his hand.

"Here is Ryan Jones, sir. Maybe he has some answers."

Ryan lifted his hand and in it dangled a dead rat. "This could be the culprit, sir. I found chew marks and charring on both the main and alternate supply cables to the emitters. There were also droppings on the floor like they were there feasting for a while."

"Are you telling me that rats killed our pilot and shut down my $20 billion airport?"

"It would appear that way, General, but I'll keep digging. I don't know what happened to the MACS yet. My crew is still working on it."

"Let me know as soon as you find anything out; I'll be in my office." Tremaine pointed at Farmer. "As for you, close this airport, and keep it that way until I advise you otherwise."

"Yes, sir." Ryan and Jack both said in unison. The general spun around and with a deep sigh walked to the transport pod.

"I'm no rat expert, Jack, but these teeth don't look sharp enough to make the clean slices I saw."

"Why didn't you say anything to the general?"

"I don't want to alarm him before I'm sure. What are the odds of losing both supplies at the same time though?"

"I don't know, Ryan, but as a bettin' man, I wouldn't have put money on it."

"Me either. I'll be back. I need to check some things."

"Okay, buster, what's up?" Sarah Perez stood with her hands on her hips, tapping her foot.

"Whatever do you mean, dear?"

"Don't play innocent with me, mister. I know something is up."

"Why? Just because I bring you flowers and gifts for the kids doesn't mean that I'm up to something."

"Joseph Samuel Perez, don't lie to me. I know when you're lying to me; your right eye twitches." Sarah's fists curled tighter.

"What? That must be why I suck at poker."

"Don't change the subject."

"Honest, dear, nothing is going on."

"Alright, I guess I'll have to believe you."

"Thank you, dear." Perez took a few steps toward the kitchen. "Umm, there may be just this one little thing."

"I knew it. Spit it out. You're such a rotten liar that you stink." She pinched her nose playfully.

"Who stinks?" Perez's oldest boy, Joshua, walked in.

"Your liar father, that's who."

"Why? What did he do now?"

"Nothing, I just brought you guys presents."

"Presents, cool, you won my vote."

"Hold it a minute. This isn't an election race. Presents and smiles are not going to wash here."

"Let's wait until we have dinner, hon. We can discuss it with the family then."

"Okay, but I don't like the sound of this. I think I may know where this is going – or not going."

"By the way, what's for dinner?"

Sarah smiled. "Whatever food you order in, dear, being that you're in such a generous mood today."

Joshua laughed at his parent's exchange. "Ooo, *dam-aged*. Dad, you're busted, and we don't even know what for yet."

Perez groaned, "Yeah, I know."

"Jenny, could you connect me with security, please?" Tremaine picked up his phone and waited.

"Right away, sir." She began typing on her computer. She reached for her phone and dialed. "Sir, I have security for you."

Tremaine lifted the phone to his ear. "Hello?"

"Security, Sergeant Dunbar speaking."

"Hello, Sergeant, this is General Tremaine." He could hear Dunbar snap to attention in his chair.

"Yes, sir, how may I help you, sir?"

"Sergeant, I need you to arrange for a ground transport tomorrow. Keep it low profile, nothing flashy. I need a van with two escorts to take a project to Hill Airforce Base tomorrow morning. Can you do that, or will there be a problem?"

"No problem at all, sir. We can do that. I'll assign crisis team Alpha to escort them. What time would you like the transport to depart, sir?"

"0900 departure will be fine."

"Consider it done, sir."

"Thank you, Sergeant Dunbar.

"You're welcome, sir."

The general released the line and dialed another number.

"Josh, pass me another slice of that heaven-on-dough, will ya?" Perez reached out to receive his veggie-covered pizza.

"I'm glad that's your favorite, Dad. It means more meaty pizza for me."

"Daddy, why was Mommy so mad at you earlier? Are you getting a divorce?" Seven-year-old Mica said.

Sarah laughed. "No dear, of course not. I was giving daddy a hard time because I think I know what's coming."

"I'm sorry, hon. I don't have a choice; we need to cancel our camping trip."

"I knew it. Dad did this, didn't he?" Sarah vigorously cut up a piece of garlic bread for their three-year-old Adam to eat.

"Well yes, but he's following orders from above."

"Hon, I knew when we married this would happen, and it often has. But knowing it doesn't mean I like it. At least you're not in combat anymore."

"Yes, I know dear, but I'm still sorry it happens."

"Can you tell me what this one's about?"

"I can say a little. I have to accompany a project to Groom Lake."

"I'm cool about it, Dad. It's okay we're not going. There's this new girl, Jodie, working at the drive-in. I got my eye on her. The timing is perfect. Billy Watson thinks I'm gone, so he'll take his time. I can scoop her first."

"Okay, Romeo, cool your jets." Sarah took a bite of her salad.

"Daddy, how long will you be gone for?" Mica said as she nibbled on her pizza.

"I'll be at least three weeks, sweetie, but I'll call every day."

She frowned in disappointment. "I don't want you gone that long. I'll miss you. You're my protector."

"Don't worry, sis, I got your back." Josh turned to his dad, "Don't worry, Dad, I got it covered here, take your time. Uh, by the way, are you taking the car?"

"Ah, the truth finally reveals itself, not on your life, kiddo." Josh just shrugged innocently.

The phone rang in the kitchen. Josh jumped up. "I'll get it. It might be Amber."

"Amber? Who's Amber? I thought he wanted Jodie." Perez laughed.

"Oh, hon, he's got three on the tow right now. Jodie could be number four."

Perez smiled. "Nice. He's a chip off the old block, isn't he?"

Sarah laughed. "Yeah, right. You wish, Mr. Stud."

"Hey, I got you, didn't I?"

"True you did, but only because of your charm and a bullet wound."

"Yeah, I know. I had to go as far as getting myself shot to meet you at the hospital."

"Was it your idea to get shot in your butt though?"

"Ha. No, it was a bad ricochet. All I know is that when the nurse said the doctor would be right in to see me, I didn't expect such a beautiful woman to come through the door. And then you followed in after her."

Sarah gasped. "Hey. You jerk." She threw a small piece of garlic bread at him.

Perez laughed. "Just kidding, hon. You're still that beautiful doctor I married so many years ago."

"Uh… I hate to interrupt this love fest, but it's Gramps on the phone. He wants to talk with you, Dad."

"If he's calling to cancel your mission, tell him he's lucky. If not, tell him to expect the stethoscope to be in the freezer for his next physical. I've connections, you know." Perez laughed and walked to the kitchen. Josh grabbed another slice of meaty pizza.

"Hey, Mom, really, I'm okay with not going. We can hang out here."

"Thanks, Josh, that helps."

"How was work today?"

"It was great. I helped a man to walk again. He now has two new bionic legs, thanks to Ghost Mountain Research."

"And thanks to you too, Dr. Perez. Hey, do you ever wonder what Dad does there?"

"Sometimes, but I think it's best we don't know. It's safer for us."

Perez walked in with a somber look on his face.

"Wow, you look sad. You must have really wanted to get away from us." Sarah laughed. "Was it canceled?"

"No, but it has been changed though."

"Really? Why do you look so sad?"

"There was a plane crash at the base today, so the airport is shut down."

"Oh no, was there anyone hurt?"

"There were several cuts and scrapes, but there was one fatality, the copilot. He bought enough time for everyone to escape the plane. He even got the unconscious pilot out but couldn't get out himself."

"Wow, what a hero."

"Yes, he is. Anyway, your father changed the conveyance from air to ground transport. We leave tomorrow at 9:00 a.m. instead of 6:00."

"At least you can sleep in a bit."

"Not really. I need to move a bunch of stuff to a ground transport now. One good thing about this is that I got permission to take my bike along."

"What? Okay, a cold table for him now too."

"You're taking that old hunk of junk, Dad?" Josh paused, "On second thought, I think it's a great idea."

Sarah glared at him with a look that only a mother could give. "No, you're still not getting the car."

"Ah, nuts."

"The funny thing is that he ordered a heavily armed escort to take us."

"Should I be worried?" Her face transformed into a look of concern.

"No dear, I'm sure it's just a precaution." He smiled his confident grin. "Everything will be fine."

"Okay." She took another bite of her salad, but this time, it didn't taste right.

CHAPTER 14

"YES, SERGEANT, I'LL HAVE IT READY FOR FIRST THING IN THE MORNING."
Ryan hung up the phone. "Ugh. I'm getting too old for this." He rubbed
his eyes. Leaning over, he picked up a base radio. "Jones to Krueger."

The radio crackled, "Krueger, here."

"Where are you?"

A long silence followed and ended when Sasha walked into Ryan's
office. "I was just down the hall."

"Oh, you're here, great. Listen. I want you to go up to the Air Deck
to help them out, and when you get there, send Kevin from C crew
back down here. I need him to do something for me."

Sasha read Ryan's upside down scribble on his notepad: Two R2-LAVs,
cargo van, Gate E, 9:00 a.m., Perez. Team Alpha.

"Sure. Do you need me to tell Kevin anything or to help him?"

"No, it won't take him long. I need him in the motor pool. I haven't
shown you that yet anyway. Kevin can take care of it. I want you
upstairs, helping."

"Okay, on my way."

"Thanks."

Sasha entered a transport pod and went to the air deck. Once there,
he stepped out to search for the crew. The room was noisy, and he had
to shout. "Which one of you is Kevin?"

"I'm Kevin."

Sasha motioned for him to come over. He put his tools down and
walked over. "What do you want?"

"Hi, I'm Stephan. Ryan told me to come up here and ask you to go to the motor pool."

"Did he say what he wanted?"

"He didn't say, just that he wants you there now."

"Okay, let me tell the boys."

"I will. Ryan asked me to stay and help."

"Okay, Freddie will fill you in. He's on the ladder. Oh, and don't mind him."

Sasha walked to the others, "Kevin had to go, but he'll be back soon."

Freddie who was on the ladder said, "Are you staying to help? It's a freakin' mess in here."

"No, I'm not."

"What? That freakin' Jones never helps us. I'm gonna call him and give him a piece of my mind."

"Don't give him too much, Freddie; you don't have a lot to spare," a crew member jabbed.

"Yeah, yeah, funny, Marty." He looked at Sasha. "Hey rookie, go get me the radio from the cart."

"With pleasure, sir."

Freddie mocked him, "With pleasure, sir. With pleasure, sir."

"Freddie, don't be such an ass," Marty said.

"Actually, you can be a real dick sometimes, Freddie," Chaz said.

"Up yours, both of you." Sasha retrieved the radio and returned. Freddie came down from the ladder.

"Gimme that." He went to grab it from Sasha who held it out palm up. Just as he was about to take it, Sasha dropped the radio and revealed a knife in his hand.

"Please shut up." Sasha grabbed Freddie by the hair and plunged the knife under his chin and deep into his throat. Freddie stood motionless for a moment until Sasha pulled the knife out and let go of his hair to let him fall straight down.

"Whoa! What the hell? What'd you do?" Marty said.

"You were right; he was an ass. If he had simply kept quiet, you'd all still be alive," Sasha said. Sasha moved toward them. Marty turned to run, but Sasha threw the knife at him with such tremendous force that it pierced his back and passed through his ribs directly into his heart.

Chaz watched Marty drop. "No please, don't kill me, I have a family."

Sasha walked toward him. Chaz quickly turned to run, but instead, as he panicked, he ran full force into a low steal bulkhead and knocked himself out cold. He dropped to the floor.

"Well, that was convenient." Sasha walked to the now dead Marty and pulled his knife out. He wiped it clean and put it back in its sheath. Sasha took hold of Marty and pulled his lifeless body into a nearby storage room. Next, he pulled Freddie and deposited him in the same manner. He walked over to the unconscious Chaz and placed his knife against his throat. He applied a slight pressure, just breaking the surface of the skin. After holding it for a moment, a tiny trickle of blood began oozing from the fresh cut. "Here's a little reminder of my mercy, my friend. Tonight is your lucky night." He lifted the knife away and sheathed it again. He then pulled the unconscious Chaz into the room with the others. Once he had him tied and gagged, he closed and locked the door. "I better get moving."

"I'll get on that right away, Ryan." Kevin left to prepare for the transport.

"Thanks." Ryan keyed the radio again. "Ryan to crew C," he stopped. "Oh yes, they won't hear it. I better go up there."

Sasha exited the transport. He looked around and saw an arrow painted on the wall with the stenciled words: *Convergence chamber.* "That's where I need to go." He walked into the chamber with his toolbox in his hand. Inside the room, he stepped onto a metal scaffold connected to stairs that went down to the floor ten feet below. He noticed several large tubes crossing in all directions and interestingly, each one led to a single large sphere in the center of the room. He descended the stairs. "Perfect, now to get to work."

Ryan left the transport and walked to where he believed his crew was working. When he arrived, he found the area deserted. "Hello? Is anyone here?" he noticed tools scattered on the floor. "Where did they go?" He continued to look around and approached the storage room that contained the bodies of his missing men. He tried the door, but it was locked. He pulled his keys out to open it, but heard crackling on his radio. "Hello?" he said into the squelching radio. "What am I doing? I can't hear this silly thing." Ryan left the chamber for a quieter spot. "Did someone call for Ryan?"

"Yes, it's Kevin. I have those vehicles prepped and waiting at staging area Echo."

"Good. Can you come back up here? I can't find your team."

"They may have just gone for a break, which I think is a great idea. I'm going to grab lunch while I'm still down here if that's okay with you, boss."

"Sure, that's fine. I might need something soon too. I'm dying here." Ryan returned to the transport and summoned a unit. He stepped in and was about to command the destination when he noticed a small smear on the console. "What the…"

He tapped on the console. "Computer," it chimed in response.

"Voice authorization: Jones-Bravo-One-One. Inquiry."

The computer answered back, "State inquiry."

"Who was the last occupant of this unit and what was their destination?"

The screen displayed a map and said, "Stephan Krueger was the sole occupant. The destination was Level 5, tunnel section north, thirty-one, convergence chamber."

"Take me there." The transport moved. "What're you doing, Krueger?"

Sasha closed his toolbox and walked up the stairs. "That should do it." He opened the door and came face to face with Ryan.

"Stephan, what're you doing in here?"

"I was checking the accelerator."

"Why? I told you to help the others. I was there, and everyone is gone."

"I told Kevin what you asked."

"Yes, I know. I spoke with him, but do you know where the others are?"

"Yes, I was going to work with them, but they decided to take a break instead. I remembered Dr. Wellington saying that there was a problem with the accelerator, and I came to check it out."

"Look, Stephan, I know you want to help, but you can't run around here doing what you want. What was the blood on the transport panel?"

"Just a little cut, I was careless near some sharp metal. I thought I wiped it off, but I guess I missed some."

"Well, you better come with me to have it looked at."

"Before we do, I've something to show you. I think I may have found the vibration problem."

Ryan took a deep breath and sighed, "Fine, show me."

Sasha opened the door and stepped inside, followed by Ryan. He brought him down the stairs and walked over to where he had been. "Up there." He pointed.

"Where?"

"Right there."

Ryan stepped in closer to look. He climbed the entanglement of tubes to allow him to better see what Sasha was pointing out. After a quick search, he found what Sasha was referring to. His eyes widened. "What the... That looks like a bomb!"

"You're right; it is a bomb."

Ryan looked down at him. "And you casually report this? How did it get there?"

"I put it there."

"You put it there? Stephan, why would..." Sasha interrupted Ryan this time.

"My name isn't Stephan; my name is Sasha. I'm not who you think I am."

"What do you mean you're not Stephan? Who are you then?"

"I'm a spy sent to discover your greatest secrets in this place, and I've found many." He pointed at the bomb. "I hope to slow you down with my little present. I'm also planning on taking a souvenir tomorrow morning."

"You're going to attack the convoy? You're crazy; they'll tear you apart. I'm calling security." He reached for his radio to call for help, but Sasha pulled his knife out and hurled it at Ryan, piercing his throat. Ryan, in shock, staggered down to the floor where Sasha waited for him. He placed his hand on Ryan to steady him while he gently pulled the knife out. "Ryan, why didn't you leave me alone?" He plunged the knife deep into his heart. "Go see your wife, Ryan."

Ryan strained to draw his last breath and gasped, "I'm coming home, Penny." He smiled at Sasha. "Thank you."

Ryan died in Sasha's arms. He gently lowered him to the floor. "I'm sorry, my friend. I genuinely liked you." He cleaned his knife and put it back into its sheath. He looked at Ryan's body and the pool of blood spreading from it. "Should I clean you up?" He thought for a moment. "It is of no matter. Tomorrow morning at eleven, this room will be rubble."

He picked up his toolbox and once again ascended the stairs. This time, he paused at the door and cracked it open to see if there was anyone else waiting. Seeing the way clear, he left and walked to the transport. Sasha returned to the maintenance bay to clear his locker. When he passed the lunchroom, he spotted Kevin eating alone with his back to the door. Kevin was deeply engrossed in a car magazine, so it was easy for Sasha to sneak up on him. Sasha cupped his knife in his hand, hiding it from Kevin's sight. Kevin turned his head slightly, and finally noticing Sasha, jumped in his seat.

"Whoa, you scared the crap out of me. Where did you come from?" He put his burrito down.

"Sorry, Kevin. I have a message for you from Ryan."

"Oh yeah, what is it?"

"Ryan said you could go home now as they found the problem, and you're no longer needed." He waited to see if Kevin would pick up the radio to confirm the message. Sasha firmed his grip on the knife, ready to strike.

Kevin's face lit up. "Hot damn! You don't have to tell me twice." He picked up his burrito and draped his jacket over his arm. He got up from the table and patted Sasha on the shoulder as he passed him. "See ya, buddy." When he reached the door, he stopped. Sasha tensed his muscles. Kevin turned and pointed at the radio. "Be a pal and put that back for me, would ya?"

Sasha nodded. "I'd be happy to."

"Thanks." He spun and left before Sasha could change his mind.

Sasha waved his empty hand and relaxed the muscles holding the knife. He slid it back into its home. "That was easy." Sasha collected everything he had in his locker and left the building. He walked to his SUV. "Tomorrow will not be so easy."

CHAPTER 15

THE SUN PEAKED ABOVE THE HORIZON AND CAST THE NEW DAY'S LIGHT upon the mountain. Ominous shadows projected onto the mountain, creating a landscape of gyrating phantoms laughing at the fate of the unwary souls inside the secret base.

"Good morning, everyone." Dr. Wellington walked into the accelerator control room, greeting the double row of scientists at their consoles. He took his seat at the manager's console at the back of the room, positioning himself to oversee the execution of the day's project.

"Good morning, sir," a chorus of replies came from the stationed scientists.

"What's our status?" He began to log into his console, overwriting the login for Project: Dark Portal. "I see Dr. Lexinger was here before us."

Dr. Carrie Boulos stood at her systems console. "Yes, sir, Dark Portal did a run yesterday. We've already reconfigured for parallel operation, and the accelerator is currently circulating a carrier stream." She pressed some buttons. "We're also standing by to ramp in the kinetic boosters any time you're ready. Current levels are below one percent with 700 TeV. What's the lot size this time, Doctor?"

"We're set up for a lot of one hundred units."

Carrie looked up from her console. "That's pretty ambitious isn't it, sir?"

"Perhaps, but we need to get as many rounds to Perez as we can. We need to test what space-time can handle with multiple test fires."

Carrie performed some calculations on her computer. "For that many at once, sir, we'll need to bake for thirty-six hours, stopping to rotate every four."

"No need to, Carrie. I had them install that rotating magnetic platform we talked about."

She made some adjustments in her calculations. "In that case, we'll need twenty-four hours at 500 PeV and a field of 3000 Tesla. We're pretty close to fracturing space-time, sir."

"It'll handle it, Carrie."

"If you say so, sir."

Dr. Wellington began his checklist, surveying the various scientists. "Cooling systems?"

"Systems engaged. Towers one through twenty-five circulating at five percent total."

"Bulk power?"

A voice came from a speaker on his console. "Jerry Luscombe here, sir. The reactor's at sixty percent, and we're currently diverting steam to condensers. We're ready to ramp up to one hundred percent reactor. X-Ray collectors are online, and the onion's currently at ten percent capacity."

"Do you have the expected peak?" Dr. Wellington readied to jot down the reply.

"Our calculations show you'll need 7000 megawatts. We've units three through ten islanded, and the aggregate is ready to ramp at 700 per minute. Standing by to regulate frequency at sixty Hz."

"Thank you, Jerry." He turned to Dr. Isabella Cortez. "Ion source?"

"The unknownium has been heated to a plasma state and is waiting in the vapor source chamber, ready to be injected."

"Okay, let's get started." He picked up the phone. It rang twice. "General, it's Dr. Wellington. We're set up and ready to begin chronon harvest on your final approval." He paused. "Yes, sir, we'll keep you apprised."

He hung up and addressed the room. "Alright, everyone, let's keep sharp. Carrie, keep a close eye when we're reaching twenty percent. I want to see if that vibration comes back."

"Yes, Doctor." She looked at her console. "Initiating power-up sequence to five percent. Power system governors are synched and ready to follow demand." She pressed a button, and the indicators on her screen moved. The power output climbed for sixty seconds. "We're at five percent, Doctor." The red hairs on her forearms began to stand. "All parameters are within acceptable range."

"Okay, let's step it to ten."

Carrie clicked the button on her console, and the indicators rose again and settled at their target. "We're at ten percent, sir. I'm detecting slight field variations in the convergence chamber but nothing to be alarmed about."

"Okay, keep an eye on that too. Let's take it to twenty."

Carrie typed in the command and hit enter. "Ramping to twenty." She watched as the power plant output slowly rose to 2000 megawatts. After a few minutes, it reached its target. "We're at twenty percent. Power input stable, generators at thirty-five percent; onion is at twenty-five." Suddenly they could feel a gentle vibration building under their feet.

"There it is again. Should we abort?"

"Everything reports okay, Doctor. Parameters are in range except for the strain gauges on the convergence mounts. They're a bit high, but I suggest we can continue."

"Adventurous today, aren't you?"

"I feel lucky today, sir."

"Fine then, take us to thirty percent."

Carrie adjusted her console and watched the indicators climb. "Twenty-five." The vibrations worsened. "Twenty-six, twenty-seven, twenty-eight." They grew stronger and stronger, causing the room to tremble, and were accompanied by a low rumble. Dr. Wellington reached for his computer mouse to hit the abort button. "We're almost there, sir, just wait." He looked at Carrie and saw the confidence in her face, then removed his finger from the mouse. "Twenty-nine… Okay, we're at thirty percent now." The vibrations subsided as she spoke. "See, I told you." Carrie smiled.

"You did, how's everything looking?"

"Good, sir. All parameters are within range. Convergence strain gauges are still a bit high but acceptable."

"Okay, let's take it to fifty percent and hold it there."

Carrie worked the console one last time and issued the command to rise to the final level. "On its way, sir." She looked at her coffee mug sitting next to her console. It was pulsating, as if it had started to breathe gently. "It looks like we're starting to get quantum hallucinations now."

"I see them too. This part always freaks me out," Dr. Cortez said.

"Okay, we're almost there. Inject the unknownium, and spin it up to near C but don't cross the streams yet."

"Injecting the matter now." The air in the complex suddenly felt electrified. Every person in the room could feel the effects of the accelerator operating at its tremendous power level.

"Cooling status?"

"Holding at ninety-five percent capacity with zero-point siphons engaged. Convergence chamber is at five femto-Kelvins."

"Start up the auxiliary collector ring." The scientist clicked her console and waited sixty seconds. "Auxiliary ring primed and pulsing at ten."

"Okay, let's crash the beams and start collecting."

"Initiating beam intersect...now." The charge in the atmosphere intensified. "Collisions are registering at 10^9 events per second. Chronon collection at point-zero-zero three percent. Anti-matter production at point-three percent."

"Divert production stream to chronon bombardment chamber."

"Activating collector ring. Diverting particles to the enrichment chamber."

Dr. Wellington leaned back and watched his cup fade in and out of existence. "Okay, now we watch and wait."

"That should about do it." Having stowed the weapon, Perez closed the cargo doors of the transport van.

"Is everything in order, Colonel Perez?" General Tremaine said.

"Yes, sir. I packed the TATES and scope in their travel cases as well as the tool case. I'm bringing all thirteen CAPs, six each in two carriers, and the last one I popped into a munitions case."

"Will it be okay loose like that?"

"Yes sir, it'll be fine in there. I didn't want to take up the extra space with an almost empty case for one CAP."

"That's fine. I have to go now. I'll be in my office if you need anything."

"Thank you, sir. I'll let you know if I do." Tremaine spun around and walked away as Lieutenant Stanley Thompson appeared with his Army Ranger team. They saluted the general, who returned it and kept on. Thompson approached Perez.

"Whew, I'm glad he didn't stick around. I always get nervous around brass."

"Hey, I'm brass too, you know."

"Yeah, but I know you, Perez." He eased up to him to whisper. "Okay, double or nothing, a new sign at four kilometers. No explosives this time."

"Dream on, Chugs." Perez looked at his watch. "Shouldn't we get started?"

"Sure thing, boss." Chugger turned to his team. "This is just a quick pizza run today, boys and girls. The pucker factor on this is a one, but keep your Spidey senses activated still. We're escorting the Colonel here with his toys to Hill Air Force Base." He pointed at his crew. "Perry, Smith, and Collins, you're with me in the Alpha car. Pippa, Decker, Walters, and Frost, you're in the Charlie car at the rear. The rest are Beta in the van, and Skippy, you're driving it. Got it, folks?"

"Hu-ah, L.T," the team responded.

"Okay, everyone geared up with ARs and Sigs?"

"Brought my slingshot too, L.T," Staff Sergeant Pippa said.

"I want standard body armor and radios, too."

"Full battle-rattle, sir," Pippa said.

"Good." Chugs pointed at a map. "We're leaving through Echo gate and going to the highway." He traced his finger on the map. "We'll take this route to here and then go north on this route. It should take about two hours to get there. Drain 'em dry now folks; we're not stopping once we're on the road. Well, except for one thing maybe."

"What's that, L.T?" Pippa said.

"Colonel Perez has taken it upon himself to ride his busted-ass motorcycle. We may have to stop to give him a ride when it breaks down."

"Hey, show some respect. This is a 1969 Honda CB750. It's a legend."

"Yes, sir. In *your* mind, sir."

"You're a Harley man aren't you, Chug?" Chugger smiled. "I'll tell you what. Last one there buys the beer," Perez said.

Chugger smiled. "Oh, you're on. Don't forget your wallet, 'cause I'm thirsty."

"Wait...crap."

"What? Trying to back out already, Colonel?"

"No, I just realized I forgot my fob upstairs."

Chugger looked at his watch. "0900 hours, time to go. Oh, the taste of free beer waits."

Perez laughed. "Don't worry, I'll catch up with you, no problem. See you out there."

Chugger nodded. "Okay team, let's mount up and move out."

"Rangers lead the way!" They all said. They got into their vehicles as Perez ran to catch the transport to his office, 8000 feet up. The convoy made its way through the tunnels to the outside hangar.

Chugger got on the radio and called Dunbar. "Protector, this is Chariot. We're departing the tunnel now."

"Roger that Chariot. Protector is watching. Opening the Echo gate now. Keep it nut to butt and watch your six."

"Roger that, thanks, Protector."

Perez ran to his office. "Man, I need to get a carrier for this thing." He looked and saw the radios. "I'll take this too. I may as well be able to taunt them as I win the beer." He jogged back to the transport pod. He was determined to collect on his bet.

The convoy drove out to the main road and turned on the first leg of their journey. After twenty minutes of driving, Chugger keyed his radio. "Protector. Chariot here. We're passing checkpoint Alpha, all clear."

"Roger, Chariot. I still have my eyes on you."

"How far can you see with those cameras?"

"About another fifteen miles, and then the mountains block the road."

"Roger."

"Chariot, be advised that Perez is catching up." Chugger laughed. He hung the radio back in its holder just as they approached an overpass.

Suddenly, an explosion tore apart the rear of Chugger's transport. The force flipped it end-over-end until it landed hard on its roof, facing backward. Dazed, he slowly turned to see the rear half of his transport missing and the former occupants dead. The two remaining vehicles stopped. Chugger watched through his cracked windshield as a smoke trail streamed toward the rear car from the overpass.

"RPG attack! Get out of your cars!" The grenade tore into the rear car, causing it to erupt into an enormous explosion. He saw his fleeing men blasted in all directions from the force. "No!" He tore off his seat belt and dropped to the inverted roof. He looked at the driver. "Collins, are you with me?" Collins moaned, showing she was still alive but stunned by the attack. He released her restraints, and she dropped.

"Come on. We gotta get cover." He grabbed her by the flak jacket and pulled her out of the transport while shooting with the other hand. Chugger looked and saw the van stopped just past the bridge. He watched his crew pour out and take defensive positions. He keyed his radio. "Protector, this is Chariot, we're under heavy attack."

"Roger, I see that two RPG's just took out your lead and lag."

Suddenly automatic weapons fire erupted around them, and bullets peppered their stricken vehicles. Chugger pulled himself and Collins from the burning wreck. They were huddled in toward the best cover he could find. He looked down and saw blood oozing through his shirt. "Damn, I'm hit too."

"Chariot, what's your status?"

"I don't see any movement around Charlie. I think six dead total. We need your help. Where the hell are they shooting from?"

"Thermals show eighteen all around you. I'm charging weapons now. Hang on." He paused. "There are six on the bridge. Four on the east side of the bridge, and two on the west. There are also clusters of six on both sides of the road." Dunbar activated his particle weapon batteries, targeted the east group on the bridge and fired. The beam traveled the twenty-mile distance in an instant, vaporizing the four attackers clustered on the overpass. "Four down."

Chugger peered over the vehicle and saw the remains of a cloud of smoke from the beam. He watched as two attackers jumped from the bridge to avoid being vaporized by the energy weapon. As they fell, Chugger aimed and shot them both. They hit the ground with a thud. "Six down, how many more?"

"There are three in the bush at your nine o'clock." Dunbar targeted the group and triggered the weapon. The beam pierced through the air as fast as lightning and hit two of the three assailants.

Sasha dove away as the two beside him dissolved into a puff of atoms. He radioed to his attack force, "Stay down! I didn't think they could target this far." He reached into his flak jacket pocket and pulled out his cell phone.

Pavel shouted out to him, "What? Do you order pizza or something now?"

Sasha waved him down, "Wait." He speed-dialed a phone number and triggered a hidden bomb in the Air Deck. "See if your weapons work now." The explosion severed the power cables to the weapons array. Sasha turned to Pavel. "I put a bomb on the weapons' power supply in case we attacked by air."

Dunbar targeted his next shot. "Steady…steady." He zoomed in on the lone figure that he had missed on his second shot. "Got ya now, boy." He was about to fire when suddenly all of his systems went black. "What the hell?" he said. "Not now dammit!" Alarms sounded as the explosion tore into the Air Deck understructure. "Chariot, I'm blind. I can't help you."

"Everyone, get to cover! We're on our own now," Chugger said. He and his team fought hard.

"Skippy, on your six." Skippy spun and fired, killing an exposed attacker. Chugger continued to call out instructions. The team killed two more attackers on the east side. They fought valiantly but suffered significant losses. One by one, the attackers killed them off, until it came down to only Chugger. Wounded, he laid there returning fire. He spent his last round from his assault rifle and threw it down. He reached into his holster and pulled out his pistol. He cried out loudly, "You want me? You're gonna have to work hard for it, you bastards!"

Pavel, Galina, and Sasha with four others broke from the bushes on either side of the road. They carefully approached, keeping the vehicles between them and Chugger. They worked their way around, slowly flanking him on both sides. Chugger saw them coming and fired his pistol. He hit two more of the attackers, but it wasn't enough. The remaining attackers returned fire at Chugger, and their bullets riddled his body. As he lay there dying, he defiantly raised his middle finger toward them; then he gasped his last breath as his hand fell.

Pavel laughed. "Well done, comrade."

"Is that all of them?" Sasha said.

"Yes," Galina said.

"How many did we lose?"

Pavel looked around. "Thirteen and I not clean up either."

"We must move quickly." Sasha ran to get the SUV.

Galina rummaged the pockets of the dead soldiers for the keys to open the cargo bay of the van. "Where are the keys?"

"Never mind keys." Pavel climbed in and pulled on the doors with his massive bulk. The doors bent under the strain of his enormous power.

Sasha pulled up his SUV and opened the back of it. "What is taking so long?" he said.

"Pavel is pulling doors open now." As Galina spoke the words, the doors released their desperate grip and surrendered to Pavel's brute strength.

"Take this." Pavel handed the broken doors to the two men waiting behind him. He reached in and pulled out the first case. Sasha and Galina grabbed it and carried the TATES away together.

"Ivan, take this." Pavel handed the scope case to him.

Galina returned for a CAP case. "Hurry, Pavel! We must go."

"Dah, I am going quickly." He waved to the next man to come. "Viktor, take this." Pavel handed him the final CAP case. Ivan returned for the tool case. "That is it, go," Pavel said. Suddenly, blood sprayed from Ivan's head. He dropped to the ground, letting the case fall. Pavel fell back into the van. He looked out and saw a motorcycle racing toward them. He smiled. "We have a visitor." He climbed out of the van and crouched low. He drew his gun and shot toward the approaching defender.

"It's Perez. Quickly, find cover," Sasha said. Galina dropped and flattened to the ground. Perez fired bullet after bullet at them. Viktor returned to help Pavel fight off the attacker and to grab the tool case.

"Viktor, take this. I will cover." Viktor took the case and left, but as he carried it back to the SUV, a bullet from Perez struck him in the back, piercing his heart. He stumbled to the ground, throwing the case toward Galina. Pavel fired rapidly at Perez, who weaved his motorcycle back and forth, evading every shot. Perez steadied his bike and returned fire with the same ferocity.

"I will get the case," Galina said. She ran to the tool case and picked it up. She shot back at Perez with her free hand while Pavel stayed firing at the rear of the van.

"Pavel, let's go," Sasha said.

"I will not back down from fight with little man I can beat."

"Come now, I order you."

Pavel grunted toward Sasha, "Coward." He picked up the munitions case and moved to leave his cover. Suddenly blood erupted from Pavel's neck. He fell back against the van and dropped the case. "I am hit." Blood sputtered from his neck as his powerful heart forced it from the gaping wound. He clutched his throat tightly and slid to the ground. Galina threw the tools into the SUV. She spun to return to help Pavel. Perez closed the gap between them quickly and was getting more and more accurate as he did.

Galina ran toward Pavel but stopped when she felt a bullet graze her head. "Pavel!"

"Go, kitten, get away," he said through the blood gurgling from his neck.

"Galina, we must go." Sasha revved the engine.

"No, I will not leave him." Another bullet skimmed her arm.

"Pavel is gone. We must go."

"Nooo…Pavel!" She reached for the munitions case but stopped when a bullet from Perez hit the case.

"Leave it, Galina. It is just bullets. We must go." She ran back to the SUV, but before entering, emptied her gun at Perez. He dodged most of the bullets except for two that hit his bike and one that grazed his helmet. She jumped in, and they sped off.

CHAPTER 16

"POWER LEVELS ARE STABLE, SIR, BUT THE STRAIN GAUGES IN THE convergence chamber are pinging high now," Dr. Carrie Boulos said.

"Can you get a visual?" Dr. Wellington said.

"The cameras were down. I'm rebooting the system now to see if that clears them." She adjusted the controls.

"Are sensors picking up anything?"

"We do have a strange reading in the chamber. It's reading like there's a damping field present, but life sign interlocks are clear." Dr. Wellington reached for his mouse to shut the accelerator down.

"Sir, cameras are active now," Carrie said, interrupting his action.

"Put it on the main screen."

Carrie sent the image to the screen. She panned the room. The vast array of tubes looked as if they were pulsating on the screen. "Wait, stop. What's that?" Dr. Wellington said.

"What's what, sir?"

"That, at the bottom."

Carrie adjusted the aim down to reveal the corpse of Ryan Jones lying in a pool of congealed blood. "What? That looks like a body." She zoomed in. "It's Ryan Jones. Life-sign readings are zero. He's dead in there?"

Wellington interrupted Carrie. "More importantly, he must have his fob in there. That explains the field." Wellington paused and looked at the screen. "What's that?" He pointed at the screen.

Carrie adjusted the camera. "It looks like an arrow...drawn in blood."

"It's pointing at something, move the camera up." Wellington closed in on the screen. The view scrolled down as the camera panned up until they could see a fuzzy picture of a box with blinking lights on it. "Can you sharpen it?"

Carrie adjusted the view until it sharpened. The scientists collectively gasped.

"What is that?" Dr. Cortez said.

"That looks like a bomb," Carrie said. "Look at the display. That's a timer, but it's counting down too fast."

"The fob must be creating a time displacement field, and it's speeding up time in that location," Dr. Wellington said as he stared at the display. "It's causing the electronics to count down faster." He watched briefly as it quickly counted down and realization sunk in. "Oh no, shut it down! Shut the damn thing down now. Emergency stop, all systems." The order came too late. The timer counted to zero. The scientists watched as the camera briefly recorded the explosion until the picture disappeared. The mountain shuddered slightly from the blast.

Suddenly, pages of alarms appeared on their computer screens as all of the accelerator systems tripped offline. On the overhead speakers, a warning tone began to sound. The scientists responded, frantically pressing buttons and flipping switches in an attempt to safely secure their systems.

"Cooling systems have failed. All pumps are offline, and we're leaking liquid N2 into the storage rings."

The voice on the overhead speaker reported, "Reactors have set back to sixty percent, core shut down initiated. Steam diverters are active, and we've rejected all generation units to full zero. We've employed all backups on emergency magnetic systems."

"What's active in the rings?" Dr. Wellington said.

"There are 10^{23} particles of anti-matter, 10^{24} particles of unknownium and…uncertain of chronons."

The voice on the speaker once again spoke, "Safeties are failing. The reactor core is running away. X-ray collectors are at one hundred percent and rising."

"Announce general alert," Dr. Wellington said. "Evacuate the mountain!" He turned to Carrie, "What's happening to the storage rings?"

"I'm recording numerous anti-matter explosions from residual particle stores. The rings are tearing themselves apart. The nitrogen coolant is providing fuel for the anti-matter, and energy is returning to the X-ray collector onion too." She pushed a few buttons. "It's at 120 percent and rising fast."

"System failures are registering everywhere, sir. Ring containment has failed," Cortez said. Suddenly, a violent wave of energy pulsed through the mountain, throwing unprepared scientists to the floor. "Storage rings are exploding, sir." Display screens showed flames erupting from the magnetic rings on virtually every view."

"Activate fire suppression systems!" Dr. Wellington said. He waited for a reply. "Well?"

"Sorry, sir, a negative response to all commands. Suppression systems are offline."

The voice on the speaker said, "We're getting feedback energy into the core. Gamma bursts from the onion are reflecting back and bombarding the core. Helium 3 booster valves are failing and are releasing into the reaction chamber. We're losing control of the reaction."

"We've lost power to reactor containment, sir," Carrie said. Dr. Wellington called up his screen to view the mountain's systems. "Instruments indicate a runaway chain reaction now in the core. Readings indicate the onion is overloaded, exceeding two per unit and systems are blowing everywhere," Carrie said. Dr. Wellington scanned his screen. Carrie looked up from her console. "Surges are reaching A-M locker containment."

Dr. Wellington keyed his mic, "Can we bleed the energy?"

"Negative, all safeties are deployed and have proven ineffective. We've injected poison into the core, but we need time. What's that? No!" The speaker turned into static.

Dr. Wellington felt the mountain shudder as he watched every indicator on his screen change to alarm for the nuclear reactor. "We lost the reactor; everyone, brace for the shock wave! Carrie, what's the locker containment field at?"

Before she could answer, the scientists, including Dr. Wellington, were all hurled around by the final energy pulse of the exploding nuclear reactor. Carrie clung to her console to keep upright. As the shaking subsided, a calm came over the room. Dr. Wellington watched as all the alarms cleared from his screen.

"Is it over?" an unknown voice said.

Dr. Wellington stood up and wiped his brow. "I think it might be." He listened as his staff began to titter in an anxious joy. He looked over at Carrie who was not smiling. He was about to silence the alarm when his screen shut off. In the background, he heard Carrie's answer, "Zero."

A complete containment failure occurred two kilometers below the scientists' feet. Fifty kilograms of anti-matter dropped to the floor of their containment vessels and instantly released enough energy to blast a new Grand Canyon. In that instant, Wellington looked at Carrie and the others. As he did, the lights of the room faded, extinguishing their hopes. The only lighting came from the small, battery-powered emergency lights mounted on the walls.

Dr. Cortez whispered as she wept, "I'm coming home, Jesus."

The scientists stood and beheld each other as the floor slowly pushed up. Cracks formed in the concrete, allowing pure light to escape and illuminate the room with its brilliance. The blast wave quickly reached the waiting scientists. Suddenly, the floor of the room erupted; concrete and rock blasted upward toward the ceiling. Each promising life in the control room ended in an instant. The wave pushed past the scientists and reached the outer limits of the rock. The unrelenting pressure forced the mountain out and into the surrounding area.

Perez gunned his motorcycle. He looked at the fallen Pavel as he rapidly passed him; Pavel's body was propped against the van. He could hear bullets whizzing by from Galina's gun. Ignoring the danger, he pressed on hard. "You're not getting away, you bastards." Suddenly from behind him, an immense flash filled the atmosphere, lighting the sky for hundreds of miles. Perez quickly glanced in his mirror but had to look away. The light from the explosion escaped from enormous fissures created in the mountain. "What the...?"

"What is that?" said Galina as they too saw the light. "How big was your bomb, Sasha?"

"Not that big. I don't know how it's so powerful, and it's too early." They saw the pressure wave of the blast radiate from the mountain. "We must find cover quickly." He spotted a tunnel ahead that led into a mountain and accelerated toward it.

As the light faded, Perez looked back. "Oh, crap." He gunned his bike in near panic as he witnessed the mountain tear itself apart. The blast sent rock and fire in every direction. He watched as the atmosphere twenty miles behind him compressed into an epic blast wave. *I'm dead on this thing if I don't find shelter now.* Perez quickly scanned his options.

"There!" He spotted a stream flowing into a culvert passing under the road.

"Come on, move it!" He forced every bit of speed he could from his old motorcycle and headed straight for the culvert. In his mirror, he could see the blast wave rapidly approaching him. As he looked, he spotted Pavel moving.

Pavel regained consciousness and struggled to his feet as he held his neck. He leaned against the van and lifted his gun, aiming at Perez. "You are not getting away, sobaka." Perez saw as the shock wave caught up to Pavel and was only mere seconds behind him. He saw Pavel vanish into the blast wave.

"Come on, come on, come on! Faster!" Perez screamed as he got closer to his refuge. When he reached the culvert, he jumped his bike down the embankment and into the stream. As he crashed, his momentum launched him into the shallow water. He scrambled into the tunnel just as the blast wave caught up. Outside at the opposite end, he saw a large buck standing in shock. He watched it disintegrate before his eyes as the wave struck. The tunnel shook under the assault of the unimaginable power the explosion released.

He covered his ears expecting an assault on them from the sound of the explosion but instead, heard nothing at all. Not a sound came from the explosion, just the shaking from the brute force of the released energy. His fob beeped frenziedly. He looked at the display and watched as random numbers appeared on it. Holding on, he braced himself against the walls of the tunnel until the blast wave subsided.

"What the hell is that?" Major Jacob Wishbone stood in the parking lot beside his office at Chalmers Army Depot 200 miles away from Ghost Mountain. He watched as the horizon lit up like a second sun. He keyed his radio. "Sergeant Winters, this is base commander Wishbone. Set the base on high alert, threat-con Delta."

"Yes, sir, right away, sir."

He looked and saw the moon high in the daytime sky. It should have been dark as it was in its new phase, but the light from the explosion momentarily lit it up, giving the earth a show of the dark side of the moon. A siren sounded across the base. "This is bad, whatever it is."

Perez sat unmoving, listening. The air was silent except for his heavy breathing and the quiet trickle of water gently flowing in the stream. He could hear his heart beating; its tempo was in contrast to the calm flow of water at his feet. He shook his head, pulling himself back from the edge of disbelief. After gathering his senses, he climbed out to look. "What just happened?" Perez stood dripping wet and in shock. He turned to where Ghost Mountain should have been. "What… Where's …Where's the mountain?" He expected to see an enormous heap of flaming rubble, but instead was astonished to find emptiness where the mountain had been. "It's gone." He spun around looking. "The mountain is gone."

He could see the town of Leviville in the distance. It was still there, but it had an atmosphere of stillness over it. He remembered what happened to Pavel and the buck. "Sarah! Kids!" Perez dropped to his hands and knees. "No!" His stomach wretched as his soul became gripped in sudden overwhelming grief. He softly whimpered, "Sarah."

In the distance, he heard the sound of Sasha's SUV as it emerged from the traitorous tunnel that had protected them. He looked and finally recognized Sasha. "You!" He watched as it sped off and out of sight. "I'll get you for this, you bastard! You're dead! You're dead!" He beat the ground with his fists. "You're dead." He kneeled motionless for a moment, letting the shock dissolve from him.

Finally, he gathered himself and switched into soldier mode. He surveyed the damage zone. "There's no debris. Where is it?" He stood up and staggered to Chugger's upside-down transport. "What? It's all rusted now." He picked at the decayed metal, and it crumbled in his fingers. "This was brand new, but now it looks like it's been here for years." He looked and saw the body of Chugger. He stood at attention and saluted, "Hu-ah buddy. Lead the way." He approached the van and saw the remains of all who had engaged in the battle. All of the remains of the attackers were dust, but his team's remains were all intact. "Their fobs preserved them."

He looked into the empty van. "Damn, they got everything." He punched the door, and it crumbled from the force of his blow. When the door disintegrated, he saw the munitions case on the ground behind. He walked to it and tried to pick it up, but the metal crumbled in his fingers revealing the cartridge inside. The cartridge itself was in pristine condition. He inspected it for damage and picked it up. "This one's for you, creep." He put it in his backpack.

Suddenly his fob beeped, and a rumble began in the distance behind him. He turned and saw the air haze over and form ripples. "Oh no, I know what that means." A time wormhole opened up, and, suddenly, an enormous flaming rock came flying out. The office building-sized rock sailed through the air like it was a tossed baseball and landed with a thunderous crash. The impact blasted a crater, which showered the area with dust and rock. "You gotta be kidding me. The mountain exploded through time?" The air around him began erupting in rocks appearing throughout time. "I've gotta get out of here, now."

He ran back to his bike to see if it was still usable. As he approached it, he saw it was like brand new. "What? How on earth…?" He looked back to the van. "A new van turned to dust, and my old bike restored to new. The blast wave must have been a time displacement shock wave. This whole area is affected. How far did it spread?" He looked at the town again. "Is everyone dead? Has everyone turned to dust?"

His fob beeped again and another massive piece of time debris emerged. He watched as it came down and crushed an entire subdivision of his town. He keyed his satellite radio. "This is Colonel Joseph Perez to any station monitoring this frequency. Are you there?" The radio crackled, but no one answered, "This is Colonel…" He stopped as more debris emerged.

Suddenly a voice came over the radio. "This is Chalmers Army Depot at Salt Lake. Identify yourself. Who is this?"

"This is Colonel Joseph Perez, INSCOM. Who is this? Is this channel secure?"

"Yes, Colonel, it is. I'm Sergeant Josh Winters, base security. What do you need, sir?"

"I need a disaster containment perimeter set up ASAP." He gave the coordinates.

"Would this happen to be where that light came from, sir? What the hell was that?"

"I'll explain later, but for now, tell your base commander it's a meteor strike and he's to mobilize immediately."

"Yes, sir. I'll pass on the message."

His fob beeped again; a huge piece emerged and struck the ground. "I have to go. Get everyone out and keep them out for at least one hundred miles from Ghost Mountain." He jumped on his bike and sped away. As he did, he watched as time debris rained down out of thin air. "Unbelievable. How can this get any worse?"

CHAPTER 17

"...MAKING THIS POSSIBLY THE WORST NATURAL DISASTER IN U.S. history." Perez stood in line at a gas station, waiting to pay for his fuel. Mounted on the wall behind the cashier, a TV blathered on about the "meteor" that had just destroyed the town of Leviville.

"The death toll from the meteor could surpass that of the Galveston hurricane of 1900, making it the deadliest natural disaster in U.S. history. Reports are sketchy as authorities are remaining tight-lipped and have the entire area under lockdown, citing public safety concerns. XNN has obtained exclusive eyewitness reports of the disaster. Reporting live from the disaster recovery camp outside of Salt Lake City is XNN correspondent Mindy Morton."

"Chuck, people here are in utter shock over this disaster of biblical proportions. More than 200,000 people have been evacuated in the past two hours, and people are jam-packed into this makeshift refugee camp here outside of Salt Lake City. Everyone is asking why, but answers aren't coming. FEMA representatives can be seen here, but seem to be taking their orders from the Army, and no one is talking." Mindy turned to her left. "With me here is Betsy Carmichael. Betsy lives fifty miles from the impact zone. Betsy, can you tell us what you saw?"

"Well, Mandy, dear."

"That's Mindy, ma'am. Mindy Morton."

"Sorry, dear. Well, Mandy, I was outside shooing my cow, Mary Beth, from my garden when, all of a sudden, I saw this huge flash of light in the sky followed by a ball of flame streaking across it. It then disappeared over the horizon and ended in that big explosion."

"That must have been terrifying for you to see."

"Damn straight, Maxi. I nearly pooped my britches. If it weren't for my Mary Beth comforting me, I don't know what I'd have done."

Mindy turned to her right. "...and on my right is Clem Pickens. Clem, can you tell us what you saw."

"Hi, Mindy. I wanna start by saying I love your reportin'."

"Thank you, Clem. It's nice to meet a fan."

"I mean, I think you're hot and all, and I get all warm when I watch you on TV, but you're much more purty in person. Me and the boys are all wonderin' if y'all is married."

"Let's not talk about that right now, Clem." On the screen, an inset of a laughing Chuck faded from view.

Suddenly another man popped into the picture. "Never mind this fool, I know what happened."

Mindy, relieved, shifted from the awkward conversation with Clem and focused on the new witness. "And who are you, sir?"

"I'm Jerry, Jerry Gary."

"Okay, Mr. Jerry Gary, what can you tell us?"

"I saw it all. There was fightin' and explosions and laser beams. Men dyin' all over the place."

Perez now very interested, stared at the TV. "Uh-oh," he exhaled softly.

"What do you mean, Jerry? Who was fighting?"

"The army men." Perez tensed slightly.

"Who were they fighting?"

"Why aliens, of course." Perez laughed, as he watched the smile fade from the reporter's face.

"The soldiers were winning too—until a giant spaceship came down and blasted the secret mountain army base that was helping the soldiers. That's what all this is; we're under alien attack."

Mindy pulled the microphone back to her and turned to the camera. She sighed, "Well, there you have it, Chuck. Speculation is rampant here as we wait for official updates from authorities. Mindy Morton reporting live for Xtreme Network News at the disaster recovery camp. Back to you, Chuck."

Perez laughed, "Sometimes even the crazies can be close."

"What was that dear?" asked a little old lady beside him.

"Oh, just commenting on the TV report, ma'am."

"Such a tragedy isn't it? Did you know anyone in the area?"

He drew in a deep breath and exhaled, "No, ma'am, fortunately not."

"Next."

Perez stepped up to the counter and handed the clerk his money. "I'll also need one of those prepaid cell phones too."

"They're $79 plus tax."

He handed him his credit card. "Make it two." Perez left the store and stuffed the phones into his backpack with the CAP. He climbed on his bike.

"Hey, buddy." A man called out to him. Perez looked at him. "Is that a pre-production, candy-red 1969 Honda CB750 Sandcast?"

"Yes, it is." Perez was amazed at his knowledge of the bike.

"Wow, it looks mint. Are you looking to sell it? Name your price."

"Sorry, it's not for sale."

The man walked over to him and handed him a card. "Too bad. If you ever change your mind, call me at this number."

"Sure, thanks." Perez read the card. *Mike Matthews – Global Transports.* He stuffed it into his pocket and sped off, leaving the man to admire the bike as it faded from his view. Perez didn't go directly to the disaster camp. Instead, he rode to Salt Lake City and found the main bus terminal. He parked his bike and entered the station. He approached a man who was mopping the floor. "Excuse me, sir, where are the lockers?" The man pointed without looking up. Perez looked. "Thanks." The man didn't respond.

He walked to the lockers and touched the video screen causing the display to light up. He followed the prompting on the screen and paid for a locker with his credit card. The machine assigned him locker number 77, which he opened and placed the CAP and other items inside. He shut the door and secured it so only his fingerprint could unlock it. He patted the door. "Insurance." Perez surveyed his surroundings and left the terminal. When he exited, he saw a tall, beautiful blonde woman standing next to his bike. He also saw two trembling men lying on the ground several feet away.

"Can I help you, miss?" Perez said.

The woman smiled, "No, I'm just admiring your bike. Have a nice day, Colonel." She walked away staring at the men on the ground who cowered from her.

"What was that? How does she know I'm a Colonel?" He watched as she vanished around the corner. Perez shook off his wonder and put on his helmet. "Never mind that, I need to get to the camp fast." He drove the distance, trying not to think of his circumstances. *Stay focused, Perez. You can grieve later.*

As he approached the camp, he could see long lines of people waiting to get in at the public gates. He drove his bike around the perimeter of the base until he found the main military gate. As he approached it, two armed guards stepped in to intercept him. One guard lifted his hand. "No civilians beyond this point." Perez reached inside his coat. The guards raised their weapons and pointed them at him.

"I'm just getting my ID, stand easy soldiers." He slowly pulled his military ID from his pocket and showed it to the guards. When they read it, they snapped to attention.

"We're sorry, sir." The other guard added, "We didn't know you were brass, sir. You know, with you not being in your uniform and all."

Perez smiled. "No problem soldiers, you're just doing your job. At ease. Where can I find the base commander?"

The guard pointed, "If you drive down that way to the second lane and turn left, you'll find him there, sir. His office is in the origami hut at the end."

"His name is Major Jacob Wishbone, sir," the other said.

"Thank you, soldiers. Stay safe."

"Yes, sir," the one said as the other opened the gate.

Perez drove to the Rapid Deployment Shelter System or RDS building the guards had pointed him to. He stopped in front of the structure and parked his bike. He was always amazed at how these truck-sized containers unfolded into such large, temporary structures for emergencies like this. He walked into the command center's outer office and flashed his ID to an already stressed-out administrative assistant. "I'll let myself in." He pushed through the door into the major's office before the assistant could protest. Inside, Wishbone sat at his desk, speaking on the phone.

"Yes, General, I'll inform you of what we find as soon as we can get into the area." He saw Perez. "Excuse me, General, but I have an unauthorized visitor." He covered the phone. "Who are you, and how'd you get in here?"

Perez held up his ID. "I can help you understand the situation, Major." Wishbone looked at it and turned a little pale. He quickly changed his tone as he was staring at the ID of a full bird Colonel with the highest security clearance ever created: Majestic level.

The major continued speaking, "I'm sorry, General, but I have a Colonel Perez here with me. He says he can help explain things." He paused and activated his speakerphone.

"Colonel Perez, this is General Kimberly Bishop. I can't believe you're still alive."

"Hello General, yes I am. I wish that I could be talking to you under different circumstances right now. I regret to say that the Ghost Mountain base is a total loss."

"What Ghost Mountain base?" Wishbone said.

"Never mind that Major. Please continue, Colonel."

"The base is completely gone, General."

"What do you mean completely gone?"

"Just as I said, ma'am, gone, vanished, and everyone's dead. But that's not all the bad news; we also lost a special package in transit. We were attacked and the entire team was killed except for me. The attackers acquired the asset that we were transporting."

"What was the asset, Colonel?"

"I'm sorry, General, but I can't divulge details on the phone or in front of the Major here. All I can say is it was project number 177 and is a catastrophic loss."

"Do you know who attacked you?"

"I believe I do. He's Russian GRU. I remember him from a joint exercise years ago, but can't recall his name right now."

"Should we call them, ma'am?" Wishbone said.

"There's no point in talking with them, Major. They'll deny everything," Perez said.

The conversation paused until the general broke the silence. "I can't believe Ghost Mountain is gone. How?"

"I don't know, General. All I know is that during our battle, Ghost Mountain just blew and disappeared."

"Disappeared? Then what's all that flying rock out there?"

"It's hard to explain, Major, just accept that it's happening. I've seen it for myself."

"Colonel, I'll read about the project when I get the clearance, but I'll need you to come here as soon as you can to give me a report. In the meantime, I can't stress this enough. Get the asset back. I don't care how, just do it. Keep it under the radar though."

"Yes, General."

"Major, I'm leaving you in charge of securing the disaster zone, but I want you to extend any and all courtesies to the Colonel. Give him anything that he needs to complete his mission, no matter what he asks for."

"Yes, General," he said.

"That's all for now, goodbye gentlemen."

Wishbone hung up the phone and looked at Perez. "So, just who is it you are again, sir?"

"You don't want to know, Major. Do you have satellite recon of the affected area?"

"Yes, in the communications hut."

"Good. Could you take me there? I need to take a look at the area. I'll also need a few things." He handed him a list.

They walked out of his office, and the major handed the list to his assistant. "Corporal, please take this list to Sergeant Colman and tell him to prepare this request immediately."

"Yes, Major, right away."

"Follow me, Colonel." The major took Perez to another expanding shelter filled with communication and sensory consoles, all manned by busy officers, "Colonel, I need to remind you this is a classified area. What you see here, stays here."

"Of course, Major." They approached one of the operators.

"Captain Jenifer Styles, this is Colonel Perez." The Captain stood to attention and saluted.

"As you were, Captain." She sat back down. Perez leaned into the console screen. "I'm here to see what you can see from the satellite."

"That's a problem, sir, I can't show you."

"What do you mean, you can't show me?"

"I think the feed is corrupt, and I'm not sure what we're seeing, sir. It looks like debris is coming out of thin air."

"Your feed is okay, Captain. It is coming from thin air. It's coming through time."

"I beg your pardon, through time?"

"Don't worry about it. Show me a wide-area view over Leviville."

She adjusted the screen and the picture panned outward. "As you requested, sir."

He pointed at the screen. "I see these all look like impact craters."

"It would appear that way, sir."

"Okay, I remember that this one hit first."

"How would you know that, Colonel? No one has seen this feed, but the Major and me."

"I was there to see it in person, Captain." The major and the captain looked at each other.

"You were in there?" the captain gasped.

"Long story, let's move on. From the pattern I see here, the outer perimeter looks bombarded first, and the debris seems to be working inward."

"Yes, that's what we think too, but we don't know why or how."

"The closer to the source of the explosion, the further in time the debris jumped." He motioned to the screen. "May I use your computer, Captain?"

"I'm sorry, sir, but it won't work for you without a login."

"Let me try anyway." She pushed away from the console, and Perez stepped in. He hit a series of keystrokes and a screen popped up.

"Where did that come from?"

"You didn't see this." He looked sternly at them both. Perez logged in and searched for the address of Stephan. "I need you to show me the area for this address." He logged off the computer. Amazed, the captain entered the address, and the screen changed, zooming into the house. "Pull it back a bit; I want to see where it is in relation to the debris field."

The screen adjusted, "It still looks clear sir, but the debris is moving inward quickly."

'Alright, thanks."

"Why? What are you doing?" Wishbone said.

"I'm going in there."

"Sir, I can't let you do that. It's far too dangerous."

"I'm not asking for your permission, Major. I'm telling you. Besides, I owe them all. I could have stopped this before it happened."

"How sir? What could you have done to stop something of this magnitude?"

"What could have I done? What could have I done? Some jerk blows up my base, killing everyone I know, and I just let him walk right in to do it. I even applauded the idiot. If only I had looked more closely… things could have been different right now."

"Sir, if I may, it's always been my habit to look forward not backward. What can you do now about the past? It's over and done. It's what you do next that counts." Perez stared at him with an empty look. "All I'm saying, sir, is this: If going into that hellish place can help fix this, then I'm all for it too, but if not, don't go in because you feel you need punishment. You don't. Sometimes things out of our control happen, and we have to pick ourselves up and deal with it – by going forward. That's unless you've got a time machine or something, sir."

Perez looked intently at Wishbone for a moment. "Is my supply request completed yet?"

"I'll check on that, Colonel, excuse me for a moment." He stepped away to make a call.

"Would you mind if I speak freely, Colonel?"

"Go ahead, Captain." Perez sighed at the continued challenge.

"I think you're nuts for going in there, but if it helps you in some way, then go. Truly though, what's so important to risk your life to go in there?"

"Answers, Captain. Answers."

"Perhaps redemption too, sir?"

"Perhaps some of that too, Captain." The major waved to Perez and gave the thumbs up.

"Okay, Captain. Keep an eye on the area, and if you see the debris closing in, call me on the radio or my cell." He gave her the number of one of the cell phones he had bought.

"Yes, sir."

"This way, Colonel, your equipment is waiting outside." Perez and Wishbone exited the communications shelter, and as they did, the quartermaster saw them and opened the back of an SUV. He stood back.

"Colonel Perez, our quartermaster, Sergeant Bill Colman." Colman saluted, which Perez returned.

"What have you got for me, Sergeant?"

"Well, sir, as you can see, we have a 4x4 Humvee. Also, your vest and radio." He tossed them aside. "I found the pistol you requested. It wasn't easy; a Glock 19 with five hundred rounds of 9x19 is not our standard issue, much to my disappointment though. Also, I got the 9 mil MP5 you wanted." He picked up a long case and opened it. "I don't have the fifty cal you wanted, so I got you an M110 instead. I hope that's okay?"

"Yes, that's fine."

"Good. Finally, a standard issue M4, each weapon with 500 rounds. I even threw in a voucher for a car wash when you bring it all back in pristine order, sir." He smirked. "What kinda bear you huntin' anyway?"

"A dangerous one, Sergeant. Did you get the recorder too?"

"Yes, sir." He opened another case. "Headset video recorder with 200 hours of recording time. Pretty tough too. It's also a lucky one, sir."

"Lucky one? What do you mean?"

"Box number seven and a serial number ending in three sevens."

"Hmm, lucky number seven. Thank you, Sergeant Colman, Major Wishbone. I'll keep in touch as I'm in there."

"Keep safe, Colonel."

"Thank you, Major." He got in the Humvee and drove off. Perez travelled until he reached the roadblock on the highway leading into the zone. The highway patrol and army were manning the blockade. Perez flashed his ID, and they stepped aside. As he drove past them, one soldier said to another, "Man, that dude's a crazy mother for goin' in there."

"Yep," was the reply.

Perez drove the route that he and the captain had pre-planned. He could see the debris materializing as he passed through the ring and made his way to his destination. His fob continued to beep warning after warning each time more rock appeared. Weaving in and out of debris, he guided his SUV to the address of Stephan Krueger. He parked in front and walked to the house. Piles of clothing and dusty human remains from the blast wave littered the sidewalk. "Perez to base, I'm entering the house now. Keep me posted." There was no response, so he was uncertain if they heard him.

He turned on his headset. "This will be either easy or hard." He drew his pistol and tried the doorknob. "Locked, I guess it's the hard way." Squaring up, he kicked the door, busting it open. He glanced outside again at the falling rock. "I better be quick." He stepped into the house. "Ugh, it reeks of death in here." He continued his commentary. "I'm searching the Krueger house for anything that might help my investigation." He worked room to room, starting on the first floor. After finishing most of the ground floor, he entered the kitchen. "Whew, bleach. He must have killed them in here." He looked inside the garage and narrated. "There are piles of dust and clothing in here." As he moved, he caught a glint from something reflecting in the dust. "What's that?" He descended the two steps to the garage floor and walked to the piles. Using a garden trowel, he cleared the dust that was concealing the objects. "Bullet slugs. This ash pile must be the Krueger family." He stood up. "You poor folks didn't know what hit you, did you?" He left the garage and closed the door, concentrating his efforts in the kitchen.

Suddenly his fob beeped. He looked at it. "Ten percent." In the distance, he heard the crash of a piece of the mountain, and after a moment felt the ground tremble. "I better hurry. These look like documents from an employment agency." He picked one up and skimmed it. "This was when you started, huh? I remember that day; it was the day I shot the sign." He continued to browse through the papers. His fob beeped again. "Fifty percent. That one's close." He heard the vortex and crash. The sound was like a distant thunder followed by a great shaking in the ground.

He turned over every paper and pushed a bowl that had been used as an ashtray, noting several cigarette butts. "Heavy smokers. Hey, what's this?" He picked up an empty book of matches. "Friendly Pines Motel, Route 7." He opened it, "Another address. I'll look that up when I'm out of here." His fob beeped again, followed by the earth shaking. "Okay, time to go." He placed the matchbook and several papers into his pack and stepped outside.

The area felt like a war zone as flying rock barraged it. "Looks like it's getting real now." He ran to his Humvee and started it. Flooring the accelerator, he forced the engine to propel the truck as fast as it could go. The fob beeped again, "Eighty-Five percent, oh crap, this one's on top of me." The sky opened up, and an enormous flaming piece of the mountain burst from a ripple. It slammed the ground, exploding into flaming fragments. The impact sent a cloud of debris outward, toward Stephan's house. Perez saw in his mirror a cloud of dust envelope the house and watched as it blasted it into fragments. *Damn, am I going to make it?* He floored his accelerator.

Steering back and forth, he threaded through the falling rock debris from the sky. An enormous chunk hit the ground near him and exploded. Giant pieces from the impact flew directly toward him. Rock shrapnel hit his Humvee, collapsing the side of it and catapulting it in the air. The Humvee landed on its roof and slid to a stop. Perez was mildly dazed from the crash. "Crrraaapppppp! I've got to get out of here." Debris continued to emerge and was becoming more frequent. He climbed out of his totaled transport and ran. "I can't believe I'm running from the same explosion, twice!" As he ran, he passed by a house with an open garage door. Inside the garage, he noticed a dirt bike. He ran into the garage to take the bike, but it was locked.

"You gotta be kidding me. Where the hell is the key?" He frantically searched, all while molten rock missiles continued to pound the area.

He looked toward the door to the house, and next to it hung a set of keys on a nail. "There, that has to be them!" He grabbed the keys and jumped on the bike. He inserted what looked like the right key into the ignition and carefully turned it, trying not to break it. He kicked hard, causing the engine to rev to life. Twisting the throttle hard, he peeled out of the garage, just as a large rock crashed into the house, obliterating it. His fob constantly beeped, sounding out warnings of the massive barrage of time debris. "They're getting faster now." Perez noticed the nimble motorcycle was better to navigate the debris and pushed the bike to its limit.

Suddenly, a large chunk emerged, cutting off his path. He skidded to a halt, as the rock sailed over him and struck the only bridge of escape from that side of town. "Damn, it took out the bridge." He rolled up to the destroyed bridge and leaned over looking down. "Okay, Perez, now what? I can't go around, and it's too steep to ride through. Forget about on foot, too." He wracked his brain and noticed the road. "It looks like the impact of the last rock pushed the road up to form a ramp." He leaned over to look into the ravine. "It's insane, but I have to jump, there's no other way." He looked around, and debris was everywhere. "I have to, or I'm dead anyway." He spun around and rushed down the road. He turned and revved the engine. "If anyone finds this recording and I don't make it, please make sure my mission is completed."

He twisted the throttle and quickly accelerated to seventy-five miles per hour. He hit the ramp and was propelled high into the air over the deep ravine. The gap was at least 200 feet across. Debris flew in all directions, and he twisted in the air to avoid being hit by flying rock as he sailed across. The bike finished its arc and landed hard, but he managed to stay on it. He hit the throttle and raced down the road away from the barrage. Looking behind, he saw the town being mercilessly bombarded by time debris; piece by piece erasing it from existence. "At least I found a lead, and I have a great video to share too." He switched off the recording device.

CHAPTER 18

"...MORE DETAILS TO FOLLOW." AFTER DRIVING FOR A WHILE, SASHA turned off the radio. "The news is calling this a meteor disaster." He laughed. "At least they didn't use the volcano story like when we blew up Mount St. Helens. They're all so gullible."

"Do you think anyone survived the explosion?" Galina said.

"Not likely."

"And our friend from the road who killed Pavel?"

"I'm not sure. I saw the blast getting close to him, but we went into the tunnel, and I didn't see if he died."

"I hope he made it." Sasha looked at her surprised. "I'm looking forward to killing him myself." Sasha acknowledged her hope.

"If he is, I'm sure you'll get your chance, Galina." He turned a corner. "We must also return to the motel and sterilize it." Galina muttered in agreement.

Once again, Perez pulled up to the gate of the disaster response base. The same two guards recognized him and saluted. "Hello, Colonel, new bike, sir?" Before Perez could respond, the other guard said, "The major is in the media briefing tent, sir."

"That's okay, I don't need to bother him again. I only need a new set of wheels, and I'm gone again." They opened the gate, and Perez passed them.

"Colman's gonna be pissed," the first guard quipped.

"Ain't that the truth?" the second said as he closed the gate.

Perez rode the "borrowed" motorcycle to the quartermaster hut. Coleman was outside in the motor pool and watched him ride up. "That doesn't have four wheels, sir." He looked over his pop bottle glasses as Perez parked the motorcycle. "You're getting quite a collection of bikes." He pointed at his other.

"Hello, Sergeant. I'm sorry, but I lost the Humvee in the barrage."

"And the weapons, Colonel?"

Perez opened his jacket to reveal his Glock. "I managed to save this."

"Thank God for small miracles, sir." Perez chuckled at his sarcasm.

"I'll need a new vehicle, Sergeant."

"All I have left are these pickup trucks, sir."

"They'll be fine. Do they have GPS?"

"Yes, sir. They even have satellite radio too. You can have the black one over there. I'll leave the keys inside it, sir. Same weapons too?"

"No need, Sergeant, just some spare mags and 500 rounds for the Glock again." He pondered, "Maybe the M110 too."

"Okay, I'll leave them in the truck, sir."

"Thank you."

"Just remember, sir. You break it, you buy it."

"Tell you what, Sergeant, if I lose or damage this one, I'll buy you a case of whatever you want."

"Make it Scotch, sir." He walked away smiling. "This'll be the cheapest drunk I'll have for the year."

Perez left and went to the communications shelter. He walked in and saw Captain Styles at her console. "Hello, Captain." She began to rise, but Perez waved her off. "Stay seated, Captain."

"Hello, Colonel. I'm glad to see you again. I can't believe you made it out alive. I was watching, but I couldn't get through to you on the phone."

"Yes, sorry about that. I left it in the truck."

"Not too useful leaving it in there, sir. That was quite a jump you did too; exhilarating to watch."

"Thanks, my next show is on Friday."

She laughed. "How can I help you now, Colonel?"

He placed the empty matchbook in front of her. "Where's this location?"

She read the written address inside the book and punched it into the computer. The screen panned and zoomed in on a wooded area with a large clearing. "Right here, sir." She pointed at the screen.

"Can you zoom in?" She adjusted the picture at his request. "That looks like a cabin."

"Yes, it sure does. Not much gets past you does it, sir?" she teased him.

"Funny, Captain. Can you get thermal on this?"

"Yes, sir." She hit a key, and the image shifted to a thermal view of the area.

"What's that?"

"That would be a single heat signature in the cabin. Small one though – it could be a child or a small woman."

"How far away is that address?"

"You'd have to go around the evacuation zone to get there, so I think… about a four-hour drive."

He turned the matchbook. "How long to the motel?"

She typed in the address. "I'd say about a two-hour drive, sir."

"Okay, I'll go there first. Keep an eye on this place and let me know if you see anything."

"Yes, sir, I will, but I need to reboot my system before I can do anything else. Our IT people have sent an update, and I'm long overdue, so they're forcing me."

"Now? It's just like them to do that. How long?"

"Two hours, sir."

"Well, we have to keep IT happy, don't we? Heaven forbid we need our computers to save the world or something. Keep me posted when you can." He turned to leave.

"Yes, sir, I will." She selected the shut-off button on her computer and the screen faded, just as heat from the engine of a car entering the driveway appeared on the screen.

Sasha and Galina arrived at their destination. He drove onto an overgrown laneway, which led into the secluded forest. Carefully, he maneuvered around preset landmines—set by his people. After a minute, he pulled into a large clearing. "There's the cabin." He drove to it and parked. They got out, and as they walked to the door, they noticed it was open slightly, allowing them to hear a noise coming from inside.

"Someone's here." Sasha and Galina pulled their guns out. He slowly pushed the door open and peered into the cabin. His eyes struggled to adjust to the dim light inside. "Perfect ambush scenario," he whispered. He pointed for Galina to take the right side. They quietly entered the cabin and swept side to side, looking for the intruder. Talking to each other in hand signals, they stealthily proceeded through the rooms of the cabin.

"Clear," Galina said.

"Clear here too," Sasha said.

He reached the kitchen and heard a soft rustling. He signaled Galina, who quietly joined him with her gun poised for action. Crouching low, he slowly pushed the door open to the kitchen. Inch by inch, his view widened to where he could finally make out who the intruder was. Smiling, he stood up straight and lowered his gun. "I think we need to call the police; we have an intruder." At the sound of his voice, a large raccoon turned to face them. Hissing, it backed away from them. Sasha, not wanting to kill the animal, walked in and opened the rear door. He backed off to allow the critter to escape, and it did, although not before it stopped and hissed one more time at them. As it left, it grabbed a last handful of food and quickly scurried off like a little fat thief. They laughed.

"We should consider moving to a safer neighborhood," Galina said

Sasha snorted through his grin, "Dah."

Once the excitement was over, the duo unloaded their prize from the SUV and took it into the cabin; they placed it on a table. "So, what does this magical gun that Pavel died for do?"

"Ah, kitten, let me show you." He took the scope and mounted it to the top, retracing the exact steps he watched Perez take. He took the assembled weapon along with one of the cases containing six of the cartridges and walked outside. "Galina, let me introduce to you the world's only weapon that can shoot through time."

She laughed, "Sure it does. Really what does it do?"

"I say this with truth. The weapon can shoot a bullet through time."

"That is incredible, show me."

"I will. Watch closely." Sasha placed the weapon on a picnic table outside of the cabin. He took the cartridge and, mimicking Perez, inserted the projectile. He activated the scope and after a few moments learned the controls. "Very intuitive and easy to use."

"It must be for their simple-minded soldiers," Galina said.

"I take the weapon and with this telescope I can see through time. I adjust the time by turning this control knob." He rotated it until he found what he needed. "Look into the eyepiece."

Galina looked into the scope and jerked her eye away to look up. "What!?" She looked in again, "I don't believe it. I see a deer, but it's not there." She pointed to the empty field.

"Exactly, it's not there now, but it was four days ago."

Galina could not believe her eyes. "How can we use this weapon?"

"Let me demonstrate." He aimed the weapon at the deer and activated the trigger. The gun discharged a bullet into the ripple hovering in the air. "Very strange," he said.

"Now you say something is strange? What could be stranger than this?"

"When I fired, the viewfinder went fuzzy. I couldn't see the deer getting hit. I don't know if it worked."

"There is only one way to find out." She walked from the table toward where the shot went.

They crossed the field searching for the deer. "Galina, go over there to look." Sasha pointed, and they doubled their efforts.

After a moment, Galina said, "Over here, I hear flies buzzing." Sasha walked over to her.

"There, I see it." They approached the deer lying dead in the tall grass. Flies were buzzing all over it.

"Too bad, I'd have liked to have had some game tonight."

"This is unbelievable. Imagine what we could do with this, Sasha."

"Yes, Russia would once again be strong." They walked back to the cabin.

"How does it work?"

"I heard a complicated explanation from the scientists, but basically, the bullet goes through a tunnel in time." He picked up a containment cartridge and showed it to Galina. "The bullet is a special type that uses time particles." She managed to open a cartridge and saw the levitating bullet inside. Once exposed to the air, it began to vibrate slightly. She was about to reach in and touch it when Sasha spoke.

"This is very odd."

Galina stopped, "What is odd?"

"Look at your watch. What time is it?"

Galina looked. "My watch says zero three hundred hours this morning. How is that? We set them before the raid this morning."

Sasha nodded. "Yes, and my watch says eighteen hundred hours but yesterday's date. I think we must be careful using this." Galina mumbled in agreement.

"Let me try, Sasha."

"No more shots, Galina. I don't want to waste bullets." Sasha's cell phone vibrated in his pocket. He pulled it out and answered it. "Hello." He paused. "Yes, Comrade General." He nodded as he listened to his commanding officer speak. "Eleven." He nodded a few more times.

"Yes, Comrade General, I'll look for the email. As for the other matters, consider them done." He pressed "end" and held the phone in his hand for a moment.

"What did the Comrade General say?"

Sasha returned his phone to the inside pocket of his jacket. He quickly pulled out his gun and firmly pressed it against her forehead. She tried to reach for her weapon, but Sasha grabbed her wrist and held it. He leaned in to whisper to her. "They ordered me to eliminate all witnesses of this weapon." He held his gun against her forehead for a moment then drew it away. "I kill you; they kill me; we're both dead. We work together, we both stay alive." He planted a gentle kiss on her forehead where he had pressed his gun.

Galina exhaled, "Were you going to kill me, Sasha?"

"Kitten, I could never kill you. I hope you feel the same to me."

"After what happened now, let me think about that."

Sasha smiled. "Understandable. We must go to the motel and clean it out now." They packed the SUV and left the cabin. "I will need your help to do this, Galina."

"I will always be here for you, Sasha." She touched his arm. He smiled, and they drove off.

CHAPTER 19

PEREZ WALKED TO HIS TRUCK AND GOT IN. HE LOOKED AT THE CON-trols and found the truck had a dash-mounted camera. He activated it to record his travels. "This has been a day from hell," he confessed his frustration to the camera in his one-sided conversation. He set the GPS coordinates, shifted into gear, and left.

He drove for over an hour and didn't speak aloud because the voice in his conscience spoke enough for them both. He could hear a taunting voice, tormenting him from the inside. *You could've stopped him if only you were a better soldier. Why did you let this happen? You could have saved them if you had been there.*

Perez shook his head. "SHUT UP!" He switched the radio on, but could only find local reports about the meteor disaster. "...Authorities are still tight-lipped about any details or images of the impact zone. Various government agencies are working hard to lay blame for this tragedy. We go to Senator Jonathan Buckney, who had a lot to say about this event."

The voice changed to that of the Senator. "What I want to know is why didn't NASA catch this thing in time for us to at least evacuate? Heads are going to roll over this."

Then it was back to the announcer: "NASA spokesman Todd Church released a statement earlier addressing NASA's critics." A video started to play in a side box on the screen and then expanded, showing a NASA scientist standing at a podium.

"Concerning the question of why NASA didn't warn anyone about this object, the answer is simple: Our systems showed nothing to warn people about – nothing at all. We search a lot of sky on a very tiny budget. We locate and record numerous Near Earth Objects. Understandably, we can't map them all, but I can assure you, we're pretty good at our jobs. We would have easily detected an object the size required to do this kind of damage, which has us both puzzled and alarmed. If we truly missed this one, this event could be defining a new kind of asteroid—one previously unknown to us, an undetectable kind, and that's a definite game changer in our business."

"...And now another eyewitness account."

"*Yeah, I know who's to blame. It's my dad, Colonel Joseph Perez, who didn't stop it. Why didn't you stop him, Dad? Why didn't you protect your family, Dad? You always promised to protect us, but you didn't. Why did you fail us?*" Perez, lost in his thoughts of guilt, jerked the wheel and nearly lost control as his truck rode on the side rumble strips. "Josh!" he screamed at the top of his lungs. He hit the radio and turned it off. He wasn't sure if he was asleep or awake, alive or dead. He pulled off the highway onto a country road exit and stopped in a deserted parking lot.

The voices tormenting him continued: *Yes, Perez, why didn't you save your family? You're such a war hero, but what did you do to protect them? Maybe you shouldn't go on; perhaps you should be with them. It'll be easier that way.* He pounded the dash of the truck. The radio turned back on to static. "Shut up, shut up, shut up! It's not my fault, I couldn't stop it!" His anguish burst out, spurred on by the relentless mental torment. It was as if demons were continuously taunting him.

He got out of the truck. A flood of avoided emotions suddenly washed over him; a tsunami of rage erupted from his soul. "WHY? WHY GOD!? I believed in you. Why would you let this happen? What have I done to deserve this?" He kicked a garbage can, sending it spinning. "Sarah's GONE!" He took out his gun and fired into the air. "My children are GONE!" He fired three more shots. "Everyone I know! Everyone I love! GONE!" He lifted the gun to shoot again, but stopped and lowered it. He dropped to his knees. "What do I have left? ...Nothing." *That's right, Perez; you have nothing left. Why do you want to live?*

"I don't want to," he whimpered. "I don't want to." The voice coaxed him on: *Then end it, Joseph.* He lifted the gun and firmly pressed it under his chin. *DO IT, Joseph! DO IT!* He took a breath and jerked the trigger – Click.

"Yes, General. Colonel Perez has been given everything he's asked for, but…if I may speak freely, ma'am?"

"Go ahead, Major."

"I think he may be too close to this. He lost his entire family, everyone he knows. He feels that he's responsible for the entire event. Frankly, ma'am, if I may say so, you put a lot of responsibility on him alone. Are you sure he can take it? Honestly, I don't know if I could."

"Your concerns are noted, Major, but I've every confidence in Colonel Perez. He may need to fight a few demons, but he'll win. In fact, I know he will. In the meantime, we need to support him however we can."

"Yes, ma'am."

As the click echoed in Perez's ears, the gray overcast sky that reflected his hopelessness, parted. A bright ray of sunshine pierced through and bathed him in its light. He knelt and allowed the warmth to soak into his face. Suddenly, the satellite radio picked up a signal. It was an old-time gospel preacher talking with music playing in the background.

Are you feeling overwhelmed? (Music plays.) Do you think you can't go on? I want you to know that there is hope. You're not alone. Perez breathed in deep, labored breaths as he listened to the new voice of a stranger on the radio. *You may feel that there's nothing left for you, brothers and sisters, but I say there's always something left for you in the Lord. (Music plays.) Turn to His grace and His mercy. Seek His love and forgiveness. There's nothing that you can ever do or ever have done that can disqualify you from His forgiveness, you simply must ask.*

A round of organ music played as he paused.

Turn and ask for His strength and hope. Turn and pray for His will and purpose for you. You'll see how faithful He is and how much He has in store for you. (Music plays.) He will never let you down. He will never fail you, and when you are in Him, you will never fail. The Bible says in Romans 8:28 that God can work all things together for good for those that believe on Him. (Music plays.) Will you believe? Will you let Him do it for you? You have a purpose in The Lord, my friend. Hallelujah and Amen.

The dark voices faded from his mind and a wave of peace washed over him. He lowered his gun from his chin and held it facing away when suddenly it discharged in his hands. Startled, Perez dropped the pistol.

The shot that was meant to kill him hang-fired in the barrel until he pointed it away. The bullet shot out and hit a new target; right in the middle of the letter 'D' on a rusted old sign that read *Devil's Tacos*. Perez silenced the evil voices, shutting the door to their persistent torment.

"Thank you," he whispered.

Perez stood up and looked across the road. Standing there was the same woman he had seen at the bus station. She called out to him, "Colonel, you still have a job to do, and things will be better if you finish it."

He put away his gun as he listened to her. He stood up and looked at her, "Who are you?"

"I'm a friend, Colonel. You must stop Mishkov. Everything depends on it." He walked toward her.

"Mishkov, I remember now." As he approached her, a large truck blew its horn and crossed in front of him. He waited the few seconds for it to pass, but when it did, she was gone. "What...?" He looked around. "Where'd she go?" She simply vanished. *Again.*

Perez felt a renewed strength. "Job to do, huh? Well, my job is to stop this monster. I'm going to find him, and when I do, I'm going to kill him, twice." He brushed the dust off and returned to his truck. As he climbed in, he heard the radio playing static. He looked at it curiously and clicked it off. He drove back to the highway and after a while called General Bishop.

"General Bishop, speaking."

"Hello, General, this is Colonel Perez."

"Colonel, I was thinking about you. Are you all right? I've had some concerns expressed to me regarding your well-being."

"Wishbone, ma'am?"

"Yes, Colonel."

"Well, you can let him know I'm fine and thank him for his concern."

"I will. Do you have anything to report?"

"I do, General. I have an address I'm going to now. I'm not sure if it will lead me to anything, but who knows? At least I won't have rock falling on me this time."

"About that, how did he get a nuclear bomb in our base? That's what it would take, wouldn't it?"

"Actually, ma'am, from what I know about the place, a well-placed conventional bomb could...," he stopped, "...did do the task. There were a lot of volatile materials in there."

"How could we build such a flawed design?"

"You know, ma'am, people always think it'll never happen to them and don't plan for it. After all, we were the most secure facility in the world, weren't we?"

"Apparently, not secure enough, Colonel. How did he get in there? Have you determined who this man is yet?"

"Major Sasha Mishkov. He's a Russian GRU agent. He was a sniper too, and a good one at that. That's how I met him years ago. Somehow, he replaced the real Stephan Krueger."

"If you know him, how could you not spot the difference?"

"I'm sorry, General. I guess I didn't pay enough attention. Suffice to say, we should check on anyone hired through the agency that recruited him. I'm certain that Ghost Mountain is not the first or last facility infiltrated."

The GPS interrupted their conversation. *In two hundred yards, make a left turn and destination is ahead – on left.* "I'm at the motel now, General, I have to go."

"Very well, Colonel. Keep me posted and be careful."

"Yes, General, I will. Goodbye."

Perez switched on his dash cam as he drove into the parking lot of the motel. He stopped at the edge and assessed his surroundings. He narrated for the camera, "I'm at the Friendly Pines motel. It's a small motel on Route 7. It looks like about thirty rooms in total. Beside it is the Hungry Mother Truck Stop. There's a lot of activity in their lot, so I think I'm going to park there to blend in." He put it in gear and drove to the truck stop parking lot.

He sat and watched the motel. Several doors opened and closed, as their occupants went in and out – some older people, some younger families with children. Others were weary truck drivers, who left their rooms to resume their treks still looking weary. He watched as a maid entered several rooms. After waiting about an hour, he felt it was safe to check it out. He got out of his truck and walked to the motel office. He entered the cramped office and immediately felt the offense of the hot, stale air on his nostrils. Sitting behind the front desk, was an older, life-weathered man.

"Hello," Perez smiled. The old man stood up his five-foot-four-inch frame when he saw Perez.

"Howdy, stranger, Bubba's the name. What can I do for ya? Do ya need a room?"

"No, I don't, but I do need to ask you a couple of questions."

"Mister, if you ain't renting, I ain't talkin'. My temper's as short as I am." Perez pulled out his cash and placed a $100 bill on the counter. "I just got a little taller, mister." He paused, looking at the money. Perez placed another $100. "I'm still growin'."

He pulled out one more $100 bill. "This is the last of my fertilizer, Bubba."

"Well, wouldn't you know it; I'm all growed up now. What'd you wanna know?"

"I'm looking for a room with several men in it."

"You don't look like that kinda fella, mister."

"I'm not looking for that, Bubba. I'm looking for perhaps, some hunters."

"Are you the law? I don't like the law."

"I'm not the law, Bubba. I'm just someone looking to return something."

"Well, the only folks I got in here like that are a bunch of them, foreign fellas. They rented the presidential suite down at the end, room twelve."

"The presidential suite?"

"Yep. Two bedrooms and a kitchen and one of them fancy bathtubs that makes bubbles, but it ain't workin' right now."

"By any chance, would you be able to let me into that room?" He held up the cash again.

"Nah, I can't do that slicker. I already got enough to get drunk tonight, and I got my guest's privacy to look after."

"Okay, I just thought I'd ask. Have a nice day, Bubba."

"You too, so long slicker." He smiled his multi-gapped grin. "And thanks for my future hangover too."

Perez left the office and walked toward room twelve. He turned on his recording device as he approached the door. He flicked the sign on the doorknob. "Do Not Disturb, huh? Well, you're about to be greatly disturbed." He knocked on the door. "Motel manager, is anyone in there?" He firmly gripped his gun in the holster and knocked harder. "Motel manager, open up please." No answer. He tried to peer through the curtains, but they were tightly closed.

He turned to walk to the back of the motel when suddenly his fob beeped. "Crap!" He instinctively dropped to the ground, behind a planter. As he did, the air rippled to his right, and a bullet emerged from a time wormhole. The bullet grazed his shoulder and embedded into the wall behind him. "That was too close." He fingered the newly created tear in his jacket. "Nice try, Mishkov, but I know you didn't see it miss, so it's my turn now."

He rose and hurriedly walked to the end of the motel and around to the back. He found a rear window, which led into room twelve. "Let's see how secure this palace is." He pushed up on the window, but it was locked. "So much for the easy way." He pulled out his knife and pried at the window lock. After a moment, he heard a soft click and slid the window up. He squeezed through the tiny window. "I shouldn't have had that last slice of pizza." He climbed in and found himself in the bathroom. He stood and looked at his fob. "Two hours before he shoots at me. I can't wait to catch you, pal."

He cracked the bathroom door open and listened. Not hearing anything, he opened it enough to squeeze through and stepped into a bedroom. He glanced at the packed bags covering the bed. "Going somewhere folks?" He lightly nudged a bag. "Yeah, you're going to hell if I have my way." Keeping low and slow, he peered into the main room. The air reeked of gun oil and cigarettes, making him quietly choke. "They smoke too much." With gun in hand, he slowly scanned the room. Although he didn't expect anyone, he was still cautious.

He searched the second bedroom and found more packed bags as well as open cots. He worked his way to the kitchen and stood up straight. "Okay, I'm alone." He talked to the camera again. "I'm in the assailant's motel room. I found enough bags for the whole crew." He walked to the kitchen and saw a full sink of dirty dishes and glasses. "It should be a regular party of fingerprints in there."

He approached a table in the main room. "What have we here?" He inventoried for the camera. "Several empty boxes of 7.62 x 39 mm cartridges, the kind that a Kalashnikov uses." He continued to search. "As you can see, there are several bottles of gun oil and wiping rags. These guys were clean and loose for battle."

He rummaged through the items. "A map of the ambush and printed emails from Ghost Mountain. So much for super security. Why didn't they c.c. him to save time?" He picked up a sketch. "This looks like the Air Deck. He must have caused that crash too." He continued looking through the papers and notebooks, searching to find any clue. Finding nothing of use, he moved on to the rest of the room.

"Jackpot, a laptop bag?" He picked up the satchel and pulled the computer from it. He opened the laptop, and it spun to life. "Fantastic, it's still on." The screen came on. "Yes, it's unlocked too. Thank God, they don't believe in cyber rules," he chuckled. He looked at random files on the machine and eventually started the email program. When running, it automatically updated, receiving a single message. He opened the file. It was written in Russian. He understood a few of the words but couldn't understand fully what the message said. He noticed an attached file and clicked on it to open it. Perez turned white when suddenly the outside door opened. Perez looked and saw Sasha walk in.

"Mishkov!" Perez dropped the laptop and pulled out his gun. Sasha saw him and immediately jumped back. He pulled his weapon out as he sidestepped behind the doorframe outside of the room. "Drop your weapon and surrender, Mishkov!"

"I don't think so, Colonel." Sasha responded to his demand with bullets. He reached around the door and fired three rapid shots where he gauged Perez was standing. All of the shots missed. Perez fired two return shots that struck the doorframe above Sasha's arm. Sparks and concrete dust from the door blew across Sasha's face.

Galina, who was sitting in their SUV, looked up when she heard the gunshots. She saw Sasha firing into the room. "What is this?"

Sasha returned fire and quickly crossed the entrance to retreat to the parking lot. He ran to a car and crouched behind it. "Why don't you give up, you weak little boy? You will never catch me; I will kill you first."

Perez ran to the open door. "Why don't you stick your head out and say that again?" he waited, aiming.

Galina saw Perez come to the door. "Ah, happy times, I get to kill him after all." She quietly got out of the SUV and crept around to come up behind him. Sasha peered over the edge of the car. Perez fired two rounds that ricocheted off of the hood, sending sparks over him.

Inside the motel office, Bubba heard the gunshots and looked outside. He saw Perez and his tenant in a shoot-out. "Return something, my ass." He picked up the phone and dialed 9-1-1, but he didn't see Galina.

"9-1-1, what's your emergency?"

"Yeah, this is Bubba down at the Friendly Pines Motel on Route 7. There's two guys poppin' shots at each other in my parkin' lot. I need the law here fast." He paused, "Stay on the line? Hell, no." He hung up and reached into a closet.

Sasha ducked down and moved to the side, running from car to car for cover, trying to work his way toward his SUV. As Sasha came to the vehicle before his SUV, Perez saw that Sasha had to cross a large gap to get to it. Perez waited, weapon poised to see if Sasha would try to run it. Sasha prepared and then fired several rounds over the car toward Perez. He lunged forward and tried to cross the gap. Perez fired several shots leading Sasha's lunge. The bullets missed but still forced Sasha to retreat. Sasha fell back against the car. He looked into the truck-stop parking lot. "There are a lot of innocent people around us, Colonel. It would be great shame for some of them to get hurt."

"Don't even think about it. You've killed enough today."

"No, not really, I need one more."

Perez dove out of the motel door and took cover behind a flower planter. Sasha, seeing him move, fired again and hit the planter. Shattered concrete showered Perez as he rolled behind a nearby car. Galina worked her way around and quietly crept up on him from behind. Sasha saw her closing in and kept his attention. "You are terrible shot. I thought you were this great warrior, but instead, you are little kitten."

"Come here. I'll show you my claws."

Galina was just behind Perez. She raised her gun and pointed it at him. She began to squeeze the trigger when suddenly the air filled with the blast of a gunshot behind them. Startled, both Galina and Perez spun around. Bubba stood with his still-smoking shotgun pointed in the air. "I don't like cheaters who shoot people in the back." Galina turned back to Perez but was too late. Perez had lined up his gun, and as she spun around, he fired, hitting her several times in the chest. Galina dropped to the ground. Perez kept his pistol pointed at her, but she didn't move again.

Sasha saw her get hit. "No! Kitten!" He let loose several angry rounds, but each one struck the car Perez was using for cover. Bubba ran for his life, hiding back in the office. Perez aimed underneath the luxury car protecting Sasha. He fired. The bullet skimmed underneath, and hit the heel of Sasha's boot.

"Enough of this." Sasha ran into the parking lot. As he crossed the path of a moving truck, he fired at the driver, who immediately jack-knifed his tractor and dropped to the floor of his cab. Sasha ran behind it and out of the sight of Perez. Perez quickly followed and used the stopped truck as cover. Through a side window, he could see the terrified driver shaking on the floor.

"Are you okay?" The driver nodded. "Stay there."

The driver lifted two shaking thumbs, "No problem." Perez peered around the truck but didn't see Sasha. Staying low, he worked down the truck making sure to keep covered. Sasha worked his way through the parking lot. Sasha turned and fired, but hit a truck cab that sent a shower of glass and sparks over Perez behind his tractor-trailer refuge. Perez finally spotted him and realized that he was working around to outflank him. He fired in front of him to cut him off.

"There are a lot of people here, Colonel. How about I start shooting some of them?"

He ran through the parking lot, which resembled a bumper-car track, with trucks moving in every direction. Perez watched as Sasha disappeared behind another truck trailer. He quickly followed, being sure to remain covered. He stopped behind his parked pick-up and clung to the side of it for cover. Perez crouched down and looked under the trucks for anyone running. He spotted many sets of walking legs, but none running. He restrained his shots. *I can't risk hitting anyone, no matter how much I want this creep.*

Suddenly, another shower of sparks covered Perez. He saw Sasha standing across the lot, firing. Perez dropped as bullets pierced his pick-up truck. Rolling and recovering, he popped up on one knee and fired two return shots. The bullets missed their target by mere inches, lodging into the now flattening front tire of a truck owned by a soon-to-be-angry trucker. Sasha disappeared behind a group of transports.

"Trying to bait me, huh? I'm not falling for it." Perez avoided the trap and veered around the back of another truck, trying to come up behind him. He ran around and fired two rapid shots at Sasha's exposed head. He narrowly missed him, embedding his rounds into wood planks on the side of a truck next to the truck Sasha was hiding behind.

"…and then the guy said, 'Hey, wait a minute, these aren't my pants.'" Inside the Hungry Mother restaurant, a tableful of sheriff's deputies laughed at Deputy Jeffery Jeffers story.

"J.J., that story never gets old," Deputy Billy Crookstop said.

"Yes, it does Billy. J.J., you need to come up with some new material," Deputy Ray Stecher said.

J.J.'s face shifted, and he quieted for a moment with a blank stare. He slowly lowered his fork. "How about a story about a guy running through a parking lot, shooting a gun?"

"A bit better, when was that?" Deputy Jack Stanfield said.

"Right now, look outside." The other deputies turned to see a man shooting at an unknown target. "Holy…" the radio interrupted.

"Unit twenty-six, are you there, Billy?"

"Yeah."

"We have a report of shots fired at the Friendly Pines Motel. Respond code three."

"Emma, this is Billy. We're at the Hungry Mother with J.J. and Ray, and we all see it. We're responding now. Got any more back up available?"

"Sorry, Billy, everyone else is at the meteor thing."

"Everyone get down on the floor and stay inside." The deputies sprang into action and ran to the parking lot. They drew their guns. Deputy Billy pointed. "J.J., you and Ray come at him from that side; Jack, you and me from this side." They rapidly flanked the shooter.

"Sheriff's department, drop the gun!" Perez looked behind him and saw four deputies aiming their guns at him. Sasha saw the deputies too and seized the opportunity to retreat to his SUV. "I said, drop the gun! Now!" The deputies closed in around him.

"I'm a federal agent pursuing a felon," Perez said.

"I don't care. Drop the gun now and place your hands on your head." The deputies pointed their guns at Perez's unprotected chest.

"I'm a federal agent pursuing a murder suspect. Back off!"

Deputy Billy fired a warning shot into the ground. "Drop the gun or the next one's in your head."

"Okay, okay. I'm dropping my gun." Perez slowly raised his left hand while crouching to place his gun on the ground with his right. After he placed it down, he slowly stood back up and interlocked his fingers behind his head. The deputies swarmed and handcuffed him. From the corner of his eye, Perez saw Sasha running away. He watched as Sasha got into his SUV and drove to Galina.

Sasha got out and looked at Perez. He pointed to his watch and then made a shooting motion with his fingers. Perez could only watch as Sasha helped the wounded Galina into his SUV. "Over there, he's right there, getting away." Sasha ran around his SUV, got in, and drove away.

"Shut up!" Deputy Billy forced Perez over the hood of a car.

"…but I.."

"I said, shut up." Billy kicked his legs out, and Perez dropped to his knees.

"Reach into my coat pocket; you'll find my ID."

"What are you? I said shut up." He leaned into Perez's ear. "Are you some hopped-up junkie? If I go into your pocket, am I gonna get stuck with a needle? Are you tryin' to stick me with a needle? If I get stuck, you're gonna be in a world of pain, boy," Billy said.

"No, I don't have any bloody needles on me." He shook his head.

Billy reached into Perez's pocket. "As I thought, nothing there. You're jerking my chain, aren't ya?"

"It was there. I must have dropped it."

"Sure, you did, and I can tap dance too."

"No, you can't, Billy. You suck at dancing," Deputy Jack said. They both laughed as they walked Perez to their patrol car.

"I must have lost my ID between here and the motel. Just let me find it. I can prove who I am."

"Sure, pal, and you promise to be right back too," Billy said. They shoved Perez into the patrol car and slammed the door. "J.J., take Ray and go look through the lot and the motel for any ID."

"What? You believe this guy?"

"Do it to shut him up."

"Okay, Billy, but it's wasting our time." He turned and walked away. "Ray, you, and me buddy, we gotta go check the lot."

Billy got into the car. Jack was already inside, typing on their computer. "Let Emma know we have a prisoner and we're returning to the station."

"Will do." Jack continued typing.

"We're taking you to jail, boy. You can call your lawyer or a general or somebody else who'll give a damn when we get there." Billy drove off. He looked into the mirror at the handcuffed Perez. "This doesn't appear to be your lucky day now does it, boy?"

Perez groaned and looked down. "You have no idea."

CHAPTER 20

THE ENGINE ROARED IN SASHA'S SUV AS HE SPED AWAY. "GALINA, SPEAK to me, kitten." Galina leaned against the door, silent. He reached over and felt her neck. "No, Galina." He stopped and reached over to her. He shook her, causing her to stir. "Galina, hold on. I will get you help." He held her and felt the wetness of the blood oozing from her chest.

She whispered through barely moving lips, "Goodbye, Sasha. If only…" She died in his arms.

"No!" He pounded the door in anger. "I will kill him right now. I'll kill them all." He turned to chase the police car transporting Perez, but stopped and thought for a moment. "The water tower, that's it. I'll take him from there with a time shot." He sped over to the water tower that was across from the motel.

"Hell, J.J., we've looked everywhere. There's no ID out here."

"Yeah, I know, Ray. I think he's screwing us around."

"This is stupid. That guy's not a fed. Let's get out of here, J.J."

"Hey, lawman." The deputies stopped as they heard Bubba call to them.

"You're not going to get on our good side callin' us that, ol' man. What do you want?"

"My name is Bubba, not ol' man, dep-u-tee, and *I called you*. I want you to take a look at this. They done gone and shot up one of my rooms on me."

"Yes, we know, pops. We arrested a suspect next door."

"Yeah, but did you get the others too?"

"What others?"

"Damn, you law types are dense, I called and said two shooters. It turns out there were three, but one was shot, a woman."

"Ray, we may have another shooter around. Where did it start, Bubba?"

"Room twelve. Some fancy pants came in looking for who was in that room. I shoved him off but not far enough, I reckin'." He walked to the door, "Look, they shot the hell out of my door and wall. Who's gonna pay for all that?"

"Please stay here. Ray, let's go." They both drew their service pistols and gently pushed the door open. "Sheriff's Department, is anyone in here?" There was no reply. "If there's anyone in here, you better tell us now, or you could get shot."

"Hey J.J., if there's someone in there, they're not too talkative."

"For sure. Okay, Ray, you go right, I'll go left."

The deputies entered the door and took defensive positions on either side. Each surveyed the room but didn't see anyone. Ray looked at the table and pointed at the empty cartridge boxes. "Someone was planning a big party." J.J. nodded. They carefully made their way through the suite.

"Everything is clear, Ray."

"Hey, J.J., there's an open window in here. Maybe Mr. Fancy Pants got in this way?" While standing in the main room, JJ looked around, "Based on what I see in here, we better call the sheriff. Something big is going on."

"Maybe the FBI, too," Ray said. Ray turned to leave the bathroom but then spotted a small black wallet on the floor. He picked it up with his glove but didn't look inside.

Across the highway, Sasha climbed to the top walkway of the water tower, cursing the entire way. The TATES was slung over his shoulder as he ascended. Once at the top, he set up the TATES and loaded a CAP into it. He switched on the Chronoscope and looked through it. Adjusting dials, he searched through time, until he found Perez alone at the front of the motel.

"I got you now, ublyudok." He aimed. "Okay, after this, I should find his body just like I did the deer. I will not remember shooting him, but Galina will be alive."

He locked in on Perez and triggered the shot. The gun spun up the round and fired it out, as the scope went fuzzy. The familiar ripple appeared as the bullet traveled to the past, where–unknown to Sasha– Perez had already evaded it.

Inside the motel, Ray started to open the wallet but stopped. "What was that?" he said.

"Don't know, a backfire maybe?" J.J. walked to the doorway. "After today, Ray, I'm not assuming anything. Let's check it out." Ray joined him at the door. They peered outside and didn't see anything unusual. The deputies stepped outside and scanned their surroundings. Not seeing anything, they holstered their weapons.

Ray opened the wallet, "Hey, J.J."

"Yeah, what?"

He held up the wallet, "Billy better learn how to tap dance."

J.J. read the ID. "Damn, this guy's a Colonel in Army Intelligence."

On top of the water tower, Sasha watched the deputies mulling about. "Why are they still there? For his body?" He looked through the scope, "No, they're ignoring where I shot. Did I miss him? I never miss." He looked again. "I don't know how, but I must have." He reached for another CAP, but stopped. "I better save them. I only have ten left and many to kill." He climbed down the tower and packed the weapon. He looked at the motel and said, "Next time, my friend, I'll not miss you. For Galina and Pavel, you're dead." He drove to the motel parking lot and watched the deputies. *I must get my belongings back. I don't want to kill them because I don't need more attention.* He watched the deputies as they talked outside.

"Ray, give me the wallet. I'll take it back to the sheriff. Stay here and guard the room until I can get back."

"Okay, J.J. Hey, bring me a new battery back, will ya? This one's running out. ...and a snack too. I never did get to eat my lunch or dinner. I'm starving."

J.J. smiled. "Always your stomach, Ray. I don't know how you stay so scrawny."

"That's because I never get a chance to eat." J.J. went to the patrol car and drove away. Ray stood and watched a man walk by eating a large sandwich. His stomach growled as he sighed.

"Here's my chance." Sasha slowly drove up to Deputy Ray and stopped. He lowered his window, and in his best country drawl said, "Hey Deputy, could y'all tell me how to get to the sheriff's office from here? I got a package for 'em, but I lost my waybill with the address on it."

Ray dropped his guard, "Sure, buddy." He walked to the SUV and leaned in toward Sasha. Immediately, Sasha pulled out a stun gun and jammed it under Ray's chin. He pulled the trigger and sent 70,000 volts into his jaw and neck, overloading his brain. Ray dropped to the ground, unconscious.

Sasha stepped out of his SUV and dropped two headache pills on his chest. "You'll need those later." He walked into the room. "What did they see?" He studied the room. "My laptop is open. He must have seen the list." He closed his computer and placed it, along with some documents, into his satchel. He took his bag but left the others.

He picked up the gun oil and squeezed it onto the scattered papers and rags. He lit a cigarette and took a few puffs. He then tossed it onto the pile of oil-soaked documents, which quickly erupted into flames. Sasha turned and calmly walked out of the room, as the fire built behind him. He put his bags in his SUV and drove. He activated his GPS button. "Washington, D.C."

Confirmed. Washington, D.C. Take a left turn...

"I've always wanted to try Russian deli at the safe house."

Sasha pulled up to the motel office where a guest stood. "Comrade, tell the clerk a room is on fire." The fire only took a few minutes to spread to the entire room. Fueled by fresh air from the open door, and an abundant supply of cheap combustibles, the fire raged, consuming all traces of evidence.

Bubba was sitting in his office, daydreaming of the big fish that wouldn't get away, when the guest ran in. "Call the fire department. You have a room on fire!" Bubba, jolted back to reality, leaned forward to pick up the phone. He dialed 9-1-1. "Yeah, it's Bubba again. This time I need the fire department." He sank into his creaky old chair. "I need a new job."

CHAPTER 21

"IT SEEMS WE'VE GOT OURSELVES A MUTUAL PROBLEM, MISTER," SHERIFF Charles T. Whitfield said.

"What problem is that?" Perez said.

"I don't know who you are."

"How's that my problem, Sheriff?"

"Well, to begin, if I don't know who you are, I have to keep you locked up until I do."

"I told you who I am. I just can't confirm it."

"And why's that?"

"Because most of the people who know me are dead and at the hand of the person you helped to get away."

"About that, we didn't see anyone other than you."

"That's because your deputies were too busy picking their banjos."

"You're not winning my love by talking like that, my friend."

"I'm way beyond wanting friends right now."

"That's too bad because we could all use a friend now and then. I'd like to be your friend."

"Great, then let me go."

"I can't until I know who you are."

"And thus, our mutual problem, right?"

"Bingo." He pointed his finger at him and winked.

"Excuse me, Sheriff."

"Yes, J.J., what can I do for you?"

"We found this at the scene, sir." He handed him the ID wallet. The sheriff studied it for a while as Perez sat, still handcuffed.

"Excuse me, Sheriff Whitfield." A middle-aged woman approached the two.

"Yes, Emma. How can I help you?" She spoke quietly to the pair for a moment. The sheriff's cocky grin faded.

"What?" J.J. said.

"Never mind saying 'what', just get back down there now." J.J. ran from the sheriff and left the building along with a few others. Whitfield tossed the ID wallet and a handcuff key on the table. "It would seem that one of our problems is solved, Colonel, but now we've got a new one." Perez took the key and unlocked the cuffs. "Apparently, I now have a deputy in the hospital, and your precious room twelve is on fire."

"No, damn it, my evidence."

"Screw your evidence, soldier boy! My deputy's brain was almost fried by – I'm assuming – your mystery man."

"He's lucky he's not in the morgue. This guy is ruthless."

"If you knew this clown was in my district, why didn't you call me?"

"The situation is classified, Sheriff."

"Not anymore, it isn't. This creep assaulted a deputy of mine, and I'm pissed."

"If your deputies had listened to me, we could have gotten him. For the record, he killed every person I know, including my entire family, so I think I'm a bit more motivated to get him."

The sheriff softened his demeanor. "Look, I'm sorry about that. I can't even imagine how that would feel. I'm also sorry that we got off on such a wrong foot. I know that it could have gone far worse for my deputy, and I thank the good Lord that it didn't." He leaned into Perez. "We have a mutual goal now. What can I do to help?"

"For starters, take me back there."

"Alright, come with me. Here are your gun and holster. You know the cocky punk even left a couple of pain pills on my deputy's chest."

"Very considerate of him." Perez put on his shoulder holster.

"Yes, I'll be sure to thank him when I shoot him in the head."

Perez laughed. "Now we're both going in the right direction."

The sheriff drove them back to the motel. As they entered the parking lot, they saw several deputies gathered by a crowd of volunteer fire fighters, all in a flurry of activity. "Damn, this guy is bad news."

When they pulled up, J.J. walked over to them. "Sheriff, I'm sorry. I shouldn't have left him alone."

"There's no way you could have known, J.J."

"Yes, there was. I could've listened to him." J.J. pointed to Perez.

"Let it go, what's done is done. Besides, I hear Ray is doing fine. He's a bit frazzled in the head, which isn't much different from normal." Whitfield tried to lighten the mood for his deputy. He pointed at the smoldering room. "What's going on in there?"

"The whole room's a loss. Any evidence in there went up in smoke."

Perez winced. "This man is insane. Your friend is fortunate to be alive. Trust me." J.J. nodded in agreement.

"Did you happen to see a laptop computer still in there?"

He shook his head. "Not sure. It's a hell of a mess in there."

Perez stepped into the room, which still had firefighters rummaging through it, breaking down any remaining hot spots. He sifted through the remains of the baggage. "What's this?" He pulled apart some clothes.

"What's what?"

"I found a sandwich wrapper for Ivan's Russian Deli."

"Never heard of it, Colonel."

"That's because it's not from around here. It's in D.C." Perez continued to search. "The laptop's not in here. He must have taken it."

"There must have been some important stuff on that thing for him to risk coming back for it."

"No offense, J.J., but it wasn't a big risk for him." Perez kneeled down and poked through the burned remains of his evidence. "There was, however, something pretty important. I caught a quick glimpse earlier, enough to tell me maybe where he's going and what he's going to do."

The sheriff perked up, "Oh really, and what would that be?"

Perez looked at him. "To kill a lot of people, Sheriff. Significant people, some I even know."

"...and where?"

Perez turned and held up the wrapper for the sheriff. "Washington, D.C."

"You don't say, huh?" They all left the room.

Perez took him aside. "Sheriff, I'd appreciate it if you kept this quiet. I don't need a major manhunt to spook this guy into hiding."

The sheriff nodded. "I understand, Colonel Perez. No worries." He made a zipper gesture on his lips, locked it, and tossed the imaginary key over his shoulder.

Perez smiled and walked to his truck, but stopped and groaned when he saw it. "Oh, man." He turned, "Hey, Sherriff, where's the nearest liquor store?"

The sheriff pointed down the road, "About five miles that way? Why, are you planning a bender?"

"No, Sheriff, but I know someone who is." He got in his truck and drove away.

"Seriously, Sheriff? Are you going to leave this alone?"

"Hell no, JJ." They watched as Perez disappeared down the road. "I just needed that slicker outta here." He picked up his radio. "Hello, Emma. Sheriff Whitfield here. Get me the number for Deputy Director Anderson Peters of the FBI in Washington, D.C., please." He turned to J.J. "Let's make this party a little bit bigger."

CHAPTER 22

"...AUTHORITIES ARE STILL BUZZING IN THE BEEHIVE STATE, AS THEY deal with the aftermath of the massive meteor strike that devastated their state just three days ago. Hope is all but gone in the effort to find survivors of this disaster. Authorities are estimating the death toll at over 30,000, with tens of thousands still missing." Sasha listened to the TV report as he cleaned his guns.

"In local news, the D.C. area is still in the grips of fear due to the D.C. serial rapist's latest attack last night. Authorities are keeping tight-lipped about the identity of his latest victim, who remains in an induced coma due to the extreme injuries caused by the assault. This attack brings the total number attributed to this rapist to twenty-three. Police are asking for the help of any witnesses who might have heard or seen anything. Correspondent Melanie Sharp is on the scene of the latest attack and is speaking with Metro Police Detective, Vince DiCarlo."

Sasha finished reassembling his pistol and racked a bullet into the chamber.

"Detective DiCarlo, this is a tragic and senseless act. What are the police doing to stop this?" She aimed her mic toward the stalky six-foot-three, forty-something detective.

"Melanie, the Metro Police are doing everything in their power to find and stop this monster, but we can't do it without the community's help. This guy is smart and careful. He doesn't have any pattern, and frankly, we're stumped."

He turned to the camera, combing his thick dark hair with his fingers. "Look, people, I grew up in these neighborhoods too. I get it. You don't like to talk to the cops. All I have to say is if you don't, then who's next on this crazy's radar? Could it be your sister? Your mother? Your daughter? Anyone, you love? You gotta help us catch this guy. If you've got any information, please call the number on the screen. If you suspect anything is happening, dial 9-1-1. For goodness sake people, let's stop this bastard. Oh, can I say that on TV?"

"You just did, Detective."

"Oops, sorry."

"We go back to our studio, now."

Music started to play. "We'll be right back with more area news on WDCA right after these messages." The music played them into a commercial.

"How'd I do, Melanie?"

"Great as always, Vince."

"So, ah, when are you and me gonna go out on a date?"

"Anytime, Vince. I don't think my ex-husband would mind."

"Just my luck, all the good ones are married. Wait. What? Ex-husband?"

Melanie laughed. "How about a coffee now? I'm free the rest of the day."

"Melanie, dear, I'd love to, but I got a thing right now. How about you and me, drinks tonight?"

"Sounds wonderful, Vince. I'll call you."

Vince jumped into his patrol car. "Melanie, keep the pressure on the public. There has to be someone, somewhere who has something we can use. See you later." He sped off.

"I'm your ex-husband now, am I?" her cameraman Tony said.

"Sorry, hon. I want him to think he has a chance so I can get more information."

"Remind me not to get on your bad side, lady."

She patted his face, "I do every day, sweetie."

Sasha turned off his TV when he heard a knock at the door. He picked up his gun and peered through the peephole. He saw the back of a man's head. "Who is it?"

"Sasha, it is Ivan from below. I am here with rifle, and I have sandwich for you too." Sasha opened the door, and Ivan stepped inside to greet

Sasha with a kiss on each cheek. "Is good to see you, comrade. I brought vodka to salute our fallen comrades."

"I will drink one toast, Ivan, but not ten."

"Then I will drink them for you." They took their glasses and raised them.

"Vechnaya Pamyat," Sasha said.

"Yes, let them be forever remembered." They drank. "How do you like place?"

"It is small and stinks like deli. People upstairs walk like elephants, too."

"But is still good place to hide. I have not seen anyone looking for you, Sasha. You are safe here. I go now. I have big order to fill."

"You truly sell sandwiches here?"

"Dah, I'm very good at it, too. Ours are the best sandwiches in the South of D.C. Even soldiers I sent to you took sandwiches with them."

"What? They had sandwiches from here?"

"Dah, what is big deal? You burned whole place."

"Let us hope." He closed the door and locked it. He walked to the window and looked down to the street below. "Let us hope."

Perez stepped off of the military transport that brought him to Andrews Joint Air Force Base in Washington, D.C.

"Good day, Colonel. Welcome to Andrews." The Air Force captain saluted.

"Thank you, Captain." Perez returned his salute.

"We've arranged to have a vehicle ready for you at the Pentagon, sir, but I don't know why you need it. We have your motorcycle here as ordered."

"Oh, I have another purpose for that, but only if I need to. Can I store it here for now?"

"Certainly, sir, we'll take good care of it. Follow me, please." The captain walked him to a helipad. "We have a helicopter ready to take you to the Pentagon, sir. It should only take about ten minutes to get there." Perez approached the running helicopter where an airman was waiting for them. "Colonel, this is Sergeant Tucker. He arranged for your SUV to be ready at the Pentagon when you leave."

Tucker saluted. "Nice to meet you, sir."

Perez saluted back. "Thank you, Sergeant, and you too, Captain. I know this was all last minute for you. I appreciate you pulling it off." He shook their hands.

"Excuse me, Colonel," Tucker said.

"Yes, Sergeant."

"I do have one request."

"What would that be, Sergeant?"

"Well sir, I know Bill Colman, and he told me about your last couple of vehicles, especially the truck you returned full of bullet holes. If you would, sir, could you bring this one back alive and unscratched?"

"I'll make you the same promise I did him, Sergeant."

"I thank you, Colonel, and I do know Billy is enjoying his Scotch after you returned his newly air conditioned truck, but I'd rather my SUV back in one piece and unharmed. That's why it's parked at the Five-Sided Puzzle Palace, sir. It's my colonel's favorite car."

Perez laughed. "I'll do my best, Sergeant." He jumped into the helicopter, and it lifted off for the Pentagon. He sat deep in thought, trying to shut out the world for a brief moment, but as he ruminated, the old voice crept back in. *How could you not have stopped this? How did he slip out of your fingers again?* The helicopter hit a pocket of turbulence, which shook Perez out of his spiral of self-loathing thoughts. He took a deep breath and exhaled. "Forget the past, just be ready for the now." His resolve silenced the voice once again.

"What was that, sir?" the pilot said.

"Nothing, I'm just thinking out loud." He sat quietly for the remainder of the flight, planning his next moves.

The helicopter came to a rest at the Pentagon helipad. Perez opened the door as the pilot said, "Have a good day, Colonel." Perez, unable to hear him, waved and smiled. He walked to the building and entered the lobby.

Inside the heliport entrance lobby, Officers Burk and Rogers stood on guard with weapons ready to confront whatever threat might come. The lobby was bustling with people, as it was at the beginning of the workday. The lines for the turnstiles were long and filled with flustered employees.

"Pretty busy this morning, huh Mike?"

"You've got that right, Charlie. I've never seen such lineups." Perez entered the lobby in his unmarked jumpsuit and walked past the lines.

"Hey, Mike, who's this clown jumping the lines?"

"Not sure, but he's pissing off lots of people if he thinks he can stroll past them. Go ask him what he's doing."

Charlie moved to confront Perez but stopped when Perez went to the unmarked door at the side of the lobby. "Wait, where's he going?" Perez swiped his card, and the LED on the reader turned green as it beeped. "No way, the light turned green on the spooky door. I've never seen the light turn green on the spooky door before. Who is that?" Charlie said.

"Well, rookie. I may not know a lot of things, even in my twenty-eight years of working here, but one thing I do know is that if the light turns green on the spooky door, you don't ask."

"Don't ask what?"

"Anything."

The door closed behind Perez, and he walked directly to the general's office and entered it. Monika Daniels, the general's secretary looked up. "Colonel Perez?" He nodded. "The general is expecting you; please go right in."

"Thank you." He opened the door and walked directly to the general's desk. He snapped to attention and saluted her. "Good morning, General." He stood rigid, fixed in his salute as the general kept her head down reading a report in her hands. After a moment, she looked up and acknowledged Perez without saluting.

"At ease, Colonel. Please sit down."

Perez dropped his salute and sat down. He casually glanced around the office as he waited for her attention. The walls were stark, with barely any mementos or personal touches that would reveal her personality. They were conspicuously void of any commendations or pictures from past campaigns or commands. The lack of decorations indicated to Perez that he was sitting in front of a commander who had ridden a desk her entire career.

After another moment, the general took the paper she was writing on and slipped it into a file that read *Eyes Only*. The folder was labeled *Project: Dark Portal*. Perez recalled a project at Ghost Mountain with that name but he was not a part of it, yet. He watched the general place the file inside her desk. She then got up from her chair and walked around to him.

"I'm sorry about that, Colonel. I needed to jot some important things down before I forgot them. What's your report?" She sat down in a chair next to him.

"As I reported before, General, Ghost Mountain is a total loss. The base was destroyed in the largest explosion I've ever seen. The unique characteristic of this event is that the debris is exploding through time. I also don't expect the meteor story to last much longer."

The general interrupted. "I read about the project, so I know what you mean by the time thing now. I know all this already, what about the weapon?"

"The weapon is currently in enemy hands. I went into the disaster area and found some information that led me to the motel where I believe they staged their raid from. I almost caught him there, but there was a bit of a problem with the local sheriff's department. I did manage to eliminate another one of them – the woman – or at least, I think I did. I doubt she'll survive her wounds."

"Who's the person you say caused all this, again?"

"Major Sasha Mishkov. He's a GRU infiltration operative. He was a sniper for their military at one time too, so he knows how to handle a weapon. Without a doubt, he will use the TATES weapon."

"How do you know for sure?"

"He tried it once on me already, so guaranteed he'll use it on others."

"How are you still alive? I thought this weapon was flawless?"

"My fob gave me enough warning to evade the bullet." He fingered the hole in his jacket, "*Just* enough."

"Who's he going after?"

"When I was in their motel room, I had a quick look at his laptop. I saw an email with an attachment and opened it. The attachment was a scan of the Time Shot demonstration roster, although I'm uncertain of who's still alive on the list and what order he'll try to kill them."

"The list is a Majestic-level document. How did Mishkov get it?"

"I don't know, General. That fact has me deeply concerned as well."

"Why do you think they want to kill our people like that?"

"My guess is to slow the project down; eliminate anyone with knowledge of it. Doing so would give them time to reverse-engineer it for themselves."

"You think the weapon is still here in America?"

"I believe it is, General. I also believe it's here in the Capital, especially if he's going after the people on the list."

"Where are you starting your investigation?"

"I found a food wrapper from a Russian deli here in Washington. I'll start there."

"Will you need backup, Colonel?"

"No ma'am, that won't be necessary."

"All right, but be careful, Colonel. We don't want to lose any more people."

"I will, ma'am. Speaking of losing more people, I think it would be prudent to quarantine everyone on the list to ensure their safety while I investigate this."

"Colonel, I understand your concerns, but if we stopped doing business every time we have a less than plausible threat, we'd get nothing done around here."

He leaned toward her. "With all due respect, General, 'less than plausible'? I would say this is highly plausible. In this case, I would take great heed. This guy is already responsible for the deaths of over 39,000 people. He means business, and he has in his possession one of the most powerful weapons in the world."

"Colonel Perez, we couldn't know for certain if he caused the incident at Ghost Mountain. After all, the entire mountain did vanish, and there's no way to tell for sure. What I do know is that the facility was ramping up the accelerator to produce a product, and there could have been an accident too."

"Yes, ma'am, that could be true. But, as I said before, he had enough knowledge of the base to put a bomb somewhere that could accomplish this level of destruction. Do you want to take that kind of chance with people's lives?"

"I'll take it under advisement, Colonel, but for now, we'll keep things business as usual."

"General, I…"

"Dismissed, Colonel."

Perez stood up. "Yes, ma'am." Concealing a soft sigh, he saluted and walked to the door. As he reached it, he whispered, "They're all as good as dead."

"Colonel Perez." He stiffened. "One more thing. Make sure you keep me posted on your findings, no matter how small." Perez turned and saw her picking up her phone.

"Yes, ma'am." He left the room. As he exited, he saw Monika placing a small audio device with earbuds into her desk.

She smiled at Perez. "Have a great day, Colonel."

"Thank you, and to you as well." As he left the office, he watched her from the corner of his eye. He saw her lift her phone and quickly dial a number.

Perez got into his newly assigned SUV and hit the button for the GPS. "Set destination: Ivan's Russian Deli."

Destination set, proceed to the marked road, and turn left.

CHAPTER 23

"OUR SUSPECT IS IN AN APARTMENT ON THE THIRD FLOOR ABOVE IVAN'S deli. He's considered armed and very dangerous and is responsible for numerous murders," thirty-year veteran FBI Senior Special Agent Adam Cross said.

"He doesn't give up easily, so stay at it until he's subdued," Special Agent Estelle Ivey, fifteen years his junior, added to the brief.

"Commander Parker, as we planned earlier, your team will enter the main lobby and go to the suspect's apartment. Agent Ivey and I will stay back until you breach and control."

"Who's covering the perimeter?" FBI SWAT Commander Parker motioned over the map.

"Metro police have loaned us a SWAT unit for support. I've placed them here, here, and here." He pointed to the diagram. "They'll also control inside movements on the lower floors in case someone walks out into the arrest." He pointed at the parking lot of an abandoned factory around the corner from the deli. "Right now, we're here. We need to approach from these three sides; the fourth side is adjacent to the next-door building, so no escape that way."

Cross looked up. "Okay, everyone; this guy keeps evading capture. We have to get him this time, so let's not mess this up." As he finished his brief, a dark blue Chrysler 300P quickly pulled into the parking lot. Cross groaned. "Speaking of messing things up."

"Uh-oh. Estelle, isn't that your favorite detective coming?" Commander Parker said.

"Ugh, really? Not now. Look, I dated him once, a thousand years ago."

"I don't know, the way he talked, you two were practically married," the Metro SWAT commander added, to stir the pot.

"Who told him we were here?" Cross said.

Detective DiCarlo stopped and got out. "Hey, how come you didn't invite me to this party? It took one of my boys in SWAT to let me know."

They looked at the SWAT leader who winced. "Sorry. I'll talk to them."

"You don't need to be here, detective," Cross said.

"What, and miss the biggest bust in history?" He looked at Agent Ivey. "Estelle dear, how come you never called me?"

"Detective DiCarlo, please don't call me 'dear,' and you know why I didn't call you. We don't need your cowboy antics to screw this up. Why don't you keep on going and grab a doughnut or something?"

Vince glared first at the five-foot-nine brunette then at the six-foot-three Agent Cross. "Seriously, Estelle? Well like it or not, I know these streets. I grew up here – right over there – before this plague took over. I want to clean up these streets, but it doesn't help when you elitist jerks, with no loyalty to the people, come in and walk all over us."

"Detective, we mean you no disrespect, but we feel we're better suited to apprehend this suspect than you are. He has unique abilities that go beyond the realm of day-to-day policing," Commander Parker said.

"Okay, now this guy I like. He's an arrogant jerk, but he does it nicely." Vince leaned in toward them. "Look, I'll play nice-nice and let you do what you gotta do. I just want to be here; you know—neighborhood presence and all. Tell you what, I'll stay outside and watch from the front of the building. You can have all the fanfare and credit you want."

"We need to get started, Agent Cross," Parker said.

"Fine, Detective DiCarlo can join the task team but only as an observer." He looked at him. "You must stay in the front and out of our way."

"Works for me, lead the way, my fearless leaders. Oh, and call me Vince."

Cross scowled and turned his attention back to the raid. "Okay, let's go."

The D.C. SWAT commander approached Vince. "Vinny, you're one crazy mother."

Vince laughed, "Don't I know it, Bobby. Watch your backs around these pretty boys and come back safe." They man-hugged, bumping chests with a firm hand grip and a pat on the back. The team mounted up and prepared to leave.

Parker keyed the radio. "Move out."

Sasha sat in his apartment, going over the details of his assignment. He pressed his pen and circled names on the list, numbering them. "First, I kill him, and then him. These other two should be easy." He leaned back and dropped the list on the table. "I don't see why they want all these people eliminated, but orders are orders. They're neglecting to mention one more kill though, me. I'm not so stupid to think that I can walk out of this alive. They'll kill me as soon as I finish this mission."

Sasha heard the screech of tires outside. He got up to look out and saw several unmarked FBI and police vehicles pulling up. He watched as their occupants quickly poured out and hurriedly deployed around the building. Sasha muttered quietly, "Ivan, you and your stupid sandwich wrappers." He hurried over to pack up the TATES when he heard a squeak outside his door. He stopped what he was doing and picked up his pistol. Sasha stood silent, his heart beating calmly in his chest. He faced the door, gun pointed, waiting for the FBI.

"Okay, quietly guys. Phelps, bring the master key," Parker said. The agent brought the fifty-pound battering ram forward. "Okay, strike here, full swing when we're ready." Phelps nodded. "Okay team, standard breach formation. Remember, this suspect is pretty tough, and if he resists us too much, we can use lethal. We can't risk him getting away again. You got his picture to verify?"

Cross nodded. "Yes, but how can you mistake that?"

He handed it to Parker. "Okay, on three." Phelps lined up and raised the ram. "One-Two-Three…"

Sasha edged closer to the door with his gun. He reached for the doorknob with his free hand. Outside the door, the agent swung the ram down as hard as he could, striking the door with such tremendous force that it exploded into pieces.

Sasha turned the doorknob and pulled it open a crack. He saw two Metro Police SWAT officers standing outside his door; their backs turned to him. The door creaked, and they reacted, "Sir, please get back in your apartment, police business."

"Yes, officer, certainly." He heard the heavy footsteps of the raiders above his head as he closed the door. He laughed and sat back down. "Idiots." The breach team poured into the apartment above Sasha's.

"Get down, get down." Another voice said, "Hands up where we can see them." And one more still, "Hands on your head."

Sitting at a table, with an Ivan's Deli sandwich in his hands, was the subject of the FBI raid. "Henry Patrick McGuire, you're under arrest. Drop the sandwich and put your hands up."

McGuire responded in a thick drawl, "I don't want to, my sandwich tastes so good." Four of the team confronted him as another four cleared the rest of the apartment.

"The place is clear, only McGuire is here," a voice of one of the raiders came from the back of the apartment.

"I repeat, drop the sandwich, and put your hands up!" Parker said.

"Okay, I'll put my sandwich down." He slowly lowered his hands and placed the sandwich down. He planted his hands on the edge of the massive table.

"Hands up, I said!" McGuire ignored the command and slowly pushed the table away. "Hands up, now!"

"Pardon? Did you say stand up?" He slowly stood up his six-foot-eleven-inch, 400-pound frame.

"No, I said hands up, not stand up."

"I *am* standing up; you have to speak louder. I can't hear too good." He firmed his grip on the edge of the table.

"Hands-IN-THE-AIR!"

"Oh, like this?" McGuire quickly lifted the table and threw it at the agents, knocking them all to the floor and making an incredible crash. He started for the door but stopped when he saw Cross and Ivey coming in with their guns drawn.

"Stop right there," they said together. McGuire turned and drove his enormous frame through his front window. An explosion of glass and wood showered the street three stories below, as he dove onto the fire escape. The platform groaned under his immense weight, but held. He stood up clumsily and lumbered toward the fire escape stairs. Cross and Ivey followed him.

"Get up, get up! After him!" Parker said.

"For a big guy, he's fast," Cross said.

Parker keyed his radio. "He's on the front fire escape. Move up from behind." The radio crackled with a frenzy of communications as the agents regrouped.

Detective DiCarlo heard the crash and looked up; his eyes widened when he saw McGuire running. "There's no freakin' way I'm jumping in front of that train." He watched McGuire trundle down the metal stairs. Vince looked around and saw a long-handled broom leaning against the building. He sauntered over and grabbed it. "This should be easy. He's not the brightest." Whistling a tune, he strolled under the platform and waited. He saw several FBI agents follow McGuire out onto the platform.

"He's almost to the second-floor platform," Parker said.

"See, I told you it would be worth following him," reporter Melanie Sharp said to her cameraman husband. "Keep recording."

Vince noticed the camera crew across the street and flashed a huge smile, "Hey Melanie, watch this."

McGuire jumped the final step to the deck and doubled back to get to the ladder that would take him to the ground. As he ran, Vince jammed the handle of the broom up through the grating and into McGuire's feet. The handle snapped off as it tripped him. McGuire yelped, as his massive bulk crashed onto the platform. The violent shaking of his fall caused the catch to release, dropping the vertical ladder down. His momentum carried him forward until he landed head first through the rungs of the falling ladder.

Vince walked to the lowered ladder and applied his full weight, pinning McGuire by the neck. He looked up face-to-face with him, "Going somewhere?"

"Get off. I'm going to kill you," McGuire said as he thrashed about, causing his foot to kick through one of the windows of Sasha's apartment.

Sasha sat in his chair watching. He laughed at the ludicrous sight on his fire escape. "Why don't you simply shoot him in head? Bang. Done. Over with."

The pursuing FBI agents reached the trapped McGuire. "Stop your fighting, McGuire." When the agents managed to get handcuffs on him, Vince released his weight, allowing the team to pull him out.

He looked up grinning. "I guess it was a good thing that I was here to sweep up your mess."

Agent Ivey looked down at him, shaking her head. "You're such a jerk, Detective DiCarlo."

Still smiling, he turned to the camera and waved, "Please, call me Vince."

The team managed to get McGuire standing again and walked him back in through the fire escape door. Sasha heard his footsteps thundering through the hall and down the stairs. He watched as they stuffed him into the back of a transport van, then a knock came at his door. He turned to answer it. "Hello? Is everything alright, officer?"

"Yes, sir, everything is fine. I'm Special Agent Ivey, and I'm with the FBI, not the police. We're sorry for the incident outside, and we'll pay for the damage to your window."

"That's very kind of you. That was quite exciting. Was anyone hurt?"

"No sir, but I can't talk about it. What's your name, sir?"

"Ryan Jones. I'm a maintenance man."

"I need your information for our claims department, Mr. Jones." She handed him a paper, and he wrote his fake information for her. She handed him a card. "Please, call the damage claim number on this card, and they'll arrange for repairs."

Sasha played it up. "Thank you, officer... I mean, Agent Ivey. I'll call right away." He closed the door and walked to the window to watch them leave.

In the background, a dark SUV pulled up and parked.

Vince stood outside with the Metro SWAT commander. He looked up and caught Sasha watching them. Sasha waved, and Vince nodded back. "I've got a bad feeling about that guy."

The commander looked up, "What do you mean?"

"I don't know. I just have a feeling we'll be seeing him again, soon."

"Yeah, but you think that about everyone, Vinny."

"Maybe, but I'm usually right when I do."

Perez turned off the ignition of his SUV. He watched as the FBI led their captured suspect away while a news crew recorded the event. "Busy place this morning."

Sasha walked away from the window and picked up his phone. "Ivan, come up here now."

"I'm busy getting ready for lunch rush, can it wait until after?"

"Ivan, now. I must leave before they come back for me. Trouble never comes alone."

"Okay, okay, but if I lose customer, you pay me back." He hung up.

"Durachit." Sasha gathered his bags and put them by the door.

There was a knock at the door. "Okay, I am here. What do you want?"

"Help me move what I need to move. Do not touch those, only I do." He pointed at the high-jacked cases.

"Dah, I be bellboy for you."

TIME SHOT

Perez waited for the FBI and police to leave. He watched as the news crew interviewed people at the deli. He noticed an older woman walking down the sidewalk toward the deli. She struggled under the heavy burden of bags filled at the local grocery store. The news crew finished with their interview and searched for a new target. The crew approached the woman, who tried to wave them away. They persisted and followed her in spite of her protests. Perez got out of his SUV and walked toward them.

"Please, leave me alone. I've been waiting for over an hour to get into my building."

"Ma'am, we only want to talk with you."

"She doesn't want to talk with you, beat it," Perez said.

Melanie reared up and protested his interference. "Who do you think you are, talking to us like that? We're the news."

"You're going to *become* the news if you don't leave right now." He pulled his jacket aside to reveal his gun.

The cameraman spoke up, "Honey, let's go."

"I'm not letting some jerk run me off like a…"

"Now, honey." He looked at Perez and pulled her by the arm. "Sorry, man, we're leaving right now."

"What? No."

"Now!" He pushed her.

"I'm not going to be intimidated…"

"Melanie, remember when I was in Afghanistan, and I told you there were people there I couldn't talk about?"

"Yes, I've never seen you look so frightened – kinda like you look right now."

"That's because I've seen this guy before. He's one of them. Let's go, now."

"Thank you for getting those vultures away from me."

"I'm glad to help, ma'am. Here, let me carry those bags for you." He took her bags. "Do you live here?"

"Yes, for the past forty-two years."

"That's a long time for a young lady like you."

"I'm seventy-eight, and I know baloney when I hear it, young man. What do you want?"

"I'm just trying to be nice. I bet this neighborhood is a lot different than it used to be, isn't it?"

145

"Oh yes, very much so. I remember when it was safe to walk around here. I'm okay because I'm too old and poor to bother with. I wasn't always. I used to own this building, but when my Freddie died twenty years ago, I couldn't manage it."

"I'm sorry about that."

"Don't be; he was an ass. Best thing to happen to me, although I wish I knew how to manage things. It turned out okay though because Ivan came along and bought the place, and he lets me stay rent-free. He's a wonderful man but keeps horrible company."

"What do you mean?"

"Take that giant monstrosity they just carted away. I always knew that man was trouble. He's lived here for a while too."

"Are there any others?"

"Why yes. There are the people in 3-C who are drug dealers. People are always coming and going at all hours of the night."

"Nasty people."

"You got that right. Next is that fruitcake in 2-D, who's always making a ruckus."

"What do you mean by fruitcake?"

"Because he's nutty like one. He's one of those crazy conspiracy nut-bars. He even thinks that sweet Ivan is a spy."

"You don't say." They got to her ground-floor apartment, and she fumbled for her keys.

"I'd invite you in, but a lady doesn't invite strange men into her home."

Perez laughed. "That's okay, ma'am. My name is Joseph."

"Hello, Joseph. I'm Helen. Helen Sullivan."

"It's nice to meet you, Helen. While I have you here, have you seen any other unsavory characters around?"

"Well, normally the apartment above me is empty, but just this week, a man moved in. He's quiet, but he gives me the heebie-jeebies." She looked down the hallway through the window of the rear door. "In fact, there's the man right now, driving away."

Perez saw the disappearing SUV. "Crap"

"I don't like to gossip, but if anyone's a spy, it would be him."

"You're very astute, Helen. I have to go now." He turned to leave.

"Joseph. Do you want the key?"

"Excuse me? Key? What are you talking about?"

"As you said, I'm astute. I know a fed when I see one, especially one as handsome and charming as you. You don't have to pretend to leave and then break in upstairs." She handed him the key. "Apartment 2-B. Slide the key under my door when you've finished, dear." She closed the door. Perez stood still for a moment and smiled. "Yes, very astute."

He ascended the stairs and unlocked the door to 2-B. He looked around and then entered and locked it behind him. He scanned the room and saw the broken window. "Wow, they were so close." He searched the stark apartment and noticed there was nothing on the walls and minimal furniture. The only item he saw was a pad of paper sitting on a table. He picked it up and carefully examined it.

"What have we here?" He tilted the pad into the light. Quickly, he searched around for a pencil, and after finding one, began to shade in the paper. Embossed on the top page was an elongated circle. He continued to color the entire page. "That looks like a three." Turning the pencil, he continued. "That's a two and a one." He kept going until he revealed the entire secret message. Drawn on the page were several circles with a series of numbers going up to ten beside them.

He pulled a page from his pocket and unfolded it flat on the table. He tore the top sheet off the pad and laid it on top of his list. He adjusted the page until it lined up. "Okay, he's already dead, and so is she. It must start here. Who's number one?" He traced his finger and stopped at one. He read the name: "Robert Maxwell."

CHAPTER 24

"ANOTHER ONE DOWN." AGENT IVEY PLACED CRISSCROSSING PIECES OF red tape across McGuire's picture on their most-wanted wall in FBI Headquarters. The room broke into a round of applause but abruptly stopped as Deputy Director Anderson Peters walked into the room. All eyes turned to him. He waited for everyone's attention.

"Well done, people, you took a monster off the street today. The public can rest a little easier tonight because of you. Again, well done," he lauded his staff.

"Thank you, Deputy Director." Several agents echoed.

"Cross. Ivey. May I have a word with you two in my office?" He turned and walked away, followed by the agents. "Please close the door." Cross closed the door and sat down beside Ivey. "Again, great job out there. I knew I could count on the two of you."

"Thank you, sir. We're happy he's behind bars now," Ivey said.

"I know you could use a break, but I was called by an old friend from Utah, and he told me about an incident they had a few days ago. I didn't want to bother you until this was over. It would seem that there's a bad man on the loose, one who may be coming our way."

"How sure of that are you, sir?" Cross said.

"This is from Sheriff Charles T. Whitfield. I'm positive. He and I were in the academy together, and I trust him with my life. We were partners for a while, but he had to leave the FBI due to a family emergency. He's a sheriff in Utah now, and we still have a casual friendship." He handed Cross a file from his desk. "They had some mysterious army colonel get into a running shootout with a bad guy at a motel. His deputies happened to be there and stepped in, arresting the colonel by mistake. This allowed the suspect to escape."

"Sounds professional," Ivey said.

Cross opened the file, "This file is empty, sir."

"That's why you're here. I want you to fill it. Apparently, while the deputies took the colonel away, the suspect fled and later returned to the motel. He attacked a lone deputy standing on guard, and fortunately, only stunned him. The deputy was guarding a room, which the suspect cleaned out and set on fire. This colonel maintains that this person is a mass killer."

"With all due respect, sir, what has this to do with our office?" Cross said.

"He feels the suspect could be coming our way. They found a sandwich wrapper on the scene that survived the fire. It was from Ivan's deli here in Washington."

"What? We just came from there."

"I know that. Maybe there's a special killer sauce or something in their sandwiches. All I know is that we could have another mass killer in our area."

Cross looked at Ivey. "Great, just what we need, another psycho in Washington."

"I want you two to look into this and see if it needs our attention; don't spend a lot of time though. Start with Tammy in forensics; she has some things to show you. Dismissed." They got up to leave. "Oh, and keep this quiet too. Apparently, this colonel asked Chuck to ignore all this, but good ol' Chuck could never stay out of things. If there are any problems, come directly to me." The agents nodded and left the office.

Estelle looked at Adam and sighed. "Just when I thought I could take a vacation."

"Why? Did you and Vince have plans?"

"I'm armed you know. Don't even go there." Adam laughed his dry little laugh as they walked out to the elevator together. "I think we should go to that deli right away."

"Hold on, Estelle. We don't know anything yet. Let's take a quick look at the items that Peters told us about first. Besides, if he's the bad guy, I'm sure he's long gone by now."

"True. If only we'd known, we could've had a two-for-one special today. Why did he hold it for three days?"

"He told us why. Besides, we couldn't be so lucky." They came to a door that read: *Forensics Office. Authorized Persons Only.*

"After you."

"Thanks, Adam." Estelle took her access card and swiped it against the reader. The reader beeped, and the door clicked as it unlatched. Cross did the same, and they entered. They looked around the room. Sitting against one wall was a big machine that worked away, analyzing a piece of evidence collected from a crime scene. On the other walls were numerous test tubes and smaller test devices, all used in the investigation of crimes.

"Welcome to Investigation Island, the annals of evidence. The land of soon-to-be-discovered answers."

"A little dramatic, aren't you Tammy?" Estelle said.

"I don't get out much."

"So, what can chief forensic scientist Tammy Blessing tell us today?" Tammy had her back to them, blocking their view of her current experiment. As they approached her, they saw her toasting marshmallows on a long metal skewer. "S'mores, anyone?" She squished a marshmallow between two graham crackers with chocolate.

"No, thank you, Tammy." Both agents turned down the offer with a smile. "The director sent us down to take a look at some evidence sent from Utah."

"Oh yes, right this way." She waved her hand to follow. "There are a few things, but the most important would be the surveillance video we got from the motel." She brought them to a video console. On a screen was the paused image of the digital video that they had received from the Utah field office.

"This is from the parking lot surveillance camera at the Friendly Pines Motel in Bakersfield County, Utah. This video is from three days ago. I've reviewed it and paused the video where the action starts." She pressed play on the screen. "As you can see, this is a wide view of their parking lot." They watched a man walk into the picture. "This is our mysterious army colonel." They watched Perez knock at door twelve and place his hand on his gun.

"What's he doing? Is he reaching for a gun?" Estelle said.

"That he is, but wait, it gets better. He knocks for a bit and walks away." Tammy paused the video. "This is where it gets interesting." She started the video again, and they watch as he suddenly dropped behind a planter. They see a small puff of material burst from the shoulder of his jacket.

"Wait. Stop it. Did you see that? Play that part again," Estelle said. Tammy rewound and played it again at half speed. "Watch him dive and look at his back… right there." Estelle pointed. "He was shot at."

"Yes, it looks that way, doesn't it?" Tammy rewound. "Watch his face. He has a look of surprise a second before he drops to the ground." She pointed at the screen. "And here, there's a blurry area where the bullet comes from."

"The shooter must be just off screen if that's a muzzle flash," Cross said.

"That may be, but would you stand up after a few seconds and stroll away? I don't know about you, but I'm not standing up for a second shot."

"The shooter only fires once, and this guy simply gets up and walks around the corner?" Estelle said.

"Yes. As you watch the video, you'll later see he comes out from the motel room. The report said there was an open window in the back." She fast-forwarded the video until Sasha walked into the picture. "Now, here's the exciting part." Tammy reached for some popcorn that was on the counter. "Estelle, Adam, I'd like you to meet the bad guy. Bad guy, here are the agents who'll be arresting you soon."

They watched Sasha unlock the door and step inside. Suddenly, he jumped back and to the side. He drew his gun and reached around the doorframe to fire into the room.

Seconds later, Cross said, "Bullets hit the doorframe. See the sparks?"

"Yes, he ran away after that. We see the colonel again, here." Perez appeared at the door.

"Wow, he charges right into battle, doesn't he?" Estelle said. "Hey wait. Is that a woman coming up behind?"

"Yes, she was with the bad guy."

"Was?"

"Wait, you'll see." The video showed an old man shooting into the air and Perez turning and shooting the woman.

Estelle reacted. "Oh, he hit her three times. She has to be dead."

"The bad guy took her away later, so we don't know if she is or who she is. Gauging from the colonel's aggressive actions, he must want this guy pretty badly," Tammy said. Perez ran out and off camera after Sasha. Tammy stopped the video.

"About a half an hour passes, and you'll see the sheriff's deputies going in with their guns drawn. After that, another forty minutes and you see the bad guy drive up and lure the deputy. He took him down with a stun gun." She fast-forwarded the video. "Five minutes later, we see him come out with a laptop case and overnight bag. A few minutes after that, we see smoke."

"Can we see the man's face?"

"I tried to pull a close up, but this is the best I could do. It's not good enough for facial recognition either." She reached for a printout and handed it to her. Estelle took the picture and studied it.

"It's hard to tell, but this could be the man from the apartment."

"What's going on here?" Adam said.

"I tried to view the video feed from earlier, but a lot of it is corrupted. It started about the same time as the meteor crash. I did catch some brief moments and enhanced them for you."

"One…two…three…five…nine… Hard to tell but at least nine men with…" Estelle squinted, "Rifle bags?"

"What happened to the rest of the video?" Adam said.

"Interference, but not just your ordinary interference. It's like nothing I've ever seen before. It's like several images are blended – hundreds of them. Putting this and the 'meteor' together, I sense something 'spooky' going on here."

"Spooky?"

"Yes, Estelle, spooky, as in the three-letter acronym kind, well except for FBI that is, because we're not spooky." Estelle looked at Cross, who rolled his eyes.

"Wait a minute, I remember something Vince once told me," Estelle said

"Oh, you mean that dreamy Detective Vince?"

"More like a nightmare." Tammy playfully scowled at Estelle's comment.

"Please, back on the subject ladies."

"He told me about his sister, Angelina. She used to be married to a guy named David Tremaine. He was a professor at a university in Utah. He ended up banging a young teaching assistant, and their marriage ended over it. She moved back here and shared some things when she was a bit tipsy."

"Drunken babbling? Is this reliable, Estelle?"

"No listen. Vince said that she had confided that David's father was a general in charge of some secret military base in that very mountain. She wasn't supposed to talk about it, but she was drunk and pretty hurt by them. I always thought that he was full of it, but now with this and suddenly a 'meteor', there's more to this than we know."

"I'm sure there is. Did you notice in the video how the colonel dropped before the bullet came?"

"Yes," Cross said.

"Well, I don't care how fast you are, you're not going to out-dive a bullet. Somehow he was warned."

"Maybe he saw the glint from the rifle or saw him just before he shot."

"Could be, but why would he stand up mere seconds later? As if nothing happened? Curious isn't it?"

"I'll need to think about that one for a while," Estelle said.

"Anyway, in case you're wondering, I've sent for the physical evidence, and it should be here in a couple of days." Tammy turned to Estelle. "You know, if Vince maybe knows something about this, I wonder if I should go question him? You know, to see if I can get more information from him about this case."

"Interview, Vince? Sure, if that's what you want to do. He's all yours, sister."

CHAPTER 25

"COME ON, HERBERT, TAKE THE PICTURE ALREADY." HE FUMBLED TO take the selfie with his wife, Shelly.

"Shut up, woman. I'm going as fast as I can. I don't know these damn fancy gizmos today."

"Here, if I may," Sasha said. He took the camera from the tourist couple and snapped a picture of them.

"Thank you, young man. Aren't the displays incredible in here?

"Yes, they are."

"What's your favorite?"

"I would say the wallpaper over there."

She looked at him curiously, "Oh, okay."

"I'm just joking. I love the architecture of this place." He had already snapped several pictures of security cameras and stairways. "I've always wanted to come to the Smithsonian Castle."

"We've been here many times before; this is our home away from home. Right, Herbert?" He rolled his eyes.

"Have you? You must know this place very well."

"Well, I don't mean to brag, but we've been taken on private tours by one of the guards we know."

"Really? Perhaps you would know this." He pointed. "Where does that stairway lead to?"

"Oh, that's easy. It goes up to the north tower rooftop. That's where they raise and lower the flag."

"I see, thank you. I must go now. Have a nice day." Sasha walked away, having finished his reconnaissance mission.

"He seemed very nice."

"Yeah, why don't you sleep with him too, you old hag."

"Shut up, Herbert. Why did I ever marry a jerk like you in the first place?"

"Because of my charm, dear, because of my charm."

"Are you certain of this?"

"Yes, Colonel. Defense Secretary Maxwell will be attending a gala at the Smithsonian Museum of Natural History the day after tomorrow. They're unveiling a display of samples from the space mission to Saturn's moons. Secretary Maxwell used to be the Secretary of Education and still loves scientific exhibits like this."

"I see. Was he informed of the threat to his life?"

"Yes, and, as I knew he would, he disregarded it."

"Okay, thank you, General. I need to get on the attendance list. Is there any way you can get me on it?"

"Sorry, Colonel. The president will be there too, so that is out of my range of influence. Besides, how will Mishkov know the secretary will be there in the first place? I have to go now, goodbye, Colonel." She hung up.

"I know he'll be there because I'm sure he has a mole in the Pentagon," he said to the disconnected phone. "I better get down there and check it out." Perez started his SUV and drove away. Several minutes later, he drove around the museum. "If I was a psycho killer, where would I shoot from?" He looked on the north side. "It's all justice department buildings on this side, so I don't believe it will come from there."

He drove to the south side of the museum and pulled over. He got out and walked around. *Expansive fields and nothing else around except for this castle.* He studied the area. *There. If it were me, I'd shoot from up there. Easy shot too.* He looked at the flat roof of the north-side tower. He got back into his SUV and drove to an inconspicuous spot to watch the tower. "Time to settle in for a long night."

Perez sat in his car and watched the castle. It was late, and he was struggling to stay awake. His head bobbed up and down continuously as he fought off sleep, but he finally gave in, dozing off. Suddenly, bushes parted a short distance away from him. Sasha stepped out and cautiously walked toward the sleeping Perez. He smiled as he pulled his gun from the holster and threaded a silencer on it. He walked up to Perez and raised the pistol. He squeezed the trigger and… Perez woke up. It was just a dream, but he still breathed heavily from the intensity of it.

Suddenly, there was a tap on the window, and Perez jumped. He turned to see a police officer standing at his window with his hand on his holster. Perez looked in the rearview mirror and saw the flashing lights of the officer's patrol unit behind him. He also saw another officer just behind, covering his partner. "Put your hands where I can see them, sir," Officer Cory Black said.

"Yes, officer." Perez added under his breath, "Not again." He placed his hands on the steering wheel.

"Slowly, with your right hand lower the window."

"Yes, sir." Perez complied, knowing he didn't want to escalate the situation.

"License and registration please."

Perez grabbed the registration from the visor. "Officer, I need to reach into my pocket to get my ID."

"Go ahead, but slowly."

Perez reached in and pulled out his government ID. "I'm a federal agent, officer. Here's my ID. I also have a sidearm in my shoulder holster."

The officer took the ID wallet and placed it on the roof. "Jordan, cover him. If his hands move from the wheel, shoot him." He reached in and took the gun from Perez. He picked up the ID and looked at Perez. "I'll need to check this out, sir. Please stay here and do not move".

"Like a stone, officer."

The two walked back to their car. "What do you think, Jordan?"

"I'm thinking he's a spook, Cory. Plates came back undiscovered, and I'll bet his ID will too."

Come on, hurry up. You're going to scare Mishkov away. Perez watched the tower intently. *Do I tell them the truth of why I'm here?* He pondered for a moment. *Yes, but not all of it.*

"Metro One Radio – Ten-One-Seven. Could you call DOD and verify an ID for me? Surname Papa-Echo-Romeo-Echo-Zulu, first initial Juliette, ID number Alpha-India-seven-seven-seven-zero-two-one – Majestic."

"Stand by." The radio crackled with the dispatcher's voice. A few seconds later, a voice came over the radio.

"Metro One radio, One-David-Fourteen, permission to relay to Ten-Seventeen?"

"Permission granted."

"Hey, Cory. It's Vince. I know that guy; he's okay. Where are you?" Officer Black gave him the details. "Okay, I'll see you in five."

Sasha stood in the shadows, watching the police with Perez. "I need to send a thank-you card to all the police who keep interfering. This'll be easier with that distraction over there." Sasha circled the castle until he found the outside phone box. He disabled the communications for the alarm and broke in. He went to the security office to disable the cameras, and when done, climbed to the top of the north tower.

"What are you up to?" He looked over the roof and scanned the area around Perez. He saw the police were still with him. He unpacked and set up the TATES to take his shot, waiting patiently for an opportunity. From his vantage point, he could see the entire area. He looked over the edge and spotted a dark figure lurking in the bushes. "Who is this? Perez, do you have help?" As he watched from the roof, a group of women walked by the unseen man in the bushes. Sasha watched him reach into his pants and pull out his member to stroke it.

"Svin'ya. Wonderful, he's a pervert." Sasha spat over the side at him.

Vince arrived and drove up to the officers. He got out and joined them. Officer Black handed him the ID and gun. "Thanks, Cory, I got it from here." They got into their patrol car and drove away.

"Dispatch, you can cancel that DOD call. We're good here."

"Ten-four." Vince tossed the radio back in his car.

"Well if it isn't G.I. Joey." He tossed the ID back to Perez but carefully offered the gun.

"You know I don't like that name, Vince." He pocketed the ID and took the pistol, placing it back into his holster. Perez got out of the SUV.

"Sorry, Joey. I guess it's because you're the only one I liked out of all of those jerks my sister was married into."

"Speaking of Angelina, how is she?"

"Much better now that she's away from that two-timing ass-hat Tremaine and his little bimbo. Angelina's back here now. She works at the museum over there." Vince pointed at the Museum of Natural History.

"How are Sarah and the kids?" Perez stiffened.

"They're all dead, Vince. All killed earlier this week."

Vince recoiled at the tragic news. "Don't that suck? I'm sorry about that, Joe. How? Was it anything to do with the meteor?"

"It wasn't a meteor, Vince. It was a murderous thug that caused the whole disaster. I'm hunting him down now."

"Really? I haven't heard anything."

"It's under the radar."

"Why? I'd be screaming from the rooftops. Why aren't you doing everything possible to get this guy?"

"It's complicated, Vince, and I'll leave it at that."

"So, why are you here at this stupid hour? You know, we thought you were the D.C. rapist. You coulda' been shot, buddy."

"I'm watching for my bad guy to show up around here. I've reason to believe that he's in town to shoot some people, starting here tonight.

"Not in *my* town if I can help it."

"Vince, I'm glad you're here. But I need you to lay low on this. These are national security matters, and I can't tell you more than that."

"Don't give me that national security crap. This is my town, and I'm a little overprotective. Start talking."

Perez thought for a moment. "Alright, Vince, you win." He shifted his stance. "I have reason to believe that there are going to be some dignitaries killed here at the museum in two days. I also believe that he's going to shoot them from the tower."

"Really, how?"

"Let's say it's speculation. Is there any way that I could get you to close down this road and the south entrance for the event?"

"On speculation? You want me to redirect the President of the United States and hundreds more on speculation? Besides, why not just put some cops in the tower?"

"It wouldn't stop him, Vince. I know I'm asking a lot of you and not telling you a lot, but I wouldn't ask if I didn't think it was critical." Vince stood quietly and thought.

"Yes, baba, I'll be careful. I walk this way every night, and I'll be fine," Rachael Chan said into her cell phone. She was walking home from her job as an assistant curator at an art gallery down the road from the castle. Rachael, a young Chinese-American woman in her mid-twenties, was oblivious to the horrors of the world. "I'll catch the bus soon, okay." She hung up.

Inside the bushes, Zachary Holt quietly waited for Rachael to approach. He spoke to the voices in his head. "No, Mom. I won't get caught. I've done this twenty-three times so far, and I haven't been yet. I have protection from my spirit guide." He hit his head several times, trying to drive the voice out. "Because I don't have a pattern, and I'm really smart Mom, not like you." He grated his teeth. "Why? Because I hate you and all women because of you. You're a whore and a drug addict, Mom. You brought me along on tricks, and when you got high, you starved me and abandoned me. That's why I killed you; you're trash." He paced inside the bush.

"I don't want a relationship with them; I want to hurt them. Thanks to you, I don't know how to have a relationship. Maybe if I kill one, you'll shut up and finally leave me alone." He peeked over the bush. "Yes, I like her too; she smells like paint when I sit behind her on the bus. Shut up now, Mom. I have to get to work."

On the castle roof, Sasha watched him pace about, but couldn't hear him. He saw the lone woman approach the bush. The man pulled out a knife and readied to attack her. "I'm going to kill this pig, but first..." He quickly aligned the TATES and looked through the scope. He dialed toward the future and stopped when he found his target. He locked in the time and set the TATES down.

He got up from his perch, just as the man jumped out of the bushes and grabbed the woman. He put the knife to her throat and covered her mouth, dragging her into the bushes. She tried to scream, but couldn't as Zachary was powerful and easily subdued her. He threw her to the ground and dropped on her, still covering her mouth. Sasha took out his pistol and threaded on his silencer. He carefully aimed, "Two birds, one stone." He fired one shot into the back of Zachary's head. The bullet struck the mark and killed him instantly, effortlessly passing through his skull to hit the ground beside Rachael. Blood and brains exploded outward, covering her. Zachary fell limp, dropping his dead weight entirely on top of her.

She laid momentarily in shock with what happened. Sasha turned and picked up the TATES. He realigned the weapon and waited patiently for her shock to wear off. "Okay, woman. Scream already." Rachael lay dazed for a few moments. Then gathering her senses, she let out a loud scream. Perez and Vince were talking when they heard the loud cries come from behind the castle.

"What's that?"

"That has to be my rapist." Vince and Perez ran toward the screams. "Metro One radio One-David-Fourteen, I need backup at my location. I think I may have the serial rapist here." Each man pulled his gun out.

Sasha waited for a couple more screams and then fired during one of her loudest. When finished, he peeked over the roof. "Thank you for your help." He quickly packed up the weapon and prepared to leave. Vince and Perez didn't hear the muffled crack of the time shot. Perez also didn't notice the beep from his fob inside his pocket. As they ran toward Rachael's screams, neither of them knew what to expect.

"It's coming from those bushes." Vince turned on his flashlight and broke through the brush with his gun pointed. Perez stayed outside looking for Sasha. "Police, freeze, get off the woman." The attacker didn't move. "I said, get off of her."

"He's dead you idiot; he can't move." Rachael screamed again and frantically tried to push his dead weight from her body, but she lacked the strength to do it.

Vince finally noticed the hole in the back of her attacker's head. "You're okay now, lady. I'm a cop. Where's your gun?"

"I don't have a gun. I thought you shot him. Get this effing thing off of me!" Vince carefully rolled the body from her with one hand while pointing his gun at them with the other. Once free, Rachael rolled the opposite direction and sat up briefly, although not for long, as she fainted from the shock.

Perez scanned the surrounding area as Sasha watched him from the tower. Seizing an opportunity, he pointed his gun at Perez, but suddenly several pigeons flew into his face, disrupting his aim. Perez looked up to see the birds flying. In the distance, Sasha could hear the building sounds of the sirens approaching from the backup units coming. He gave up on Perez, collected his weapon, and fled the roof. He ran down the stairs and burst out the front doors, bolting directly for his SUV. He stowed the weapon and drove away slowly as the police closed in.

Suddenly, Perez realized, "The front!" He ran around the castle in time to see a set of taillights driving away in the distance. "Damn, I missed him again." He jogged back to the rear of the castle and forged through the bushes to check on Vince.

"Where the hell did you go?" Vince glared at Perez as he kicked Holt's body.

"I was looking for the man who did this." He pointed at the dead rapist. "He used this to distract us for his escape. I saw him driving down the road."

The sirens came closer and closer. "I called for backup and an ambulance. You better vamoose amigo, unless you want to be answering questions all night." He handed Perez a card. "Give me a call later."

"I will. By the way, talk to your sister and get me into that museum too."

"Don't want much, do you?"

Perez pointed at the dead man. "Hey, you're a hero now. Milk it, buddy." Perez left quickly on foot. As he walked away, he reached into his pocket and pulled out the fob. He looked at it. "Just as I thought; he already made his shot."

CHAPTER 26

We go live to City Hall where hero Metro Police Detective Vince DiCarlo is about to receive his commendation for stopping the D.C. serial rapist.

"Detective DiCarlo has shown exemplary service throughout his entire career and has earned this Medal of Honor," Police Chief Peter Shewnam said. He turned to Vince, "Detective, congratulations on a job well done."

"Thank you, sir, but as I said before, it wasn't me."

The Chief leaned into Vince. "Take the accolades and smile detective; that's an order." The chief took his hand and shook it for the cameras. "We don't want to credit a serial killer for this victory."

"Yes, sir." They concluded the press conference with a few quick questions. Afterward, Vince walked down the stairs and into the crowd of backslappers and reporters. He looked across the road and saw Perez standing there. "Excuse me, folks, I gotta go." He walked toward Perez, who started to walk down the sidewalk.

"Hey, Joey."

"Congratulations, Vince. I hear the mooing."

"The what? Oh yeah, mooing… milk it, right."

"So, what have you got for me?"

"I got you in on a guest pass under Angelina." He handed him the ticket. "You won't be able to go near the President, but at least you'll be inside. By the way, she's looking forward to seeing you, too."

"And the road?"

"I got it closed down too. But it wasn't easy and, because of my interest, I'm on the outside detail now."

"Great, thanks, Vince."

"So, what now?"

"I've got a few things to get ready, and I'll see you there tomorrow."

"Okay, Joey. Be careful."

The next day, Perez approached the museum and presented his pass to the guards.

"Thank you, sir, please step through the detector." Perez stepped through and when cleared, walked in and mingled. He looked for Maxwell but couldn't find him. As he scanned the room, a soft, sultry voice spoke from behind.

"Hello, Joey. How are you?" Perez turned.

"Angelina. Hello, I'm okay." She hugged him tightly. Angelina was an intensely beautiful woman in her early forties. Her long, straight, black hair flowed over her broad, strong shoulders and accentuated her stunning curves. Perez noticed how incredibly alluring she looked.

"Wow, you look amazing. You let your hair grow too. It suits you. No glasses either?"

"Thank you, Joey, for noticing. Yes, I like the long hair, and I had laser eye surgery."

"I'm sorry about what David did, how he betrayed you. I still can't understand how he cheated on such an amazing woman as you. Are you okay?"

She smiled. "I'm fine, Joey. In fact, it's a wonder what dumping 180 pounds of useless flesh can do for your wellness. The kids are still a bit hurt; the fool doesn't even call them."

"His loss."

"Never mind that, I'm so sorry about Sarah and the kids. Vince told me. I can't imagine it. You must be devastated; Sarah and the kids, gone." She embraced him again in a tighter hold but held on long enough for reality to sink a little deeper into his soul.

Perez fought back his emotions, "Thank you, Angelina, it means a lot coming from you." She released her hug.

Perez shifted the focus from him. "So, what's going on with the kids, Ang?"

"They're almost grown up, Lisa starts college next year, and Jeff is in grade eleven. I'm not dating, and except for the kids, work has been the majority of my life. Things have been crazy around here with the new exhibits and all. It's been a long while since I've had a vacation. I could use one right about now. I'd love to take the kids and go up to the cottage." Perez smiled and nodded in agreement.

Outside the museum on the north side, a mysterious man quietly milled about. On his back hung a heavy backpack that appeared quite full. He held a camera and would snap occasional photos of interesting building architecture. Sasha had discovered that the south side of the museum was to be shut down by the authorities and had created a plan to get that changed. Sasha had placed a bomb inside his backpack. The timer was set for twenty minutes, but it was not yet running.

Inside the museum, the President of the United States, Bernard Chambers, mingled with the crowd of dignitaries. Secretary of Defense Robert Maxwell had joined him. "I don't want to talk about that meteor thing, Robert. I need a break from that." He looked at a display and mused, "So, this is what $50 billion will buy us now—a bunch of rocks." He pointed at the new display.

"It doesn't seem like much, sir, but the scientific breakthroughs are staggering from this discovery. We've even found a new naturally occurring element, unknownium."

"Unknownium? That's a stupid name. Who called it that?"

"Uhh, I'm not going there, sir."

Chambers looked puzzled, "Where did this stuff come from again?"

"The moons of Saturn, specifically Phoebe and Hyperion. We're checking the others too, but some are much harder to explore."

"What do you think about it, Robert?"

"It's very exciting, sir. We're already learning so much about the new element. It promises to be a significant part of our world's newest energy resources, although we only have a small amount of it right now."

"If it's so important, why is it in this case and not in a lab somewhere?"

"That's not the actual material, sir. It's a hunk of rock that we took from a field and salted with a fake element. The real stuff is $250 million a pound and will never see the light of day. It's still nice to pretend though."

The President sighed. "Is *anything* in here real?" He pointed at a display in an adjacent room.

"Sorry, Mr. President, we have to put on a good show."

"Well, in that case, I guess I should be on my way." He turned to his secret service detail. "Bring the car out front; I want to leave."

"Right away, Mr. President. We'll go out the north entrance in five minutes." The agent keyed his radio. "Perimeter, Benchpress is ready to leave the building. Bring the cars up to the Alpha entrance."

Outside at the north entrance, stationed agents received the call from the protection detail inside and signaled for the motorcade to come and set up for the President. "Excuse me, folks, but we need you to leave the area now." The agents drove the bystanders away from the protective zone.

Sasha had been standing in place for a while and placed his backpack on the ground next to him. "It's about time." He walked away and disappeared into the crowd, leaving his pack. As Secret Service agents made their final sweep, one of them noticed the pack propped against the wall.

"Hey, what's that over there?"

"It looks like a backpack. Better hold Benchpress until we check it out."

He keyed the radio. "Hold Benchpress; we need to clear a potential threat."

An agent stopped the President. "I'm sorry, sir, but we need to hold for a moment."

"Why? What's wrong?"

"We're just being thorough, sir. It'll only take a few minutes."

"Fine." He turned to speak with Robert.

The agent turned to another. "Get the bomb squad here now." After a few minutes, a bomb tech arrived with a sniffer pack. He carefully approached the bag and pointed the probe at it. He pushed a button on his tester, and a gentle current of air began to flow into the probe. Inside the device, delicate sensors tested the air for explosive compounds.

Sasha, knowing that they would do this, made sure they found some. Not wanting to waste good explosives, he only salted the outside of the bag with enough Semtex to trigger a tester. The lights on the device lit up, indicating the bag contained explosives. The tech's eyes widened, as he gently turned and signaled that the threat was legitimate. He slowly backed away from the bag.

The outside agent keyed his radio. "Rabbit, Rabbit, Rabbit. The threat is real. I repeat the threat is real. Evacuate Benchpress out the Beta doors." Secret service agents inside sprang into action.

"Sir, the threat is genuine; we need to move you out now."

Chambers looked at Maxwell. "You should come with me, Robert."

"Thank you, Mr. President, I will. I greatly appreciate it." The lead agent took them to the south entrance, away from the bomb.

Perez saw what was happening and walked toward them. "No, No, No! Not that way." As he approached, a group of panicked people blocked his path to Maxwell.

The call was made for the motorcade to come to the other side of the building to pick up the President. Agents flooded out on to the south stairs and quickly cleared bystanders. Perez watched from a distance and tried to wave off their exit but was ignored. He worked his way to get closer again but was quickly shoved aside by a giant secret service agent, who was not interested in what anyone had to say. Perez retreated back to Angelina.

"Clear the area and set up a perimeter," an agent called into his radio.

At the south exit, police, FBI and secret service agents arrayed themselves on the stairs and visually scanned the surroundings, looking for any identifiable threat. Vince was part of that contingent of law enforcement and remembered what Perez had said the other night.

"Hold them for a minute. I need to check something before Benchpress comes out. Wells, Rayner, Holden, and Hearn, you guys go check the roof of the north tower." He pointed at the castle.

"Sure, Vince, right away." They ran to the castle.

"Hold Benchpress again." They stopped inside.

"Do we need to go to Charlie?"

"Negative, hold on Beta."

"Yes, now stay there," Perez said.

The officers quickly made their way the short distance to the castle and ran up the stairs to the tower roof. At the top, they drew their weapons and burst out onto the roof, spreading out. "Metro police, anyone here? Identify yourselves." They quickly searched the small roof.

One of the officers went to the edge and radioed, "Vince, the tower is clear, top to bottom. You're good to go."

"Okay, stay there and watch the roof." Vince turned and signaled the secret service, "Good to go."

"Okay, Benchpress can exit via the Beta." Inside, the lead agent gave the go-ahead for the President and Maxwell to move.

"It's about dang time," Chambers said. The group exited the building and rushed to the now waiting cars.

The officers on the roof were watching the activities, when suddenly one of them noticed a haze form in the air about twenty feet from the castle. "Hey, what's that?" Before the others could answer, the air rippled, and they heard a loud whooshing sound followed by a pop. The CAP had caught up with their time. Having emerged from the time wormhole, the projectile flew directly to its target, Robert Maxwell. The bullet tore into Maxwell's body and pierced his heart, killing him instantly.

The radio sprang to life, "We've got a shooter, get Benchpress out of here now! Secretary Maxwell is down." Secret Service agents, all with drawn weapons, scanned the surrounding area and pointed them at the tower. They covered the President and rushed him to the safety of the armored limo and raced away. Chambers turned inside his car and watched as the lifeless body of his friend, quickly faded from his sight. The President, shocked at what had happened, muttered, "Somebody will bloody well pay for this."

On the roof, the officers all stood stunned. Police tactical and Secret Service agents rushed toward the tower and ran to the top. They burst through the door and pointed their weapons at the officers, "Drop your weapons! Drop your weapons!"

The four rooftop officers stood bewildered. They slowly took their guns out of their holsters and placed them on the rooftop. They then raised their hands in perplexity.

"You're under arrest for murder and the attempted assassination of the President." Each one was arrested and led from the roof. Back on the ground, agents surrounded Vince.

"You ordered the shooters up there. Drop your weapon, now."

"Hey, I'm the one who said not to use this bloody entrance. I didn't have anything to do with this."

An overzealous FBI agent approached Vince from behind and struck him hard with the butt of his rifle. Vince dropped to the ground, dazed. Other less enthusiastic agents descended on Vince and carefully hand-cuffed him. They rolled him back over and got him to his feet. He shook his head and looked at the agent who hit him. "Buddy, I'm going to get you back for that cheap shot." The agent grinned and mocked a little kiss toward Vince. "Yeah, you can kiss my ass, punk," Vince said. They rushed Vince to a dark unmarked SUV, shoved him inside, and drove away at high speed.

The atmosphere inside the museum was chaotic. With a bomb at one entrance and shooting at the other, there was nowhere for people to go. Everyone was trapped and panicking. People were crying, fearful of the bomb outside while others tried to push their way past the Secret Service and FBI agents who were ordered to contain the building at all cost. Everyone was being held in limbo inside, with few answers. Perez, standing off to the side, gently took Angelina by the arm. "We need to get out of here, fast."

"Come with me. I know a way out."

They quickly walked away together. She navigated a labyrinth of corridors and tunnels, zigging and zagging in one door and out another, until finally ending up further down the street at the National Gallery of Art. Once outside, Perez hugged her. "I need to go now. I think it would be a good time for you to take that vacation you were talking about." She nodded and hugged him, and then Perez walked away.

On the north side of the museum, bomb techs approached the bomb to diffuse it, but Sasha had built the device so that it couldn't be. As the agents made a small cut in the pack, it triggered a secondary system detonating the bomb. The top of the pack tore open, sending the tech falling backward. A giant cloud of confetti was violently ejected from the bag and covered the area. A sign popped out that read: *Thanks for the help.*

The bomb tech sat stunned, staring at the falling confetti as others watched in disbelief. Sasha laughed as he stood in the distance, watching the chaos. "One down, many to go." He turned slowly and strolled away, whistling a happy tune.

CHAPTER 27

"I DON'T LIKE IT, BUT I DON'T HAVE A CHOICE, AND I WANT ANSWERS now." Deputy Director Anderson Peters slammed his phone down. He opened his desk drawer and reached for his emergency pack of nicotine gum just as there was a knock at his door. "Come in." The door opened, and Special Agents Cross and Ivey walked in.

"You wanted to see us, sir?" Agent Cross said.

"Yes, Adam, Estelle. Please, come in and sit down." They closed the door and took a seat. "I imagine it's no surprise why I called you here."

"No, sir, no surprise," Ivey said.

"This isn't your regular crap storm. This one's a crap hurricane, and it's coming all the way from the President."

"It's still hard to believe what happened: an attempt on the President by one of the most decorated detectives in D.C. I still can't believe it," Cross said.

"If I may speak freely, sir?" Estelle said. Peters nodded. "I don't believe it. I know Vince, and there's no way he was a part of this. I..."

"Let me stop you there. You and some friends in high places don't believe it either. It's a good thing you feel that way. I'm assigning you two to this investigation." The director handed them a file. "I want you to get to the bottom of this and fast. I have the White House breathing down my neck, and I want this gone, now."

"Yes, sir." They sat still for a moment.

"Well, why are you still sitting here? Get going." They stood up.

"Go see Tammy in forensics first." They left the room, closing the door behind them. The director breathed a deep sigh; he reached into his drawer and pulled out an empty pack of nicotine gum. He stared at it intensely for a moment and tossed it back into his drawer. He slowly pushed it closed. "Crap."

"I haven't seen him that stressed before," Cross said.

"I have."

"Really, when?"

"Don't ask; it's a long story." The elevator dinged as the doors opened. They stepped in.

"Speaking of long stories, what's with Vince setting up the President?" A floor passed with a ding.

"I don't think he did, and this is getting bigger and weirder by the minute. I think this mysterious colonel has something to do with it too." The elevator dinged and the doors opened. They hurried to the forensics lab.

"Hopefully, Tammy will have some answers."

"Let's hope so, because I know Vince is better than this. That means somebody else is getting away with it."

"Not on my watch," Adam said as they entered the lab.

"Hey Adam, what's that smell?"

"What smell? I don't smell anything."

"That's my point; she's always cooking up something in here. I don't smell anything this time."

"You know that brings to mind a question I've had for a while now." He looked at Estelle. "How does she stay so trim when she's constantly munching on something in here?"

"That, my friends, will be my little secret." Tammy walked in. "All I'll say is, it's clean living, exercise, and keeping stress-free."

"Hi Tammy, we're here about…"

"I know why you're here."

"What is it with everyone interrupting me today?"

"I'm sorry, but I'm struggling to be stress-free today."

"Do you have anything then?"

"Yes, a headache." She dropped a clipboard on the counter. "Do you know how much stuff they sent me?" The agents shook their heads. "Well, a lot. I have a million pieces of confetti. Why would they collect individual confetti pieces? I also have a fake bomb, a backpack, several police officers' weapons, and even their clothes—right down to their underwear." She looked at them with a creepy look. "Oh, and I'm keeping Vince's." The agents both cringed. Tammy smiled and laughed. "Got ya."

"This is serious, Tammy. Someone tried to shoot the President."

"No, they didn't."

"What do you mean, 'No, they didn't'?"

"I'll get to that soon. Let's look at what we have first."

"What? Explain now…" Tammy pressed her finger to his lips to stop him from talking.

"Oops, I should have washed that before I touched your lips. Let me know how you're feeling in a few days, will ya?" He scrambled for a paper towel and spat into it. Tammy smiled. "Well, to begin, the two events were related. The bomb was meant to shift their exit to the south doors."

"Why do you say that?"

"Well Estelle, it's because it was a total fake; a high-tech fake, but still a fake. The assassins knew it would force the President out and through the south exit." She grabbed it and plopped it on the counter. The agents twitched. "What? I said it was a fake. Look, it had the usual electronic timers and wires, but instead of explosives, there were two cylinders. One was filled with confetti and one with compressed air."

"Why would they do that?" Cross said.

"My guess, this is for a nondestructive dirty bomb."

"It's for a what?" Estelle said.

"A non-destructive dirty bomb – that's a bomb that spreads radioactivity but without the explosive carnage."

"What, this thing could be radioactive?" They winced.

"Oh no, how did I miss that? I was touching the confetti with my fingers too. Oh, what will I do?" Cross frantically wiped his lips again. "Oh, stop it. I checked for that first thing. It's just confetti." Cross calmed down as Tammy smiled. "You get riled pretty easily, don't you?" He gave her an angry stare.

"Moving on…" Tammy said. Estelle laughed. "Anyway, my guess is, whoever did this wanted to get the pack past explosive detection systems, so real explosives were not an option."

"So why did the bomb techs go crazy over this then?"

"There was enough Semtex salted on the pack to be sensed by a close-up bomb probe. This way, they were guaranteed to force the President to leave by the south exit."

"Whoever did this, knew what they were doing and what we would do," Estelle said.

"It does point to Vince's masterminding of the shooting, doesn't it?" Cross said.

"Maybe, except for a few things."

"Such as?"

"I've checked everything, and I mean everything, and there's not one speck of gunshot residue or explosives on anything. All of the uniforms of the cops on the roof were completely clean – well except for the pizza sauce on the one officer's uniform, probably from his lunch. There's no way any of them fired any weapon of any kind… which reminds me, we also found no rifle in the area, at all. Their handguns weren't fired, and they couldn't do this anyway. And, from my knowledge of events, Vince was the one who closed down the south entrance in the first place."

"Yes, he did," Estelle said.

"Anyway, I have some other puzzling information. Follow me." They walked to the adjacent room. "I managed to check out the slug they recovered from Secretary Maxwell. There were no unique markings, and it was of no recognizable caliber. I've no way of identifying the type or origin of the bullet or the weapon that fired it." She picked up the bullet with forceps. "I have no idea where this came from. I scraped a sample to analyze in my mass spec machine, and the results just made things even more puzzling." She held up the bullet. "This thing is made of some pretty crazy materials. The mass spec is showing all kinds of rare elements, including one that's not even on the periodic table. There's also something strange about it. It's still warm."

"So, why is that strange? It's warm in here," Adam said.

"It's strange because conventional materials eventually adjust their temperatures to that of their ambient surroundings, in our case, room temperature. This one though is fifteen degrees above room temperature and every ambient temperature I subject it to."

"That is strange," Estelle said.

"Darn straight, it is. I started to think *radioactive*, so I checked the radiometric signature of the material, and there were no standard signatures." She showed a paper. "There was no way I was going to let this little thing get the best of me, so I pulled out the big guns. I used a Tri-Axialating Radiometric analyzer and tried to identify the signature. I ended up with some peculiar results." She showed a paper with a graph.

"The signature has a harmonic frequency distortion that is off the charts, to the tune of gamma rays on steroids, which is supposed to be impossible, by the way. This radiation is more energetic than gamma rays but not lethal. I can't explain it, but there it is. Another thing is that the harmonics register slightly offset in their vibrations, which tells me their creation was at different times. Although it is the same material, different parts of it have different time signatures." A beep sounded from the other room.

"Finally, want to watch what happened? I got the stored video from Rayner's and Wells' vest cams. I just finished processing the Wells feed." They walked to the computer, and Tammy sent the feeds to displays on the primary wall monitor. "I synchronized both feeds, and I'm showing them side by side here."

The agents turned their attention to the screens. Tammy pointed to the left screen. "This video belongs to Wells' camera." She paused to drink. "Okay, here we see them running to the roof and searching it. Next, we see officer Rayner radio Vince and clear the roof. Rayner's camera shows the museum from his view. The video shows they were standing around and talking about an upcoming grill party they were planning for next Saturday. But then Officer Rayner's camera flickers and fails." The picture went static.

"I tried to fix it, but I couldn't. It was just like the motel feed from Utah. The other feed from Officer Wells, however, was still good and about to show something *very* interesting." They stood quietly and watched the feed. Estelle pointed to the screen. "Officer Rayner is standing near the edge."

"Hey, the air is getting hazy behind him, just like the motel video," Cross said. The air rippled, and a bullet shot from the center.

"What the hell was that?" Cross said.

"That's a bullet that just came out of thin air," Estelle said.

"Like the shootout at the motel," Tammy said. She crossed her arms and tapped her nose. "In fact, I believe that the physical evidence for that case just came in. I haven't looked at it yet. It's over here." Tammy went to a pile of boxes and read the manifest. "Box number nine." She signed the evidence continuity sheet and opened the box. She sifted through several bags. "It's in here somewhere."

"What is?" Estelle said.

Tammy picked up the bag containing the recovered bullet that Perez had evaded. "This is." She waved the bag and picked up the other evidence bag with the bullet that killed the secretary. "Look familiar?"

Cross and Estelle stared at the bags and then looked at the picture of Perez and each other. "We need to find this colonel," they said together.

"Great job, Tammy. Check the video footage and see if this mysterious colonel shows up at the museum today or before," Cross said.

"With pleasure, anything for my Vince, the prince."

"Oh, puh-lease…" Estelle said.

CHAPTER 28

VINCE DICARLO SAT IN THE STARK INTERROGATION ROOM LOCATED IN FBI headquarters. His hands were cuffed together and bound to a rigid bar fixed to the cold steel table that separated him from his interrogator.

"Seriously, your clock isn't working? Did you take the batteries out of it so it's stuck at ten past two? Are you trying to *psy-op* me or something? Trying to wear down my mental resilience to affect my guilty and paranoid mind with time deprivation?" Vince mocked him.

"Why do you ask? Is it working? Are you getting paranoid? Something you want to confess, perhaps?"

"Please, all you're doing is pissing me off. Look, we've been at this for, I'm assuming, hours now. I don't know what you're talking about." Vince shifted his weight, searching for comfort on the hard steel chair.

His interrogator was the same enthusiastic agent who had struck him from behind. He leaned into him, almost touching cheeks. "Come on, Vince, just admit it, and we can all get out of here. Simply tell me that you orchestrated this whole thing, and we're done here."

"Oh, we were done a long time ago. I want my damn lawyer."

"Lawyer? What do you mean, lawyer? You're a terrorist, my friend. You don't get a lawyer."

"I'm going to enjoy wiping that smug look from your face, pal."

"We better get in there before Vince hurts him," Estelle said. She and Adam had been standing in the adjacent room, watching the interrogation through the one-way mirror. The feed from a camera was displayed on a monitor in the observation room.

"What and miss this great show?"

"Look, Adam, I know Vince can be a jerk, but this isn't right."

"Fine, let's go." They walked into the next room and opened the heavy steel door.

"Look, dude, brush your teeth too," Vince said to the agent. The agent backed off checking his breath and rounded the table when Cross and Ivey walked in. Vince saw them. "Finally, someone who can straighten this out. Estelle, please tell this idiot that I had nothing to do with this."

Estelle looked at Vince. "We think otherwise, Vince."

"What? Are you freakin' crazy?"

"Vince, we know you're not part of the shooting, but you do know something about this."

"What? How?"

"How?" Estelle placed a photo of Perez on the table. "Who's this guy?"

Vince looked at the picture. "Never seen him before in my life."

Estelle looked at Cross and dispensed two more pictures. "Care to look again?" She slid the photos across the table. Vince looked at them and exhaled a long breath. "So, this isn't you talking to him? By the way, this is from your own cruiser's dash cam."

"Damn, I meant to erase that."

"And this one?" She slid the second photo to him. "This, of course, isn't your sister with him at the museum the day Maxwell was shot, right?" Vince was about to speak, but Estelle interrupted him. "We also have this…" She pulled a final picture of Perez, pointing his gun. "This was taken from a truck stop surveillance camera when he was in a running shoot-out with someone last week." Vince sat back and pursed his lips. The room was filled with silence until Cross broke it.

"You see, Detective, we thought we could get the name of this man from NCIC records, but when we ran it, there was no record to be found. There wasn't even a record of the Metro Police inquiry the other night. It's as if this man doesn't exist; erased from reality, *Men in Black* style."

"That's because he doesn't exist. Look, I do know what his name is. I also know who his wife was. What I don't know is who he is, other than somebody I wouldn't want to mess with."

That part caught Estelle's attention, "Vince, you're not afraid of anybody."

"Well, sometimes you should be. The man's name is Joseph Perez, and he's a colonel in the army, Army Intelligence, I think. He married into the same family that my sister Angelina did. I told you about this family before. Anyway, my sister's father-in-law was some high-ranking army general at a base out in Utah, and Perez was there too." Vince paused to take in a long breath. "The only reason I ran into him was that patrol unit calling on the radio for an ID check. I went down there to meet him. It looked as if he was on a stakeout."

"This was the night of this photo?"

"Yeah, that was the night I found Zachary Holt dead, you know, when he attacked Rachael Chan. Perez told me he was hunting a fugitive and was certain there would be a shooting attempted during the exhibit. He asked me to shut down the south entrance to the museum."

"And you believed him?"

"I shut it down, didn't I?"

"How did he know to tell you to shut the entrance down?"

"I don't know how, he just did. He also asked me to get my sister to get him an invitation to the exhibit. That's all I know. I don't know where he is now or even how to get in touch with him."

"We can help you there." Estelle pulled out Vince's phone. "He sent you a text." She showed him, and he read it, *Vince, meet me at the Basilica of the National Shrine of Jesus' Birth as soon as they let you out today. Joey.*

"How does he know if you're letting me out today?"

"Well that's another interesting thing," Cross said. "Right after this text, the deputy director got a call ordering us to release you. You're free to go."

"What! This text came in hours ago, and you let me sit here with this idiot, badgering me the whole time? Oh, I'm pissed." He rattled his cuffs. "Get these freakin' things off of me. Now!"

The enthusiastic agent took the key and unlocked the cuffs. "Sorry, man, I was doing my job. No hard feelings?" Vince stood up and walked around the table to him. He firmly gripped the agent's hand with his right hand to shake it.

"Sure, pal, no hard feelings." He held the grip and then punched the agent in the jaw, knocking him to the floor. He walked away and said, "Yeah, no hard feelings. That's why I used my left to slug you."

"Are you certain of this?" Sasha said.

The caller on the other end of the line spoke, "I heard the confirmation myself. It's most certainly there."

"And does my friend know this too."

"As I said, I heard the call myself letting him know. Colonel Perez will be at the Basilica today."

"Excellent, and so will I be."

Andy Carson from World Satellite Services was driving to his next appointment. He looked at his worksheet and sighed, "No lunch again. Well screw them. I'm taking one." He had a full schedule planned out, including the last-minute call from the National Leadership of Churches Conference Center.

"Urgent, huh? Well, you can wait." He headed to his first appointment but was blocked by a stalled car across the road. The driver had his head stuck under the hood. Andy, his usual impatient self, leaned on his horn. "Come on, buddy! I'm busy here. Move it out of the way!" The driver poked his head around the edge of the hood and waved. He quickly walked to the van to apologize.

"I'm sorry, mister. I don't know what's wrong with my car. It's too heavy for me to push out of the way by myself," Sasha said.

"That's too bad, jerk. Call a tow truck or someone else who'll give a damn." He followed with a slew of expletives as he picked up his clipboard. He looked at it for a moment and jammed the van into reverse to back away.

"Excuse me, sir." Sasha placed his hand on the sill of the open window. "You know you really should be more polite."

Andy jammed the van into park and stepped out, cursing, ready for a fight. Sasha smiled and pulled out his silenced pistol. "Thank you for making this so easy." He squeezed the trigger, placing a shot between the cursing tech's eyes. Andy dropped like a stone. Sasha walked up to him and bent over to take his ID. He placed his pistol into Andy's mouth and said as he pulled the trigger, "This is for having such a foul mouth." Sasha threw Andy's body into the stolen car and moved it to the side of the road. He dressed in his clothes and got into the van.

He picked up the work list. "Let me see." He circled the recent add-on. "It looks like it's your lucky day today, Bishop Domenic. You've just been moved from number twelve to number one." Sasha drove off to keep his critical appointment.

Vince drove up the circular driveway of The Basilica of the National Shrine of Jesus' Birth. He parked and walked to the front stairs, where he looked around and noted his surroundings. Several construction vehicles, including a large crane, were parked by the front entrance. The crane was set up to lift an enormous gilded iron cross from the back of a flatbed truck to the roof peak hundreds of feet above.

"Hey, what's with the cross?" he asked a random construction worker.

"It's for the peak. Big funeral here in a couple of days. They want everything looking sparkly for the President."

"Never mind him, look around for Perez," Estelle said into Vince's earpiece. "Do you see him yet?"

"Don't worry, princess. I'll let you know when I see him." He looked around. "What did I ever see in her?"

"I heard that, Detective DiCarlo." Vince smiled.

"You may as well get comfortable. I don't know how long this will be..." Suddenly the radio crackled and squealed in his ear, loud enough for him to quickly yank it out, "Mother..."

"Now, now, Vince. Let's keep the language clean." Perez pointed to the cross as he stepped out from behind a parked truck. "Now that we have the FBI out of your ear, we can talk." Perez held up a jamming device.

Sasha pushed his tool cart into the lobby of The National Leadership of Churches Conference Center across from the Basilica where Perez and Vince were meeting. "Excuse me, I'm here to fix your satellite."

The receptionist was about to speak but was cut off. "Oh, thank the Lord, that was fast. God truly does favor us with miracles. I'm Bishop Domenic Rasinga, the administrator of this facility."

Sasha pointed at his name tag. "Andy. How can I help you?"

"Our satellite is down, and we have a big conference starting in an hour."

"No problem, Bishop. I need to go to the roof where the dish is."

"Okay, come this way, but you can't get the cart on the roof."

"No problem, I only need it close to me. I can carry what I need to the roof."

"In that case," Bishop Dominic said, "please follow me."

"I'm sorry to drag you into this, Vince."

"No worries, Joey, but this sure is a cluster..." Perez pointed at the cross again. Vince sighed. "This sure is a mess. Where's my sister?"

"After we left the museum, I told her to leave town for a while. She went to the family cottage for a vacation."

"That'll be the first place they'll look."

"No, Tremaine's family cottage." Vince nodded.

"Okay, fess up. How the hell did Maxwell get shot? My guys were standing on the roof. They said a bullet came out of thin air. Nobody believed them, and that's why they – we – all got arrested."

"It did come out of thin air, Vince. That's why it's so important that I find this Russian guy."

"Russians, huh?" Agent Cross said behind Perez. Perez turned and saw both agents pointing their guns at him.

"It's about time you got here." He turned his attention back to Vince.

"Put your hands up," Estelle said.

"I wouldn't advise that Agent Ivey, or should I say, Agent Peters?"

Estelle lowered her weapon. "How did you know that? Nobody knows that." Cross looked at her with a puzzled look.

"Give my regards to the Deputy Director, or should I say your husband?"

Vince looked at Estelle. "Well, I'm certainly not going to date you now, Estelle."

Cross took a long, hard look at Estelle. "And you were going to tell me this when? For how long now?" He dropped his guard. Perez quickly disarmed them both.

"Two years. Now listen. I don't have time to play these games. I'm with Army Intelligence at a security level higher than the President's. I'm here to catch a killer, just like you are – only I was trying to do it quietly. It looks like I can't do that anymore. I can't tell you much other than I'm looking for Major Sasha Mishkov also known as 'The Reaper'. He's a Russian agent who's responsible for over 39,000 deaths, including my entire family." Perez handed their weapons back. "I want this guy badly too, but all of you law enforcement types keep getting in my way. He keeps escaping because of you."

"Keep talking," Cross said.

"This agent stole a valuable prototype weapon from the government, and I need to get it back. I can't tell you what it does, but needless to say, we're highly motivated."

"It shoots through time, doesn't it?" Estelle said. Both Cross and Vince stood surprised.

A bit surprised himself, Perez said, "Oh, what the hell. Yes, it does. I need to get it back, and fast."

"Shoots through time? So, you're saying there's no way that we can protect against this? Wow, the President is as good as dead."

"Well that might be true if he were an intended target, but concerning the last shooting, the actual target was Maxwell."

"How can you be so sure of that?" Estelle said.

"Well, to begin, Mishkov never misses," he rubbed his shoulder, "and I mean *never*. Second, Maxwell was a sponsor of this weapon. Mishkov is systematically eliminating anyone who knows about this weapon, which could include you three now."

"I saw the video recordings. This creep shot at you, didn't he? At the motel? But he missed you?"

"Only because I had this," he held up his fob. "This beeps a second or two before the time shot. When properly trained, it can give you a small chance." Estelle opened her mouth to speak, but Perez interrupted. "I know, you think we could give this to the President, but you can't. Each one is synched specifically to your DNA. My fob wouldn't work for him, and the only place that could make one for him is a giant crater right now."

"The meteor?"

"Yes, the 'meteor'," he air-quoted. As they talked, Sasha made his way to the top of the conference center and walked to the edge of the roof. He looked at the satellite dish and noted the damage that his remote drone had done earlier in the morning, which had prompted the call for repair. Sasha looked toward the front of the Basilica and saw the group of agents talking.

"Like fish in a barrel."

The bishop now standing beside him asked, "What was that you said?"

Sasha reached into his jacket. "Nothing. By the way, are you all confessed up today?" Before the bishop could answer, Sasha pulled out his knife and plunged it deep into the bishop's heart. "I guess you're not so lucky today after all." Sasha went downstairs to the cart and pulled out his surprise. He had his standard sniper rifle with him. "No mystical shots needed this time." He set up for his shot. He lined up his target, aiming directly at Perez. He breathed and said, "Dlya moikh brat'yev. For my brothers." He squeezed the trigger, unleashing a devastating bullet directly at Perez.

As the agents talked, crews were lifting the new cross from the truck. The crane lifted it up without effort but the foreman shouted, "Hey, that's not the right rigging." Suddenly one of the straps snapped from the strain. The cross swung toward the agents when the second strap broke, releasing the cross to fall the short distance to the ground. The group of agents heard the shouts of the workers and looked up to see the cross falling toward them. Suddenly they saw a shower of sparks come from the cross and heard the sound of the bullet striking the metal. They quickly dove behind the truck for cover. Workers ran in all directions.

Sasha watched in disbelief. "How do I keep missing this man?"

"Did anyone see where it came from?" Vince said.

Both Estelle and Cross replied in unison, "No."

"Keep down, and don't give him a target." Perez looked around the corner of the truck he was hiding behind. He quickly drew back when, from of the corner of his eye, he saw the flash of the next shot that Sasha fired. A split second later, the bullet struck the frame of the truck, spreading a shower of shrapnel. A stray piece of metal broke off and grazed Adam's head, causing blood to ooze out of the shallow wound it created.

"Crap. That was way too close. You okay, Adam?" Vince said.

Adam nodded as he pressed his hand on the wound. "Yes, I'm okay. How are we going to get to him?"

Perez had anticipated the attack, as he suspected a leak in the Pentagon. He had brought a surprise for Sasha with him. He crawled into the bushes under cover of the truck and retrieved his sniper rifle. Hidden by the shrubs, he could see out, but Sasha could not see him. The others remained hidden behind the cover of the trucks.

"Vince, take a quick look and draw his fire," Perez said.

Estelle smiled. "Yeah Vince, take a look."

"Ha, ha. Right."

"No, seriously, I need to see where he's shooting from."

"What? I'm not sticking my head up there."

"You big baby, I'll do it then," Estelle said.

"Fine, I'll do it, but just a quick glance."

"That's all I need." Vince quickly stood up, looked, and dropped his head back down again, seconds before a shot cleared the truck and hit the stone behind them.

"That was way too close; I'm not doing that again!"

"No need, I see him now." Perez looked through his scope and zoomed in on Sasha on the rooftop with his rifle. He lined up his sight and fired a round directly at Sasha. The bullet traveled the distance to him but struck his weapon at the breach instead. "I missed him."

"What?"

"It's okay. I hit his rifle. He's not going to be using that anymore. Wait, what's he doing? He's throwing a rope over the side." Perez fired another round but missed him again. He jumped up. "He's climbing down the back."

"Okay, let's get him then. Get in my car," Vince said.

Perez ran to the car. As he did, he kissed his fingers and patted the cross that was now embedded crooked in the concrete courtyard. "Thank you for the cross."

Vince looked at Estelle who was attending to Adam. "Go! We're fine. Go get him!"

Vince jumped into his cruiser and started the engine. It roared to life. He threw it into gear and took off. "Over there, at the leadership conference building." Vince drove to the building and crashed through the gate arm and into their parking lot. They saw Sasha run to a van and get in. The van sped forward but stopped and turned around to face them. "There he is. He's looking right at us."

"Go. Go. Go. Look, he's turning around again. The back gate, he's going to the back gate." Sasha spun his van around and sped toward the exit, narrowly missing a group of nuns crossing the parking lot.

"What are you doing, Perez? Shoot the jerk!"

"I can't. I might hit someone. Get us closer." Vince activated his lights and siren to warn the bystanders in the lot. Sasha drove straight for the sliding iron gate at the back of the lot. It was closing after the last car exited. He pressed hard on his accelerator and aimed for the ever-shrinking open space of the gate. He struck it at full speed with the greatest force that he could muster. The front end of the van crumpled as it impacted the gate. In turn, the gate absorbed the energy of the impact and exploded from its track, flying out onto the road.

"Come on, get out of the way." Vince blasted his siren to clear the gawking spectators who were blocking his path. They slowly worked across the lot to the broken gate.

Approaching drivers reacted to the enormous barrier that had been violently cast into their path; they panicked, and they slammed on their brakes, causing a domino effect of rear-end collisions. One driver of a brand-new Maserati Levante avoided hitting the others and came to a stop in front of Sasha. A bit shaken by the crash, Sasha staggered out of the van and toward the Maserati. He pulled out his gun and pointed it at the driver.

"Get out." The driver sat defiantly, ignoring the request. "I said, get out, now!"

"What? Get another car, you moron." Sasha walked around to the driver's side and approached the man who started to roll up his window. Without the slightest hesitation, Sasha shot through the side window and into the driver, killing him. He then reached over the exotic SUV and shot several rounds at Perez and Vince, as they quickly approached.

"Look out," Vince slammed on his brakes. Both men ducked for cover. Bullets passed through the windshield, pierced the front seat and embedded themselves into the rear of the car.

"Okay, that was too close. Perez, shoot that idiot."

"I can't, too many collaterals."

"Screw them! He's going to kill plenty more than that if we don't stop him now."

Sasha pulled the lifeless body of the Maserati owner out onto the street. He jumped in and sped away. Vince hit his accelerator and snaked through the collection of wrecked cars. He picked up his radio microphone. "Metro four radio, this is One-David-Fourteen. I'm in a high-speed pursuit of a homicide suspect in a stolen, black Maserati Levante SUV. Maryland plate: India-Lima-Victor-Michael-Oscar-November-Echo-Yankee. I repeat *I LV Money*."

Sasha quickly increased the distance between him and his pursuers with the aid of his newly acquired, more powerful SUV. Vince's squad car, although fast, was no match for the Maserati's performance. "I'm heading north on Harewood Road NE, approaching Taylor. I need backup and lots of it. Send EMS and a unit to Michigan and 4th."

"Ten-four. All available units, assist One-David Fourteen in pursuit of homicide suspect. The suspect vehicle is a Black Maserati Levante and is heading north on Harewood. Responding units, approach from Taylor."

The radio sprang to life.

"40-42 responding from Ritchie and 13th. Four minutes out."

"40-51 and 40-53 responding from Michigan and 18th. Six minutes out."

"50-21 and 50-23 responding from Franklyn and 10th. Seven minutes out."

"40-71 responding from Grant Circle."

The dispatcher acknowledged each responder and began to coordinate them. Sasha pushed his stolen Maserati hard, gaining a steadily increasing distance from his pursuers. Vince drove his car to its limits.

"No way are you getting away this time." He keyed the radio. "Dispatch this is One-David-Fourteen. I can't keep up with this guy. Where's my help? Does his car have remote tracking?" Sasha turned right. "He turned east on Taylor."

"40-71 joining pursuit at Taylor." Vince saw the unit coming up from behind to join.

"40-42 on Taylor at Michigan. I've blocked Taylor, and I'm setting road spikes."

"40-51, 40-53 join 40-42 at Taylor and Michigan."

"Roger. We're coming up fast—be there in two minutes."

"50-21 and 50-23 coming north on Michigan. Two minutes away."

"1-David-14 approaching Michigan. We see you, 42." Sasha weaved the SUV through traffic. As he approached the blockade, he jumped the curb and drove around the spikes. "1-David-14, suspect has turned northeast on Michigan."

"40-51 and 53 joining pursuit."

"40-42. I'll be active in thirty seconds."

"40-43 to dispatch, I'm joining the pursuit. I'm on Michigan at the boundary. I've set spikes here too."

"Radio, 1-David-14, east on Michigan. Approaching South Dakota. 40-43 we'll be at your location in less than three minutes."

"50-21 and 50-23 joining pursuit now."

"1-David-14, better call Brentwood and Hyattsville and advise we're probably going into fresh pursuit through their jurisdictions."

"10-4, eight units heading to fresh pursuit."

Sasha pushed on, cutting off cars as he passed them. Some spun out, forcing the pursuing police to slow down. Sasha looked ahead and saw the next blockade. As he approached the cruiser, he drove over the median again and gunned the engine. This time, however, when Sasha crossed the median, the SUV ran over a newly planted tree that was being held by short pieces of T-bar, driven into the ground. When he ran over it, a bar jammed up into the oil pan, puncturing it. Oil poured from the tear in the pan. The barricade officer shot at him as he passed. Sasha crossed into the neighboring state's district.

"Radio, 1-David-14. We're entering Maryland; we're now in fresh pursuit." He drove around the spikes as the officer pulled them back. Suddenly, he skidded sideways on the oil from Sasha's SUV. "Whoa! Oil slick." He fought to regain control and drove up on the sidewalk. Behind him, he saw cars spinning, and crashing in the intersection blocking the way. The other pursuing units had to stop and wait for the blockage to clear.

Sasha saw the oil light come on as well as the tire pressure gauges drop. "I better ditch this soon. The mall, I'll go there."

"Radio, 1-David-14, any chance of some Brentwood or Hyattsville help?"

"Negative for now, they're all 10-7."

He looked at Perez. "It's you and me, buddy."

"Attention all units, any available units to respond to two priority calls. Active shooter on Van Buren St. NW at Fort Luzon Community Center. Also, an active shooter at Rock Cliff Tennis Park on Bazinga Street NW, District four units to respond?"

"40-53. We'll break pursuit and take Van Buren from Webster. Seven minutes"

"40-71 Same here. Mark me responding to Van Buren as well, from Varnum six minutes out."

"40-51 breaking from pursuit for Van Buren. From Webster seven minutes out."

"Any units for Rock Cliff?"

"40-71, I'll take that instead of Van Buren. Mark me eight minutes out."

"10-4. 40-71 is responding to Rock Cliff, 40-51 take Rock Cliff as well.

"40-51, 10-4, taking Rock Cliff from 16th, now six minutes out."

"Radio, 4-David-11 responding to Van Buren."

"10-4, 4-David-11 responding to Van Buren,"

"Radio, 4-David-13 for Rock Cliff, four minutes out."

"10-4, 4-David-13 responding to Rock Cliff."

"All units, code five still in effect for pursuit."

"Vince, did you hear all that?"

"I'm a little busy now, Joey. Hear what?"

"Two more shootings. I bet Mishkov just took two more time shots."

"All the more reason to stop him now." Sasha turned toward the mall.

"Radio, 1-David-14, the suspect has turned north on Belcrest from Queens Chapel."

"He might be going to the mall," Perez said.

"What? Stopping in for a little shopping, is he?"

"No, but there's a lot of innocent people to hide behind."

"Yep, he's turning on the 410 and into the parking lot." He keyed the radio again. "Radio, 1-David-14. He's going to the Metro Mall. All units converge on the mall."

"Radio, 40-42. We're all two minutes behind 1-David-14. Hang on Vinny, we're almost there."

"1-David-14, Radio, Hyattsville is sending three units now. ETA three minutes."

Sasha sped down the entrance lane of the mall and jumped the curb. He drove across the grass until he hit two large planters at the entrance. The SUV rode up and over the barriers and was launched into the air, crashing through the entrance doors. Terrified shoppers scattered, jumping away from the airborne SUV.

"Radio, 1-David-14. Suspect has TC'd. I repeat suspect has TC'd." Vince approached carefully, and as they neared the crashed SUV, Sasha jumped up from behind a planter. "Crap, where did he come from?" Vince hit his brakes.

"Get down, Vince." Perez ducked behind the dash. Sasha rapidly fired several shots, letting loose a hail of bullets at them. The bullets penetrated the windshield with ease, and several rounds hit Vince squarely in the chest, sending his body into wild convulsions. The shots narrowly missed Perez, showering him with shards of glass from the shattered windshield. Their now driverless car crashed into the stone barriers. The airbags deployed, and they were violently pushed back into their seats.

Sasha hurriedly walked to Vince's crashed car. He held his gun out toward them waiting to fire again. Perez regained his senses after the crash and thrust his Glock through the windshield and fired several shots at Sasha. One of his bullets hit Sasha in the arm, grazing him. Sasha jumped back and ran into the mall. Inside the mall, he fired his weapon into the air, causing a stampede of people to run toward the exit where the two cars had crashed.

Vince sat still, gasping for breath. Air from his lungs gurgled through the blood streaming from his chest wounds. He reached over to Perez and grabbed his arm. With a mixed look of fear and contempt, he said softly through the blood, "Joey. Go get that mother fu…" His words trailed off as he died.

"No! Son of a…" He jumped out of the car and ran after Sasha. Other police units began pulling into the parking lot. The first unit came up beside Vince.

"Oh no! Radio, 40-42 on the south side of the mall. 10-33 – Officer down, officer down. Get an ambulance here now. We need to set a perimeter around the Metro Mall."

"40-42, Radio, 10-4. All units, 10-33 officer needs assistance, set perimeter around Metro Mall. Units 50-21 and 50-23 proceed to northeast and northwest sides of the mall and control."

"Radio, 40-43, I'm on the west side of the mall. Send Hyattsville to the south side and east side. We're going to need the watch commander here, asap."

"10-4."

Sasha ran through the mall, turning to see if Perez was following and occasionally fired a random shot behind him. People scattered at the sight of Sasha, who didn't care who he shot. He ran to the nearest exit on the opposite side of the mall. Outside, he found a woman, loading her minivan. He quickly approached her pointing his gun. "Give me your keys, now." The woman, in shock, slowly reached out her hand with the keys. He snatched them and slowly backed away from her. She stood in terror until Sasha got in and started the van. As he began to drive off, she came to her senses and screamed.

"NO!" She ran after the van.

Sasha looked into the rearview mirror and saw the running woman, but then something else caught his eye. He immediately stopped and got out. The woman caught up to him, screaming. He pointed the gun at her again, "Stay there, or I will kill you." She stopped and dropped to her knees, crying. Sasha opened the side door of the van and reached inside. He pulled out a baby seat. The woman cried in fear for her child. Sasha placed the carrier on the ground and then pulled out her diaper bag. He placed it down beside her baby.

"I'm many things, woman, but I'm not a monster." He turned and got back in the van and sped away as police units converged on the mall. Sasha saw the woman run to her baby and pick her up, hugging her tightly. They disappeared from his sight. In the distance, Perez witnessed the exchange with the baby and watched as Sasha drove away.

"Damn it! How does he keep getting away?" He looked back. "Vince, I'm sorry buddy, but I have to leave you too. Goodbye, my friend." Seeing that the place was swarming with police, Perez took advantage of the chaos and walked away.

How did he know where we were today? How does he know my every move? There has to be someone helping him, but who? Who has this level of information? His thoughts bombarded him as he walked away. In a flash of inspiration, he had an idea, but it made him sick to his stomach. "The general," he said. "It has to be the general."

CHAPTER 29

"IT'S BEEN NEARLY TWENTY-THREE YEARS SINCE AREA CITIZENS HAVE felt the paralyzing levels of fear that grip the city today. Residents, who once again believed it was safe to go outside with the capture of Henry Patrick McGuire and the death of D.C. rapist Zachary Holt, are now trembling in the confines of their homes, afraid to go out in the wake of the unprecedented number of murders that occurred today." News anchor Chuck Wendall turned to a new camera.

"Topping today's gruesome list are Secretary of the Army Patrick Milne and Secretary of the Navy Allison Beauregard, each being gunned down at the same time as police resources were already stretched to their limits with a wild, car chase through northeast D.C." A video clip showed coverage of Vince being carried away by a coroner. "The chase ended with the suspect evading capture, but not before he murdered hero veteran police detective Vincent DiCarlo. Three additional deaths are also directly attributed to the subject of the chase, who authorities are now calling The Grim Reaper killer."

A video showed the bodies of each victim. "Technician Andy Carson and real estate broker Anton Marvel were both murdered as the suspect carjacked each of them for their vehicles." He turned to a new camera. "The final victim of today's carnage attributed to the Reaper was Bishop Dominic Rasinga, director of the National Leadership of Churches Conference Center, who was found dead on the roof of the center, stabbed by the suspect. Chief of Metro Police, Peter Shewnam, had this to say." The video changed to the chief.

"Today marks a grim day in the history of the metropolitan area. We give a sad farewell to our friend and colleague Detective DiCarlo mere days after awarding him a medal of valor on this very spot. We also say goodbye to friends and family of many others. We're doing everything in our power to halt this madman's crime spree and are working with several agencies in a cooperative effort led by the FBI. If you have an encounter with this suspect, I urge you to comply and surrender what he wants. Doing this could save your life, just as we saw with Christine Lippenshults and her baby today. If you see him, do not confront him, but rather call 9-1-1 immediately."

FBI Deputy Director Peters turned off the television at the front of the briefing room. The room was at capacity with more than 200 FBI agents, police, and intelligence agents, except for Perez. Standing beside Peters were Agents Estelle Ivey and Adam Cross. Cross sported a fresh new bandage on his right temple from his close call. Peters spoke, "Okay, everybody, listen up. Our number one priority is to find this man." He showed a picture of Sasha. "As the news said, we're calling him the Grim Reaper." He clicked his presentation forward. "Reaper is responsible for countless deaths, now including three top government officials and Metro Detective DiCarlo. We need to stop him, and fast." He clicked again showing the next picture.

"We also need to find this man." A picture of Perez appeared. "Agents Cross and Ivey support that he's a good guy, but I've yet to believe it. I've tried to get in touch with the intelligence community, but they're not saying a thing about him. In fact, according to the Army, he doesn't exist. Well, I'm here to say that he does exist, and his name is Joseph Perez. He's a colonel in Army Intelligence, even though they deny it. According to them, he's a ghost, killed in the meteor event out west, to which I say *bull*." He slammed his fist on the podium.

"All of Reaper's targets so far are high-level government officials, but it also seems he doesn't care who he takes out. If they're in his way, he kills them. According to this colonel, he's not after the President, but don't breathe easy because that could change. I'm ordering all leaves, vacations, and soft duties canceled until further notice, and I'm authorizing double shifts until this man is apprehended. Agent Cross is the SAC on this with Ivey second in command. We've also issued a warrant for this colonel's apprehension as a material witness. With that, I hand it to you, Agent Cross."

Adam stepped to the podium. "I'll make this brief. What I'm about to say to you cannot leave this room. We're in dire circumstances until we get Reaper. Although the military will deny it, the suspect is in possession of an extraordinary weapon, stolen from a destroyed research base out west. I know you're not going to believe this, but he has a rifle that can shoot a bullet through time." The audience broke into a frenzy of comments of disbelief. "We don't know how it works, but understand this, it does work. No one is safe until we get this suspect. Our official line to the press is that the Reaper is part of a terrorist organization called Al-Aelaa and anyone seeing him is warned not to approach him but to call 9-1-1 immediately."

Estelle took over. "Listen, we've all lost someone close here. Vince may have been an annoyance to most of us, but he was a good cop and a friend. We need to get Reaper for Vince. Now this other guy, he's trying to catch Reaper too, but isn't doing so well. We need to help him. Take this package and spread it out everywhere. Shake down every snitch, weasel, every lowlife that you know, find every contact or wannabe wise guy, and squeeze them hard."

Adam continued, "We have calls into the state department, who are using their connections with the Russians directly. I want you to use all of your Russian connections too. He has to have support from somewhere. We shut the deli down, but there could be more. Squeeze every Russian contact, and let them know that we're going to be climbing up their butts until we find him. Let's make it impossible for this scumbag to hide anymore and make sure that he's not getting any help from his Russian friends either." Adam stopped for a breath and lightly rubbed his bandage, "I want this guy gone. Let's do it for Vince and the thousands who are dead by this maniac's hands so far. Dismissed." Everyone in the room stood and shuffled out, talking to each other in a buzz of chatter. Once the hall was empty, Agents Cross and Ivey looked at each other.

"Okay boss, now what?" Estelle said.

Cross just stared back with a blank look. "Beats me, but I need coffee." He grabbed his jacket. "The fresh air will do us some good too."

They walked to the café across the street from FBI headquarters and approached the counter. "Two coffees, cream, no sugar in mine. Estelle, same for you?" She nodded. Suddenly, Estelle's cell phone rang, and she pulled it from her pocket. She looked at it and saw the caller ID for Vince DiCarlo, just as Adam received his coffee. She quickly patted his arm, almost causing him to spill it. "Hey, watch it; I haven't even had a sip yet."

"Shut up, Adam and trace this call." She showed him the display.

"I'm on it," he quickly set the coffees down.

She let it ring a couple more times to give Adam a chance to call for the trace. She hit the answer button, "Who is this?"

"Not a very friendly way to answer the phone now is it, Agent Ivey?"

"Hello, Colonel, do we ever have a lot to talk about," she switched ears. "Like why you left Vince to die."

"I'm sorry, Agent Ivey. I was with him, but there was nothing I could do. He died almost instantly, and I needed to keep after Mishkov."

Estelle interrupted, "Well, being that he got away from you again, that didn't seem to work, now did it?"

"You know as well as I do that we have to play by the rules, where he doesn't. I'm frustrated that he keeps escaping too. A new problem is that the entire world knows about him now, and he'll likely go into hiding, or, at the very least, change his appearance. If he does, we'll never find him."

"Oh, we will find him."

"Don't flatter yourself. Mishkov is trained to be a ghost. You won't find him; he finds you. We need to flush him out–give him something that he can't resist."

"Why don't you come in and you can work with us then?"

"Hmm? Let me see. I've been arrested and detained, and I've been held at gunpoint by you and others. Now to top it off, there's a material witness warrant for me, which spells shackles."

She covered the phone, "How does he know about that? We just issued it."

"I can't risk any more interference from you law enforcement types, especially since I don't know if your agency's been compromised."

"FBI compromised? What the hell are you talking about? He seems to keep getting away from you."

"Let's just say that there are a lot of secrets getting out, and they've been deadly so far. Somebody's feeding information to Mishkov, and I don't know who. I've an idea, but that's all I have, an idea."

"Well, who do you think it is?"

"I'm in one of the most secure sections of the Pentagon. There're only a few people who have access to this level of information."

"Okay, spit it out already!"

"Well, Agent Ivey, if you're looking for something to do, you may want to have a chat with General Kimberly Bishop. You may also want to look at her secretary, Monika Daniels."

"Listen, pal, I'm not your errand girl, and I'm most certainly not here to do your dirty work for you. Why don't you do it yourself?"

"I'm checking a few other leads. Listen, the stakes are too high here. Do what you need to do, and let me do what I need to do. I know what I'm doing."

"Well, Colonel, your ways haven't accomplished much so far, have they now? Three government officials are dead, Vince, and who knows how many more to follow."

"I can't change my way of doing things, but I may be able to help you out with that last point. I have a classified list of names that may be his hit list. I really can't show it to you, but I might accidentally drop a copy in the café across the street from your headquarters. You know, the one you're standing in now. I can't help myself if I'm careless now and then." She quickly looked around.

She covered the phone, "He's around here somewhere."

"Yes, I just found out they triangulated him to this café. If nothing else he's ballsy." They scanned the café, searching for Perez and ran outside looking around.

"Now that you know where I am, I guess I'll need to go. As I said, I have a few things to take care of right now. I'll leave a clue on how to find me next, but in the meantime, if you want to secure each person still alive on that list, it might help. Remember, he can get to them from any time. Bye for now." Perez hung up the phone. The two agents searched for him as other agents ran from across the street to help.

"You two go that way, and you two go down there. The rest of you go inside. Close the café off; nobody gets out." Estelle looked through the window into the café. She watched as a waiter removed a bag from the top of a table. On the table, she spotted a cell phone resting on top of a folded piece of paper. "Adam, over there," she pointed. "He just hung up, he must still be in here."

The agents spread out and searched. Estelle put on gloves and picked up the phone and paper. Carefully, she unfolded the paper and looked at the list of names printed on it.

"Top Secret – Majestic Level Only. Man, I could go to jail just for looking at this."

"What are the names?" Adam said.

"This is a who's who in Washington, Adam. I see several people on here who are already dead, and there's a few redacted too."

"Did he leave a way to contact him?"

"Nothing else here."

"And the phone?"

She looked at it. "No numbers, but there's a picture on it. It's of the Washington Monument."

"Did he give a time?"

"No, nothing else."

"So, I guess we're expected to drop everything for our precious little colonel and wait, batting our eyes?"

"It looks that way."

Cross rubbed the bandage on his temple. "Well, screw him, I'm not setting myself up again."

"Wait, the metadata."

"The meta-whata?"

"The metadata on the phone." She skillfully navigated the phone menus. "Damn, wiped clean somehow." Estelle stared at the picture for a moment and then smiled, "I got it."

"Got what?"

"Look at the picture, I mean, *really* look at it."

"Okay, what am I looking at?"

"The bus, it's a D.C. circulator. What time does it pass the monument?"

"Right, let the picture do the talking. We'll have to check the bus routes. That could still be a dozen times in a day. What else do you see?"

"These people here."

"What about them?"

"They're on those two-wheel Segway things. I count at least ten of them. Could this be one of those tours?"

Adam nodded, "Yeah, it could be."

"It looks like we have our clues. Let's make some calls, Adam."

"Why doesn't this idiot just tell us how to find him?"

"Who knows, spook habits maybe?"

"Okay, let's see if he's still in here." They turned their attention to the visibly agitated and captive patrons.

Perez leaned against the wall of FBI headquarters where the two had walked past him, moments earlier. He pocketed his phone, which he had used to call forward to Vince's phone on the table. "Clever girl.

Hope I see you soon." He turned and walked away as the FBI tore the café apart looking for him.

"You want to do what?" Deputy Director Anderson Peters said.

"As I said, sir, I want to place surveillance teams on some Pentagon staff and place some others in protective custody." Cross watched the color of his boss' face redden.

Peters fell back into his chair and threw his hands into the air. "And where on earth did you get these ideas?"

"From our secretive army guy, Perez."

"You trust this guy? How can you trust him?"

"I don't completely, sir. He's evasive, but he hasn't steered us wrong yet. We now have access to a list of potential victims of the Reaper." Cross handed him the list that they received.

Peters examined the list for a moment and then looked at Cross over top of his glasses. "You know, we can't even admit to having this list, right?"

"What else can we do, sir? I've got nothing."

Peters gently placed the list back on his desk. He took a deep breath and held it for a moment. "Fine, but for goodness sake, don't let any of them know they're under surveillance."

"Yes, sir, and the protection?"

"I'll make a few calls and see if I can drum up some help from Secret Service or DOD." Cross nodded and turned to leave. "Agent Cross."

Adam stopped and turned. He could see the frustration on Peters' face. "Yes, sir."

"Adam. Get this guy, will you?"

"Yes, sir." He turned and left the office of the Deputy Director.

CHAPTER 30

A BLACK SUV CONTAINING TWO AGENTS FROM THE ARMY PROTECTIVE Services Unit (PSU) sat in front of a house, guarding the next potential victim. Inside the SUV, Lieutenant Jerome Stanford and Corporal Mitch Billings diligently watched for any intrusion into the neighborhood.

"Corporal, who's this coming?"

"I'm checking the plate now, sir." He paused. "They're okay, sir. They live up the laneway."

"Thank you, Corporal."

"You're welcome, sir."

"So, Corporal, why did you volunteer for this duty?"

"Well sir, I heard that you folks in PSU didn't have enough help to watch everyone, so I thought I'd volunteer to help out. I don't want to see any more people die, at least not on my watch, sir."

"Do you know who the principal is here, Corporal?"

"Yes, sir. Chairman of the Joint Chiefs of Staff, General George C. Paxton."

"Very good. By the way, our driver called in sick for tomorrow morning, so I'll need you to drive the principal's car in the morning."

"Yes, sir, I can do that."

"There goes that guy again, sir."

"Must have forgotten the milk," Stanford laughed.

Sasha slowly drove past the pair, back out of the dead-end court. His license plate had been adjusted to an address on the general's lane by his operative in the DMV. "General, I see that you have a lot of watchers now. No worries, tomorrow morning will come quickly." He drove away to the entrance, and as he turned, he looked across the ravine at the end of the general's lane and saw an opportunity. "Perfect."

The sun slipped below the horizon, and a thick darkness enveloped the city. Sasha drove up the gravel laneway, taking advantage of the moonless night, and stopped at his destination. He stepped out of his car and went to the trunk. He pulled out the TATES and set it up. Sasha activated the scope and scrolled through time, looking for an opportunity to shoot the general. "I can't find a good shot from here." He thought for a moment. "Of course, that's what I'll do." Smiling, he repointed his weapon and selected a time. He aimed and activated the trigger, firing the TATES.

"I will never get tired of that. Time to get to work." He packed the weapon in the trunk and pulled a box out as well as two tools. He closed the trunk and descended into the ravine. About thirty minutes later, he finished his work in the crevasse. "That will do the job, just fine." Sasha walked back to his car but was met by a light shining on him.

"What are you doing down there in the dark?" Manny Gomez said. Surprised by the sudden appearance of the Metro police officer, Sasha quickly thought.

"Hello, officer, I'm looking for my son. He ran away two days ago, and I don't know where he is."

Gomez looked him up and down. "Have you filed a police report yet?"

"No, sir. He does this often, and I don't want to burden you, folks."

"It's no burden, sir. That's why we're here. Do you want to make a report now?"

"If it's at all possible, officer, I want to check two more places first. If he's not there, I'll call and report him missing."

"Alright, sir, have it your way. But while I'm here, could I see your ID for my log entry?"

"Certainly, Officer." He reached into his inside pocket but stopped. "Oh no. I think I lost my wallet in the ravine."

"That's unfortunate, sir. I need you to identify yourself before I let you go. I may need to bring you down to the station otherwise."

"Oh wait, I remember now. I left it in my trunk." Gomez's face showed concern.

"You may get it, sir, but move slowly." He placed his hand on his gun as Sasha unlocked the trunk with the remote. Sasha made sure to block the officer's view inside. Gomez repositioned to look, but Sasha reached inside quickly and grabbed his knife. He spun and threw it directly at the throat of Officer Gomez, who didn't have time to react. The knife pierced the officer's throat, and he instinctively grabbed at it. Gomez dropped to his knees as he struggled to breathe through the blood pooling in his windpipe.

"I'm sorry that you found me, officer..." he looked at his name tag, "...Officer Gomez. I didn't want to kill anyone else tonight." He took hold of the knife and pulled it from the officer's throat. He stepped in behind Gomez. "I'm also sorry for this." He forcefully drew the blade across his throat, from one side to the other. Gomez convulsed as blood poured from his neck. He dropped face forward into the gravel. Sasha casually wiped the blood from his knife on the officer's uniform and put it back in its sheath.

He smiled at the dashboard camera in the patrol car. "I see I'm on camera." He walked around the car and removed the video storage device from the trunk. Surveying his work, he tossed the hard drive into his trunk and closed the lid saying, "That should keep them busy for the morning."

The slain officer lay still in the cool night air, as his life-giving blood drained from his neck onto the gravel roadway. Sasha started to get in his car, but stopped. He turned to face Gomez. "I'm not your typical opponent, officer. You didn't stand a chance against me, but yet you still come out to protect these people. There's a lot of evil that you and others like you stand in front of, and I salute you and your comrades for trying to put yourselves in between evil and innocent people. May the night salute you for your selfless bravery until you are discovered in the morning." He got into his car and calmly drove away, leaving the death scene behind him, knowing that Gomez wouldn't be alone for long.

CHAPTER 31

"I HATE THIS CRAP, SPENCER. IT'S BEEN A TOUGH WEEK, FIRST VINNY, now this."

"I hear ya, Ray. You don't get used to this."

They pulled their car up to the scene behind several other patrol cars and got out. "Are there enough uni's here tromping all over our crime scene?" Ray waved his hand. "Detective Ray Donovan and Spencer Alves taking command of the scene. If you don't need to be here, then don't be. Everyone else, make sure you sign the log."

They walked up to the scene and met the first response officer. "He's over there. The camera storage drive is missing too."

"Of course, it is," Ray said. "Who is it?"

"Officer Manny Gomez. Eleven-year veteran."

Spencer knelt down beside him. "What?" He lifted the sheet covering him. "Oh, Manny, goodbye buddy."

"Did you know him?" Ray said.

"Yes, I was his T.O. ten years ago. He was a good kid, always working hard, always prepared...." He stopped speaking and looked at the first officer on the scene. "Did you say the hard drive was missing from the dash cam?"

"Yes, unfortunately. We may never catch who did this now."

"Maybe we still can." Spencer looked at Ray, "Remember I was saying that Manny was a good cop and always prepared? Well, I remember that when he went solo, he got a backpack that he would drape over the front passenger seat to keep his gear and reports handy. He also used it to keep a second forward facing camera as a backup. It might still be there." He stood up and hurried to Gomez's patrol car. He opened the passenger side door and saw the bag. He reached in and pulled it out, placing it on the hood of the patrol unit to examine. "See right here; this is a buttonhole camera."

"Open it. Let's see if it caught anything." He opened the pack and searched through it for the camera storage unit.

"Oh damn."

"What? Is it missing?"

"No, I just found a picture of his wife, Stacy, and the kids. Wow, they've grown." He shook his head and put the picture down. "Just be there, damn it." A new surge of determination washed over Spencer as he tore through the pack until he found the recording drive. "Bingo, right here." He pulled the storage unit from the bag and looked at it. "It's not working," Spencer said.

"Looks like the battery's dead," Ray said.

"Yeah, it is, but knowing Manny..." He reached into the side pocket and found a spare battery. "Let's hope this one's good." He inserted the new battery, and the display came to life. "Okay, let's see what happened." He activated the playback and searched. They stood staring at the screen. "Here, he's pulling up the laneway." They watched the events unfold, wincing at the violence of the attack. "Mother..." Spencer bit his lip. He pressed pause on the video, as Sasha coldly smiled toward the camera. "You are so dead, you creep." Spencer pointed to the pathway descending into the ravine. "He came up from there."

"Yeah. What was he doing down there?"

"Let's find out." Spencer looked at the others, "You guys stay up here and watch out." They climbed down into the ravine to see what Sasha had been doing.

A short distance across the ravine, General Paxton walked to his staff car. "Good morning, Joel...Hey, you're not Joel."

"No, sir, I'm Corporal Mitch Billings. Joel called in sick today, so I'm taking his place until the Pentagon, sir, and then they'll replace me."

"Very well, Corporal, carry on."

"Yes, sir." He keyed the radio and signaled the escort team. "The general is ready to go."

The lead driver responded, "Hold for a moment, we're just inquiring about what's going on across the ravine."

"Oh, that's a crime scene for an officer killed last night. They've been there all morning."

"Do you see any reason to abort?" the general said.

"Negative, sir. That many cops in one place, all morning, I don't see anyone trying anything right now."

"Okay, let's go then."

"Yes, sir." He keyed the radio. "The general said we're a go."

"Roger." They drove off.

The convoy was three cars: The lead protector was up front, the general's car second, and a third followed closely behind with more guards. The first car of the convoy approached the end of the lane and when clear, turned. The general's car came to the intersection and stopped. Billings checked traffic and prepared to turn right to go down the main road.

Down in the ravine, Ray and Spencer had been searching for anything out of the ordinary. They systematically searched until they ended up on the opposite side of the shallow gorge just below where the general's lane met the main road. The duo saw a handle sticking out of a bush.

"Hey, Spencer, what's that?"

"Looks like a shovel."

"Was that guy down here burying something?"

"Way over here?"

"I didn't say he was smart."

They looked for signs of recent digging. As they searched, the air above them began to get hazy, followed by a rippling, a loud pop, and the typical whooshing sound. The two detectives stood startled for a moment at the event, wondering what had just happened. The bullet caught up to their present time and traveled the short distance to the general's car, piercing the windshield, hitting Corporal Billings in the chest. The shot killed him instantly. Now driverless, their car slowly moved forward toward a gate that separated the road from the ravine.

"What the hell was that?"

"Get down, Ray!" The detectives dropped for cover when they heard the shot. Other officers heard it too and ran into the ravine.

The general ducked down in his car as it rolled forward. It came up to a gate on the opposite side of the road, but instead of meeting a locked gate, it gently swung open. The car pushed through and over the cut chain on the ground.

The detectives crouched for a moment when they heard the crashing sound of a car breaking its way through the light brush from above.

"Look out, Ray." They jumped aside, as the car passed them. They watched as it rolled down into the ravine, eventually coming to rest at the bottom. Inside, the general was still alive but shaken up. He sat still, stunned from the crash.

In the quiet, he heard the muffled beeping sound of the newly buried bomb under his car. The timer, precisely set to coincide with the crash, counted down the final few seconds. The bomb's detonator triggered and set off a pound of C4 plastic explosives. The bomb sent a massive blast up into the underside of the car, propelling it high into the air, and killing the general. The mangled car crashed back down into a crumpled, flaming heap. The two detectives were knocked off their feet by the shock wave and laid on the ground stunned.

The general's protection detail quickly turned around and closed in with their guns drawn. They ran down the ravine and pointed them at the detectives. "Hands in the air." The detectives still dazed, couldn't react. "Hands in the air, or we'll shoot."

The other responding officers interceded. "Back off, they're cops! Don't shoot." They all pointed their guns at the protection detail to cover Spencer and Ray.

Sitting quietly in the distance, Sasha watched the scene to confirm his kill. "A good night's work. I think it is time now to lay low."

CHAPTER 32

"THE NEWS IS HAVING A FIELD DAY WITH THIS, AND PEOPLE DON'T want to leave their homes anymore." Deputy Director Peters paused to listen on his phone. "Yeah, well everything is getting out of hand, we have to figure out how to stop him." Peters paused to listen again to the response and countered, "Look, the Joint Chief and a D.C. cop murdered in five hours? The body count is getting way too high." He listened again. "I don't care if we have to sit on that monument for the next six months. I want this guy found!" He slammed his finger into the off button with a vengeful force.

He pocketed his cell phone and reached into his other pocket to pull out his last piece of nicotine gum. Savagely, he tore off the wrapper and jammed it into his mouth. He chewed a few times. "Hmmm, a little piece of heaven." He returned to his office and unlocked his door. Expecting the automatic lights to come on, he charged right in. He was well into the room before he realized it was still dark. "What? Great, now the lights don't work." He returned to the now closed door and tapped the light switch, which still didn't activate. "You've got to be kidding me."

Feeling in the dark, he made his way to his desk lamp and switched it on. The light filled the room with a soft glow from its weak bulb. "Better than nothing." Peters sat in his chair and opened the file he had been carrying. As he continued to read, he took his hand and reached into his desk drawer. He slid it open and slowly lowered his hand inside, searching for a mystery object. Suddenly, he pulled out his service pistol and pointed it at what he thought was a figure in his peripheral. Peters drew his gun so quickly that by the time he focused on the spot, there was no one there. "Wow, I must be tired. I'm seeing things now." He started to put his gun back when a hand appeared from behind and settled beside his face.

The soft voice of his intruder whispered into his ear. "You may want to put this back in your gun." The intruder tossed the gun's striker pin onto the desk. Peters reacted by swinging his gun around to hit his surprise guest, but the intruder sidestepped and avoided the swing. The person backed away into the light and paused for Peters to focus.

Peters face flushed, "Oh, it's you. We've been looking for you."

Agents Cross and Ivey opened the door of the forensics lab. When they went in, they found Tammy sitting at her desk, crying. She held in her hands pictures of Vince and the Gomez family. Tammy looked up, "Why did God create such a monster?"

"He didn't, Tammy. He didn't."

Tammy placed the pictures down and stood up, staring at them. "I'm going to get this jerk for you now. I promise." Tammy turned her attention to the agents. "I've been looking at all of the evidence collected so far, and I have nothing. I promise though, I'll find something; anything to wipe that smug look from this creep's face."

"We know you will, Tammy. Why don't we start here?" Adam dropped his finger onto the evidence bag with the attendance list in it.

"The paper itself doesn't have a single trace of evidence on it, other than the remains of a caramel latte, likely from the table it was sitting on."

Cross took the bag and looked at the list. "This list is getting shorter by the day. Who's next?"

"I wish I could tell you that, but one thing I can tell you is when you're to meet your mystery colonel."

"Oh, joy. Okay, when?"

"Well, Mr. Grumpy, nine minutes after nine, tomorrow morning."

"That's pretty precise timing, Tammy. How'd you get that?" Estelle said.

"I looked at the bus schedule and the tour schedules and cross-referenced them to three occurrences."

"Why this specific time?"

"Well, if you'd let me finish, you'd know, Mr. Chatty." Cross folded his arms and stopped talking. "That's better. I looked at the shadows of the bus and people and calculated the angles and came up with this time." Tammy paused. "Then I noticed something interesting."

"Okay, I'll bite. What did you notice, Tammy?"

She zoomed in to reveal Perez. "Well, Estelle, as you see here, I noticed a certain mysterious colonel standing in the middle of monument field number two. I zoomed in and enhanced, and he was holding up two hands with nine fingers showing. If you were to look at the monument from the top and think of north being twelve o'clock, the colonel was standing at the nine o'clock position."

Unable to resist the opportunity, Estelle said, "Don't you mean eight fingers and a thumb?"

"Smart ass."

"Okay, so we know the time. How do you know the day?"

"Oh, that part's easy. Look at the sign on the side of the bus; it's for a show that's opening tomorrow."

"Okay, so do we meet him in the field or do we meet him at the theatre?"

"That I can't tell you. I guess both."

"Great. Estelle, you take a team to the monument, and I'll go to the theater with my team. When one of us meets him, arrest him, and bring him in. I've had enough of this fool."

The following morning, the sun shone brightly. Both Cross and Ivey signed out cars and organized two separate surveillance teams to watch over their respective locations. Each arrived early to set up their teams. At the appointed time, the agents took their positions. Cross stood at the theater entrance, and Ivey walked to the center of the field.

Time passed with no rendezvous, and Cross looked at his watch. "This is stupid. He's not coming here." He started to walk away when a cab pulled up.

"Hey man, are you Cross?"

"Very!"

Not getting his pun, the driver said, "Huh? Are you Agent Cross or not?"

Cross sighed. "Yes."

"Some guy paid me a hundred bucks to give this to you at this specific time." He handed him an envelope. Cross looked inside and pulled out a keycard, the kind that you would use to open a locked door.

"Is that it?"

"Yeah." He sat staring at Cross.

"Okay, you can leave now."

"Hey, don't I get a tip?"

"A tip? Get lost! Now!"

"Yeah, he said you'd be like that." He sped off, but not before giving him the one finger salute.

"Idiot," Cross said, as he grumbled on his way to his car.

At her location, Estelle waited patiently in the middle of the field. She noticed a group of Segways traveling along the sidewalk. She also heard the engine of an approaching bus and looked to see it coming. "Okay, everything's in place, where's Perez?" She watched as the tour guide stopped the group and broke away from them. The guide rode straight to Estelle.

"Are you Estelle Ivey?"

"Yes."

"I've something for you," she pulled out a large envelope from her pack. "The guy who gave this to me said you'd know how to get in contact with him."

"Oh really?" She took the envelope from the guide. "Is this everything?"

"Yep, I've got to get back on schedule now." She turned and hurried away on the two-wheeled machine.

Estelle called to the retreating guide, "When did he give this to you?"

"Two days ago." The guide turned and continued with her tour. "The Washington Monument is…"

Estelle opened the envelope and found a page inside with several phone numbers typed on it. She shook the envelope upside down. "That's it?" She keyed her radio. "Okay everyone, that's a wrap. Perez is a no-show." Estelle walked back to her car, which was parked away from the monument. She unlocked it and got in.

As she placed the key in the ignition, she was startled by a figure in her rearview mirror. "Oh crap! Colonel Perez, you scared the hell out of me. What is it with you and all this cloak and dagger bull?"

"Sorry, Agent Ivey, but with the way you guys are after me, I don't want to risk getting arrested or some stupid thing. Right now, I'm not sure who to trust, and with Vince gone, you're the only one I do."

"What about your superiors?"

"They are why I'm doing this. I've some critical information to share with my superiors, but I don't know who to trust. I believe there's a mole in the Pentagon."

"A mole? What do you need from me?"

"I need you to tap some phone numbers for me. You have the list in the envelope. They're all at the Pentagon."

"You want me to tap the Pentagon? Are you crazy? It's impossible. They are way too secure."

"They are less secure than you think. Don't worry. I've the authority to do it, but I need your help."

"You realize Cross is going to be pissed for you wasting his time at the theater and then asking for this."

"No, I threw him a bone to make him feel important, too. Tell him it's for the Pentagon parking lot, and yes, he's a grouch."

"Sometimes, but after having to deal with you lately, I understand why."

Perez opened the door. "Be there tomorrow with your surveillance van." He closed the door, and she rolled down the window. "Oh, and don't tell your husband. I want to keep this between us for now."

"How do you know I won't tell him?"

"I don't, but if you do, I won't be there and the card won't work either." He walked away.

Estelle quickly looked at the list again and started the car. She reached for her cell and called Cross. "You aren't going to believe this but..."

"Are you sure about this, Colonel? After all, I'll be committing treason with this if you're wrong," Major Wishbone said. He shifted his phone to his opposite ear.

"Major, it's the only way I can flush out the mole."

"Okay. I know the general said to do whatever you asked, but I still want this in writing."

"Done, but keep it quiet. I'll send an encrypted email right away. How soon can you do this?"

"I can get this together by tomorrow morning's briefing."

"That'll be great. Let's catch us a traitor, and if we're fortunate, a killer too." Perez hung up.

CHAPTER 33

THE NEXT MORNING'S SKY WAS OVERCAST, REFLECTING THE BURDEN on Perez's mind. He stood briefly on the steps of the Pentagon, contemplating his actions to come. He walked in to bait the trap devised to catch a traitor. Perez dialed his cell phone. "Hello Agent Ivey. I'm going in. Are you ready?"

"Yes, Colonel. All lines you requested are monitored and ready to intercept."

"Thank you, Agent Ivey, let's do this." Perez entered the spooky door and went straight to General Bishop's office. As he opened the outer office, he saw Monika quickly pull her earbuds out and hide them. Perez pretended not to notice and walked in. "Good morning, Monika. How are you this fine day?"

She smiled. "I'm fine, Colonel. How are you?"

Perez put on his best-acting face. "On top of the world. I've great news to tell the general."

"Really, would that be anything you could share with me?"

"I really shouldn't be saying anything before the general knows, but I'm too excited about this. Let's keep it between you and me." She smiled and nodded in agreement. "I was speaking with Major Wishbone from the disaster recovery camp, and he told me they found survivors from the base explosion."

"Really? How wonderful."

"For sure. They found Dr. Wellington and two of his team members. They'd hidden in an empty anti-matter vault, which had just enough shielding to protect them during the explosion. They're being flown here this afternoon, and then we'll transport them to Atlantis, our underwater base off of the coast of South Carolina."

"Wow, Colonel, that's fantastic news."

"It is. Do you want to know the best thing about it though?" She nodded. "The best thing is they said they could create a device that'll render the TATES unusable, and it could be ready by tomorrow. We can issue devices to make targets safe again."

Monika's tone became subdued. "That's good too, sir."

She looked at her telephone. "The general is free now, Colonel, you may go inside."

Perez flashed his smile. "Thank you, Monika."

He walked into the general's office and approached her desk. He saluted and waited for her to respond. The general saluted back. "Take a seat, Colonel. What's so important that I had to cancel my meeting? Could an email have done?"

"General, it's worth it. I received news from Major Wishbone that they found survivors."

"Why didn't he tell me? I'm going to have to speak with him about that."

"Ma'am, it's my fault. I asked him to keep it quiet and told him I'd inform you in person."

"Fine, who survived?"

"Dr. Wellington and two of his lab assistants, ma'am. They're returning here this afternoon via air transport and will be transported to the Devil's Attic deep underground base in New York."

The general smiled. "That's wonderful news, but next time I want it to come directly to me."

"I'm sorry, General. It won't happen again. I just wanted to deliver this news myself." He passed her a page. "Another thing you need to know is that Dr. Wellington said he can manufacture a damping device that'll render the TATES useless as early as tonight. Any shots taken after midnight tonight will no longer go through time, basically rendering the weapon useless. But we still need to get past tonight."

"Well done, Colonel. We can at least stop the killing from the weapon. When they get here, bring them directly to my office."

"Oh, I'm sorry, General, but they need to be transported to the base and stay isolated for a short period due to their radiation exposure. They should be ready for a visit by the day after tomorrow."

"Very well, I'll see them at the base later." She waved her hand at him. "Dismissed."

Perez, shocked by his abrupt dismissal, got up, saluted, and turned to leave the office. As he left, he stopped and turned. "Oh, and General…"

"Yes, Colonel?"

"This doesn't mean I've given up on finding Mishkov. I'll be doubling my efforts now."

The general's voice softened slightly. "I wouldn't have it any other way, Colonel."

As Perez left the office, he again saw Monika removing her earbuds. He exited the outer office, but as he rounded the corner, he stopped and listened. Monika watched as he left and immediately put in her earbuds. She picked up her phone to dial out.

"I got ya." Perez quickly left the building and went to the van. Cross and Ivey, along with a technician, sat in the communications van parked in the Pentagon lot. As he got in, Agent Cross met him with a stern look. Perez smirked and in an innocent tone said, "Agent Cross." He placed his hand over his heart and smiled a mischievous grin. "What a pleasure to see you. Sorry for the wild goose chase."

"You son of a…" Estelle nudged him.

"Behave, Adam." Cross stopped talking.

"I saw that it didn't take long for Monika to make a call. Did you get anything?"

The two agents looked at each other and returned the smirk to Perez. The technician suppressed his smile too and said, "Yes, we did." He paused. "Your main suspect likes to listen to the radio while at work. While you were inside, she called into a local radio station at least ten times. She's trying to be caller number seventy-seven. Eventually, she was and won a pair of concert tickets to a band I've never heard of, but she was happy about it."

"What?" He pounded his fist on the console. "I was positive it was her. That means… What about the general's line?"

"Nothing yet, sir. She did make a call, but it was of a personal nature that I'm not sure we should share with you."

"Listen, pal, it's important that I get all of the information. She could be speaking in code."

Cross smiled. "How do you like being in the dark, chump?" Estelle glared at Cross, who slowly suppressed his smile.

"Perez, Adam is right. That's a sample of how you've treated us the whole time."

Cross interrupted, "If it weren't for your little visit to Agent Ivey's car yesterday, I'd be arresting you right now too. If you must know, the general is going through a personal crisis; she's getting a divorce. Your visit interrupted her previous call and delayed a meeting with her lawyer. It would seem her husband is running off with his twenty-two-year-old yoga instructor." Perez groaned.

"So now what?" Estelle said. Perez paused to absorb the information. He didn't know.

"I guess we continue with the plan until we do hear something. I'm going to the helicopter landing pad now. I know Mishkov is gonna get the message one way or another. His only chance to take them out will be tonight."

"How can you be so sure this will work?"

"Well, we'll soon know two things for sure: One, if the chopper's shot at in a few minutes, then I failed tonight, and I'm likely dead." Cross smiled.

Estelle gave him a stern look then turned back to Perez. "And two?"

"And two… is that he got the message, so I need to dig deeper for the mole."

"…and if it isn't shot?" Cross said.

"I guess we'll find out for sure tonight." Perez lightly slapped him on the knee and left. He walked away, but was only a few steps from the van when the door slid open. "Perez!" He looked back at Cross. "Get back in here, we might have something."

Sasha sat in the front room of his safe house in Georgetown; this one in a more affluent part, away from prying eyes. "Are you certain of this?"

"We still have Trojan Horse on the line. Ask them yourself."

Sasha issued his question to the Pentagon mole, "Comrade, what did that relentless pest say again?"

"He said that there were survivors found at the destroyed base, project members from the team that made the weapon." Sasha's ears perked, "He said that the scientists are hastily building a device to stop the weapon from working anymore. They'll be coming to the Pentagon by air soon and will be transported to the Devil's Attic tonight."

"What's that?"

"It's a base, which you'll never be able to get into, and with that, you'll only have until tonight to get them. Once transported to the base, you won't get the chance again."

"How do I know this isn't a trap?"

"He'd never lie to a general."

"Yes, we got her." Perez lightly thumped the console of the van.

"It's electronically distorted, how do you know who it is?" Cross said.

"It's also not on any of the assigned numbers you gave either," the technician said.

"I gave different versions of the story. That one is the general's version, but I don't know why she left her office to call." Perez was preparing to arrest the general when suddenly the general's line activated.

"Hey, someone's calling from the general's office," the technician said.

The phone rang, and a man picked up. "Hello."

The general's voice came over the speaker. "You son of a bitch! If you think you can get away with this, you've got another thing coming. There's no way you're getting my dogs!"

"Wait. Who were we listening to on the other line? Who's the general talking to right now?"

"I believe her soon to be ex-husband, sir."

"What line was the first call on?"

"Extension 551347," Ivey said.

Perez paused to review his memory, "I didn't give you that number."

"No, you didn't, but we had to tap a full range of numbers, and that one was in the range. I guess we lucked out on this one."

Perez inquired, "Let me see the list I gave you." Cross passed it to him. He looked at it, quickly scanning the numbers. He looked at a second list he had and in a quick motion opened the door. "There's no way she could have gotten from there to her office in that time. It has to be someone else." He ran toward the building.

"Well, where is it?" Ivey said.

"The sector custodian's office." Perez ran the two minutes to get to the custodian's office. He stopped outside of it and listened. Inside, he could hear a man's muffled voice but couldn't make out what was said. *Where did this guy come from?* He heard the conversation end and a chair slide as if someone was getting out of it. Perez quickly retreated around a corner, away from the door. Glancing around, he watched as the custodian left with a wastebasket in his hand.

"Hmm? Could it be?" When alone, he walked to the office and used his access card, which was programmed to open every door in the Pentagon without record. He casually looked around for a few moments. He picked up the phone and hit redial, "Damn, the cache is cleared out." He noticed several wastebaskets on the floor next to the desk. "Odd. Why would he have so many wastebaskets here?" He picked one up and examined it. "It's heavy and the bottom looks thick."

He turned the basket over and picked up a screwdriver from the desk. He pressed on the bottom until he found a spot that had a little more give than the rest. Finding a small cover, he pried it off and discovered a small electronic card inside. "Is this a recording device and a transmitter perhaps? So that's how he does it. Our leak is the custodian. How many offices has he compromised?"

"This is a restricted area. What are you doing in here?" the custodian said as he entered the room. Perez set the basket down and faced him. He noticed the custodian reaching behind a storage locker beside the door.

Perez slowly moved behind a utility cart. "Hi there, I'm looking for a rag to wipe up a coffee I spilled."

"Try again, Colonel Perez." The custodian jerked a pistol from behind the locker and fired at him. The gun made a small puffing sound, due to the noise suppressor threaded onto the barrel. Perez dodged behind the cart, which he had strategically placed between them. He pulled out his pistol and rolled from behind the cart. He fired two quick shots, striking the custodian in the shoulder and upper chest. The custodian fell back from the impact of the bullets.

The hallways echoed with the sound of Perez's shots, setting off security alarms. The sirens sounded, alerting the surrounding people of the threat. Doors closed all down the hallways as security quickly responded. Guards, armed with submachine guns, converged on the scene within seconds and pointed them at Perez and the wounded custodian.

"Drop your gun, now," a guard ordered as he looked down the barrel of his gun.

"Don't shoot me, I'm INSCOM. Here's my ID. I just exchanged with a mole." The guards looked at his ID and lowered their weapons.

"What happened, sir?"

Perez approached the custodian and found him still alive. "He's a Russian agent. He's wounded and losing a lot of blood. Call a medic. He needs medical attention."

"Yes, sir," the guard keyed his radio. "Base, get a medic down to Sector 5D1 and call for an ambulance."

"Tell your commander I'll need to speak with him shortly, but for now, have every trashcan in the building collected."

The guards looked puzzled. "I'm sorry, you want us to do what, sir?"

"I said, get all of the trash cans from every single office, label them, and bring them to security."

"That's what I thought you said. That could be thousands." Perez looked sternly at the guard, who stopped protesting. "Okay, you're the Colonel. Dispatch, we need to sweep the house for all trash cans." Perez began to walk away. "Sir, where are you going?"

"I have to go outside for a minute."

"Sir, we need you to stay and explain all this."

"I'll come back, but I have to get to the helipad right now." He left the protesting security officers standing in the custodian's office and went to another to pick up a large cardboard sign. Perez left the building and rushed to the helipad, being careful not to expose himself to a time shot. As he neared the landing pad, he saw an ambulance race up to the entranceway. EMTs got out and quickly rolled a gurney inside for the stricken spy. When Perez reached the helipad, he met three soldiers dressed as scientists, who had been waiting out of sight.

"Colonel, the helicopter is about two minutes out," the lead soldier said.

"Good."

The soldier looked at the cardboard sign, "What's that, sir?"

"A little salt for what I hope is a massive wound." The soldier stared at him, puzzled.

"Okay, everyone, I hear the chopper coming now. Stay out of sight."

"Do you think he'll try to shoot the bird down? Are you just gonna let him do it, sir?"

"I plan to get him first, but just in case, I ordered shielding put in to protect the pilot." He looked up, "There it is. Thirty seconds out. He's coming in fast, too."

"I don't blame him, Colonel. Would you wanna be an easy target?"

"No, definitely not." Perez clung tightly to his fob. The chopper swooped in and settled on the landing pad without incident. Barricades had been erected to block the view of the fake scientists getting into position. After a minute, the chopper powered back up and left.

"He didn't shoot the helicopter, sir. You must have got him."

"Maybe? Time for the salt now." He held the cardboard sign high over his head and directed it toward the Arlington cemetery, facing where he predicted Sasha would shoot from. He held it for a few moments and not hearing his fob, he smiled and lowered the sign. "Now, watch and wait."

As they waited, EMTs, escorted by security, wheeled the wounded custodian from inside to their ambulance. Suddenly, Perez saw a pocket of atmosphere haze over. His fob beeped in his hand. "Everybody, get down!" His warning came too late. The familiar rippling pattern appeared in the air and a time shot emerged. The bullet quickly closed the gap to its target and tore into the already wounded chest of the captured spy.

Perez watched, as the gurney toppled over from the force of the bullet. Security personnel and EMTs scrambled for cover in response to what they thought was an active shooter. With the single shot, the subversive was killed, along with all hopes of extracting any information from him. "No. We needed the intel. Everyone, stay down." The fake scientists stayed hidden behind the barricade. Perez had already dropped his sign and stared at his fob. "Is a second shot coming?" He stayed low but a second shot never came.

Perez quickly left the helipad and returned to the FBI van. Inside, the three agents had watched the event unfold. Perez opened the door. "It has to be from the cemetery."

"We've got it from here, Colonel. Let us do our jobs now and you stay out of it." Cross forced the door shut, and they quickly drove off. Perez stood unmoving, feeling as if he had been ditched at the altar by a reluctant bride. He collected his thoughts and shook off the humiliation he was just doused with. He watched the van withdraw, growing smaller in his sight.

"I don't think so, pal. I'll see you tonight, although you won't see me." Perez walked to the Pentagon armory. "Hello, Captain, have you got that special order for me?"

"Yes, sir, but it wasn't easy. What do you need with that anyway?"

"I can't tell you the details. I just need you to expedite it to Major Wishbone at the evacuation base in Utah."

"Yes, sir. I've set you up where you specified too."

"Thank you, Captain. It's time I go fishing."

"I don't trust this colonel. I want all areas around the Pentagon covered," Peters said.

"But sir, we don't have the manpower for such a large area."

"I don't care! Call in the Metro if you need to. I want every square inch around there under surveillance."

"Yes, sir, I'll make the calls."

"Deputy Director Peters."

Peters turned to see the Director walking toward him. "Director."

"Come with me, Anderson. We need to talk about a few things."

"Sir, I need to…"

The director interrupted. "No, you don't. Special Agent Cross has it."

"Yes, sir." They walked away together.

"Okay, Estelle. Let's make some calls."

"You know, we could have used the colonel's help in this."

"I've had enough of him for a lifetime. Just make your calls; we need to brief in an hour."

"Okay, boss; see you in an hour."

CHAPTER 34

"MAY I HAVE YOUR ATTENTION, EVERYBODY?" DEPUTY DIRECTOR PETERS said. The room quieted. "I just had my butt chewed out for an hour by the director. We need to get Reaper today. If we don't, we may lose him for good. The sure thing is we know he's somewhere in the area because he made one of those time shots." He turned to the map.

"We're also sure he understands that tonight is his only chance to get the survivors, and events prove he tried to capitalize on it. He believes his target area is the north Pentagon helipad and landing path. Our less-than-reliable colonel believes he shot from the cemetery here." Peters pointed at the southeast corner of the Arlington National Cemetery. "I'm not taking any chances though. I want saturation coverage in all of these areas." Sweeping with his hand, he waved over the map in all of the surrounding areas other than the cemetery.

"I want everything covered. Everyone should already know their assignments, but if not, see Special Agent Cross. We know Reaper's in there somewhere because he's already killed his spy. Because the helicopter wasn't shot down, we hope it means we got him. Don't let this belief make you cocky though. I want full awareness maintained until we get him." Peters took in a deep breath. "To complicate matters further, the funeral of General Paxton is being held at the cemetery today, at six o'clock this evening. They won't change it either."

He closed his notebook. "Look, I want this guy caught alive if possible. The intelligence data we could extract would be incredible; the director made it very clear to me about that. But, I'm more interested in your safety, and I pre-authorize lethal force if needed. If you can't take him alive safely, then terminate him. I don't want him to get away again, and I certainly don't want to lose any of you. As always, keep in mind, there's collateral potential in the area, especially with the funeral. Keep concealed; don't tip him off. If you do see him, call for backup before you make a move."

He leaned forward. "People, Reaper is trained to kill you without breaking a sweat. Get that in your heads: He's not an ordinary target; he's dangerous and disciplined. Keep in pairs, and keep safe. Oh, and if you see Colonel Perez anywhere near the place, arrest him for obstruction. I'm tired of his screwing us around." He waved his hand. "That's all, dismissed and be careful out there."

He stepped away from the podium, and gestured to Estelle. "Special Agent Ivey, may I have a word please?" Estelle walked over to him. Peters leaned in toward her ear, "Honey, I know this is your job, but I don't want to send you out there today." Estelle took in a deep breath to protest. "...but, I also know that I need you out there. All I ask is that you be extra careful, no heroics. I want Reaper but not that bad as to lose you in the process." He placed his hands lightly on hers. "Be sure you come home tonight, please."

Estelle looked down at their touching hands. "I will." The words sounded final as they hung in the air. Peters walked away as Estelle stood still, pondering.

"Hey, lover girl, are you done?"

"Don't Adam. I'm worried, he's never done that before."

"Well, something else is strange too. I told Peters where Perez thinks the shot is coming from, and as much as I don't like the guy, I think he's right." Cross pointed to the map, "Your hubby, however, assigned us to the North Pentagon parking lot, and if you look here, he only assigned six junior agents to watch the entire cemetery."

"Yes, I noticed that too, but maybe he's trying to keep me safe."

"Yeah, well, I don't want to lose him, so I think we need to reposition to here." He pointed to the southeast corner of the cemetery.

"That's against direct orders, Adam."

"Maybe, but he did say I was in charge of assignments, so I say we need to go there."

"Okay, let's do it. If we're wrong, we'll only get chewed out. If we're right, well let's say, we better bring our 'A' game with us."

"Okay, let's go. We need to get there before Reaper."

All of the agents quietly set up in their assigned areas, trying to remain as concealed and inconspicuous as possible. Of those attached to the cemetery, there were two agents in the mausoleum, two working the grounds, and two other agents who walked around, pretending to be a couple. Agents Cross and Ivey entered the cemetery and parked their car near the main mausoleum. Cross went to the trunk.

"Aww, you brought me flowers, how sweet," Estelle said.

"Only if you're already dead, Estelle. Let's pick a random grave over by that maintenance shed. We can slip into it quietly and watch from there." They walked to the shed area and picked a grave that read: *Private Raibert Mungo MacDonald, January 19th, 1899 to March 16th, 1917. He died to save countless others.* "Nice epitaph. Let's leave them here." Cross placed the flowers. They looked around and slipped into the shed and sat patiently watching.

As the day slowly passed, the radios kept silent, except for the occasional squelch. All of the agents watched as people came and went, visiting lost loved ones. Some placed flowers; others would stand and talk to the ground. A younger man came and bitterly wept over a grave. "That grave looks fresh," Cross said.

"Yes, I saw it earlier. It must be his wife. Her marker indicated she was Killed-In-Action last month." When the man left the grave, he placed a small stuffed animal against the headstone and walked away, crying. He walked to a black Ford Mustang and drove away to the edge of the cemetery where he parked and got out to sit on a bench as he stared into the sky. A nearby clock tower rang. Once, twice, three times… up to six gongs. Right on time, a procession of black cars drove through the entrance of the cemetery.

Cross keyed the radio. "Paxton's funeral is here. Everyone keep sharp and be aware of your backstops." The hidden agents watched as the hearse drove into the cemetery, followed by a long procession of cars. They slowly navigated through the entanglement of roads until they found the resting place prepared for the slain general.

The FBI radio channel crackled, "Keep focused, everyone."

Agents watched, as attendees assembled. The casket was carried to the grave by six sharply dressed soldiers, each stepping in a somber choreographed walk. Other soldiers, marched along with them carrying rifles for the salute, and finally, a soldier stepped in with a bugle. The bearers placed the casket on the loading straps at the grave. There wasn't much remaining of the general from the explosion to put in a coffin, but the family and friends needed the closure. People gathered tightly around the grave, many crying and visibly mourning their tragic loss. The pastor stood at the head of the grave and began his interment sermon.

"We're gathered here on this sad occasion to say goodbye to a dear friend…" The agents watched in silent respect for the murdered general. The sermon continued with a handful of family members standing up briefly to say a few words.

During the service, none of the agents noticed the driver of the Mustang slipping into the side brush. As the two walking agents searched through the bush, they passed some trees. A clump of grass rose behind them, and a set of eyes opened to watch them walk away. These eyes also watched the funeral. Sasha laid still on the ground, concealed in his sniper camouflage. He lifted the TATES and looked through the time-scope, scanning the Pentagon to find the time he wanted to shoot the helicopter down. He carefully scrolled through the time line, searching, and suddenly stopped.

"It is a trap." Inside the view of the scope was an image of Perez holding up his sign, which read: *Gotcha*. Sasha looked back into his scope. "You think you got me? This time, my friend, you're the one who won't get away." He aimed at Perez but while he adjusted his sights, he noticed a commotion off to the side, "What's this ambulance?" He pointed at the building and focused on the ambulance when he saw an occupied gurney coming from the building. "Trojan Horse. That's why I haven't heard from you today. How'd they get you comrade?"

The pastor finished, "…as we celebrate the life of our fallen friend and hero. In Jesus' name, Amen." Sasha readied his aim.

An American flag draped over the general's casket was picked up and stretched tautly. The officer in charge called out, "Honor Guard. Present arms!" The seven soldiers readied their rifles to fire the salute.

"Sorry comrade, but your lips cannot speak our secrets." He locked in the time and waited for the right moment.

"Ready," the Honor Guard raised their rifles.

"Fire!" They shot the first volley. Sasha aimed.

"Fire!" The team fired the second volley. Sasha pressed the fire button, attempting to sync the shot with the final volley. The officer in charge started to call, but his voice croaked for a second, delaying his command.

Suddenly the agents heard the sound of the TATES across the cemetery. The Honor Guard looked around to see where the third shot had come from. The air rippled, and the projectile left to go back in time after its intended target.

"Did you hear that?" the radio crackled.

"Yes, where did it come from?"

"It sounded like it was from the bushes over by the wall. Move in, but keep low. We've got him now." Agents slowly and quietly worked their way toward the shot.

Sasha lay still, except for his finger pressing the transmit button on his radio. "Go." Suddenly a man ran from the bushes to the waiting Mustang. He started it, and the engine roared to life. Inside, the driver shifted into gear and squealed his tires, loudly racing away.

"He's in the Mustang. Get after the Mustang!"

"All units, he's in the cemetery. Get over here now. Close the roads leading from here." The agents ran to their cars to chase the fleeing shooter. Other units left their watch areas and raced to the cemetery. The attendees of the funeral, shocked at the noise of the fleeing car and the sudden appearance of FBI agents, scattered in fear, all remembering the news about Reaper.

Escaping guests got into their cars and choked the roads, preventing FBI agents from passing. The pursuing agents jumped curbs and drove over ground-level grave markers, trying to get by. One even hit a headstone, knocking it over. Cross and Ivey saw the Mustang leaving as well and reacted. They abandoned their hiding place and quickly ran toward their car to join the pursuit. They were a farther distance behind and had to run.

"What do we have here?" Perez said. Perched on the roof of the Pentagon, he watched the mayhem unfold. He was set up with his sniper rifle, ready for any opportunity should Sasha show himself. He looked at his fob. "He made his shot." Perez had seen the ripple and compared its location to the target of the afternoon shot. He did a quick calculation and guessed where it had originated from. As he scanned the bush, he saw the man run to the parked Mustang and take off.

"I don't think so, not this time." Perez aimed at the fleeing car and adjusted his focus to see the driver. He followed it with his scope as it sped toward the exit to freedom. He lined up his rifle to take his shot, finally ending the nightmare. The car weaved in and out of the winding roads of the cemetery. "Come on, and show me that ugly face of yours, Mishkov."

Perez patiently waited, calculating in his head, looking for the right chance to take his shot at the speeding car. His chance finally came as it made a final turn and fully faced him. He lined up but then lifted his eye from the scope. "Damn." He lifted his rifle away, and the car sped away with the pursuing FBI units hot on his trail. Perez quickly aimed his rifle to scan the bush area. He saw Agents Cross and Ivey running from their hiding place toward their parked car. Suddenly, a glint of reflected sunlight flashed from the bushes. The sun had betrayed Sasha's position, although Perez wasn't sure exactly where Sasha was.

He picked up his phone and dialed Estelle. In his scope, he watched the two running to their car. Estelle stopped and looked down at her belt. He saw her grab her phone, but instead of answering it, she pushed on the screen to silence it. She continued to the car. He redialed only to be silenced again as their vehicle began to move off. "Answer the phone, Agent Ivey." He tried a third time.

She answered, "Not now, Perez. We're after him."

"No, you're not. It's not him!"

"What do you mean? He just made his shot and took off."

"I'm watching you from the Pentagon roof. I got a look inside the car, and it's not him."

"So, what? He could have a driver." Their car rapidly moved further and further away from the glint.

"You're letting him get away again."

"Goodbye, Colonel."

"Listen you, idiot. The car has only one person in it, and it's not Reaper. I just saw a glint in the bushes where you were, so the bastard is still there. You're going to lose him again if you keep going after that car!" Perez heard a muffled voice on the other end and watched as their car screeched to a halt. It spun around and raced back to the bush area.

Sasha watched as one of the pursuing cars stopped and turned around. "They know I'm here." He pulled out his pistol and threaded his silencer on to it. He lifted and readied it, pointing at them as they drove closer.

Agent Cross hit his brakes and stopped about fifty feet from where Perez had told them. "Watch yourself, Estelle." Cross keyed the radio. "Attention, Reaper is still in the cemetery; the Mustang is a decoy. All agents get back here now."

They got out and crouched behind their doors for concealment. The other agents were blocked by fleeing guests and couldn't get back to help. Perez watched through his scope as Cross suddenly flew backward with blood spraying from his neck. He watched as Agent Ivey reacted to him going down, but she was too late. He saw her fly back as well. "No, damn it. Come on, show yourself, Mishkov."

Perez felt helpless, being so far away. He couldn't tell where the shots had been fired from. The source was close to the fence line and passing truck traffic on the roadway occasionally interrupted his view. Suddenly, he saw a lone figure emerge from the bushes; it was Sasha. He slowly walked toward the stricken agents.

Agent Cross lay on the ground gasping in pain and holding pressure on the wound in his neck. He frantically felt for his gun, but couldn't find it. Sasha walked up to him and lifted his pistol. "I'm sorry for this, but I must kill you now. You cannot apprehend me. I'm going away now, and so are you."

Perez lined up his shot and pulled the trigger, releasing a bullet toward Sasha. It traveled the vast distance between them, getting closer and closer, but a passing truck intercepted the round. Sasha was safe. "Damn." He lined up for another shot when he saw Sasha raise his gun at Agent Cross.

Sasha squeezed the trigger and fired a bullet into Cross' forehead, killing him. He casually walked around the car to Estelle. She was lying on the grass, bleeding from her shoulder wound. Crumpled on the ground, she didn't have the strength to lift her gun. Fear gripped her mind as she saw death approaching.

"Don't do it. Please, don't do it."

Sasha lifted his pistol and pointed it at her. "I was ordered not to kill you, but I'm sorry, I must kill you so I can…"

Suddenly the side of Sasha's head exploded, and his body flew sideways from the force of Perez's second shot. His gun dropped, and his lifeless body fell to the ground with a satisfying thud to Estelle's ears. Sasha was dead; the Reaper finally stopped.

Estelle collapsed back onto the ground, relieved her life was spared. However, she was still in shock from watching her partner die. "Perez, why didn't you save Adam?"

Returning agents finally pulled up and swarmed the scene, including Peters. "Estelle!" He jumped out of his still moving car to run to her side. He grabbed her, being careful not to worsen her wound, "What the hell were you two doing in here?" He looked at the body of Sasha lying at Estelle's feet and saw the gaping hole in the side of his head. "Did you do this, Estelle?"

She struggled to speak, "No." She pointed to the Pentagon.

Peters looked at the Pentagon and saw a silhouette standing on the roof with a rifle. "Thank you, Perez." He gripped his wife's hand tightly.

Perez stood quietly, reflecting on what brought him here and watched the flurry in the cemetery. "I'm sorry I couldn't save you, Adam." He placed the rifle on the roof and wiped away tears of joy and anguish from his eyes. He watched as agents poured over the scene, moving around like ants defending their anthill from an intruder. He saw an agent carry the TATES from the bushes and place it into the trunk of a car. Perez slumped back onto the roof, exhausted from the ordeal. He picked up a roof stone and lightly tossed it. "That's one."

CHAPTER 35

"LADIES AND GENTLEMEN, IT IS WITH MIXED EMOTION THAT I MAKE this announcement," Deputy Director Peters said. Standing before him, hundreds of newsprint and television reporters shouted questions, desperate for an update. Peters waited for a quiet moment to continue. "I'm happy to announce that the subject known as the Grim Reaper was shot and killed last night in an FBI-led operation. Metropolitan police, as well as Department of Defense resources, provided a small level of assistance in ending this villain's reign of terror." Cameras flashed as Peters spoke.

"The success of the operation did not, however, come without a great cost – the murder of one of our agents. Senior Special Agent Adam Cross lost his life in the pursuit of the suspect. Another agent was wounded during the operation and is recovering well, following a brief visit to the hospital. It's expected that the Metropolitan area will finally be able to breathe a deep breath of relief. Residents can once again go about their lives without fear. At this time, I'd like to present the agent who aided in the stopping of this monster." He gestured for Estelle.

"Special Agent Estelle Ivey-Peters, will be receiving the FBI Star for her injuries sustained in the pursuit and the FBI Shield of Bravery for her part in the stopping of this terrorist. Senior Special Agent Adam Cross will be posthumously awarded the FBI Medal of Valor for his heroic service to the FBI." Estelle stood still with her arm in a sling, posing for the cameras.

She leaned toward her husband, "I told you, I don't deserve this. Perez shot him."

Peters leaned back. "Remember, he doesn't exist. Go with it." He looked at the scrum of reporters, "I want to close this off by thanking all of the agencies and departments who helped in stopping this man's spree of violence, including an unnamed agent from Army Intelligence who helped in the manhunt. Our FBI spokesperson will now answer your questions. Thank you." He stepped away from the podium. "Estelle, I want you to go home and rest."

"But…"

"That's an order. Minimum two weeks away from here." He kissed her and returned to his office. He opened the door and stepped inside. The lights failed to come on again. As he walked to his desk, he said to the darkness, "I wish people would stop breaking into my office." Peters sat down in his chair and turned on his desk lamp now with a stronger bulb. He looked and saw Perez sitting in the chair opposite him, shrouded in the shadows of the room. "To begin, thank you for saving Estelle's life."

"I wish I could have saved them both."

"I wish that too, but I'm still grateful you at least saved hers." He moved a file to the side. "Okay Colonel, why are you here?"

"I think you know."

"You want your toy back, don't you?" Perez nodded slightly. "I'm sorry, but you can't have it just yet. The weapon is evidence linked to multiple homicides, and even though the suspect's dead, we need to keep it."

"I'm sorry too because that's unacceptable. The military must get this weapon back and under our control. You have it stored here, don't you?"

"I'm not at liberty to discuss the current whereabouts of the weapon, Colonel. Besides don't you trust us to keep it safe?"

Perez's smile faded. "I don't trust anyone at this point."

"Colonel, I'm not saying that you can't have it back, just that you need to go through the proper channels. In one or two years, we may be able to release it back to you. If you fill out these forms, we can start the process." Peters turned to get the documents from his file cabinet and smiled as he turned back to face an empty room. "Darn, I hate it when they do that." He smiled and picked up his phone. He dialed a number and listened as the phone rang.

The other end was picked up. "Hello."

"Hello, After-Life. This is Deep Sleeper. The Reaper's dead and I have the weapon."

Perez sat in his car and spoke with General Bishop over his cell phone. "Firstly, Colonel, I'm not happy about your ruse directed at me, however, under the circumstances, I understand. I'll let it go this time without court-martialing you, but you're lucky it worked, and you got him."

"Thank you, for your understanding, General. I'm glad we stopped him, but now we have another problem. Peters isn't giving up the weapon."

"I'll work on it from my end, but I think we'll need you to render your unique assistance in the field."

"Yes, General. I understand. I'll get started on it right away." The phone disconnected, and Perez sat in his SUV, pondering what to do next. He picked up his laptop and opened a recording file. He listened to the voice of the Deputy Director on his recent phone call, which had been recorded by his bug.

"I'll arrange for immediate transport of the weapon from the FBI evidence storage. I'll have it sent to the secure storage facility in Virginia tomorrow. While they're traveling to the site, you can intercept and acquire it then. I'll send a single car with two junior agents, so you'll have minimal resistance."

He paused. "Unfortunately, I don't know where he put the remaining ammunition, but I'll keep looking for it." He paused. "Okay, I'll let you handle that. I'll make sure Colonel Perez gets the blame for the hijack too. We need to eliminate him for good. Tell Uri I'll send them in a tan sedan tomorrow morning from the garage at 8:30 a.m. sharp."

Perez sat in his car, listening to the recorded conversation. "Oh, you will, huh? Now it makes sense. We'll see who gets arrested." He started his SUV. "At least I know who I'm dealing with now." He drove off. "I think I'll start by hijacking the lambs you sent to slaughter first, then deal with you later." He reached into his pocket and pulled out the card that he had gotten from the stranger at the gas station. He dialed the number.

"Hello, Mike Matthews here."

"Hello, Mike. I'm Joe Perez. You gave me your card recently. Are you still interested in the Sandcast?"

"Am I? You name it."

"Okay, let's talk."

Another day passed. A single unmarked sedan pulled out of the garage of FBI headquarters at precisely 8:30. Inside the car, sat rookie agents Don Parks and Bob Miller. They discussed how they would complete their mission.

"Wow, Peters himself picked us," Don said.

"Yeah, I know. Isn't it great? We must've done something right to get this detail."

"So which way are we going, Bob?"

"Let's take the scenic route; we don't need to rush this cushy one."

Perez watched from his SUV as the car pulled out. "Good morning, chaps. I'll be your friendly neighborhood hijacker for today." He set off following from a distance, careful not to alert them. It was tough in heavy city traffic, but he managed to keep up with the oblivious agents. He shadowed them out of the city and onto the rural highways where it became easier to follow them. He, himself, did not see the car behind him. An hour passed.

"Hey, Bob, I *really* gotta take a whiz. Pull over at that rest stop."

"Seriously, Don? I told you to go before we left."

"I know, but I can't help it. I had a lot of coffee this morning."

"You can hold it because I'm not stopping."

"Okay, fine, hand me your thermos then."

"Hand you my what? Wait, what? No way, man. You're not gonna piss in my thermos."

"Well, it's either that or the floor of this car, so take your pick."

"Fine, we'll pull over. But I'm stopping at the side to stay out of the way."

"Whatever, just stop now."

Perez watched as the agents pulled off into the rest stop and drove around to the side. The passenger got out and awkwardly ran for the building. "Now's my chance." Perez pulled up quickly and stopped. He looked around and saw what he needed. "Bingo." He walked past the gas pumps and took a handful of paper towels and a squeegee from the reservoir. He trotted up to the agent's car with a giant smile on his face, as if working for a great tip. He washed the car's windshield. "Lovely day isn't it, mister?"

"Excuse me, what are you doing?"

"Cleaning your windshield; it looks filthy."

"Please stop that; I'm on official FBI business. Move away from the vehicle!" Perez ignored the request and continued to wash the windshield enthusiastically. "Are you deaf or just stupid? I said, get away from the car." The agent showed his gun in the holster.

"Whoa, mister, I only want you to be a happy customer," he kept cleaning. Finally, at his breaking point, Agent Miller opened the door and stepped out. As he did, Perez quickly reached over and hooked the agent's neck with the squeegee. He pulled him into the hinge area of the door and pressed his weight against the car door, trapping the agent's legs. Perez pulled out his gun and held it against the agent's throat. "What happens next will determine whether you live or die. Do you understand?" The rookie nodded slowly.

"I want you to slowly take your gun out of the holster and toss it into the back of the car. Do not move quickly or I will kill you." Perez carefully watched him, while keeping an eye out for the other agent. Miller slowly pulled his gun and tossed it into the car. "Okay, I want you to walk with me when I take my weight off of you, but no sudden moves. Do you understand?" Miller nodded again.

As Perez released the pressure, the agent pushed back forcefully. Expecting this, Perez countered with a quick strike to the agent's neck causing a brachial stun, momentarily dazing the agent. Perez holstered his weapon and gently guided the stunned agent to the side of the building where he cuffed him to a gas meter. He jumped into the agent's car. "I'm doing you a favor here. You two get to go home alive tonight. Tell Peters 'hello' for me." He sped away before the other agent returned.

In the distance, the following car with four Russian agents watched the hijack unfold. "Excellent move, I must remember that one," one agent said.

"Dah, too bad he's not on our side," said another.

"Only one guy, easier for us now too," said a third.

"I don't know. The FBI agents were soft and cuddly. This one looks like he knows what he's doing. He could be pretty tough."

The rest looked at him. "Soft and cuddly?" The agent shrugged his shoulders, and they laughed as they sped off after Perez.

A moment later, Agent Parks walked out of the rest stop to find his partner cuffed and their car missing. "What?" He ran to the cuffed agent. "What happened? Where's the car?" Agent Miller sat still dazed from the blow. Parks looked around. "Peters is going to kill us."

Perez planned his next move, as he drove down the road. *I need a different car.* As he drove, he noticed a car quickly approaching from behind. He could see four men, and one was holding up a gun. "Looks like I have company." The car bumped him from behind. Perez pressed down hard on the accelerator, gunning the engine of the borrowed FBI car. It slowly revved up. "Police package, my butt. This thing's a pig." The pursuing Russians agents had no difficulty keeping up with him. Perez used every skill he had to keep them from running him off the road. He weaved in and out of heavy traffic, trying to lose them.

"Sergei, shoot the wheels."

"Dah," he rolled the window down and leaned out. He fired several shots at Perez but missed the wheels. The bullets struck the rear windshield causing it to explode into fragments.

Perez ducked down. "Damn, that was close. I need to deal with these idiots, now."

"Are you drunk, Sergei? How could you not hit wheels?"

"Hey, at least I hit window."

"I said wheels, not window. Do you want to climb down mountain to get weapon?" He pointed to the 1000-foot drop beside them.

"No, Uri, I don't."

"Then shoot wheels."

Perez slowly accelerated up the mountain highway. As he approached the top, he saw his chance. The road widened enough for him to execute a surprise maneuver on his pursuers. Perez took the middle lane of the now three-lane highway and waited for the Russians to come up on his side between him and the edge. He waited for just the right time to act and watched as they raised their weapons to shoot at him. Suddenly, Perez slammed on his brakes and turned his car hard to the left causing it to spin. As the car spun, he reached his pistol out of the window and fired at the driver of the pursuing car. His bullet tore through the window and hit the driver in the head, killing him instantly. The Russian's car became an uncontrolled missile. "Sergei, take the wheel and stop the gas."

"I can't reach!" The car headed directly for the low guardrail at the edge of the road. "I have it now."

Sergei had the wheel but too late. Perez spun in behind them and fired another shot into the leading tire of their car. It lunged to the right and caught the edge of the road, sending it into an uncontrolled spin. When it hit the guardrail, Perez sideswiped it and pushed it up and over the rail to plummet over the edge. Perez saw the look of horror on the three agents faces as they realized they were about to plunge 1000 feet to their inevitable deaths.

He waved his hand, "Bye, bye." Perez regained control and steadied his car on the road. "Any more contestants?" He looked in the mirror but didn't see anyone following. "I need to ditch this car fast. One thing's for sure, when Peters finds out, I'll be a fugitive."

CHAPTER 36

PETERS SAT AT HIS DESK. "YOU WERE HIJACKED?" HE WAS SURPRISED to hear the voice of the expendable rookie.

"Yes, sir. He took the car and everything," Agent Miller said.

"He? What do you mean, he?"

"He, as in the hijacker, sir."

"You mean to tell me that there was only one hijacker? How did one hijacker take both of you?"

"It was only me, sir."

"Only you? Where was Parks?"

"Agent Parks was in the restroom, sir."

"How could he have so easily taken you?"

"Well sir, he was very good. He took me completely by surprise."

"So, you weren't watching?

"No, sir. I mean, he tricked me when he washed my windshield."

"You let him wash your windshield?"

"Well, no sir. He just ran up and started washing and…"

Peters took in a long, deep breath. "Never mind. I don't want excuses. Did he say anything?"

"Yes, sir, he did. He said to say *hello* to you, sir."

Peters inhaled and let his breath out slowly. "Get your butts back in here. I know who it is, and we need to find him."

"About that, sir. We could use a ride back." Peters looked at his phone and gently hung up on the bewildered agent.

Agent Miller looked at Agent Parks. "Crap."

Peters slammed his desk. "Perez, you sneaky bastard." He remembered his crew and picked up his phone. He called their cell phones but got voice mail. "They're all dead, I'm sure. Perez, you're more dangerous than I imagined." He hung up and dialed his dispatch.

"National communications, Foxwell speaking."

"This is Deputy Director Peters, authorization Tango, Tango, one-six-three. I want a nationwide fugitive bulletin for Joseph Perez. I'll email the details." He hung up. "Try to get away from us now, Perez."

Tammy Blessing sat in her small office that adjoined her lab, listening to her phone, "Do you understand my instructions, Ms. Blessing?"

"Yes, Deputy Director. I've already completed the facial profile, and I'm uploading it now. I'm going to need your login credentials to activate the protocols because I don't have the authority."

"Fine. I'll log in and transfer to your terminal. Be sure to log out when you're finished."

"Yes, sir, I will. Goodbye, sir." Peters grunted out a short acknowledgment and hung up. Tammy held the disconnected phone against her ear. "What a jerk." She slowly placed the receiver down as she watched her screen pop up with the Deputy Director's login. "Okay, Mr. Mysterious Colonel. You can run, but you can't hide." She entered the command to start the search for his face. A picture of Perez appeared on the screen. "Colonel Perez, meet the FBI/Homeland Security National Surveillance Network facial recognition system called Ubiquitous. Ubiquitous, meet your first target." She hit the enter key, and millions of surveillance feeds activated, feeding their data to the Ubiquitous computer.

"What's Ubiquitous, Tammy?" a nearby agent said.

"It's a classified system that came online today that automatically scans every single source of surveillance from public cameras, all the way to the hidden cameras on your smart TV. Everything is visible to us now."

"Why's it coming on today?"

"It's a new system that's replacing an old one that tried to kill the President and the entire government. The Reaper case prompted a rush on its completion. It's a new artificial intelligence that has a moral conscience. We hope to help criminals find new accommodations in their local prisons with it. What's scary is that once it's set to find you, it usually can within minutes."

"Remind me not to go outside or to the gym anymore," she left the lab.

"The gym!" Tammy looked at her watch, "Oh no, I'm going to be late for class." She shut off the screen, gathered her things, and ran out to her early evening fitness class.

Perez, sporting a disguise, stood outside watching the FBI building. In his talks with Ivey and Cross, he had heard about Tammy and waited for her to come out. He saw her running, waving good night to the guards, and followed her to her class. He waited outside while she worked out. When her class was over, Tammy gathered her belongings and walked out to the bus stop. Perez had been sitting on the bench at the stop. The bus pulled up, and the doors opened to let them on.

"Hi, Herb, how are you tonight?" she swiped her bus pass.

"I'm great, Tammy, now that you're here. How about you?"

"I've had a tough day today, Herb." She sat down at the front. Perez dropped in his money and walked toward the back.

"Well, you're going home now. It'll all get better as soon as you settle into your soft chair."

"For sure, Herb." She looked around the bus at all of the regular riders and smiled at them. Each one smiled back or waved. She noticed the new face of Perez in the crowd and smiled at him, but he avoided eye contact. She shrugged, "Your loss, mister."

"What was that, Tammy?"

"Oh nothing, Herb." After a twenty-minute ride, the bus rounded a corner and approached the stop that Tammy needed.

"Are you going to the market today?"

"Not today, Herb, just home."

"Okay, Tammy, here's your stop." He pulled the bus over and opened the doors. "Have a great night."

She stood up and glanced at the stranger again. "Thanks, Herb, you too. See you tomorrow." She climbed off the bus and the doors closed as the bus pulled away.

"Excuse me, driver! Was that 'T' Street?"

"Yes, it was. Why was that your stop too?"

"Yes, it was. I'm sorry, but I gapped out and missed it. Is there any way you could stop to let me off?"

The smiling driver, still glowing from his encounter with Tammy said, "Sure. I'm not supposed to, but I'll do it this time."

"Thank you so much." He jumped off the bus and hurried back to Tammy's street. *Are you still there?* He looked around the corner and caught her just as she was going up the stairs to her reclaimed townhouse. He could see that parts were still under renovation. He walked to her townhouse and stood across the street. The day's light was quickly fading, and he saw a light come on inside her home. She walked up to the window, now in a bathrobe, and pulled the curtain closed.

"Perfect, she's in the shower," he walked to the back of her house. *I hope she doesn't have dogs.* He climbed the stairs to the rear entrance and saw two cats sitting in the flanking windows. *Good, she's a cat person.* He picked the lock and stepped inside. The cats hissed, but, otherwise, put up no defense against the intrusion. He went up the stairs and looked for her. He heard the water running from the shower and music playing in the bathroom. He heard her singing to an old-time rock-and-roll song. "Hmm, she listens to old rock and renovates houses, interesting woman."

His wait was not long as he heard the water stop and the music get quieter. Tammy walked back into her bedroom in her robe. The room was now dark, as the day had finally faded to night. She reached to turn on the light, but nothing happened when she flipped the switch. "Not again, I just fixed that." She flipped it a few times and gave up. She walked to her nightstand, feeling her way in the dark she clicked on the bedside lamp, when Perez quickly but gently reached around and grabbed her from behind, covering her mouth to suppress her screams.

Tammy struggled to free herself from the grip of this malicious intruder but couldn't. She began to cry and stopped fighting, trying to lull her attacker with her apparent submission. Seeing her calm down, Perez leaned forward and whispered in her ear, "Don't be afraid, Tammy, I'm not here to hurt you. I only want to talk." He lifted his hand from her mouth.

"Then let go of me, creep!" He released her, and she fled to the far side of her bedroom. She reached into her bedside table and pulled out her revolver. She cocked the hammer and, pointing it at him, pulled the trigger. She only heard a click. "What?" She pulled the trigger again and again.

"You're going to need these?" He held up a palm full of bullets. She threw the gun at him and grabbed a shoe from the floor. "You're the man from the bus. What do you want?" Tammy stood, shaking.

"Let me explain." Perez pulled off his disguise.

"It's you, we're looking for you. Why did you come here?"

"I need to talk with you, Tammy. I need your help."

"Sure, I'll get right on that for you, creep! The director said you're the one who shot Adam to get your precious rifle back. He also said you were about to kill Estelle when he stopped you." She approached him with a renewed vigor, fueled by her anger for him, "And you stole the gun back anyway, almost killing the agents who were transporting it."

"Okay, the stealing the rifle part is true, but I left them unharmed. In fact, I likely saved their lives as Peters' thugs tried to get me after."

"Whose thugs? What are you talking about?"

"Deputy Director Peters. He's a bad man, Tammy. I didn't kill Adam. Mishkov did. He was about to kill Estelle too, but I took him out first. Ask Agent Ivey. Peters is a Russian mole. I don't know how, but he's infiltrated to the highest levels of the FBI."

"I don't believe you. You're lying." Perez lifted his hand and played a recording of Peters ordering the hit of the FBI transport. Tammy settled down and listened. "What? Peters is a mole? I'm going to get that son of a…"

"Slow your horses, girly. I have a plan for him." He put the recorder down. "I needed the rifle back, first, for national security reasons, and second, the weapon is the only way that I can set everything right again."

"What do you mean, set everything right?"

"I have one more time bullet, and it has Reaper's name on it."

"But he's already dead."

"True, but he's still alive in the past."

A smile formed on her face. "Oh yeah, I get it."

"If I can get the right shot, I could end this before it all started. Vince would be alive again as well as Adam and thousands of others, including my family."

Tammy got excited about bringing her friends back, "What can I do to help?"

"I thought you'd never ask."

"You heard me: I want surveillance teams on every Army base between here and Utah." He paused. "I don't care, get it done. We can narrow this down when the NSN system gets a hit, but for now, every base. I want him found! Now, get on it!" Peters slammed the phone down.

He reached for his nicotine gum from his drawer and stopped. "Screw that." He shoved the drawer shut. He spun in his chair and lifted the lid from a container behind him. He pulled out an 'emergency' pack of cigarettes and hungrily shoved one into his mouth and lit it. He inhaled deeply, pulling in a long, deep drag of the smoke. After holding it in his lungs for a few moments, he slowly exhaled. "That's better."

Perez explained to Tammy, "I need to get back to Utah, but I know he'll have all of the airports and military bases watched. I'll need to get there some other way. I can wear a disguise, but it won't fool your program for long. I need Ubiquitous to stop looking for me, or at least this face. Is there any way you can do that from FBI HQ tomorrow?"

"I don't know, Peters has it locked down, and we can only use it under his authorization."

"No problem, use this login and he won't know a thing." He handed her a piece of paper. "There's a bigger problem though. When I take the time shot to kill Mishkov in the past, I'll reset the timeline. Everything we've learned so far will be forgotten, and all the other bad guys will still be in full operation. I need to somehow get a message back to the new timeline about this. Peters, the custodian, the employment agency, everything, but I don't know how."

Tammy sat and thought for a while. "You have that fancy little gizmo you carry around for dampening the time displacement field, correct?"

"Yes, how'd you know that?"

"I figured it out. Anyway, if we can ramp up the power to it and connect it to a recording device, it may carry the data back to the past."

Perez thought for a while. "I may have just what we need. I have a headset video recorder."

"Will your fob have enough power?"

"No, it's a passive device that gets power from the field of a time bullet. The problem is, I think if I use the energy from my last shot to protect the recorder, it won't have enough to go through time." Perez sat back and sighed. "Will I ever get a break?"

Tammy thought for a moment. "What if I can get you the spent rounds from all the murders? Together, they could have enough residual to do it, wouldn't they?"

Perez sat up. "You know, they just might."

"Okay, that settles it. Tomorrow, we change history. You can sleep on the couch. Now get out of my bedroom."

"I guess I'm recording a long message tonight."

The next day came quickly for the eager-to-help Tammy. Perez had already left her home before she awoke. She promptly readied herself and rushed to work. "Good morning, Tom. How are you today?" She greeted security like every other day.

"Good morning, Tammy. You look a little troubled this morning."

"I'm just a bit overwhelmed with everything lately, Tom."

"I think things will get better, Tammy. I can feel it." He pointed to the extra-large travel mug she carried. "You know the routine."

"Yes, of course." She placed it on the scanner belt and watched as it passed through and lit up the lights. As usual, the mug set off the detectors.

"I don't know why we do this every day. You need to get a new mug, Tammy."

"But this is my favorite mug." She smiled.

"Try to get a new favorite."

"Well, at least it's decaffeinated today." She picked it up and continued to her office. She carded into her lab and went straight to her desktop to log in to her computer. The screen faded on. "Hey, NSN is still active with the director's login. Fantastic, I won't need this." She pocketed the paper Perez gave her. "This will be easier than I thought." She adjusted the parameters of Perez's picture, so as to throw off the search.

When finished, she logged off the Deputy Director's account. "That should do it." Tammy got up, grabbed her coffee mug, and walked to the evidence locker. One by one, she gathered the spent time rounds from each box and dropped them into the mug. She closed the last box, put it back on the shelf, and left the room, but on her way out, she ran into Deputy Director Peters.

"Good morning, Tammy. I tried my login for Ubiquitous, but it was still logged in by you."

"Yes, sir. I'm sorry. I left in such a hurry last night to get to my class that I forgot to log out. I logged out first thing this morning, sir."

"No problem, Tammy. Try not to do it again."

"Yes, sir." She turned and walked away. Peters watched her, alternating his gaze between her and the evidence locker door.

"Tammy," she froze, "what case are you working on right now?"

She held up her coffee mug. "Nothing, sir. I just forgot my coffee mug in there from yesterday."

"You know you're not allowed to bring anything into the evidence locker, Tammy."

She frowned. "Yes, sir, I know. I'm sorry, I forgot. It won't happen again."

"It's alright, Tammy. I know we're all stressed lately. I'm smoking again, too." He turned and walked away. Tammy breathed a sigh of relief and headed toward the lobby. She got to security again with her cup in hand, and the guard waved her through.

"Thanks, Tom. Can I get you something while I'm there?" The sensor beeped as she passed. She stopped, but Tom waved her through.

"No thanks, Tammy." She crossed the street and entered the café. From the window, Peters watched her for a moment and then stepped away.

CHAPTER 37

"HAVE YOU MADE ANY PROGRESS ON THE COLONEL'S REQUEST, CAPTAIN Styles?" Major Wishbone pulled up a chair and sat next to the captain.

"I may have found an opportunity for him, Major." She scrolled through the archived satellite and drone surveillance data and stopped at a location she had previously marked.

"Is that Reaper's SUV?"

"It does look like the one the colonel described."

"Will he be able to shoot him there?" he pointed at the house on the screen.

"Colonel Perez asked for the earliest possible date to erase as much damage as possible, sir. I found him here at the house on this date, but as for the best moment, I traced him back to an intersection on the morning of April 7th. I took into account the location and current accessibility, and, in reviewing the satellite data, this is pretty much the only spot that is ideal to shoot from. That is, for now. I don't know for how much longer though."

"What about further back, outside of the area?"

"No, sir. The colonel said the time bullet is limited to its original manufacture date, in this case April 6th. We also don't have data on the outside of the area."

"Okay, send him the coordinates and keep monitoring for any changes."

"Yes, sir; I will."

Perez sat alone at a table in the café across from FBI headquarters. He sipped his coffee from his travel mug and read the morning newspaper. He was careful to be aware of his surroundings, making sure he wasn't recognized through his disguise. Tammy walked into the café and exchanged a quick glance with him. He smiled and looked at his newspaper. Suddenly there was a soft beep from his phone as a text came into him. He read the message, "Yes."

Tammy placed her cup on the counter. She looked at the barista. "A small latte, please."

"This is a large cup, lady."

"I know. I'm so clumsy that I always order a small in a big cup so that I won't spill."

"Okay." He opened the lid. "Hey, there's something in here already."

"It's all right, just pour the latte over them."

The clerk merely shrugged. "It's your coffee." He busily prepared the drink.

"That will be five-fifty, lady." She paid him, and he handed her the cup. Tammy walked outside and stopped at Perez's table to look at her phone. She placed her mug next to Perez's identical cup.

"Okay, I changed the parameters, so you have a short window of time to travel. Peters is suspicious though, so I don't know how long this will work." She played on her phone.

"I only need about ten hours to get there and set up."

"I doubt if you even have five."

"I guess I better not stop for a movie then."

"This is serious, Colonel. If you screw up, I'm dead, and the others stay dead, so don't screw up."

"Don't worry, Tammy; you'll be forgetting all about this soon."

Tammy grabbed Perez's cup. "Not soon enough." She walked away, sipping the coffee she got from Perez and had to stifle her reaction to the bitter taste of black coffee. "Yuck. Sure, he gets a nice latte, and I get this crap."

Perez watched as she walked away. "Wow, what a natural."

Hours later, Perez sat in the seat of an airliner bound for Salt Lake City. He made it through security at the airport without incident. He simply strolled past several FBI agents who merely glanced at him and continued to scan the crowd with their facial recognition scanners. Perez entered the intercept coordinates sent to him on his laptop and

reviewed the target area. "Okay, not a bad spot. I can shoot from there."
He touched the screen.

"I beg your pardon?" A lady within earshot said, "Did you say shoot?"

"Sorry ma'am, I was speaking to myself. I'm a photographer." She
smiled her relief, but he chose to keep quiet for the rest of the flight. The
plane landed at Salt Lake City on schedule. He grabbed his carry-on
and quickly exited the plane, passing FBI agents who were still holding
the corrupted scanners with the wrong picture. He took off the disguise
the instant he was alone.

"So far, so good, the program is ignoring me." Perez left the airport
and got into a waiting taxi. "City bus terminal, please."

"Boy, you must like to travel a lot, huh?"

Perez snorted a quick laugh. "You have no idea."

"Damn it." Deputy Director Peters slammed down his laptop screen.
He picked up his phone and dialed.

"Forensics, Tammy speaking."

"Tammy, could you meet me in the evidence locker? I need to talk
with you."

"Yes, sir, right away." Peters hung up and reached into his drawer. He
pulled out his service pistol and racked the slide to chamber a round.
"It's time for us to have a friendly chat, Tammy." Peters marched to
the evidence room and entered it. While he waited for Tammy, he
looked through the evidence boxes and noticed all of the spent time
rounds were missing. "She must know something." He looked at his
watch. "Where is she? She should be here by now." He called the front
entrance security.

"Security…"

"Deputy Director Anderson Peters here. Who am I speaking with?"

"This is security officer Tom Groves, sir."

"Have you seen Tammy Blessing come through there?"

"Why yes sir, she just came through and is walking out the front
door right now."

"What? Stop her!"

"Just a minute, sir," he placed the phone down, and Peters could hear
muffled talking and scuffling. He grew impatient as he waited; then
Tom picked up the phone.

"I'm sorry sir, but she vanished before we could get to her."

"Damn," he hung up his phone.

On the other end of the line Tom hung up his phone. "Yep, she's too fast for us." He stood holding a shiny new coffee mug filled with fresh hot coffee. He waved at Tammy who mouthed *Thank you*, as she quietly slipped out the door. The guard sipped his coffee. "Mmm, I love my job."

Peters raced back to his office and opened his laptop. He logged in to the Ubiquitous program and viewed the search parameters for Perez; he found a different picture instead. "What the…? Very funny, Tammy. Paris instead of Perez. That explains why we don't have a hit yet. I can fix this in a hurry." He hit a few keys and reverted to the original image Tammy had posted and hit enter, sending the update to all systems in seconds.

Perez sat in his cab, unaware that he was compromised. He thought about what he had to do next. The taxi pulled up to the bus station, and he handed the driver a $100 bill. "Wait for me, and there'll be another one of these in it for you."

"Hey, no problem, take your time, mac." He put the car in park and shut the engine off. Perez got out of the cab. As soon as he stepped out, his face was picked up by a video surveillance camera, which instantly transmitted his face to the Ubiquitous program, alerting the FBI.

The laptop on Peters' desk chimed. He looked at the picture. "I got you." He picked up his phone and dialed the Utah field office. "This is Deputy Director Peters. Connect me with the Special Agent in Charge." He waited and then heard a click.

"SAC's Office, Denise Gray speaking."

"Agent Gray, Deputy Director Peters here. I just had a hit on Ubiquitous for the fugitive Perez."

"Yes, sir, it pinged here too. We're already on it, sir."

"He's at your city bus terminal; get there now. Close down the entire city if you have to."

"We're stretched a little thin to close a city, sir, but we'll do our best to close a street or two."

"Don't get smart with me, Agent Grey."

"I'm not trying to be, sir, but we're tired, and I don't have a lot of available agents. I sent several to the base already. Do you want me to pull them from there, sir?"

"No, leave them there; but get someone to the bus station pronto."

"Yes, sir."

"Well, when are you sending them?"

"As soon as you stop talking to me, and I can get off the phone, sir."

"Fine," he hung up.

She looked at her phone. "Ivory tower brass-holes." She dialed a new number. "Dispatch, this is S.A.C. Gray. Send what we have left to the Central bus station. Perez is there."

Perez walked into the station and went straight to the cargo claim area. He gave the clerk a claim slip. "I'm here to pick up a package."

"Give me a minute, pal." The clerk took the ticket and walked to the back. Perez waited, watching his surroundings for any curious lingering onlookers. He felt relief when he saw the clerk returning with a long box in his hands.

"It just came in this morning. You got any ID?" Perez showed the clerk his ID and signed for the box. He opened it and pulled out the TATES inside a carry case.

"Is that a rifle?" the clerk said. "If it is, I have to report it."

"Nope, just some golf clubs." He handed him a $100 bill.

"Enjoy your game, buddy." He walked away.

Next, Perez went to the lockers. He leaned the TATES against the lockers and pressed his thumb against the reader. The door of his locker buzzed and clicked open. He reached in and pulled out a small satchel and a gym bag. The satchel had the last remaining CAP in it. The gym bag had cash, a cellphone, and his gun with several loaded magazines. Perez collected his belongings and quickly went for the exit. Outside, FBI agents had arrived and were surrounding the station. Perez saw the approaching agents through the windows.

"Looks like I've got company." He looked at the other entrances and saw agents entering the doors. He searched around and noticed a woman come out of a restricted area, leaving the door to close slowly behind her. He hurried to it and caught it before it closed. Inside were the building's central heating and cooling systems, among other utilities. He weaved through the machinery until he got to an outside door.

"Hey, what are you doing in here?" a worker who had spotted him challenged.

Perez smiled and opened the door. "Air inspector." He left before the response. The door was around the corner from his waiting taxi. As he walked to it, he saw four agents standing between him and the cab. They hadn't seen him yet, so he took advantage and surprised them. "Hey!" They all turned, and Perez shot each of them before they could react. Down they went, wounded but alive. "Sorry, fellas." He kept going to his cab. "Here's that hundred I promised, now drive." The cabbie took the money and drove off.

Other agents heard the shots and rushed around to find the stricken agents on the ground. "What happened? Are you guys okay?"

"We're all hit, but we'll live. He left in a cab over there." They pointed to the cab, which was disappearing down the street.

The agent keyed his radio. "Dispatch, the suspect is in a cab heading north on South 600 West. We also need multiple ambulances; we have four agents down." He looked at the stricken agents. "Okay guys, help is coming."

"Never mind us, we're fine. Go get him."

Agents rushed to their cars and sped off after the fleeing cab. The pursuing agents quickly caught up to the cab and stopped it. Surrounding it, they pointed their guns and ordered, "Driver, turn off the car and get out."

Slowly, the terrified driver exited his cab with his hands held high in the air. "Don't shoot! Don't shoot! He just gave me a hundred bucks and told me to drive away quickly."

The agents looked in the empty cab and at each other. "Damn…"

Perez sat in the rear of his original cab, as it slowly drove in the opposite direction, away from his pursuers. After several minutes, they came to his planned rendezvous point. "You can stop here, driver." He pulled over and Perez got out of the cab with his cargo. He came around to the driver's window and handed the cabbie five crisp one-hundred-dollar bills. "You never saw me."

The cabbie took the money and smiled. "Who said that?" Perez smiled and walked away as the cabbie drove off to spend his new mini-fortune.

CHAPTER 38

BASE QUARTERMASTER, SERGEANT BILL COLMAN, CLOSED THE REAR doors of the transport van he had just finished packing. Major Wishbone came out of his office and walked to Sergeant Coleman, who saw him approaching. He saluted the major. Wishbone saluted back. "Sir, I have the special cargo loaded for Colonel Perez."

"Excellent."

"But I'm not sure how we're getting it to him. The FBI has the exit blockaded."

"Don't worry about the FBI, Sergeant. I have that covered. Get to the front gate and be ready to leave on my command."

"Yes sir, understood."

Wishbone paused for a moment, allowing the severity of the situation he was entering sink in. "I hope you know what you're doing, Colonel. This is full out a football bat." He dialed his cell phone, and when he heard the answer on the other end, he said, "This is Wishbone. Deadlock is a go."

Dozens of heavily armed FBI agents held their position outside the main gate of the evacuation base. The agents stopped and searched every vehicle that passed through the gates, whether they were going in or out. Senior Special Agent Gary Chan, the agent in charge, addressed a new group of FBI SWAT members who had just joined them.

"Deputy Director Peters has ordered us to arrest and detain anyone who resists our search. We're pretty confident that, as a refugee base, they don't have enough force to challenge our presence. We have the authorization to engage them with any force we deem necessary, especially if this colonel shows his face. We just heard that he's in Salt Lake City and may be coming here."

"Sir, a van's coming from inside the compound." They watched as a white panel van approached the gate, driven by a very nervous-looking soldier. The two gate guards stood with their weapons ready in their hands.

"Okay, this doesn't look good. Get ready to stop it." They watched as the van eased to a stop at the gate and waited. "This one doesn't get through, understood?"

One of the new tactical team leaders, Captain Vito Battelli, approached him. "Are you for real? We're going to war with the U.S. Army?"

"Direct orders from Peters," Chan said.

"I don't care if it's direct orders from Hoover's ghost. I don't agree."

"Neither do I, Captain Battelli, but orders are orders."

"Yeah, that's what the Nazis said too."

"Pardon me, what was that you said?"

"Nothing SAC, you're the boss. Sounds like thunder, is a storm coming?"

In the distance, both Sergeant Colman and the surrounding FBI agents could hear a low rumbling, gaining in intensity. Coleman said a quick prayer and signaled the guards. They opened the gate for him, and he pulled out. He stopped about one hundred feet from the FBI blockade. "Anytime now, Major. Where's that rabbit you promised me?"

Suddenly, Major Wishbone raced up in an unarmed Humvee. He exited the gate and passed Colman, pulling up to and stopping mere steps from the FBI agents. Wishbone stepped out and lifted a bullhorn to his mouth. "Attention FBI, my name is Major Jacob Wishbone, and I'm the commanding officer of this base. I wish to inform you that you're impeding the operations of this base and as per Joint publication 3-68 Noncombatant Evacuation Operations, Appendix A, Subsection A, I am authorized to use force for force to execute my duties at this base. With that, if you do not cease this blockade, I'll be authorized to use force to move you."

Agent Chan stood a few steps away. "I'm sorry, Major, but you're not going anywhere. I don't see how you're going to force anything, and why the hell are you speaking through a bullhorn?"

The major raised the bullhorn, as the rumbling got louder, "So you can hear me."

"We can hear you fine, Major."

"Not for long." Suddenly, across from the base, a squadron of five AH-64 Apache attack helicopters crested a hill and approached the FBI blockade. They hovered behind Wishbone and set their targeting systems, pointing their 30-mm chain guns at the agents.

The lead helicopter pilot announced over his PA speaker. "Weapons are hot, sir. Please step aside for us to go kinetic." Wishbone lifted his hand and signaled for them to hold. "Waiting on your command, sir," the pilot said through the speaker again for all to hear. By this time, hundreds of people were lining the fence to watch the standoff.

Wishbone raised the bullhorn again. "Can you still hear me?" The surrounding FBI agents all retreated to behind their cars and pointed their weapons, waiting for Chan's instructions. "There's no point in hiding behind your cars. These helicopters will turn them into Swiss cheese in seconds."

Agent Chan tried to shout over the noise of the helicopters. "You wouldn't fire on federal agents, would you? That would be a criminal act of treason."

Wishbone calmly replied, "Try me. I won't hesitate to fire upon you. I'm authorized by federal mandate to use whatever force, I deem necessary to get my job done."

Inside the van, Colman nervously watched the stalemate unfold. Agent Chan looked at the helicopters and then back at Wishbone. He turned to Battelli. "This is crazy. I'm not going to die for this."

"Damn straight, I know I'm not." Battelli waved his team to lower their weapons.

Chan turned and faced his agents. "Stand down, stand down. Open it up, and let them through." The agents all lowered their weapons.

Wishbone turned to Colman and waved him through. "Get moving and don't stop." He turned to Chan. "Good choice." Colman gunned the engine and took off through the blockade. A few of the agents jumped into their cars to chase Colman, but a helicopter maneuvered ahead of them and dropped into their path, aiming its 30-mm chain gun at them. The pursuing agents screeched to a halt.

Agent Chan watched, as the van drove off. He turned and looked at Battelli. "Peters is going to kill us."

"Yeah, he may chew us a new one." Battelli pointed at the helicopters. "But at least they won't. Besides..." Battelli held up his hand.

Chan looked at what was in his hand and smiled. "Alright, Captain."

Wishbone stood facing the agents. Although he had his victory for the moment, there was going to be hell to pay for this. A sweating Colman looked into his rearview mirror as he sped away. Seeing that no one was pursuing him, he calmed slightly but knew it wasn't celebration time yet. He still had to get this payload to Perez. Unfortunately for Colman, he hadn't seen Battelli fire a weapon at the van. Fixed snuggly on the rear door was a blinking tracking device, reporting his whereabouts.

Colman drove an hour to the rendezvous location; unaware he was tracked the entire time. He took the appropriate exit and stopped at an underpass on the westbound highway, leaving Salt Lake City. A short distance behind him, FBI agents stopped and waited, trying not to give their position away. Agent Chan looked through his binoculars and saw a lone figure come out of the bushes with a pack and rifle bag on his back. Chan squinted into the glasses. "That's him! He's got the rifle too. Let's go. Go! Go! Go!" The agents revved their engines and peeled out toward Perez and Coleman.

Colman got out of the van to open the rear doors when he spotted the tracking device. Perez approached him. "Oh no, I'm sorry, sir." He pointed at the device. "I didn't know." Perez turned and looked down the road; he saw several cars approaching at high speed. He threw his packages into the van and took out his gun to hammer the tracking device from the door.

"Don't worry about it, Sergeant." He closed the doors and quickly got in the driver's seat.

"Hey! What about me? How do I get home?"

Perez pointed at the FBI. "I'm sure they'll give you a lift home, eventually." He tore off, fleeing from his pursuers.

Colman looked at the approaching FBI and dropped his shoulders with a big sigh. "I should've had lunch." The agents quickly passed Coleman, who stood in the middle of the road, waving. One car with two agents stopped, and they got out with their guns drawn on him. He looked at them and smiled, "Going my way?"

Perez accelerated down the highway, heading west into the salt flats.

Agent Chan watched. "Where the hell does he think he's going? There's nothing but desert out there." He keyed his radio. "This is Chan. I need a roadblock set up on the I-80 at Wendover. He might be going for the airport there." He looked at his driver. "We have him now. He's got nowhere to go."

Perez drove as fast as the overloaded van would go. He fought hard to maintain the gap he made, but the pursuing agents were catching up quickly. He picked up his cell phone and dialed a number.

"Hello, Mike here."

"It's Perez. Are you ready for me?"

"I'll be there in five minutes."

"Five minutes, I doubt I have three!"

"Sorry man, that's the best I can do."

"Fine, I'll have to buy some time."

He slammed on his brakes and stopped on the highway. He jumped out, grabbed a rifle Coleman had left, and fired at the pursuing cars. The cars screeched to a halt, and the agents poured out, taking cover. He fired several shots, forcing the agents to duck down. Some of his bullets struck the tires of two of their cars, flattening them. While the agents were all down behind their cars, he jumped back into his van and sped off.

Holding position behind his car, Agent Chan peered over the hood. "He's running again. Let's go."

"No can do, boss. My tires are flat."

"Yeah, same here."

"Move them off the road and get in the good ones." The agents pulled their disabled cars off the road and got into the remaining ones. Perez had successfully bought a couple of minutes. Agent Chan pulled out his pistol. "I'm getting tired of this. Get me close enough to end this." The driver nodded. Inch by inch, the agent-laden cars closed the gap, slowly gaining on Perez, despite his efforts.

Suddenly, the rear window of the van shattered. Perez looked in his mirror and saw Agent Chan leaning out of his window, firing at him. "You want to play that way, do you?" Perez weaved the van back and forth as bullets whizzed by him, cracking the front windshield and lodging into it. The pursuing cars drew closer and closer, allowing Chan's aim to improve. Suddenly, as Chan was lining up for another shot, a huge shadow passed over them.

"What was that?"

They looked up and were stunned to see a massive C-130H Hercules aircraft with a Global Transports logo pass fifty feet above them. The driver eased his foot off the gas. Chan looked at him. "Hell no, you get going." The driver sped up the car again.

Inside the plane, Mike Matthews sat at the controls. He keyed his radio. "Colonel Perez, it's nice to see you again."

"Is that you, Mike? It's about time."

"Sorry, Colonel. I had to admire the nice new motorcycle I just got."

"Funny, just come and get me before the FBI does."

"Oh, don't worry about them; I have something special for them." The plane dropped lower to the ground, and the rear loading ramp opened. Suddenly, several boxes of metal car parts fell out onto the road. The boxes exploded from the impact and scattered debris across the highway. The parts slammed into the pursuing agents, blowing tires and smashing through windshields. The bombardment stopped all the cars except for Chan's.

"That should slow them a bit." Matthews maneuvered his plane over Perez and lowered his gear. He dropped to the ground until his bay door was dragging and shedding sparks. "Okay, Colonel, time to get aboard. Hurry up! I want to go for a ride soon." Matthews matched the speed of Perez's van the best he could. Perez gunned his engine as more bullets flew past him from Chan's gun.

"They're still shooting at me!"

"We got you covered, Colonel." A man appeared in the back of the plane with a rifle and fired at the pursuing car.

"Hell no, that's enough!" Chan's driver hit the brakes and quickly stopped.

"Come on, let's go, after that son of a…"

"Screw you, you fool. The chase is over." Chan hit the dash with his fist. The man in the plane fired one more round into the front of Chan's car, which set off the airbags. Forced by the airbag, Chan's fist came back and hit him in the nose.

He took a second to regain his senses, and wiped the blood from his face. "Damn."

Perez floored his accelerator and hit the dragging ramp. The van lunged forward and into the moving plane. "Okay Mike, I'm in."

"Hold on. My loadmaster will tell me when we're good." The loadmaster threw a net over the van and quickly clamped it down. He flipped a switch, which turned a light green in the cockpit. "Okay, now we're good." Matthews pulled back on his yoke and thrust the throttle levers full forward on his four powerful engines. The plane quickly climbed as the loadmaster closed the rear doors. Perez shut off the engine and got out.

He looked in the plane and saw his motorcycle strapped to a pallet. "I'm going to miss you, baby, at least for the day anyway."

The loadmaster leaned into him and spoke over the noise of the aircraft. "The captain wants to speak with you up front. Come this way." Perez followed him to the cockpit. When the sixty-something Matthews saw him, he handed him a headset to put on.

"Welcome aboard, Colonel Perez."

"Thanks for doing this, Mike, and call me Perez."

"Well, Perez, I was serious when I said I wanted that bike."

"It couldn't have gone to a better person, Mike. Take good care of it."

"No worries there."

"I'm surprised you brought a marked plane."

"Didn't you hear? This plane was stolen right out of the airport this morning. They even took out the transponder. It's a shame, isn't it?"

Perez laughed. "A great shame."

"Besides, I could use a newer plane anyways." He laughed and adjusted some controls. "Well, Perez, where do you want to go now?" Perez handed him a set of coordinates.

"I need to get to here." Mike punched the coordinates into his navigation computer.

"Whoa, I want the bike, but not that bad. I'm not going in there."

"It's okay. I don't need you to take me right in. I need within thirty miles. Is that possible?"

"I can handle thirty miles, but there's nowhere I can land to let you out."

"You don't need to land. I'll jump the rest."

"What about your van? Are you gonna walk the rest?"

"Consider the van a bonus, and no, I'm not walking. I've other plans."

"I suppose you would. Okay, you should start getting ready, 'cause we'll be there in about thirty minutes."

"Okay," Perez extended his hand to shake. "Thanks again, Mike. You're a lifesaver."

"You're welcome, Perez. You know, deep down inside I knew I was supposed to help you and getting the bike makes it even sweeter."

"Oh, you mean, I can have my bike back then?"

"Not on your life, kid." Perez laughed. He took off the headset and patted Mike's shoulder goodbye. He climbed back down to the cargo area and approached the loadmaster.

"Hey, what's your name?"

"Hunter."

"Well, Hunter, can I get you to help me set up?"

"Sure." Perez opened the van doors, and Hunter looked inside. "Are you kidding me?"

Perez smiled. "Just another walk in the park for me."

"Damn, I'm glad I don't have your job."

Twenty-five minutes passed, and Matthews keyed the PA system. "Okay, Perez, we're two minutes from your coordinates. We're at twenty, do you have air, or do I need to drop to twelve?" Perez didn't respond. Matthews keyed the mic again. "Perez, did you hear me?"

Hunter keyed back. "Sorry, sir, the colonel can't come to the com. We only need to depressurize, and he can drop from here. I have my mask ready, and once we depressurize the rear compartment, I can open the cargo doors."

"This is for real; he's jumping out into the middle of nowhere? Okay, commencing depressurization." He watched as the gauges in the cockpit moved, indicating the pressure drop in the cargo bay. Once equalized, he saw the indicator light on his panel showing the rear cargo hatch open. A few moments passed, and the light went off.

"Passenger away, sir. You may want to look out your port-side window, too."

Matthews looked out his window. "Well, I'll be. He's a crazy one, isn't he?"

"Definitely a crazy one, sir."

"I hope he knows what he's doing because he's about to enter hell."

"Report, Captain."

"Major, I have the area on the screen, and I think the main explosion is about to arrive."

"Are the destination coordinates still clear for him?"

"Barely sir, he better get in there soon. It's raining fire in there."

"Do you know where he is?"

"I'm looking now. The plane the colonel was in turned a minute ago, so he must be solo by now. Wait, there he is."

"Where?"

"Right there, sir. See that tiny little dot? He's on his jet-wing pack, and he's going in fast."

Perez had entered hell; fire and molten rock shot from the sky in a steady assault on the ground beneath. Perez maneuvered his jet wing pack, narrowly missing the onslaught of flaming debris. Time ripples filled the sky as the mountain mercilessly cast its deadly ruins through time.

"Perez to Wishbone, are you there?"

"Wishbone here, Colonel, we can see you."

"Is my landing zone still good?"

"Yes, it is, Colonel, but not for long. We think the main explosion is coming."

"I can barely get through now. How long until I clear the debris ring?"

"About another three miles and you'll reach the inner edge, but it's shrinking fast. Get in and get out quickly, Colonel."

"This is a one-way ticket, folks. I'm not getting out of this one, just pray this works." Perez looked into the distance, and all he could see was a wall of rippled air. He pushed the twin engines of the eight-foot-wide jet wing to their limits. He could feel the strain of the G-forces on his body as he dodged the debris. Stones pelted his facemask and upper body as the jetpack propelled him through the shower of exploding rocks.

A mere ten miles away, he saw his target landing zone; however, they were the longest ten miles he had ever faced in his life. He started his descent and prepared for a rapid landing. On his wrist, his fob incessantly beeped, indicating time events almost to the point of his ignoring them. He flew lower, passing 15,000 feet, then 10,000 feet. He quickly dropped to 5000 feet and started to slow down for his final approach as he planned on parachuting down from 2000 feet. Perez knew he had little time to spare and pressed hard. Suddenly, the horizon became fuzzy, and the entire sky filled with time ripples.

"Oh sweet…" Suddenly, a wall of burning rock appeared through time. "No, I need more time." He immediately took his pack into a power dive. The wall of rock was unimaginably vast, taking up his entire view. One of the sloped sides of the mountain, at least two miles high and five miles wide, had been pushed vertical through time; pushed by the force of the anti-matter explosion. As if on a hinge, the rock pivoted to stand at attention and stopped. It teetered precariously, balanced on its edge. "Oh yes, it stopped." He kept diving but slowed for his jump. Suddenly, he heard an enormous boom and watched as the rock crumbled under its own immense weight. A wave of thunder came from the breaking rock, and the two-mile-high wall teetered forward, falling slowly toward the town.

Perez set his thrusters to maximum and dove straight to the ground. He had only precious moments until sixty billion tons of flaming rock would crush the entire town. Further and further, the mountain fell toward Perez and his target. He could feel the force of the air pushed by the falling rock wall.

"Get out of there, Perez. You're not going to make it," Wishbone said over the radio.

"I have to get in there; this is going to destroy everything." His dive took him closer and closer to the ground. He looked at his altimeter, 3000 feet, 2000 feet. The ground raced up to him, 1000 feet. When he hit 500 feet, he pulled up and out of the dive, leveling out. He was going phenomenally fast, a mere 200 feet above the ground. He ripped the release cord of the jet wing, which separated from his back, allowing it to fly away. He glided forward at hundreds of miles per hour as he dropped to the ground.

When he came close to the landing zone, Perez tucked his body into a somersault, which brought him feet first into his glide. He wrenched the ripcord of his parachute, which immediately unfurled and quickly caught the speeding air. He felt the enormous G-forces of deceleration rip at his body, as his speed plummeted rapidly. He dropped the final distance as he slowed and glided to the ground. In the distance, he saw his jetpack strike the mountain with a massive explosion.

Perez stepped out of his descent as he touched the ground at near zero forward velocity. The leading wake of air from the falling mountain caught his parachute and tried to push him back, lifting him away from the ground. He yanked on the chute release and dropped back to the ground. With the mountain bearing down on him and flaming loose stones raining down, he pulled the TATES from the case that was strapped to his body. It was already loaded and set for the correct time.

With the TATES in his hands, Perez sprinted the final hundred yards, as rock pelted him. He could feel the weight of the air being forced down on him from the falling mountain. Perez dropped the recording device wrapped in the spent time rounds and dove to the ground. He activated the scope and looked through it finding Sasha back in time. The mountain was almost on him. With mere seconds left in his life, he lined up his shot and fired, releasing his final bullet through time, hoping to end the madness he was living. In his last few seconds, he said, "I told you I was going to kill you *twice*." He smiled as he disappeared under the mountain. Perez was dead.

CHAPTER 39

"THIS IS THE BEST GRUB YET, PEPPER," G.W. SAID. HE SAT AT THE counter of the Utah 70 truck stop. The calendar on the wall read April 7th. His server, Pepper Johnson, stood in front of him.

"Well, I'm glad you enjoyed it, G.W. I'll be sure to compliment the chef on your behalf."

G.W. smiled through what was left of his rotten teeth. "Ya. Be sure to tell 'im that it don't suck this time."

"I'm sure he'll be thrilled to hear that." She cleared his empty plate, stained with hot sauce and the remnants of his scrambled eggs. "So where are you headed today, big fella?"

"I got a load of logs I'm taking about three hours upstate." He looked at the clock and saw 5:30. "I gotta be there at nine, so I got lotsa time."

Pepper looked at the clock, "Oh, I hate to tell you this G.W., but that clock ain't right. We didn't move it forward yet for daylight savings time, so it's really 6:30."

G.W. almost choked on his coffee. "What? It's 6:30? Damn, I'm late. If I'm late again, I get fired from my contract." He grabbed a $20 bill from his pocket and tossed it on the counter. He took a last chug of his coffee and leaned over to give Pepper a quick peck on the cheek. "I gotta roll, see ya, doll." She waved goodbye as he ran out to his truck. He opened the door, which read George Westonbrook Trucking and nimbly climbed into the idling truck. George thrust it into gear and revved the engine, taking off down the highway muttering, "By tunderin', I gotta do a three-hour drive in two and a half. I better skip the inspection stations. I know, I'll take the Leviville bypass."

"Are you going to be able to complete your mission, Sasha?"

He looked at his clock as it changed to 7:35. "Yes Galina, I'm going there now." He raised his hand to block the early morning sun, which kept him from seeing the haze forming in front of him. "This blasted sun is blinding me." Suddenly the air rippled and the shot Perez had fired in the future emerged. It quickly closed the gap to the SUV and struck the windshield with the full force of the wrath deserved from the future timeline. The bullet pierced the surface of the glass and forced its way through each layer toward its intended target, however, it stopped at the final film of the bulletproof glass of Sasha's custom SUV.

"What the hell?"

"What is it, Sasha?"

"Somebody shot at me."

"You must go now, abort mission."

"No, I must keep… Noooooo!" Sasha missed the stop sign and drove straight into the path of the speeding truck of George Westonbrook.

"Whoa! What are you doing?" George's pupils widened as he slammed on his brakes, although he didn't stand a chance of avoiding the doomed SUV that had strayed into his path. His truck, complete with the enormous weight of a full load of lumber, struck Sasha's SUV with more than 300 tons of force, instantly crumpling the side of it and crushing Sasha in the driver's seat. The momentum of the truck launched the SUV across the intersection, causing it to tumble wildly, crashing through fences and highway signs. It finally came to rest upright, far into a field that flanked the junction. Its tumble only stopped after the front end slammed into a tree. Sasha sat stunned by the impact. He tried to move but couldn't; he was trapped.

Watching from a distance, the local sheriff's deputy saw the wreck and immediately responded. He keyed his radio. "Dispatch, Wildfeather here. I've got a major wreck here at the fishing hole. Get fire and ambulance here, pronto."

George got his truck stopped a short distance down the road but, being shaken, he sat unmoving in his seat. The responding deputy pulled up to the scene and got out of his patrol car. He ran to the crumpled SUV and saw a bleeding Sasha sitting motionless, but still breathing. "Hey mister, how bad are you hurt?" As the deputy made his final few steps, he was able to see into the wreckage. "Whoa. Oh, man. Uh, I mean… it's all gonna be okay, mister."

Sasha saw the color drain from the deputy's face. Using all of his strength, he moved his head to look down. Sticking out of his abdomen, he saw the remains of a street sign that had gored him. The sign read: *Providence Road*. Calm washed over Sasha as he realized his fate; he knew he was bleeding out too quickly. Knowing he was about to die, he struggled to look at the deputy. Sasha opened his mouth to speak, and the deputy leaned in to hear. Sasha with his last breath forced out his final whisper, "So close." Sasha died. Again.

"It was nobody, dear." Stephan replaced the phone onto the cradle. He had just finished talking with the mysterious caller who had given him his passcode when he heard a knock at the front door. "Wow, busy morning." Placing the note on the counter, he walked to the door. He opened it and saw in front of him, two sheriff's deputies with surprised looks on their faces. He read their nametags: *Wright and Carter*. The deputies looked at each other and then back at Stephan.

"Is this the Krueger residence?" Deputy Wright said.

"Yes, sir, I'm Stephan Krueger. Is there a problem?"

Wright looked at Carter. "You're Stephan Krueger?" Stephan nodded in agreement.

"Do you own a black SUV, and would you happen to have a twin brother?" Stephan was puzzled by their questions.

"No, to both questions. Why would you ask that?"

"I'm sorry, sir, but have you been here all morning?"

"Yes, I'm preparing to start work at the base this morning." Stephan's voice was showing his growing impatience with the strange questioning from the deputies.

"Wait, do you mean that creepy army base at Ghost Mountain?" Stephan again nodded in agreement. Wright looked at Carter and then back to Stephan. "Never mind, sir. Sorry to have troubled you." He turned to Carter, "We better get back to our John Doe at the wreck." He gently pushed him. "Right now."

Carter caught the drift of what his partner was suggesting and looked at Stephan. "Sorry to bother you, sir. Have a nice day, or whatever it is you do at that place." They turned and hurriedly walked back to their patrol car. Carter said to Wright, "I want nothing to do with that accursed place." Wright nodded in agreement. "That's for sure."

Stephan slowly closed the door, "What was that all about?"

"Who was that, honey?" Anna called down from upstairs.

Stephan paused to ponder. "Nothing dear, it was nothing, but I will say that this morning has been strange."

"Okay, you better get ready. You don't want to be late on your first day, you know."

"Yes, I'm dying to get there." Stephan finished getting ready. Anna rejoined him after sending the kids off to school.

"You have a wonderful first day, my love. Remember, you deserve this." They kissed and Stephan walked to his old pickup and got in. He checked that he had all of his papers and started it up. Shifting it into gear, he drove off for his appointment.

A short distance away, he saw the collection of emergency vehicles at Providence Road. As he slowly drove past the crumpled front end of George's truck, he saw rescuers carrying a stretcher with a body bag on it from the wreckage. "That must be the John Doe from this morning." He contemplated his own life as he speculated on the tragic events that led to this person's death. Feeling sadness for this poor unknown soul, he remembered how fragile life was and how blessed he had been. He looked up, "Thank you." Looking back down the road, he smiled and accelerated away. "Yes, things are finally looking up for me, this time."

CHAPTER 40

EARLY THAT MORNING, GENERAL ISSAC TREMAINE FINISHED HIS EMAIL and sent it to the long list of guests he invited to the upcoming TATES demonstration. With a press of the enter key, he sent his important message out. As it vanished from his screen, he took a candy from the bowl on his desk and said, "Life is good."

Thousands of miles away in Brentwood, District of Columbia, Vince DiCarlo jumped into the air and splashed his shot into the basketball net that was mounted to his sister's garage. "Ooh yeah, I win." Vince strutted about celebrating his victory over his athletic nephew Jeff. Angelina stood at the door, watching her brother play with her son and smiled. Vince looked at her and said, "I kicked his butt."

Jeff in the background mouthed, "I let him win." Angelina laughed. Jeff said, "Oh dang, Uncle Vince, how'd you do that?"

"I still got lots of life left in me, kid."

"No doubt," Jeff smiled as Vince gave him a big headlock hug.

Colonel Joseph Perez walked up to his family breakfast table. "Good morning, family."

"Mornin', Dad," Josh said.

"Good morning, Daddy," Mica greeted him with a gleeful smile.

Sarah walked in carrying a plate of French toast for them all. "Good morning, dear," she said after they kissed.

He took two slices from the plate and stopped. "I don't know what it is, but I feel like today is going to be a great day. Like something new is going to happen."

"In that case, Dad, can I…"

"No, you can't have the car."

"Ah, nuts."

In the supply room of the western district supply depot for the U.S. Army, Quartermaster Bill Colman sifted through a recent shipment of equipment. He pulled out a case of recording headsets and one by one inspected each box. When he unpacked box number seven, he opened it and pulled out the recording set. He noted that the serial number ended in three sevens. "Hmm? Lucky number seven." After checking it, he began to repack it but noticed a small flashing light indicating its memory was full, "Hey, Captain."

"What?"

"This recorder is indicating full, sir."

His Captain showed little interest. "Just erase it, Colman. We don't have time for this." Colman shrugged and pressed the delete button. The display of the recorder then read: *Are you sure you want to delete? Yes or No?*

Colman paused and pondered his choice. "I'm not that busy. There might be something interesting on here."

"Colman, are you finished with that thing yet? Get over here."

"Right away, sir." He took his finger and lined it up, pressing the button that said…

Printed in Canada